RESTLESS IN THE GRAVE

In 1991, Dana Stabenow, born in Alaska and raised on a 75-foot fishing trawler, was offered a three-book deal for the first of her Kate Shugak mysteries. In 1992, the first in the series, *A Cold Day for Murder*, received an Edgar Award from the Crime Writers of America.

DANA STABENOW

"Kate Shugak is the answer if you are looking for something unique in the crowded field of crime fiction."
Michael Connelly

"One of the strongest voices in crime fiction." *Seattle Times*

"Cleverly conceived and crisply written thrillers that provide a provocative glimpse of life as it is lived, and justice as it is served, on America's last frontier." *San Diego Union-Tribune*

"When I'm casting about for an antidote to the sugary female sleuths… Kate Shugak, the Aleut private investigator in Dana Stabenow's Alaskan mysteries, invariably comes to mind." *New York Times*

"Fast and furious adventure." *Kirkus*

"Stabenow is blessed with a rich prose style and a fine eye for detail. An outstanding series." *Washington Post*

"Excellent... No one writes more vividly about the hardships and rewards of living in the unforgiving Alaskan wilderness and the hardy but frequently flawed characters who choose to call it home. This is a richly rewarding regional series that continues to grow in power as it grows in length." *Publishers Weekly*

"A dynamite combination of atmosphere, action, and character." *Booklist*

"Full of historical mystery, stolen icons, burglaries, beatings, and general mayhem... The plot bursts with colour and characters... If you have in mind a long trip anywhere, including Alaska, this is the book to put in your backpack." *Washington Times*

THE KATE SHUGAK SERIES

A Cold Day for Murder
A Fatal Thaw
Dead in the Water
A Cold Blooded Business
Play With Fire
Blood Will Tell
Breakup
Killing Grounds
Hunter's Moon
Midnight Come Again
The Singing of the Dead
A Fine and Bitter Snow
A Grave Denied
A Taint in the Blood
A Deeper Sleep
Whisper to the Blood
A Night Too Dark
Though Not Dead
Restless in the Grave
Bad Blood

DANA STABENOW

RESTLESS IN THE GRAVE

First published in the UK in 2014 by Head of Zeus, Ltd.

9 7 5 3 1 2 4 6 8

A CIP catalogue record for this book is available from the British Library.

ISBN (BPB) 9781908800800
ISBN (E) 9781781850527

Printed and bound by CPI Group (UK) Ltd,
Croydon, CR0 4YY

Head of Zeus, Ltd.
Clerkenwell House
45-47 Clerkenwell Green
London EC1R 0HT

www.headofzeus.com

This one is for the Danamaniacs,
and especially for
Cathy Obbema,
Cathy Rose,
Carolyn Bright,
and
Sandy Nolfi—
Liam returns, just for them

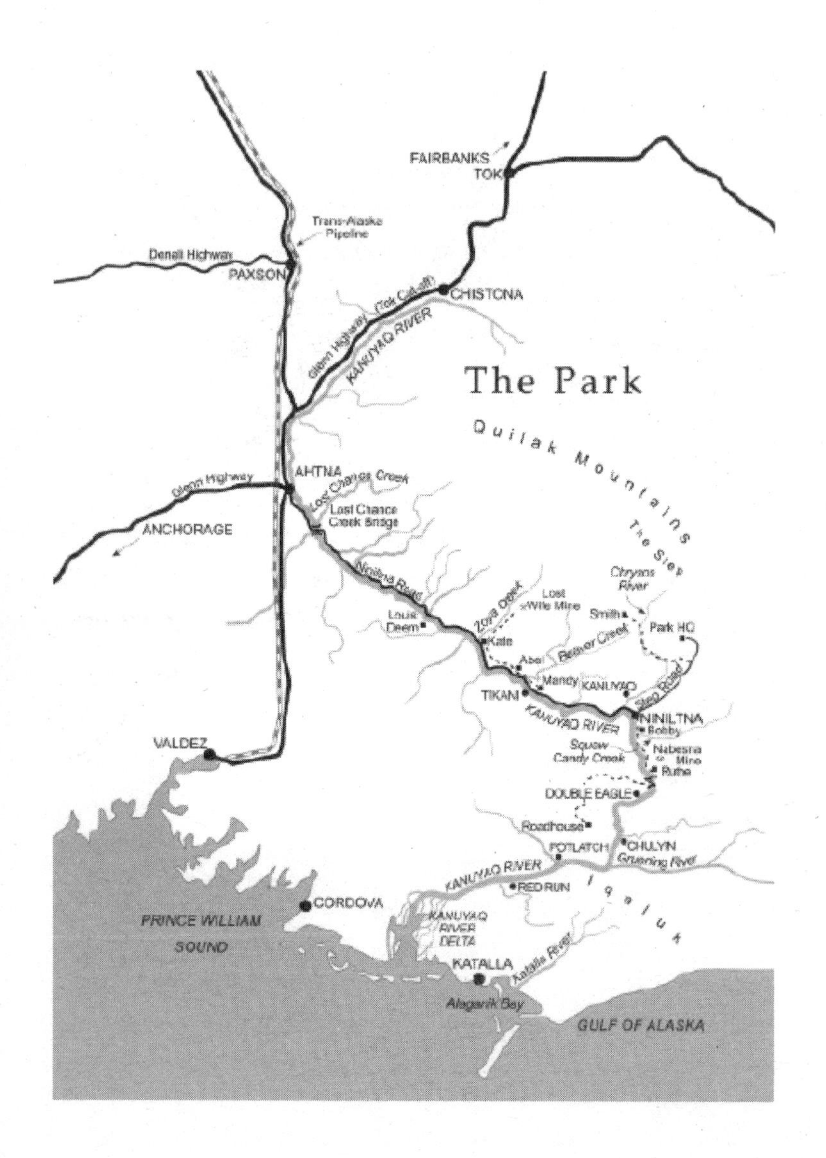

The Park
FAIRBANKS
TOK
Trans-Alaska Pipeline
Denali Highway
PAXSON
CHISTONA
Glenn Highway (Tok Cutoff)
KANUYAQ RIVER
Quilak Mountains
AHTNA
Glenn Highway
Lost Chance Creek
Lost Chance Creek Bridge
ANCHORAGE
The Step
Chrysos River
Lost Wife Mine
Smith
Park HQ
Louis Deem
Kate
Abel
Beaver Creek
Mandy
KANUYAQ
TIKANI
KANUYAQ RIVER
NINILTNA
Bobby
VALDEZ
Squaw Candy Creek
Nabesna Mine
Ruthe
DOUBLE EAGLE
Roadhouse
POTLATCH
CHULYIN
Gruening River
KANUYAQ RIVER
RED RUN
Igaluk
CORDOVA
PRINCE WILLIAM SOUND
KANUYAQ RIVER DELTA
KATALLA
Katalla River
Alaganik Bay
GULF OF ALASKA

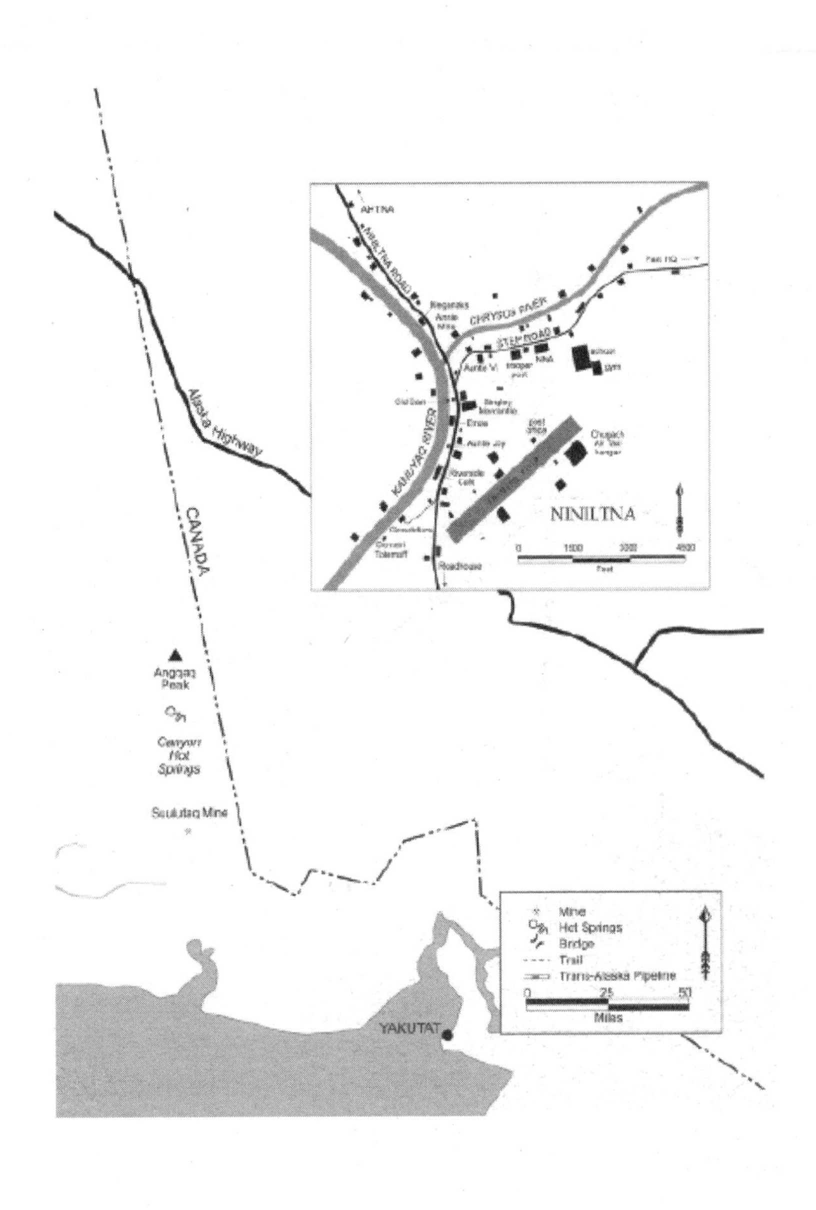
AHTNA
CHRYSUS RIVER
KANUYAQ RIVER
Elmos
Riverside Cafe
Roadhouse
Chugach Air Taxi hangar
NINILTNA
0
1500
3000
4500
Feet
Alaska Highway
CANADA
Angqaq Peak
Canyon Hot Springs
Suulutaq Mine
Mine
Hot Springs
Bridge
Trail
Trans-Alaska Pipeline
0
25
50
Miles
YAKUTAT

"... It's with us in the room, though. It's the bones."
"What bones?" "The cellar bones—out of the grave."
—Robert Frost, "Two Witches"

1

NOVEMBER

Sangin District, Helmand Province, Afghanistan

THEY KEPT IT SIMPLE. They could cut off his right hand, or he could use it to learn how to fire the weapon they gave him.

They had even picked the target. He knew before they told him it would be American. By now he could repeat the Imam's Friday harangue to do jihad on the invaders word for word.

All he had wanted was to go home. Pakistan was a hungry place for a young Afghani man with no family or friends. His father had been killed when the Americans invaded in 2003, and his mother had taken the children and fled over the border, joining the hundreds of thousands of other refugees in the camps. When she died, he found his way back to his own country, where he had not been so much recruited by the Taliban as kidnapped.

At least they fed him.

The camp three hundred yards up the narrow valley was small, an outpost dug into a small saddle between two hills, consisting of forty American soldiers. The top of the hill in front had been leveled to provide a landing place for a helicopter. He had been waiting for it for three days, broiling by day and freezing by night beneath the camouflage netting that had been stolen, they told him, from the enemy in another firefight in another valley.

The weapon was beautiful and deadly, brand new, light of weight, black in color, made of heavy plastic married to a dense, dark metal with a dull shine. A zippered sheath kept it free of the dirt and sand that filtered through the netting to layer his clothing and coat the inside of his nostrils so that he could barely breathe.

In the distance, a few tumbledown buildings marked a primitive landholding. A boy herded goats toward a patch of earth that showed the barest hint of green and hosted a few wormword bushes twisted into nightmare shapes from lack of water. Those fields he could see lay fallow, the only cash crop this area had ever known rooted up by the invaders.

A faint sound of wings disturbed the air. He looked up. A steppe eagle had been hunting this valley every morning and evening, soaring overhead on brown wings spread six feet from wingtip to wingtip, black tail spread wide.

This sound wasn't the eagle, though. It was the helicopter, coming at last.

It hurtled up the valley, barely time enough for him to get the rifle out of its protective sheath. He settled his eye to the scope, as he had been taught, and sighted in. The magnification of the scope threw the aircraft into startlingly immediate relief. The windshield was scratched and sandy and the sun rendered the Plexiglas nearly opaque, so that the figures at the controls on the other side were barely visible to him. He caught the merest glimpse of a smooth cheek, nearly hidden beneath helmet and sunglasses. Too young yet to shave. His age.

One shot was all it would take, they had told him, so long as he hit the target. He blinked the sweat out of his eyes as his finger pulled the trigger, slowly, firmly, even gently, again as they had taught him. The stock recoiled against his shoulder as the high explosive round left the barrel. The sound of the shot rendered him temporarily deaf.

Before he could raise his eye from the scope, the helicopter touched down on the pad and on landing seemed simply to shatter into a thousand pieces. The three-man crew died instantly, shredded by fragments from their own splintering aircraft, as did the one soldier on the ground standing fifteen feet from the landing pad, skewered by a flying piece of one of the rotors. All six of the soldiers waiting for their ride home fifty feet from the landing pad were injured as well, two of them mortally.

The watcher upslope granted him just enough time to be amazed at the destruction he had wrought before putting a bullet into the back of his head precisely where his skull ended and his spinal column began.

2

JANUARY 14

Niniltna

EACH OF THE 103 Pyrex baking dishes was scraped clean. The mountain of gifts was reduced to a floor-covering rubble of plastic clamshells, price tags, and instruction books. The last person with a story to tell about Old Sam had finally and reluctantly abandoned the microphone. The heavy wooden double doors slammed shut behind the last guest with a finality that echoed off the hard sufaces of the gym.

"A good potlatch," Auntie Vi said.

"Lots of the people come to say good-bye," Auntie Balasha said, nodding.

"Too many," Auntie Edna said. "Look at this mess. Pigs."

Auntie Joy said nothing.

"Vern Truax he come, too, see you?" Auntie Vi said. "And he don't stay too long, just pay his respects. Good manners. Good business."

"You see Peter Kasheverof's daughter canoodle in the corner with Lizzie Collier's son?" Auntie Balasha said. "A marriage there soon, I think."

"There better be," Auntie Edna said.

Auntie Joy said, "I get the bags and the dust pans."

Auntie Balasha and Auntie Joy moved from one end of the

room to the other with mathematical precision, a garbage bag in one hand and a dustpan in the other, scooping up debris. Auntie Edna and Auntie Vi followed with push brooms. When Auntie Balasha and Auntie Joy reached the far end, they exchanged the bags and pans for buckets and mops, followed in their turn by Aunties Edna and Vi with dry mops and polish. In both efficiency and productivity, it was an operation that would have made Henry Ford proud to be an American.

In the kitchen, in bright yellow rubber gloves, Annie Mike presided over a double aluminum sink almost as deep as she was tall, filled with steaming, soapy water. Kate ferried in the dirty dishes, and when she set down the last load she said, "That was a good story Demetri told, the one about Old Sam and the sheep hunt. I hadn't heard it before."

"Me, either," Annie said. "For all that he lived right next door to us for the last thirty years, there's a lot we don't know about that old man."

Kate turned to look at the other woman.

"Like the icon, I meant," Annie said. She had seen Kate's shoulders tense at her words, and wondered. "I'm ashamed to say I'd never even heard of it before now."

"Me, either," Kate said. She was silent for a moment, thinking of the Sainted Mary, an ancient Russian icon triptych depiciting Mary and Jesus as mother and baby, mother and corpse, and mother and ascending son of God, that had only recently returned to the tribe due to the one-person scavenger hunt—that one person being Kate—orchestrated by Old Sam from beyond the grave. A century before, tribal members had credited the icon with everything from healing the sick to granting wishes to finding loved ones lost at sea. After a sufficient amount of spiritual groveling first, Kate was sure. "You think Emaa knew about it?"

"She was of his generation. Be strange if she didn't."

Kate looked through the pass-through at the four aunties in the gym. "By that definition, most of them would have known about it, too. I wonder why they never said anything."

Annie ran more hot water into the dish encrusted with the remains of the Olga Kvasnikof special, macaroni and cheese with Spam. "Put yourself there, in that time. A third of them were dead from the Spanish flu. They were fifty-plus years into American sovreignty. There were ongoing repercussions from the Klondike Gold Rush and the Kanuyaq Copper Mine. White encroachment on Native lands. What amounted to a foreign government taking over. The introduction of the notion of private property when before, the whole state and western Canada, too, had been their oyster, without border or boundary." She rinsed out the Pyrex dish and set it on the drainboard. "Their parents' generation was being pushed, hard, by Western civilization. Could be their pride couldn't take the extra hit, that they just couldn't face up to losing an artifact the tribe regarded as holy. Be easier just to pretend it never existed in the first place."

"Yeah, okay," Kate said, "but that icon had to have come into the Park relatively recently. We didn't have a written language, but there were newspapers around in 1920."

Annie raised an eyebrow. "How many of them wrote about Alaska Natives?"

Kate thought. "Yeah. So bottom line is, we don't know when the first Kookesh brought in the icon. Assuming he did."

"Ask a Tlingit," Annie said. "They never forget anything."

Kate laughed, and sighed. "God, I'm going to miss that cranky old bastard so much."

Annie looked through the pass-through, at the four aunties who were now getting out the folding chairs and setting them in neat rows for the next day's annual January shareholder meeting. Auntie Joy was wearing an unusually solemn expression. "You're not alone."

"Where is it?" Kate said. "The icon?"

"We've got it locked down in the NNA headquarters for now, but people are going to want to see it. It's theirs, they ought to be able to, but I'm not prepared to spend shareholder money hiring a single employee dedicated to locking and unlocking the room it's in every time someone walks in the door." She paused. "We've also had some inquiries from scholars wanting to study it."

"And?" Kate said. Annie Mike was never this long-winded except when she wanted something.

"We should give some thought to building something to house it and display it."

"A museum, you mean?"

"Why not?"

Kate remembered the oil lamp made of stone that Emaa had donated to a museum in Anchorage. No reason that kind of thing couldn't have remained in the Park, had there been a place for it. "In his will, Old Sam told me that if and when Phyllis Lestinkof and her baby moved out of his cabin to turn it over to the tribe and make it into a museum."

Annie smiled. "The Samuel Leviticus Dementieff Memorial Museum."

Kate smiled, too. "He'd have loved to make fun of that. You want to bring it up at tomorrow's meeting?"

"God no," Annie said, rinsing the last dish and pulling the plug on the sink. The water gurgled out as she stripped the gloves from her hands and annointed herself liberally with the lotion in the push-button dispenser on the drainboard. Her hands were square and brown and strong, the nails short and neatly trimmed. "The next board meeting is soon enough. For one thing, we don't know that Phyllis and the baby will be out of Old Sam's house anytime soon. Better to have a whole plan, with a site selected and a budget before we ask them to vote on it. It's never a good idea to allow the shareholders to think too much for themselves."

Kate gave her an appraising glance.

"What?" Annie said. She was a matronly woman in her mid-fifties with a fondness for polyester in primary colors. Today she was resplendent in a lipstick-red double-breasted suit with black shiny buttons the size of dessert plates and shiny patent leather loafers to match the buttons. Be easy for someone to be fooled into thinking the bright plumage was the most interesting thing about this plump-breasted, bright-eyed woman.

But when the blinding effect wore off, there remained a dignified, self-assured tribal elder with a direct, steady gaze and an air of quiet authority. It gave pause to anyone who might imagine they could bully or intimidate her in matters concerning the shareholders of the Niniltna Native Association, starting with board member and fellow shareholder Harvey Meganack and extending all the way up to Vern Truax out at the Suulutaq Mine.

A good thing, since she was Kate's handpicked successor as chair of the NNA board. "I used to think you were an auntie in training," Kate said.

There was the barest hint of a smile behind Annie's solemn expression. "And now?"

"And now I'm wondering if you aren't the next Emaa." Emaa being Kate's grandmother, dead these six years. Sagacious, prescient, patient, iron of heart and of backbone, Emaa had been more a Machiavellian force of nature than a human being, and had steered the Association's ship of state from its creation by the Alaska Native Claims Settlement Act until her death. She had been succeeded by Billy Mike, who upon his own death was in turn succeeded, with extreme reluctance, by Kate. It had been the two longest years of her life.

Annie's face relaxed into a smile. "Be careful what you wish for, little girl."

Kate laughed again. It was getting easier.

On the other side of the room, Auntie Joy looked up at the sound. Kate met her wounded eyes for a brief moment before Auntie Joy turned away again. Kate's laughter faded.

"Were they especially close?"

"Sorry?" Kate said.

Annie nodded at Auntie Joy. "Old Sam and Auntie Joy. She seems a lot more torn up than the rest of them."

After an infinitesimable pause, Kate said, "They went back a long way."

She was sure her expression hadn't changed, but Annie gave her a sharp look before she turned to reach for a dishcloth.

3

JANUARY 15

Niniltna

JIM'S CELL PHONE VIBRATED against his belt. He jumped and swore.

His dispatcher laughed. Shamefaced, he joined in. "Can't get used to it," he said.

Maggie looked out the post window on the uphill side, through which could be seen Niniltna's brand-spanking-new tower, a three-hundred-foot-tall behemoth (taller than Bobby Clark's, and didn't that just torque the hell out of the owner and proprietor of pirate radio station Park Air) that loured up from behind the school gymnasium, a massive presence in the brief light of a January afternoon. Through the openwork steel frame, she could see the alpenglow painting the snow-covered breasts of the Quilak Mountains a pale magenta. Less than a month after construction, the tower already bristled with a dozen antennas and dishes, some directed upriver toward Ahtna and the Glenn Highway, an equal number down, in the direction of half a dozen villages and, more to the purpose, the Suulutaq gold mine.

The tower and the gymnasium were both surrounded by parked vehicles of every kind, make, and age—pickups, SUVs, snow machines, four-wheelers—and Maggie could even hear the howling of dogs, signifying the presence of teams tethered to dogsleds. Evidently some shareholders had mushed in to the annual Niniltna Native Association shareholders meeting.

"This is probably how the old folks felt when the Kanuyaq Copper Mine ran the first telephone wire the whole four miles between Kanuyaq and Niniltna," she said, and went back to writing the crime report for the *Ahtna Adit,* which could now, courtesy of one of the antennas on said tower, be emailed directly to the local weekly from her very own computer. Previously, she'd had to save the document, download it to a thumb drive, and trudge up the hill to the school, where until last month had resided the only Internet access to be found in Niniltna.

Not that it was all joy, because with this all new and improved access to communications, the Park rats had taken to cell phones with a vengeance, and all of them seemed to have the trooper post on speed dial. *January 10,* she typed. *A caller reported the theft of a four-wheeler from a residence on Riverside Drive,* the third one this week. Jim had found it, like the other two, abandoned near the Suulutaq Mine, the product of yet another McMiner stealing a quick ride back to work.

"Everything old is new again," Jim said, still fighting to get his cell phone, still buzzing, out of his belt pouch.

January 11. A caller from the Riverside Café reported a pickup being driven erratically down the Step Road.

That had been the Park's Chief Ranger Dan O'Brian, bringing his truck down from Park headquarters on the Step to Herbie Topkok's shop in the village, without benefit of brakes. And *erratically* was Maggie's euphemism for what Harvey Meganack had really said, which was distinctly inappropriate for a family newspaper, not to mention an official state record.

January 11. An anonymous caller reported three individuals spray-painting slogans on the side of the Last Chance Creek bridge.

Salvador Totemoff and two of his junior high peeps exercising their right to free speech. Maggie and Jim were less bothered about the graffiti than they had been about the fact that said bridge was three hundred feet above creek level. Not that, in the event of the very worst happening, it wouldn't have been a case of self-correction on the part of the gene pool.

The snap finally gave and Jim looked at the display. UNKNOWN it said. He bowed to the inevitable and answered anyway. "Jim Chopin."

January 12. An anonymous caller objected to cross-country skiers wearing parasails as they came down the bunny hill.

Well he might, as a launch from the ski hill had a trajectory that could put a parasailing skier on course with the windows of several homes of Niniltna's most illustrious citizens, among them Demetri Totemoff and Edna Shugak. The aforesaid Harvey Meganack, in pursuit of his eternal quest to make his fortune, had cleared a path through a stand of spruce on a slope off the foot of the town's airstrip, installed a rope tow, and built a shed from which Harvey's cousin, that unrecovering alcoholic and heretofore unemployable Elias Halversen rented out sleds, skis, and snowboards. Harvey's plan had been to entice some of those Suulutaq McMiners into paying for a little harmless fun during their off time, totally ignoring the fact that said miners were mostly young men in their twenties and that when they got off their twelve-hour shifts all they wanted to do was score transportation to the Roadhouse, the only purveyor of alcohol within a hundred miles.

Well. The only legal purveyor.

January 13. An anonymous caller reported two individuals were selling pints of Windsor Canadian in front of Bingley's.

It didn't take a rocket scientist to figure out who the two individuals were, but as usual Howie and Willard had been long gone by the time Jim got there.

This was the last item, and she saved and sent with a flourish.

Jim was still standing in front of her desk, and something in the quality of his silence brought Maggie's head up. His eyes had narrowed and his mouth was a hard line. After a moment he said, "Where are you?"

He glanced through the window. "Cross the strip and follow the road down the hill. The post is the third building on the left after the school."

He hung up and went into his office, and she went back to work wondering what all that was about.

Ten minutes later, the door to the post opened, and Maggie looked up. In purely instinctive feminine reaction, she sat bolt upright in her chair, sucked in her gut, raised her chin to smooth out an incipient wattle, and resisted the temptation to raise a hand to check her hair. "May I help you?" she said, and was proud her voice didn't squeak.

"I'm here to see Sergeant Chopin," the Alaska state trooper, also a sergeant, said in a pleasant baritone, pulling the ball cap from his head. His name tag read L. CAMPBELL. "He's expecting me."

"Certainly," Maggie said. Jim's door was closed, which was unusual. The only time Jim's door was closed was when both he and Kate Shugak were on the other side of it. It took Maggie a moment to find the intercom button on her phone. "Sergeant Chopin? A Sergeant Campbell to see you."

"Send him in."

She released the button and nodded at Jim's door.

"Thanks." He looked at her name tag. "Maggie." Sergeant Campbell's smile made her heart skip a beat. Tall but not too tall, thick dark red hair that just begged to be rumpled by a caressing hand, eyes the color of the sea at sunset, strong, square shoulders, narrow hips, and long, muscular legs. There just wasn't anything not to like. When he turned to knock on Jim's door, she couldn't help noticing that the view going away was equally entrancing. His uniform was neither off the rack nor made of a material even remotely synthetic. It fit like it, too.

A laconic "Yeah" sounded from behind the door.

Campbell opened the door. "Jim," he said.

"Liam," Jim said, and the door closed behind them.

"Wow," Maggie said softly. She had worked every day of the last three years with a man who was, to put it mildly, easy on the eyes. She would have thought she'd become inured to it.

She'd always wondered if recruiters for the Alaska State Troopers selected for height. Now she wondered if they selected for looks, too.

• • •

On the other side of the door, the two men in the almost identical uniforms exchanged a long, expressionless stare. Finally Jim said in a voice entirely without inflection, "Liam," and nodded at a chair. "Have a seat."

"Thanks, Jim." Campbell unzipped the heavy blue jacket and sat down.

There was silence. "How long you been here?" Campbell finally said.

"Going on three years," Jim said.

"Little different from Wasilla."

"That it is," Jim said. "Not busting near as many meth labs and marijuana grows in the Park. Thank god."

Campbell nodded. "You looking to retire out of here?"

He was referring to the Alaska State Troopers' seven-step duty posts. The more rural the post, the higher the pay. The higher the pay when a trooper retired, the bigger the pension. "Not planning on retiring anytime soon," Jim said, and wondered if that were true.

"You just like the village life, then."

A faint shrug. "This village, yeah."

Campbell raised an eyebrow. "Hear tell there might be another reason."

"There might." Jim did not elaborate.

"Never took you for a one-woman man."

Jim shrugged and returned no answer.

Another silence. Campbell started to fidget in his chair, and thought better of it. "You're not going to make this easy, are you."

"Any reason I should?"

Campbell looked past Jim, at the impenetrable cluster of spruce trees crowding in at the window. "It's not like I don't know I screwed up."

"Five people dying because you were asleep at the switch constitutes a little more than screwing up in my book," Jim said.

"That was six, almost seven years ago now," Campbell said, his voice level. "Maybe time to let that go."

"Like you have?"

Campbell met Jim's eyes squarely. "Not an option for me."

A third silence. Jim took a long breath, held it for a few moments, and then let it out slowly. "What the hell happened?"

Liam told him. He spoke simply, in words devoid of emotion, but the obvious determination to remain matter-of-fact told its own tale. "There's no excuse, Jim," he said. "I just wasn't paying attention. I fucked up, and five people died."

"You're right, you did," Jim said. A pause. He sighed. "But so did they. They drove down an unmaintained road in February, out of cell range, with no arctic gear, and didn't tell anyone where they were going." His mouth twisted. "A friend of mine calls it suicide by Alaska. Usually it's Outsiders with no clue. But sometimes..."

Campbell was silent.

"I should have asked before," Jim said. "I'm sorry."

"You tried," Campbell said. "I wasn't real ... receptive."

They were men. That was as sentimental as it was going to get.

Jim leaned back in his chair and crossed his feet on his desk. "Newenham. Lot of big cases, all closed pretty decisively, and all of them on film at ten, too. Been an interesting post for you."

Campbell's expression lightened at the relaxation of tension in the room. "You could say that."

"And I see you're already back up to sergeant."

"Yeah."

"Fast tracker." Jim smiled for the first time. "Good work on Gheen."

Campbell shrugged. "He finally kidnapped the wrong woman. She escaped and led him right to us." A shadow passed across his face. "And getting him didn't come for free."

"Heard that, too. Still."

Liam nodded. "Still."

"Heard you didn't even have to go to trial."

Liam shook his head. "Oh, he wanted to tell us all about it. Whether we wanted to hear it or not."

Jim smiled. "A full confession, plus enough probative evidence to slam-dunk a jury full of card-carrying ACLU members, might make some practicing law enforcement professionals think they'd died and gone to heaven."

"When the perp, tail wagging, led them to the grave of his tenth vic, where was found not only her skeleton but also the skeleton of her unborn child, some practicing law enforcement professionals might think otherwise. I'm just glad it didn't come to that."

Their eyes met in perfect understanding. By profession, their noses rubbed in the worst of human behavior every day of their working lives, they were de facto unshockable. People behaved badly. It's why there were cops. But Jim and Liam wouldn't have been human if the criminal, conscienceless inventiveness of certain deeply bent individuals had not, in fact, deeply shocked them on occasion.

Campbell settled back into his chair. "I've got a problem."

"Figured. A big one, too." He saw Campbell's look and shrugged. "Had to be something big to get you on a plane all the way out here." Jim laced his fingers behind his head. "I grant you full and free access to the wisdom of your elder and better."

Campbell didn't smile. "I caught a murder." He paused. "I think."

"Interesting," Jim said.

Campbell's laugh was explosive. "That's one word for it. I could use some help on it."

"I thought you had help. Didn't Barton send Prince down there?"

Campbell's brows came together. "He did."

"And she can't help you?"

"No," Campbell said.

"Why not?"

Campbell's lips tightened. "Because she ran off with my father."

When Jim stopped laughing, he saw that Campbell was regarding him with a marginally lighter countenance. "Yeah, very funny."

"Clearly, it is," Jim said, wiping an eye. "USAF Colonel Charles Campbell, trooper thief. Who'd a thunk it."

"Anybody who knew him for more than five minutes," Campbell said.

"Wouldn't have thought it of Prince, though."

"No," Campbell said glumly, "but all bets are off when it comes to my father and women. But about this case."

Jim frowned. There was something else, other than perfidious fathers absconding with faithless sidekicks. "What about it?"

"If I were investigating this officially," Campbell said, his voice bleak, "my prime suspect would be my wife."

4

JANUARY 15

Niniltna

AT THE VERY SAME moment Sergeant Liam Campbell was unburdening his heart to Sergeant Jim Chopin, Niniltna Native Association board of directors chair Kate Shugak was back in the Niniltna School gymnasium for the second day in a row. As usual, a longing eye was canvassing the room for the nearest exit. While yesterday's potlatch for Old Sam had inspired its share of grief and tears, she infinitely preferred it to presiding over the annual shareholders meeting.

Although it was going unusually well, the customary infighting, backbiting, and power-jockeying were in suprising abeyance. In part this was due to their current chair's leadership abilities. Kate marched them through old business like Alexander went through Asia, doubling the budget for the Niniltna Public Health Clinic against easily suppressed opposition from Ulanie Anahonak and her anti-everything clique, refining two clauses in the NNA contract with Aurora Communications, Inc., the document governing the construction of cell towers down the three-hundred-mile length of the Kanuyaq River, and reporting on ongoing talks between the Association, the State of Alaska, and the federal government on just who could fish where, when, and take how much out of the three-hundred-mile length of the Kanuyaq River.

New business didn't take much longer, being chiefly concerned with the return of the Sainted Mary to the tribe. Kate reported on as much of the history of its one-hundred-year perambulation and subsequent restoration as she thought it was good for the shareholders to know, and gave all the credit to Old Sam. Tradition held that the Sainted Mary reside with the current chief, but there wasn't a current chief, that position having been gradually superseded over the last thirty years by the chair of the NNA board, and the shareholders agreed that the safest place for the Sainted Mary at present was locked up in the NNA's headquarters here in Niniltna. Kate proposed and Herbie Topkok seconded that a committee be formed to work out more permanent accommodations for the Sainted Mary's future, and five people, including two aunties, promptly volunteered to serve.

"Is there any more new business?" Kate said.

There wasn't. Really, one of the least confrontational shareholders meetings in the history of the Niniltna Native Asscociation.

Or, she thought, everyone was just in a hurry to get to the main event, which was the election of a new board of directors, and a new chairman of that board.

She was in something of a hurry to get there herself.

"Very well," Kate said. "There being no new business, I move that we open the floor to nominations for the board seat left vacant by the death of board member Samuel Leviticus Dementieff."

The move was seconded, and Auntie Vi raised her hand.

"The chair recognizes Viola Moonin."

"I nominate Axenia Shugak Mathisen for Old Sam's seat," Auntie Vi said, and the glower she directed at the assemblage dared anyone else to put up a rival candidate.

Some of the shareholders would go up against Kate any day all day long, but Auntie Vi was another kettle of fish entirely. Harvey Meganack, of all people, seconded the nomination.

"Axenia Shugak Mathisen has been nominated to serve on the board of directors," Kate said. "Ms. Mathisen?"

Halfway down the center aisle formed by two rectangles of gray metal folding chairs, Axenia rose to her feet, dark brown eyes calm, black hair cut in a tidy pageboy with artfully feathered bangs. "Madam Chair?"

"You have been nominated to a seat on the board of directors. Do you accept the nomination?"

"Madam Chair, I do."

"Very well." Kate surveyed the two hundred shareholders. "Are there any other nominations?"

Auntie Vi maintained her glower. Prudently, there were none.

"Very well," Kate said. "Is there any discussion on the nomination of Axenia Shugak Mathisen to the board of directors of the Niniltna Native Association?"

Iris Meganack raised her hand. "Axenia lives in Anchorage. I thought all board members had to live in the Park."

Kate looked at Annie. "The chair recognizes Annie Mike."

Unflustered, Annie looked at Iris. "Residency is unrestricted, according to our bylaws. The founders"—by which she meant Ekaterina, Kate's grandmother, who had been most responsible for the final form of the bylaws governing the Association—"were mindful of the fact that the Association was and would be for the foreseeable future very small in number of members. They knew it would have been a mistake for the founders to exclude any shareholder on the basis of residence."

"Yes," Iris said, "but have we ever had a board member who didn't live in the Park before?"

"No," Annie said. "Again, this is a matter of tradition only, not of bylaw."

The shareholders took a moment to digest this. Kate looked at Axenia, who had remained on her feet for the discussion. She was dressed in worn jeans, a faded plaid shirt, and waffle stompers that looked older than she was. She had brought both of her children with her, and they were playing quietly with the rest of the kids in back of the rows of folding chairs. She'd been front and center at the potlatch yesterday, circulating through the crowd to speak at least a few words to every single person there, and taking her turn at the microphone to tell an unexceptional story about Old Sam and the time he'd built a bed for her Barbie doll. She'd been a wild child in her youth, before Kate conspired against their grandmother to get her cousin out of the Park. Her Park rat dress and quiet, assured demeanor, not to mention her well-behaved children, had gone a long way toward erasing the Park's memory of that wayward teenager.

Someone else raised their hand. "The chair recognizes Debbie Ollestad."

Debbie raised herself ponderously to her feet, wincing when her weight came down on that bunion on her left big toe. "Axenia's husband is an attorney for the Suulutaq Mine." A murmur went around the room. "Isn't that a conflict of interest?"

Annie Mike raised her hand. "Madam Chair, if I may. The bylaws do not define conflict of interest, per se. They do require all board members to conduct themselves in a manner that is transparent, at all times putting the interests of the Association before their own." Annie paused briefly, and when she continued, the more observant noticed the steel entering into her voice. "If a board member is at any time observed by any shareholder in violation of these precepts, the bylaws provide a mechanism for bringing the matter before the shareholders." Annie paused again. "At which time the shareholders will be asked to decide if they wish to retain the services of said board member."

Her tone was so dry this time that a ripple of laughter ran around the room, and Debbie nodded and resumed her seat in obvious relief.

"Is there any further discussion?" Kate asked, bending an intimidating eye on the assemblage. There was not, and Axenia Shugak Mathisen was elected to the Niniltna Native Association board of directors by a voice vote. Amid applause, she walked to the stage, climbed the stairs, and took the empty chair next to Auntie Joy.

Which brought them to the last item on the agenda. Kate took a deep breath and did her best not to look overjoyed. "As you all know, two years ago I was named NNA chair, to serve out Billy Mike's term. It's up. I'm out."

This time the laugh was louder and lasted longer. Behind her, Kate could hear the enthusiastic thump of Mutt's tail on the wooden floor of the stage.

Try as she would to maintain the dignity of her office, Kate couldn't stop the grin from spreading across her face. "Therefore, today we elect a new chair. I declare the floor open to nominations, and as my penultimate act I'm going to co-opt the first one. I nominate Annie Mike."

"I second," Auntie Vi said promptly.

Kate had spent the last two months speaking in person to each and every one of the 276 shareholders to ensure that there would be no other nominations and no discussion. In addition, she had put the aunties into the field, a five-pronged attack that had not failed of effect. Ulanie Anahonak looked angry, but she could take the temperature of a room as well as any other politician, and Annie Mike was elected to the board without a single dissenting vote. Indeed, the shout of acclamation was almost as loud as the shout that greeted Lars Ahkiok's winning basket in last year's annual grudge match between the Kanuyaq Kings and the Seldovia Sea Otters.

Annie, who had spent the last fifteen years sitting in a corner taking minutes of board meetings, was unaccustomed to so much direct attention. She came to the podium to accept the gavel, a little flushed. She kept her acceptance speech short and sweet, thanking Kate for the nomination and the shareholders for their votes and promising to work hard to keep their confidence and to help lead the Niniltna Native Association into a profitable and sustainable future. Her first act as chair was to announce that Phyllis Lestinkof had been hired as the new Association secretary. This found favor with everyone except for Phyllis's family, boon companions of Ulanie's, who had cast Phyllis out when she became pregnant with an illegitimate child and whom they had fondly hoped to find in a ditch sometime during the past winter, dead of hypothermia and despair. Instead, their sinful daughter now had a daughter of her own, a home with a supply of wood sufficient to last through two winters, and a good job. Dark and direful mutterings came from their section of the chairs. Phyllis, sitting in the front row, baby Samantha on her lap attired in a hot pink onesie, displayed a newfound composure and ignored them. She was a woman of substance and a mother now.

As Annie spoke, Kate looked over the audience and found not a few faces turned her way. Most seemed to be waiting for the other shoe to drop. No one had quite believed her, however many times she had said it, that she was uninterested in being chair for another term, or for life.

She looked at the new board. Auntie Joy, Harvey Meganack, Demetri Totemoff, who between them represented a minimum of sixty years' time served on the NNA board. And the newer members, Einar Carlson, Herbie Topkok, Marlene Colberg, Ulanie Anahonak. The newest member of all, her cousin Axenia. Axenia met Kate's eyes calmly, but Kate fancied she could detect suprise and disbelief in her cousin's eyes, and perhaps just a hint of contempt as well. Axenia could not imagine anyone ever willingly giving up power.

Kate had the sudden uncomfortable feeling that her cousin and their grandmother had a lot in common.

"Very well," Annie said, giving the gavel a tentative rap. "With thanks to our outgoing chair, who has agreed to continue to act for our interests in an advisory capacity, and in memoriam of Old Sam, who will be with us always in spirit, I declare this annual shareholders meeting of the Niniltna Native Association adjourned." Before anyone could get to their feet she added with a stern look that would have done Ekaterina proud, "Please, everyone who can, stay behind and help us clear the room."

Her request was unnecessary. The Kanuyaq Kings would be playing the Cordova Wolverines this weekend, junior varsity and varsity, men's and women's teams, in a two-day matchup beginning tomorrow. Bernie Koslowski would have their collective heads with one fell swoop if so much as a crumb of fry bread were left on the wooden floor of the school gymnasium. "Free throws win ball games," the coach was fond of saying, but so did a clean, dry floor to play on, and the cleanup crew was every one of them heart and soul a Kanuyaq Kings booster.

Not to mention which, they didn't want to be banned for life from the Roadhouse. As any miner in Suulutaq could tell them, the Roadhouse was the only watering hole around.

5

JANUARY 15, THAT EVENING

Niniltna

IT WAS A CLEAR night with a waxing crescent moon and the temperature way below zero. The exuberant manner in which Kate hit the panic bar on the gym door on her way outside would have given anyone watching the idea she was headed for Hawaii. Even Mutt had to scramble to keep up. By the time they reached Kate's snow machine, Kate had her parka zipped, her hood up and buttoned, and her goggles pulled down over her eyes. The snogo came to life at a touch and Kate swung a leg over the seat and hit the throttle. Mutt gave a startled yip and it took her two strides to catch up and scramble up on the seat behind Kate. She had to snatch her a mouthful of parka shoulder before forward momentum tumbled her off again.

The only official speed limit through the village of Niniltna was the one observed by common sense and a decent respect for the lives and property of others, neither of which did Kate have on display that January evening. She used the hill down from the school as a launchpad and hurtled the snogo into a long, heart-stopping skid of a right turn onto Riverside without letting up on the throttle, worthy of a 911 call all on its own. The Meganacks house flashed by on their left and that's when Kate really hit the gas. Mutt let out another startled but this time also exhilarated yip and took a firmer grip on Kate's parka.

The snowgo's top speed was ninety miles an hour, or it had been when it was new, but Kate had kept it in good shape. Eight feet of accumulated winter snow had been packed down by two months'-worth of traffic so that the road home was a hard, fast surface that more nearly resembled a luge run. Traffic was mostly going in their direction. Kate blew past them like the Road Runner outrunning an Acme rocket, with Wile E. Coyote still back in Niniltna. The only oncoming traffic was Willard Shugak's ancient International pickup, and while Willard wasn't the brightest bulb in the box, even he had enough smarts to pull over as far to his side as he could without going into the ditch when he saw Kate's rooster tail coming at him.

Well before the turnoff to the homestead, Kate applied brakes and body weight in injudicious proportions to put the snogo into another death-defying sideways slide that jostled Mutt's teeth loose from their hold on Kate's parka. With a sound that could only be described as "Yikes!" Mutt tumbled from the back of the machine and went rolling off the road to be buried headfirst in a snowbank. Kate, laughing like a maniac, came to an exceedingly momentary stop with the nose of the snogo pointing precisely at the trailhead. She gunned the engine again and shot down it. Behind her she heard Mutt barking madly and she laughed again.

The trail was narrow and twisting and she hit only the tops of the bumps. Woman and machine slid to a superbly executed hockey stop in the clearing, raising a spray of snow in another rooster tail that reached as high as the shop roof. With a war whoop that could have been heard fifty miles away in Niniltna, Kate vaulted off the seat, but Mutt, hurtling down the trail and into the clearing, was one second before her. On the fly she grabbed the hem of Kate's jeans in her teeth and dumped Kate on her ass. Kate rolled to her hands and knees and tackled Mutt into a pile of newly snoveled snow that under the impact went up like a small atomic bomb. For the next ten minutes the 120-pound woman and the 140-pound wolf-husky hybrid roughhoused all the way around the clearing, a circumnavigation that shook the stairs to the house, nearly knocked the cache off its stilts, and knocked the door to the now blessedly retired outhouse off one hinge. They somersaulted into spruce trees that unleashed more clouds of snow from heavily laden branches and banged against the big sliding door of the shop before winding up once more at the foot of the stairs to the house.

By now Kate's short cap of black hair was frozen into icy dreadlocks, she had snow up her pant legs and down the back of her shirt, her parka was half off one shoulder, and she was losing her right boot. This called for drastic measures. She grabbed Mutt's head in both hands and covered her muzzle with loud, lavish kisses. Mutt leaped back in horror and gave a mighty sneeze. Kate knew an opportunity when she saw it and in a flash she was on her feet and taking the stairs two at the time. There was an outraged "Whuff!" from behind her and Kate took the last three steps in one jump and hit the door with a crash that shook the house.

She flung it open hard enough to shake the house again and took a giant leap inside. She landed on the floor with bent knees and raised arms, struck a pose like a Pamyua dancer and shouted, "With one bound, Kate was free!"

Mutt romped in behind, scattering snow from the kitchen to the living room. Velocity overcame friction and she slid into Kate with a hard thump, knocking Kate off her feet, and the tendency of bodies in motion to stay in motion rolled them up into a ball that thudded ingloriously into the kitchen counter.

Kate was laughing so hard she couldn't speak. Mutt, more conscious of her dignity, or perhaps just readier to reengage the enemy, made a mad scramble to reachieve the vertical.

She froze in place. A tentative growl emerged from her throat.

Kate blinked up at her, and raised her head.

Johnny stood at the stove with a spatula in his hand, Jim sat at the dining table, and a total stranger sat on their couch. All three of them were regarding Kate and Mutt with identical quizzical expressions.

"Oh." She sat up. A hank of frozen hair fell into her eyes, and she made an ineffectual attempt to bat the ice out of it. "I didn't know we had company."

"We noticed," Johnny said, a grin spreading across his face.

Jim's attempt not to laugh was a little too obvious. "You okay?"

"I'm fine," Kate said, and got to her feet.

"Kate," Jim said, "this is Liam Campbell. Liam, this is Kate Shugak."

Kate squelched over to shake hands. Liam's was large and strong, Kate's cold and wet. "Jim was your training officer in the Valley," she said.

"He was." Liam looked at Jim. "She knows of me by repute."

"Trust me," Jim said dryly, "you're not our only topic of conversation."

Liam grinned down at Kate. "I should hope not."

Mutt, satisfied that she was not going to be summoned to repel boarders, broke the silence by shaking herself vigorously, spraying the entire first floor with ice pellets, and went to scuff up her quilt and sprawl in front of the fireplace.

Kate let go of Liam's hand and turned to look at Johnny. "Do I have time for a shower?"

He flipped a burger in the cast-iron skillet. The resulting sizzle followed by the pungent aroma of crisping moosemeat was enough to make Kate weep. "Barely," he said.

"Excellent."

She waited until she was upstairs with the bedroom door closed safely behind her before whispering to herself, "Wow."

This Campbell guy was *hot*.

Dinner was massive mooseburgers with stacks of lettuce, cheese, onions, and tomatoes on buns toasted crisp and lathered with relish, mustard, and mayonnaise. Johnny, not just a boy but a prince, had made homemade fries to go with, and everything was washed down by Auntie Balasha's homemade root beer, two cases of which she had been induced to part with in exchange for a cord of firewood. Old Sam had been the traditional provider of firewood for the aunties, and Kate foresaw a full-time future career with an ax in her hand if she didn't find a reliable substitute. Something the NNA could organize, she thought, a group of teen shareholders paid to make sure their elders had adequate fuel supply for the winter.

She would have to be careful how she suggested it, though, or Annie Mike would rope her in to run the committee.

And she was so done with that.

Johnny retired to his room with a fistful of dessert, aka Auntie Joy's browned butter sugar cookies, fuel to spur the Googling of prospective colleges. Thanks to the small dish hanging off the eaves outside and the string of cell towers down the road from Ahtna to Niniltna, Kate's homestead now had Internet access, or it did as long as she didn't run out of fuel for the generator.

She didn't know quite what to think about this. It was just so unbearably uptown. At any moment someone was going to revoke her citizenship for frontier living.

The adults moved into the living room, Kate and Jim on the couch and Campbell on the La-Z-Boy. He'd unbuttoned enough to have divested himself of jacket, tie, and boots, although he still looked like he'd just stepped out of an ad from *GQ*. He applied himself to dessert with the same enthusiasm he had shown toward dinner. Kate did like a man who enjoyed his food, whether she'd done the cooking or not.

She licked the last of the sugar from her fingers and looked at Campbell. "This isn't just a social call."

Campbell looked at Jim, who raised his shoulders in a faint shrug. Campbell looked back at Kate. "No," he said. "I need help."

"What kind of help?"

"Investigatory help."

Kate raised an eyebrow. "I thought you were some kind of trooper."

Unoffended, Campbell grinned. "The uniform sort of a giveaway? Yeah, well, that's where it gets a little tricky. My vic was killed in a plane crash last month." He got up and walked to where his jacket was hanging over the back of a chair. He fished a plastic bag out of a pocket and tossed it to Kate.

She caught and examined it, frowning. It was an evidence bag, containing a nut threaded onto a tube. "What is this?"

"It's off a Super Cub. Holds on the bell housing over an oil screen."

She handed it back. "Why is it in an evidence bag?"

Campbell set the bag down on the arm of the La-Z-Boy

and regarded it. "December eleventh, pilot and businessman Dagfin 'Finn' Grant took off from Newenham in his Super Cub, headed for his FBO south of town."

"FBO?" Kate said.

"A fixed-base operator," Jim said. "A privately or publicly owned commercial business created to provide aviation support at a local airport." He saw her look and shrugged. "What it says on Wikipedia. FBOs provide fuel, parts, maintenance, aircraft parking, aircraft rental, pilot housing, pilot entertainment." He hesitated over that last word just long enough for Kate's eyebrow to go up. "You name it," Jim said, "an FBO has it on offer. Basically whatever they figure they can make money selling to pilots, air taxies, and small airline operators."

"Grant figured he could sell quite a lot," Campbell said, "and he was right. His FBO was—is—located on the site of a former air force base about twenty-five miles south of Newenham. BRAC closed it four years ago—"

"Base Closure and Realignment Commission," Jim said.

"—and Grant snapped it up for pennies on the dollar. Prior to that, he had been operating a flightseeing and air taxi service out of Newenham. Bristol Bay Air Freight. He renamed the business Eagle Air LLC and moved it to Chinook—the air force base—and started to expand. In two years he had bought up nearly every tourism-related business in the area, air taxies, fishing charters, hunting lodges." Campbell paused. "I understand that sometimes he bought them whether the owners wanted to sell or not, although I've never been able to get anyone to say any more than that." He shrugged. "And, of course, absent complaints, there was no reason to investigate one way or the other."

"He independently wealthy, or what?" Jim said.

"Good question," Campbell said, "and one I don't have an answer for." He looked at Kate. "Which may be where you come in. He married local royalty."

"Who?"

"His wife's maiden name was Clementina Tannehill."

"Tannehill." Kate's lips pursed together in a silent whistle. "That's not local, that's state royalty. Hell, that's territorial royalty, and it might even be actual Romanov royalty if you go back far enough. You said Clementina? That'd be, at a guess, Thad and Lillie's daughter. And..." She thought. "Carter's sister?"

Campbell consulted a notepad. "Yeah. She's the sole survivor of her generation. I'm told they've had a finger in every business pie from Unalaska to Bethel, and that Thad staked the first platinum claim at Platinum."

Kate nodded. "They're statehood stakeholders, all right, and high boat seiners, and stampeders, and before that fur traders. You name it, they've done it and made a pile of money at it. You were right about the royalty. If Grant married into that family, he was made in Alaska from that moment on. Although..."

"What?"

"I remember some rumor or other about the family falling on hard times. Nothing substantial, just a whisper on the wind." She shook her head. "And it wouldn't count locally, anyway. If the Tannehills let him marry into the family, it wouldn't matter how high the number was on his driver's licence. The old farts would take him at face value." She looked at the part in the evidence bag. "He your vic?"

Campbell nodded, too. "When he moved operations to Chinook, he commuted between Newenham and Chinook in his Super Cub." His voice was very dry, just the facts, ma'am.

"On the morning of December eleventh, at 10:06 A.M. according to the flight service station, he took off for Chinook."

"10:06 being just about daylight?" Jim said.

Campbell nodded. "Wy says it was at most a fifteen-minute flight. At eleven o'clock, one Tasha Anuyuk, Eagle Air employee, called Grant's house looking for him. His wife, Clementina, reported him overdue to flight service, and local pilots went up to look for him."

"Weather?" Jim said.

"Cold," Campbell said, "but clear and no winds to speak of. Wy—my wife, Wyanet Chouinard, she's a pilot with her own air taxi operating out of Newenham—spotted him first, about two miles short of the Chinook runway."

Kate got the distinct impression that Campbell would have preferred almost any other pilot in the world to have found the wreckage of Finn Grant's airplane.

"I took a four-wheeler out to the wreck. It's all delta out there, built of glacial silt that came down the river. Lot of rolling hills and little lakes, thick brush, scrub spruce, lots of alders."

"I've flown over it," Jim said. "Pretty lumpy landscape and none of the lakes are very big. Hard to find a smooth stretch long enough to set her down in if you were in trouble."

"Wy said Grant did his best to get her down in one piece," Campbell said. "So did the NTSB guy. You could see where he'd tried to slow down on a couple of hillocks, but it had been cold for a while and the snow was frozen pretty hard. He couldn't get the Cub slowed down enough before he plowed into the last hill."

"What caused the crash?" Jim said.

Campbell picked up the part in the evidence bag and pointed. "See the nut?"

They did.

"It was loose," Campbell said.

"How loose?" Jim said.

"NTSB says loose enough to start leaking oil as soon as he started the engine. Not loose enough for him to spot if he opened the cowling for a look-see, and not loose enough for it to show on his oil pressure gauge until he was well in the air."

"Yikes," Jim said.

"That's what the NTSB guy said when he found it," Campbell said.

"Explain," Kate said, looking at Jim.

"The nut holds the bell housing over the oil screen," Jim said. "If the nut is loose, oil leaks out through the screen and the housing. Oil pressure would drop to zero and the temperature would redline." He saw Kate's expression and elaborated. "The moving parts inside the engine would lose lubrication and coolant and start running rough and heating up. Take, what, ten minutes for the engine to seize up?"

"Fifteen, max, the NTSB guy said," Campbell said.

"He should have known he was in trouble almost immediately," Jim said. "Why didn't he just turn around and put her back down in Newenham?"

"NTSB guy speculated a little about that for me," Campbell said. "Said it depended on just how loose the nut was."

Jim nodded. "Could have backed off in the air from the vibration of the engine."

"Yeah."

"Who serviced his engine?"

"Grant himself was a licensed A&P mechanic, and he employed another, who was working on a Cessna in Naknek when Grant went down."

"Annual up to date?"

Campbell nodded. "He was an asshole, but he wasn't a sloppy asshole. Even the people who hated him admit that he was a first-class pilot."

There was a short silence. "So a screw came loose," Kate said.

"A nut," Jim said.

"Whatever," Kate said. She looked at Campbell. "Sloppy or not, what makes this a case of anything other than pilot error? Or mechanic error? Or in this case both?"

Campbell sighed and leaned back to look out the tall windows that constituted most of the front wall of the little house in the big woods. The crescent moon in the clear sky combined with the frosting of snow on the ground beneath to generate enough reflected light to fill nearly all the shadows in the room. In front of the fireplace Mutt snorted in her sleep, her thick gray coat turned a lustrous silver in the moonlight. "First of all, motive," he said.

"Who?" Kate said.

"Nearly everyone in Newenham," Campbell said. "Including my wife."

"The aforementioned Wyanet Chouinard?" Kate said.

"The very same."

"Awkward," Kate said.

"I'll say," Campbell said.

"She hate him enough to kill him?" she said bluntly.

Campbell's gaze lingered on the scar on Kate's neck. A thin rope of ridged skin that was only a little lighter than the surrounding skin on the strong brown throat, it reached nearly from ear to ear. "I don't think she does, or ever did hate him," he said, "but she was damn near the only independent operator left in the aviation business between Anchorage and Unalaska other than Grant. He wanted to buy her out. She refused. He got pretty nasty about it, in front of witnesses, and they had words. Witnesses say he threatened her, and those same witnesses say she threatened him right back. Everybody who saw it says it got pretty lively."

Kate had thrown out the question partly as a means to gauge just how committed Campbell was to finding out the truth of Grant's death, as opposed to finding his wife innocent of any wrongdoing in conjunction with it. Jim saw that Liam's sangfroid had passed the test, and he breathed again.

"When did this argument take place?" Kate said.

Campbell sighed. "Oh, that would be the day before he died."

"He have any public fights with anyone else?"

"Who he didn't fight with would constitute the vast minority of the Newenham population," Campbell said. "As I said before, he strong-armed a lot of the businesses he bought into selling."

"How?"

Campbell shrugged. "Bought up their debt and foreclosed. Bought the buildings they were doing their business out of and raised the rent on them, or just booted them out. Bought out their competitors and lowered prices to drive them out of business."

"Ruthless," Kate said. Her fingertips were starting to tingle and her nose was beginning to twitch. From the corner of her eye she saw Jim repress a smile.

"You could say that," Campbell said. "The last three, four years, he was not our most popular citizen. Not that he ever had been before, but he did ramp things up after he bought Chinook."

"Was this right after he married Clementina?"

"What?" Campbell said. "No. No, he was fifty-nine. He'd

been married to Clementina for thirty years."

However much inherited wealth had been made available to Grant when he married so very well, his recent buying spree must have accounted for a great deal of it, and even inherited wealth ran out at some point. Even Tannehill inherited wealth. Kate wondered why it had taken Grant so long to begin spending it in such a high, wide, and handsome fashion. "Okay, so you're kind of overflowing with motive," she said. "What else?"

"Means," Campbell said. "The bell housing and the bolt that fastened it on is immediately obvious the minute you unbutton the cowling. Even to me. Wy showed me on her own Cub. Anybody with an open-end box wrench could have reached in and given that bolt a half a turn and buttoned her back up and walked away. Takes about sixty seconds. Wy did it for me, twice. I timed her."

"But how many people would know how to do that?" Kate said.

Jim snorted. "How much have you assimilated just by riding in small planes all your life? How many private pilots in Alaska, what is it, one in thirty-seven? How many of them have families who have been raised around planes?"

"Including Grant's," Campbell said. "His brother, Fred, is a pilot. Two of his kids are pilots. Well. One, now."

"One?" Kate said.

"The oldest daughter, Irene, was a helicopter pilot serving in Afghanistan. She died in combat in November."

Kate winced. "Ouch."

"Yeah," Campbell said, "not a good year for the Grant family."

"So," Jim said, coming back to the point of Liam's presence in the Park, "you don't really know if you have a crime, ou've just got a dead guy and a bunch of people happy he is."

Liam raised a hand. "I know. I know. And no one cares. They'd all be just as happy if Finn stayed buried and they got on with their lives." He brooded. "Including his family. Maybe even most especially his family."

He frowned down into his mug. "I like Newenham, Jim," he said. "It was meant to be exile, punishment—"

Kate looked at Jim, who gave a tiny shake of his head as if to say, *Later.*

"But I like the place," Liam said. "I like the people, I like the lifestyle." He pulled a wry mouth. "It's the fucking Wild, Wild West. I like being three hundred plus miles away from John Dillinger Barton, with no road. We've got espresso and satellite television, just like downtown. Has a one-room library but Jeannie's a demon for interlibrary loan, and if she can't get it for me, there's always Amazon. The people are never boring. I'm learning tai chi, if you can believe that, from an old fart down there." He sighed. "And there's been plenty of action on the job. A little too much, if you want to know the truth. But I'm handling it, I think pretty well. I feel ... dug in."

"You've found a home," Jim said.

Campbell looked around, at the moon shining through the tall windows, at the crackling fire in the fireplace, at the enormous half wolf-half husky sprawled in front of it, the quilt crumpled beneath her, and finally at the woman with the short dark hair and the disturbingly direct gaze curled up next to Jim. He looked back at Jim and their eyes met in mutual understanding. "Yeah. I think I have."

"But," Kate said, "you're not even sure a murder has taken place."

"No."

"And your problem is that without more evidence, you

can't justify investigating it yourself."

"Plus press of other business," Campbell said. "Moccasin Man's started a meth lab somewhere, I'm certain of it, and I'm riding herd on the usual assortment of drunks and thieves and abusers." He hesitated. "I won't be able to pay you anything close to what he—" He nodded at Jim. "—says you usually get."

"Hmm." Kate pretended to think it over. "Once in a while, I like to polish my halo by taking on a case pro bono."

Campbell's expression lightened. "I can front you a thousand for expenses."

"I'll take it," she said promptly. "What if I don't find anything?"

Campbell was silent for a moment. "You'll find something," he said at last. "I don't know what, but something." He shrugged. "Call it a hunch."

Kate's eyes narrowed. Cop hunches were not to be ignored. "And?"

Campbell's expression was bleak. "And it has to be laid to rest, either as an accident or murder." He drained his mug. "Or Wy and I are going to have to leave."

"That won't help," Jim said. "It'll follow you."

"Tell me about it."

Later, Jim said, "You going?"

They were cuddled spoon fashion in bed. He had filled her in on Campbell's backstory, all of it this time. She rolled over to face him. "It would get me out of town at a very good time."

He thought about it. "You don't want to be around for Annie to lean on while she's finding her feet as the new board chair."

"You are smarter than the average bear, Chopin."

"And," he said with caution, "maybe clear out some cobwebs, too."

She knew immediately what he hadn't said. "You mean Old Sam."

"Yeah."

Her turn to be silent as she thought back to October and November of the previous year. The lives of childhood gods should never be too closely examined, but Old Sam had been determined to leave her no choice. At last she said, "You're right about that, too."

"It doesn't change who he was, Kate."

"I know that," she said. "Nothing he ever did could change my opinion of him. It's just, sometimes I wonder..."

"What?"

She sighed. "How well we ever know anyone."

"Pedestals are dangerous things."

"Especially the highest ones."

He had no answer for her, and fell back on misdirection. "The real reason you want to take this on is because you can't wait to tear into a real case. Your snoop's blood is itching."

"Well," she said, drawing it out. "There is that, too." She smiled into the dark. In fact, her nose was eager to poke itself into the personal business of a bunch of people she'd never met, to sniff out the distinctive aromas of means, motive, and opportunity, to boldly go where no nose had gone before. She laughed, a deep sound that rasped against the scar, the remnant of another case, long ago and far away but never wholly forgotten.

"Just try to wrap it up in a week," he said, sounding a little grumpy even to his own ears. "Otherwise I might have to come down there and clear it myself."

"Oooh, big talk from the big trooper." She investigated. "And getting bigger."

In one swift movement he rolled her over on her back, kneeing her legs apart and settling himself between them. "I'll just mark my spot."

The next morning she packed a bag and Jim drove her and Campbell to the airport. It was another clear, cold day, and the snarl of sharp peaks on the eastern horizon increased in menace with the late arctic dawn.

The gloom dispersed as George Perry preflighted the single Otter turbo and a Beaver full of horny, thirsty Suulutaq miners came in from the mine, more than ready for their week off.

The sun peeked over Big Bump as they boarded. Kate, having taken an extra moment for a fond farewell from Jim, was last in line, and as she put her foot on the bottom step of the airstairs she noticed another plane parked nearby. It was a small, elegant jet, twin engines, very sleek, clad in anonymous white paint, the N-number lettered in very small black letters on the engines. She couldn't quite make them out.

"Nice, huh?" George said, looking behind her from the doorway. "Grumman Gulfstream Two."

"A corporate jet?" Kate said.

"Yeah. Some Suulutaq bigwigs. Frank took 'em over to the mine in the Beaver this morning." George, tall, thin, a cavernous face with a five o'clock shadow present at eight o'clock in the morning, looked just a little smug. "Good thing we got the runway paved last fall."

Yet another example of Suulutaq's largesse, and it grated on Kate, but only a little. Maybe when the city of Niniltna finally incorporated, they could start charging landing fees.

"You getting in or not, Shugak?" he said impatiently.

Kate got in and sat down across from Campbell. Mutt padded in behind her and lay down in the space between the pilot's seat and the rest of the passengers. George put on his headset, and the turbine engine started to whine.

The last thing Kate saw as they taxied away was the sexy little corporate jet lording it over the end of the runway. When the Otter turned for takeoff, the sun finally tore free of the clutch of the Quilaks and escaped to the sky, and a shaft of light caught the engine facing Kate, illuminating its identification number. The first letter was a C.

Interesting, Kate thought. All U.S. tail numbers began with an *N*. *C* for Canada, maybe? Global Harvest Resources, Incorporated, was an international conglomerate, and Canada was the world's third largest producer of gold. Maybe they were in town to investigate the possibility of investing in the Suulutaq. Make sense if they wanted a piece of the action going on next door.

George turned the Otter loose and they lifted up off the end of the newly paved runway, and it was with no little relief that Kate left the newly minted international gold capital of North America behind, at least for a while.

Watching from the ground, Jim remembered the view of Kate following Liam Campbell into the plane, and wondered how smart he'd been to send her off with a man whom he knew from personal observation was irresistible to the ladies. There had been some brisk competition for the fairer sex between the two of them, that wild time in the Valley.

His gaze followed the Otter until it was out of sight.

6

JANUARY 18

Newenham

NEWENHAM WAS THE LARGEST city in southwestern Alaska, the market town for the dozens of tiny, mostly Yupik Native villages surrounding it for hundreds of miles in every direction. Some of them had begun as fish camps, where the Natives went every summer to catch their year's supply of salmon, either to eat or to sell it for money to buy fuel.

Other villages got their start as remote canneries back in the day, when Bristol Bay salmon went into a can instead of being flash frozen and shrink-wrapped, and when by law you could fish for them only from a sail-powered boat. Some began as mining camps for gold, platinum, or coal, and some as fuel stops and mail and freight dumps for the Alaska Steamship Company. A few were the result of adventurers looking for a place far enough away from the madding crowd to put down a quiet root and prosper on the 160 acres of land provided for in the Homestead Act.

Very few were viable in the long term due to a lack of anything remotely approaching a year-round industry. Salmon were being farmed now in Europe, Canada, and South America in quantities and at a price that had severely impacted Alaska's wild salmon catch, and the nascent ecotourism industry was barely worthy of the name. Especially since that determinedly sole-source provider, Finn Grant, had bought up everyone else in the flightseeing, fly-in fishing, and big game hunting business. With his death, tourism out of Newenham was at a standstill.

First and foremost, Newenham was the regional market town. In winter on snow machines and four-wheelers, in summer on boats, year-round in airplanes the villagers came to Newenham to buy groceries and supplies, get their eyes checked and their teeth fixed, visit relatives, stand trial, fly to Anchorage to go to the AFN Convention in October or to catch another plane to Hawaii for spring break in March.

But Newenham wasn't only their market town, it was also the headquarters for three national parks, four national game preserves, a dozen wildlife refuges state and federal, and an offshore petroleum reserve, access to which had been stymied in a series of court decisions over the fifty years since statehood. It was also the seat of the regional government, state judiciary, and state law enforcement. Although the latter had lately been reduced to a sole-source provider, one Sergeant Liam Campbell.

Liam yawned and steered his vehicle back over to the right side of the road. He couldn't remember one single night's uninterrupted sleep in the past year. This could not go on. It wasn't the first time he'd said that to himself, but this time, dammit, he meant it. Mayor Jim Earl was going to have to find the wherewithal to hire some city cops, and Major John Dillinger Barton, the Lord High Everything Else of the Alaska State Troopers, was going to have to chisel enough funds out of the state to assign Liam at least one more trooper. Two would be better and three ideal, but he'd take what he could get. If he were closer to retirement, he could really make a statement and threaten to quit over it, but he liked his job and he wasn't independently wealthy. While Finn Grant's death had sent a lot of business his wife's way, her air taxi was still barely self-supporting. Not to mention the kid they had in trade school.

He yawned again, his jaw cracking this time. Over a third of the Newenham population was under eighteen, which didn't make his job any easier, the hormonally challenged being terminally and all too often fatally prone to acts of stupidity.

There was also the problem of village flight, people leaving the villages for the big city in hopes of finding a job so they could feed their kids. The population of Newenham had increased by almost five hundred over the past two years, to almost twenty-five hundred in the last census, which made Newenham city-sized in Alaskan Bush terms. Most of them were Yupik and a lot of them were living out of town on Native allotment lands, which put them outside the city limits, which meant they didn't have to pay city taxes but also meant they couldn't vote in city elections. This had incurred a lot of acting out on property both civic and private. That this was the outward adolescent manifestation of a lot of inward adult resentment, Liam was well aware.

He did his best to stay the hell away from local politics, but there was no way he could avoid the fallout from all of the above in the form of domestic disputes, alcohol-related abuse, the blood feuds that went back generations, and the usual civic disharmony on a scale that was, so far, mostly misdemeanor, and mostly manageable. But if Hizzoner and His Eminence didn't get their acts together, soon, Liam was going on strike.

He topped a small rise and pulled over to the side of the road, and checked the rearview mirror. No traffic for the moment. He rolled down the window and took a deep, invigorating breath of cold, clean winter air.

A raven croaked at him from a nearby treetop, and he looked up to meet a cocked head and a beady black eye.

"Don't even think about it," Liam said.

The raven looked at him out of his other eye and gave a mocking series of throaty croaks and clicks.

"I mean it," Liam said.

The raven must have decided Liam meant it because he spread his wings and dropped off his branch to do a death-defying strafing run over the top of Liam's vehicle, before vanishing over the trees on the opposite side of the road.

Close encounters of the *Corvus corax* kind. To this was he reduced. Liam rubbed his hands hard over his face and looked at the view.

Newenham sprawled up and down forty square miles of riverbank, about a thousand buildings, twenty-five hundred people, three fish processors (couldn't really call them canneries anymore), a town hall, a courthouse with its very own public prosecutor and public defender, two cop shops (one of them vacant except for two dispatchers working twelve-hour shifts seven days a week and who knew how long that would last), a hospital, and what Liam thought had to be a contender for the title of world's largest boat harbor. From this vantage point, it sprawled along the waterfront the way the town sprawled along the riverbank, a veritable floating forest of masts and booms and flying bridges surrounded by two immense gravel arms, breakwaters separated by an entrance that looked minuscule even when you were on a boat going through them. Liam heard tell that time was, most of those boats had been hauled out of the water every year before winter ice could crush their hulls into matchsticks. The harbor hadn't frozen once since he'd been assigned here. Nobody bad-mouthed global warming around Newenham.

At Newenham the incoming tide mixed with the outflowing snowmelt and the Nushugak River was wide enough to require a clear day and a squint to see from one side to the other. It was here that another, smaller river whose name was lost to the ages had provided rich provender for the Yupik who had worked seasonal fish camps there. In 1818 the Russians showed up, established a settlement, and called it Rika Redoubt. Twenty years later the Russian Orthodox Church followed, establishing a mission and building a church that still stood, if a little tentatively. In 1897 the U.S. Army Signal Corps brought in a telegraph line, in 1903 the Alaska Steamship Company added Newenham to its western route, and in 1905 the first Alaska Packers salmon cannery opened its doors, followed by a rush of others, all Outside interests. Alaska Natives were catching their own fish during the summer months and too busy to work for anyone else, so the canneries brought in crews from Mexico and China and the Philippines. At one time, according to Moses Alakuyak, the drunk shaman who was older than god and the generally acknowledged patriarch of Bristol Bay, not to mention Liam's father-in-law, there had been nine salmon canneries operating in Newenham.

Which might go a long way toward explaining why the salmon population was not what it once was.

Something flashed in the sun, the window of a pickup moving in his direction. Wouldn't do to have the state trooper, the law of the state made manifest, found pulled over only to admire the view. And dozing off while he was at it. Liam shook himself out of his drowse and started the engine and went on into town.

Most of Newenham was built off one main road, variously known as the main road, the airport road, the lake road, and the Icky Road. The road went north, along the riverbank, passing the Anipa Subdivision five miles out, the airport ten miles out and turning inland to end forty miles later on the shore of One Lake in the village of Ik'ikika.

The road also went south along the river, twenty-five miles to Chinook Air Force Base, or it had until the winter the senior senator from Alaska lost a twenty-year congressional battle and the base was closed. Everything movable was loaded onto barges and towed around the Aleutian Peninsula through Unimak Pass to Dutch Harbor, where it was loaded on a container ship headed south. What was left now belonged to Finn Grant's estate, and on the plane home Saturday Liam had heard a rumor that Angayuk Native Association was negotiating terms for lease or sale of the property. Two very nice paved runways in prime condition came with it, not to mention a barracks big enough to sleep fifty and administration and support buildings to go along with them, so it would be a very attractive property to someone with a use for it.

Which only opened up motive for another couple of hundred people, all of them Angayuk shareholders, he thought gloomily.

The town's only supermarket appeared on his left. Alaska Commercial Company, known locally as the AC, had the usual full parking lot, with the expected congregation of kids playing hooky standing around the door, smoking cigarettes, playing grabass, and killing time. He slowed down as he drove past, letting them see him and returning look for look.

Next to the AC the liquor store opened up. Out of habit Liam checked the clock on the dash. Eight A.M. on the money. Martha Pauk was first in the door, followed by Jimmy Creevey and Manuel Chin. It would be two more long hours before Bill's Bar opened up, and they couldn't wait.

He thanked his lucky stars yet again for being posted to a place with only two bars and one liquor store, unheard of in Alaska for a city this size unless the community had by a miracle voted itself dry. Jim Earl and the town council kept a death grip on liquor licenses, and no amount of encouragement from the Alaska liquor lobby was going to shake a fourth license loose. The only way somebody could open a new bar was if Bill or whoever owned the other bar this month died and the new business bought or inherited the old business's liquor license. Bill's bar was never a problem, partly because of the .30-06 she kept behind the bar and partly just from sheer force of personality.

The other bar—Seaside Inn? Breeze Inn? Dew Drop Inn? He honestly couldn't remember what it was called at present—was a dive that had changed hands twice and possibly three times since Liam's arrival four years before. It never seemed to become stable enough to become a base of drinking operations for reliable patrons like Teddy Engebretsen and Kelly McCormick and Johnny Kvichak, so it was no wonder it kept going out of business in the same location.

Besides, everybody went to Bill's. Bill never watered down her drinks, Jimmy Buffett and the Neville Brothers were always on the jukebox—nowadays on the SoundDock—and if on that rare occasion someone was clueless enough to cause a ruckus, why, it so happened that Bill Billington was also the Newenham magistrate. It had a calming effect on the customers, while in no way dissuading them from having a good time.

Of course, the downside of only two bars was nine churches, but half of them were teetotalers, and Liam was professionally in favor of teetotaling. Sobriety cut down the workload, especially in rural Alaska.

Personally, he liked his Glenmorangie straight up. Probably a throwback to his Scots ancestry. Bill kept a bottle behind the bar just for him, and even if the hamburgers hadn't been the best in town, that would have been enough to guarantee his loyalty. Besides, he liked a quiet drink in good company as much as the next man, and Bill took misbehavior in her bar personally, especially when said misbehavior resulted in destruction of property. It was widely known that in her magistrate persona she could get a little punitive in her sentencing. It had a bracing effect on her patrons' manners.

Failing that, Moses Alakuyak could always see fit to prophesy on your ass if you gave his girlfriend, Bill, any trouble.

The Bay View Inn, Newenham's only hotel, passed on his right, across the street from city hall. Alta Peterson, the hotel's owner, looked up from breaking ice from the patch of asphalt in front of the door and waved. Sometimes he wondered if the woman ever slept.

Boat harbor, harbormaster's office, bulk store slash Costco wannabe, a bunch of chandler's stores, a four-space strip mall with a Subway holding down one end and apartments above, the Newenham Telephone Cooperative, the Newenham Electrical Association, a stubby set of town houses with a river view. He turned right and went up a hill, past some old clapboard houses with snow hiding collections of leftover lumber and fifty-five-gallon drums—no one in Bush Alaska ever threw anything away—and around a corner and pulled up in front of the trooper post. It was a small building with one office and two temporary holding cells. The impound lot behind, surrounded by a twelve-foot chain-link fence, was twice the size of the building and currently corralled a posthole digger belonging to Crawdad Homes, who on one of his semiannual benders had seen fit to take it for a joyride up the road to Icky. That would have been fine with Liam if Crawdad had managed to keep it on the right side of the road, and out of Elias Anayuk's living room.

Crawdad was now enjoying the hospitality of the Pre-Trial Correction Facility in Anchorage, where he would be smart to stay for as long as possible, given Sally Homes's sworn oath to yank his liver out through his mouth when he got home.

He got out and was greeted by a soft croaking. He looked up and found the raven on a branch near the top of a tall spruce, peering down at him with the same beady black eye.

"What now?" he said, and his voice wasn't friendly.

It croaked and clicked at him again.

"You forget," Liam said, "I don't speak raven."

The raven clicked some more.

He waved a dismissive and probably foolhardy hand and said, "Yeah, yeah," and went inside, closing the door firmly behind him.

He slung jacket and cap on the coatrack and put his sidearm in a drawer, and sat down to fire up his computer with no little dread. Dispatch called him directly for emergencies, which he actually preferred to the picayune reports that would have stacked up overnight online. The Newenham City Council, like every other city council in the state and the nation, was in a perpetual knot over finances, and filling the vacant positions at NPD had dragged out over two years. Dispatch worked out of one dingy little room in the city hall basement and triaged 911 calls before they got to his cell phone, but that didn't mean they didn't all eventually wind up in his in-box, requiring some response on the part of what remained of law and order in Newenham.

Maybe the next time he got a call to respond to a domestic dispute in Delinquentville, he should just roll over, put his arm around his wife, and go back to sleep.

Yeah. That'd happen.

The door opened, and he looked up to behold Jo Dunaway. "And this started out to be such a good day," he said.

"Great to see you, too, Liam." she said. She came in and draped herself decoratively across a chair in front of his desk.

A thirty-something zaftig blonde with short corkscrew curls and sharp green eyes, Jo was a reporter for the *Anchorage News,* the state's newspaper of record. Normally that would be more than enough for him to escort her right back out his door and look not upon the order of her going.

Normally didn't include Jo being his wife's college roommate and lifelong best friend. He bared his teeth. "Great to see you, Jo. How soon will you be leaving us?"

She bared her teeth right back, and they were sharper than his. "Gary sends his love."

Gary being her brother, an Anchorage building contractor who had something of a history with Liam's wife. Liam felt, not for the first time, that the world was a little too tolerant of the amount of Dunaways in it. "What can I not do for you, Jo?"

She slid fully into her chair and made an elaborate pretense of getting out her reporter's notebook, heaving a dramatic sigh, and putting it back in her pocket. "Remember Wes Hardin?"

He looked and indeed, felt, blank.

Jo elaborated. "John Neville Hardin, nicknamed Wes? After the famous Wild West gunfighter?"

"The name rings a bell," he said cautiously.

"It should." From between the pages of her notebook she pulled a piece of paper folded into quarters and handed it to him.

It was a printout of an obituary from the *Anchorage News*. "Coastie, State Legislator, Businessman, Philanthropist," Liam read out loud. "John Neville 'Wes' Hardin, a hundred and three, died December twenty-sixth, at the Pioneer Home in Anchorage." He looked up. "So?"

"Keep reading," she said.

A celebration of his life will be held at 2 P.M. Saturday at the Wendy Williamson Auditorium on the University of Alaska–Anchorage campus. The public is invited to attend. He will be interred in Anchorage Memorial Park Cemetery in a private ceremony in the spring.

Born and raised in Westchester, Connecticut, and a graduate in engineering of the U.S. Coast Guard Academy, Wes served 20 years in the U.S. Coast Guard, half of it under way. He rotated ashore for the last time into the job of harbormaster in Juneau, where he was instrumental in the smooth integration of the cruise industry into Southeast Alaska. At the age of 65, he formed his own cruise line, Hardin Cruises, with a fleet of small ships that eventually numbered 10, specializing in luxury cruises with an ecotourism theme. At 70, he sold the line and ran for the state legislature on the Republican ticket, where he served Southeast Alaska for 10 terms. He never won by less than a landslide.

At the age of 90, he retired from the legislature to start By Your Bootstraps, a nonprofit organization to fund microbusiness start-ups in Alaska employing less than five people and generating less than $300,000 in revenue. Within five years, By Your Bootstraps had awarded grants to over 100 small businesses, and as of the end of the last fiscal year, 76 of those businesses had moved into self-sustaining profitability. For this he was awarded the Presidential Medal of Freedom, the first Alaskan to be so honored.

Among many other things, over the years Wes endowed the Hardin Chair of Engineering at the University of Alaska–Fairbanks, and founded the John and Geraldine Hardin Cancer Wing at Gastineau Hospital in Juneau, the Geraldine Reid Haven House in Ketchikan and the Geraldine Reid Girl Scouts Jamboree Center in Sitka. He was a past president of Rotary Club Alaska, the Boys & Girls Clubs of Alaska and the Alaska Chamber of Commerce. He was the recipient of honorary PhDs from the University of Alaska and Alaska Pacific University. He and Geraldine leave behind a combined estate valued at over $500 million.

Wes was preceded in death by his wife of 60 years, Geraldine Reid Hardin, daughter of historic stampeders Elvira and Edward Reid, and by his son, John Reid Hardin, who died in combat in Vietnam. He is survived by his granddaughter, Alexandra.

He looked up again. "Okay. All-around Alaskan powerhouse and do-gooder dies after a long and useful life. Figure his name was familiar to me in the same way it probably would be to anyone alive and breathing in the state of Alaska during the last century. Can't say I ever met him personally. I don't remember arresting him for anything."

Her green eyes narrowed on his face in a way he particularly disliked, mostly because he was afraid she could see right through to his brain to read what was sparking between his synapses. "His name hasn't come up in conjunction with any investigations you can't comment on at this time?"

His eyebrows snapped together. "No."

"How about his daughter's name? Ring any bells?"

He looked down at the obituary. "Alexandra? No."

"Hardin left a lot of money behind," Jo said. "Settled in a trust for his daughter, Alexandra."

"So far, I can see no reason to rush out and cuff and stuff anybody."

She gave him a sweet smile. "A lot of Alexandra's money has gone missing."

Her words sank in, and his heart sank.

Jo Dunaway was a first-class snoop, with a string of awards to her credit, one of them for a recent story in which he had had a prominent role. Since a certain ex-governor had turned Alaska into must-see TV, Jo had also become a regular talking head on various news channels. If Jo was following money to Newenham, it was all too depressingly certain that there was money here to be found.

When he didn't say anything, she sat up and leaned forward, elbows on her knees, green eyes intent on Liam's face, alert to any change of expression. "Alexandra suffers from early-onset Alzheimer's. She requires twenty-four-hour care. Her affairs, including the counting of something on the order of five hundred million dollars in cash, securities, and real property, rest in the irreproachable hands of Chapados, Reid, Reid, McGillivray, and Thrall." She waited, and when he didn't say anything, continued. "Which, you may remember, is also the law firm of the estate of the late, unlamented Dagfin Arneson 'Finn' Grant."

He remembered. Hugh Reid had sprouted on the scene within twenty-four hours of Finn Grant's death, and appeared to enjoy the full confidence of Finn's wife and family. His heart sank further but he maintained what he hoped was a neutral and impenetrable expression. "And?"

"And," she said, her eyes narrowing again, "there have been rumors filtering north that Finn Grant may have been the victim of foul play." She stood up and glared at him. "There have also been rumors of possible suspects. Your wife being one of them!"

As adversarial as their relationship was, both professional and personal, the one unquestionably laudable thing about Jo Dunaway's character Liam knew for certain was that she was absolutely, unswervingly loyal to Wy Chouinard, college roommate and in-everything-but-blood sister. So this trip to Newenham was personal for her, which only increased the pressure on the professional him.

Not to mention the potential nest of snakes it opened up in regards to Finn Grant's possible murder.

When he did not respond, she said, "Well?"

"I have no comment at this time," he said.

"Is there an ongoing investigation into Finn Grant's death?"

"I have no comment at this time," he said.

"Is there any reason to suspect that his death was caused by anything other than mechanical error?"

"I have no comment at this time," he said.

"Sure you don't," she said. "I'm staying on for a few days. Oh, don't worry"—a sardonic note when she saw his expression—"I won't be crowding the newlyweds, I've got a room at Alta's." Again with the smile so sweet, it made his teeth hurt. "Burgers and brew at Bill's tonight, though. I already checked with Wy."

He was on his feet before she got a step closer to the door. "Jo," he said, his voice coming out like the crack of a whip.

She had backbone, did Jo Dunaway. She didn't jump or

respond in any way until she got a hand on the doorknob. Just by way of reinforcing the First Amendment. "Yeah?"

His eyes bored into her. "If you have any information germane to an ongoing investigation, you have a duty to be forthcoming with that information."

She shook her blond corkscrew curls back from her face and said in a gentle voice, "But according to you, Liam, there is no ongoing investigation. Or not one you can comment on at this time."

He waited for the door to close behind her and put his head down on his desk. "Fuck," he said with deep and sincere feeling.

He wondered how best he could impart this latest wrinkle in the maybe-murder of Finn Grant to Kate Shugak, and if, faced with another couple of hundred suspects, she might not rightfully be expected to turn tail and head back for Niniltna as fast as she could run.

He raised his head and reached for the phone to call the boss. If there were any rumors floating around about this non-case, he might as well be the last one to hear them.

7

JANUARY 18

Chinook Airport, twenty-five miles south of Newenham

THE HANGAR WAS PAINTED white with green trim and boasted the name *Eagle Air* in large, dashing script with an attendant, requisitely fierce eagle logo, wings spread, beak open, talons extended. It filled up the entire hangar door.

"Looks big enough for a 747," Kate said, meaning the hangar.

"Plus three single Otters and four Caravans. All three Otters are turbo, too."

"Pilot envy," Kate said.

The pilot smiled. "Maybe a little. Makes 'em go faster, all right, but the downside is they need a lot more space to land and take off in."

"Leaves the shorter strips for you."

"True enough. I wouldn't mind getting my hands on one of their Caravans, though. Be great for moving the mail, especially at Christmas. You know what Christmas is like for mail to the Bush."

Kate nodded. She knew.

Wyanet Chouinard was half a foot taller than Kate, with brown eyes wrinkled at the corners from squinting at horizons. Her hair was dark blond with bronze streaks, and she wore it pulled back in a thick ponytail that ended well below her shoulders. Her Carhartt bibs were black with oil and grease stains and her XtraTufs looked like they'd been used to teethe ferrets. Kate had felt at home with Chouinard from their first meeting.

They and Mutt were standing next to Chouinard's Cessna, a well-loved 180 with plenty of miles on her. Nevertheless, she looked a hell of a lot cleaner than her owner, smart and trustworthy in white paint with brown and gold trim, *Nushugak Air Taxi Service* spelled out in fancy black script down her fuselage. The two backseats had been pulled to make room for the mail from Manokotak and Togiak. Togiak was where Chouinard had picked up Kate.

Chinook Airport, latitude 59-02-40.8000 north, longitude 158-30-19.8000 west, elevation eighty-one feet, twenty-five miles south of Newenham, home to Eagle Air and Eagle Air FBO, sat at the corner of two runways, 1/19 and 8/26. Paved runways were in many Alaskan communities an almost unimaginable luxury, as witness the newly paved strip at Niniltna that had made George Perry look so smug last Saturday morning. Chinook had no control tower and the nearest flight service station was in Newenham, but it had a bright orange windsock at the end of Runway One-Zero, at present indicating a steady ten- to twelve-knot wind out of the northwest.

The paint job on the hangar was so new, it made their eyes water from fifty feet away. The first building was complemented by a second, equally oversize building next door, two stories high. Kate estimated it at ten thousand square feet, or about half the size of the hangar. A communications tower bristling with antennas and dishes loomed in the background and made Kate feel like she was back in Niniltna.

"Pretty ritzy for a one-horse operation," she said.

"Oh yeah," Chouinard said. "Finn Grant had an open house when it was finished, we all got the tour." She added a little grimly, "Whether we wanted it or not."

"And?"

"And while it might not look like it, those buildings are actually original to the air force base."

"Nice remodeling job."

"You should see the inside. Offices that look like they were designed for Donald Trump. A ready room for pilots that's even plushier. A business center complete with six state-of-the-art computers with high-speed wireless Internet access, a printer the size of a baby grand, and two fax machines. Speaking of baby grands, there is even an upright piano."

"You're kidding." Kate laughed. "This Finn Grant guy watch a lot of World War Two movies about the Royal Air Force?"

"Could be. There's also a self-serve café stocked with delicacies flown in daily from City Market and Alaska Silk Pie—"

"Alaska Silk Pie?" Chouinard had all of Kate's attention. "They have Chocolate Silk Royale?"

"And," Chouinard said, "there's a lounge full of squashy dark blue leather furniture and a flat-screen television the size of a barn door, with a built-in cupboard stocked with DVDs they can watch on the big screen in the adjacent mini-theater. Everything from *Finding Nemo* to *Debbie Does Dallas*. There's even a rock fireplace. With a slate hearth."

That sounded a little like fireplace envy. Kate eyed the row of windows across the second floor. "What's upstairs?"

"Individual bedrooms, each with its own bathroom and a sitting room, for those aviators needing to spend an extra day or, more likely, for those who got weathered in going one direction or another."

"Wow," Kate said, awed in spite of herself. She'd spent most of her air time in airplanes that smelled of clam juice and moose blood, not to mention the puke of the last drunk passenger to throw up in it. When she got weathered in, she usually spent the night on the floor of the high school gym.

"Yeah, I know," Chouinard said. "That, and the quarter-million a pop it cost to turn three single Otters into turbo, and pretty soon you're talking real money."

"Where'd he get it?"

"Married it." Chouinard closed the Cessna's door and hoisted the brown canvas mail sack over her shoulder. Mutt trotted off to mark new territory. The two women began to walk toward the hangar office. "Clementina—his wife—was a Tannehill. Old-time Southwest family. I think her grandfather had a stake in the mines in Platinum."

"Wow squared," Kate said, properly respectful. As an Alaskan she would have heard of the Tannehills, but she and Campbell had agreed that it would be better all around if his wife didn't know who Kate really was, at least not at first. It was hard enough to keep a secret when two people knew it. Three people and you might as well call CNN. Until now, Kate hadn't been south and west of Tyonek, or at least not ashore except at Dutch Harbor and on one of the Aleutian Islands, which memory still made her feel like a popsicle. Alaska was a big place. Having Mutt along might stretch the bounds of an undercover identity, but the plan was to get in, get the job done, and get out again before anyone remembered a certain speech at the AFN Convention some years back.

Besides, Mutt had made her objections to being left behind vigorously, vehemently, and vociferously known, and Kate hadn't been willing to go through another scene like the one at Canyon Hot Springs last October, when Mutt had come this close to quitting the firm. The last two years had tested their partnership enough for one lifetime.

By prior arrangement, she had flown PenAir to Togiak and spent the night. When Wy arrived on her mail run, Kate bought a seat to Newenham. Her cover story was a girl and her dog on the run from village life. It wouldn't hold up for long, she didn't look much like a Yupik—legs too long and not enough chest—but she wasn't worried. So many people saw Alaska Natives as interchangeable.

And after all, she had her orders from Jim. *Just try to wrap it up in a week.* She smiled to herself.

The glitter of sun on snow was painful to the eye. It was a relief when they stepped into the shadow of the second building. As they reached the office door, it crashed open and bounced off the wall. Both of them jumped back out of the way just in time, as a well-nourished twenty-something clad in tight jeans and an even tighter T-shirt with the Eagle Air eagle's wings lovingly cupping her breasts came trotting out of the office. She was not wearing a bra and her shoes had four-inch heels. The shoes were a bright yellow to match the eyes, beak, and talons of the Eagle Air eagle, so Kate had to assume they were part of the uniform.

Four-inch heels? In January? She'd kill herself first.

"Hey, Wy," this vision said on the fly. "Got a flight coming in, the mailbag's on the desk."

"Sure, Tasha." The pilot vanished inside.

Tasha opened a door into the hangar and wheeled out a short airstairs. By then Kate could hear the approach of an airplane, a jet by the sound of it. She squinted against the sun and found it on approach off the end of one-zero. As she watched, the gear descended out of the fuselage and the aircraft touched down light as a feather, using the friction of tires on pavement and all eight thousand feet of runway length to chew up speed. By the time it reached the apron in front of the hangar, it was moving at a pace decorous enough to satisfy the most aviophobic passenger, as well as the most persnickety FAA checkrider.

It was another private jet, to her untrained eye the twin of the one she'd seen parked on the Niniltna airstrip when she and Campbell had flown out Saturday morning. Austere in anonymous white paint, no logo and no tail numbers. Even the hushed sound of the engines seemed reticent and circumspect.

"That's the 550," Chouinard said, reappearing at Kate's side. "New York to Tokyo in fourteen and a half hours."

"Gulfstream?" Kate said, which was the only possible remark she could have made that might sound reasonably intelligent. She'd learned it only three days before.

Chouinard nodded. "I'd heard about this one, but I've always just missed seeing it."

"You know the owner?"

"Fifty-one thousand feet cruising altitude," Chouinard said, eyes fixed on the jet. "No commercial traffic to worry about, or weather either, for that matter. Mach point-eight, with four crew and eight SOBs. Rolls-Royce engines, fifteen thousand pounds of thrust each. And they've got an integrated avionics suite—PlaneView, they call it—LCD displays, EVS—"

"You realize you might as well be speaking tongues," Kate said.

"Oh." Chouinard laughed and said a little sheepishly, "Sorry. Got carried away there for a minute."

The engines wound down and stopped, and the hatch

popped open. A bunch of guys trooped out. They looked like guys, if a little better-looking and in a lot better shape than most.

Especially the one in the lead, who looked very familiar. "Who's that?" Kate said.

"Huh?" Chouinard was still looking at the jet.

Another man came bustling out of the office, hand outstretched. He was short and a little pudgy with thinning hair and an unctuous manner. He wore a khaki safari suit and a red scarf knotted around his neck that made him look like he might be partnered up with Crocodile Dundee, a natural mistake he corrected at once. "Hugh Reid, Mr. McGuire," he said in a nasal voice. "We met once before, I'm sure you don't remember. I am—I was—I am Finn Grant's partner."

McGuire took Reid's outstretched hand in a brief clasp. Reid seemed to want to hang on, but McGuire managed to divest himself and gestured vaguely at the posse behind him. "Hugh Reid, guys. Finn's partner. Are you a pilot, Hugh?"

"Er," Reid said, "I'm afraid not, no."

"I see. Then in Finn's, uh, regrettable absence, who will be taking us out to the lodge?"

"Why don't we just take the jet?" This from a short, thin man with thick glasses and a nervous manner.

"Because, Willy," one of the other guys said, "no way is Gabe landing this baby on gravel."

McGuire smiled at Kate over Reid's shoulder. "Lester would kill me if I did. Hi. Gabe McGuire."

"Hi," she said, and didn't smile back.

Reid trotting at his elbow like he was attached by an invisible leash, McGuire reached her in one long stride. His grip was warm and firm, and like Reid's had a tendency to hang on. He looked her over and didn't mind letting it show that he liked what he saw.

"Sorry," she said, baffled, "have we met?"

A quiet laugh went around the entourage. McGuire held out his hand to Chouinard. "Hello. You're Liam's wife, right?"

"Uh-huh."

"And if memory serves, you're a pilot."

"Uh-huh." Chouinard was still staring at the jet.

He glanced at the hangar. "You work for Finn Grant?"

That did get her attention. "No," she said, very definitely. "I run my own business." She jerked a thumb at the Cessna behind them. "Nushugak Air Taxi Service."

"Yeah? You rated on single Otters?"

"Yeah," Chouinard said, realizing this conversation was heading toward money in the bank. "You need a ride out to your lodge?"

He nodded. "Five passengers total, and a daypack each."

Chouinard jerked another thumb at Kate, now reduced to baggage. "I've got to run my passenger to Newenham and drop off the mail first."

"No problem. We'll make ourselves at home here while we wait." He smiled at Tasha, who visibly melted right down into her four-inch heels. "If that's okay with Tasha."

In a fluttery voice Tasha said, "Of course, Mr. McGuire."

"Gabe."

Tasha blushed. "Gabe."

Reid said, "Okay, Tasha, show these gentlemen to the lounge. We've got showers, Internet access, beds if you feel like a nap. Satellite television, DVDs, a full bar, Tasha can whip you up some sandwiches—"

He stood back, holding the door open and beaming over his shoulder at McGuire—*See how efficient I am? How well I am taking care of your people? May I sacrifice a goat at midnight in your honor?*—as the other men filed inside.

Chouinard said, "Okay if I ask your pilot for a tour of your jet?"

McGuire was amused. "Sure." He waved a hand at one of his men. "Les, show Ms. Chouinard the baby."

"I haven't seen anything that perfect since the first salmon steak of the season," Chouinard said, walking toward the jet.

She wasn't talking about McGuire. He grinned and got out of her way.

Mutt came up, having marked out her territory at Eagle Air, and cocked an ear at McGuire. He went down on one knee and held out his fist, palm down. "Hey," he said. "I'm Gabe. And you are?"

She sniffed his hand. They both looked at Kate.

"Mutt, meet Gabe," Kate said, forced into it.

Mutt gave Gabe's hand a tentative lick, and then another, more enthusiastic one. He had passed the taste test. Unfortunately.

McGuire rubbed Mutt's ears, and her tail hit overdrive. He rose to his feet. "Mutt, huh?"

"She is one," Kate said. He turned slightly, to get the sun out of his eyes, and something clicked. "You're the actor."

McGuire did not look thrilled at the recognition. "Some say yes," he said. "Some say no."

From the moment he'd stepped off the plane, she'd been a little off balance. She forced herself to examine him in an analytical light, as if he were a suspect she would later have to pick out of a lineup. He was tall, long-limbed, and muscular, moving with a confident kind of grace. His dark eyes were set deep beneath a broad shelf of a brow, his mouth was mobile and prone to humor over a very firm jaw, and he had eyebrows and cheekbones like George Harrison. He wasn't handsome, but he was memorable. On camera, sneaking across the desert in camos with an RPG over his shoulder, he was rugged, rough-edged, and sexy as hell. His jeans were undoubtably designer, but they showed their miles without shame, and no Alaskan man would have been embarrassed to wear the faded red plaid shirt under the scruffy blue anorak.

Their eyes met, and Kate was alarmed at the slight shock of recognition, almost familiarity.

He reminded her of Jack.

Not a lot, they weren't twins or anything, but there was something about Gabe McGuire in person, in the rough angularity of his features and the directness of his gaze that brought Jack Morgan forcibly to mind, in a way it never had the times she'd seen him on-screen.

She didn't like it, not one bit. She felt herself teetering on the edge of taking a step back, and pulled herself together. He wasn't Jack, of course, Jack was dead, had been dead for over four years.

"What's wrong?" he said.

And he was observant, too, damn him. "Not a thing," she said. "I've seen some of your films. You do good work."

"Thanks," he said. "What do you do?"

"I'm on my way to Newenham."

"You're Alaskan?"

"Born and bred."

He looked at the eyes that in shape were Asian but a changeable hazel in color; at the thick hair cut in a short cap that shone blue black in the sun; at the high flat cheekbones clad in clear, olive skin; at the wide, full-lipped mouth. He considered the now thin and much more faint white scar that crossed her throat almost from ear to ear, and moved on without so much as a raised brow. She was all of five feet tall, clad much as he was, in jeans, a battered down jacket over a T-shirt, and a pair of Rimrocks that had seen hard use. His eyes came back to her face. "Aleut?"

She couldn't hide her surprise. "How did you know?"

He shrugged. "I've spent some time here. Put myself through college working at the processing plant in Akutan."

"Really," Kate said, warming to the man in spite of herself. "Minimum wage?"

He grinned. "Yep. But time and a half for anything over eight hours a day and forty hours a week, and double time for holidays. You, too?"

"No, thank god," she said, "I worked it from the other end, I deckhanded on a fish tender."

"Bristol Bay?"

She shook her head. "Prince William Sound."

He nodded. "Gorgeous there."

"Not so bad here, either."

He followed her gaze to the Wood River Mountains looming on the northwestern horizon. "Not quite so in your face as they are in Prince William," he said. "There, they're always a reminder that you've got the sea at your back."

She looked at him, surprised again.

He quirked an eyebrow, as if to say, *What, you thought I was just another pretty face?* For some unknown reason, Kate felt herself flush. She was relieved when they heard the approach of another aircraft. They both turned to watch it land and taxi up to the fuel pumps. It had no windows except for the cockpit.

"Caravan," Kate said, not really as a challenge, but he took it as one anyway.

"Super Cargomaster," he said. "Almost nine-hundred-nautical-mile range with a payload of almost two tons. FedEx uses them for a lot of their short hops between small towns and hubs."

She looked at him, remembering the comment about him not landing the jet on gravel. "You're a pilot."

He nodded, looking perhaps just a little complacent, and perhaps a little expectant of admiration, if not reverence. He was a pilot, all right.

"Or just an aviation nut," she said.

The complacence vanished. "I'm a pilot," he said, and might actually have been reaching for his wallet so he could show her his license when Chouinard came down the steps of the Gulfstream, talking over her shoulder to the pilot. "He flies?" she said. "Seriously?"

"Seriously."

"God in heaven," Chouinard said devoutly. "Please don't let him hurt it."

Kate laughed. McGuire gave her a look, which relaxed into a reluctant smile when he realized she was riding him.

"I won't," Les said gravely. He was a tall, thin man in his sixties, with an untidy thatch of thick, pure white hair, a stubble to rival McGuire's, and a twinkle in his eye if you looked for it.

Chouinard saw Kate and was recalled to duty. "Thanks for the tour," she said, shaking hands with Les. "Happy to show you around my outfit in return, such as it is."

"If we're around long enough, I wouldn't mind a ride-along on your mail route," he said.

"Sure. Depends on how much mail I've got to carry." Chouinard walked over to Kate and McGuire. "Sorry about the delay, Kate."

"No problem," Kate said. "I know better than to stand between a pilot and an airplane. Especially one like that airplane."

Chouinard and McGuire both laughed. “Thanks for the tour, Gabe.”

“No problem, Wy. Tell Liam I said hi.”

And with that, America’s Number One Box Office Draw in the bone-chilling, spine-tingling, heart-pounding *Invincible*—the thrilling story of an intrepid Navy SEAL armed only with a Leatherman rescuing a beautiful American heiress kidnapped by an army of Muslim extremists—saw the three women to Chouinard’s Cessna, gave Mutt a farewell ear rub that left her panting in ecstasy, closed Kate’s door, and gave her a warm smile through the window before waving them off.

They taxied out onto the runway as McGuire’s entourage followed him into the building. “He’s like an actual human being, isn’t he?” Chouinard said.

“How long to Newenham?” Kate said.

8

JANUARY 18

Newenham

BILL'S BAR AND GRILL was a big square building with pale vinyl siding and a galvanized tin roof. It squatted on pilings three feet above the ground, and stairs and a switchback ramp led to a solid door flanked by large windows in which no neon beer signs shone. The business inside was advertised by one medium-sized sign over the door, its name in black script next to a cartoon mug of foaming beer.

Kate, carrying her pack and Mutt padding behind her, walked into one large room that looked to take up two-thirds of the building. A kitchen took up most of the rear third, a pass-through allowing the transference of saliva-inducing aromas of beef crisp on the outside and pink on the inside and the FDA food pyramid be damned. Through an open door in one corner Kate glimpsed a small office crowded with a desk, a couple of chairs, and a filing cabinet.

In the main room, a bar with a dozen stools ran along the back wall. Booths lined both sides, with half a dozen very small Formica-topped tables and mismatched dining chairs in between. The exposed rafters were draped with green fishing nets. Suspended in the nets between the rafters were lengths of leadlines and corklines, floats and buoys and Japanese glass balls. The walls were crowded with more commercial fishing detritus: a pair of crossed boat hooks, single oars, a mounted king crab, bad oil paintings of boats, a brass steering wheel, and from the accumulated rust what might have been Captain Cook's lost anchor.

It wasn't the Roadhouse, but nevertheless Kate felt instantly at home. She walked up to the bar, set down her pack, and climbed on a stool.

The woman behind the bar had white, straight hair that hung below her shoulders and a splendid figure cinched in at the waist by a wide leather belt, between a faded blue denim work shirt unbuttoned far enough to show serious cleavage and jeans worn white at the seams where her butt threatened to burst them. Her eyes matched the color of the shirt.

"What'll you have?" she said to Kate, swiping a rag down the bar.

"Still serving lunch?" Kate said.

"Serving lunch from when we open till when we close," the woman said.

"Cheeseburger and fries?" Kate said.

"It's what we do best. Anything to drink?"

"Diet Seven Up? Lots of ice?"

"Fresca okay?"

"I didn't know they were still making Fresca," Kate said, charmed. "Sure."

The woman shouted the order through the pass-through, which was immediately followed by the agreeable sound of meat sizzling on the grill. "Here you go." A tall glass full of ice and a frosty can appeared.

Mutt poked an inquisitive nose over the bar.

"And who might you be?" the woman said.

"This is Mutt," Kate said. "My partner. Mutt, meet..."

"The name's Bill, Bill Billington," the woman said. She gave Mutt's head a hello scratch and looked at Kate.

"Kate," Kate said. "Kate Saracoff."

Besides herself and Mutt, there was only a man with his head down on the bar and what looked like a mother and son at one of the booths. As Kate looked, a second man joined them. Bill brought him a Bud Light without waiting for an order. "Slow afternoon," Kate said when she got back.

Bill shrugged. "They're always slow this time of year."

"So you're probably not looking for help."

Bill looked her over, her blue eyes appraising, and a little too speculative for Kate's comfort. "Got any experience?"

"Bartending?" Kate said. "No. But I show up on time, and I'll work while I'm here."

Bill looked at Mutt. "Well, she'd make one hell of a bouncer."

Mutt gave a yip of assent, and watched with hungry eyes as Bill set Kate's plate before her. "Oh hell," Bill said, and another plate full of chopped ground round with a raw egg mixed in showed up shortly thereafter. Mutt displayed suitable gratitude and waded in with enthusiasm.

"Like to see people enjoying their food," Bill said, watching Mutt. "So you're new in town." It wasn't a question, and Bill didn't wait for an answer. "You need a place to stay?"

Kate nodded, and Bill raised her voice. "Tina?" The woman in the booth looked around. "Talk to you a minute?"

The woman stood up and came to stand next to Kate. "Kate Saracoff, Tina Grant."

Tina for *Clementina*? As in *Clementina Tannehill Grant*? As in Finn Grant's widow? Kate loved small-town Alaska.

"Kate's my new help, as of today. She needs a place to stay. You were saying you had a place over your garage you were looking to rent."

Tina and Kate looked each other over. Mutt sat up, prepared to be polite, even if it was only a woman, and a woman with no food on offer, either.

"Looks like a wolf," Tina said.

"Only half," Kate said.

Mutt did her best to look more canine than lupine.

Tina looked at Kate. "It's a one-room studio with a three-quarter bath."

"Kitchen?" Kate said. No point in seeming too eager.

"Small stove, barely room enough for four burners, but you can fit a whole chicken in the oven. Microwave, under-the-counter fridge. It's clean and partly furnished. You can use what's there."

Kate made it a rule never to flout serendipity when it offered itself up free of charge. "May I take a look at it?"

"Sure. You got transportation?" Kate shook her head. Tina nodded at the door. "I was on my way out. I'll give you a ride."

Kate looked at Bill, who gave her the barest suggestion of a wink and said, "Come back when you're settled in, and I'll walk you through the job."

As they left the building, Tina nodded at the men in the booth. "See you back at the house, Oren."

Oren Grant. That would be the son. Kate noticed he did not look thrilled at the prospect. There was some resemblance between him and the man sitting next to him. Grant's brother, Oren's uncle, maybe, Frank? Fred, that was it, Fred Grant.

Kate felt his eyes follow her out the door, but when she looked back it was Tina he was watching.

• • •

It was a one-car garage, separate from the house, the room at the top reached by a flight of unpainted wooden stairs. Tina led the way. The door at the top was unlocked.

Going counterclockwise around the room from the doorway was an armchair with an ottoman and a pole lamp, a twin bed with a bare mattress and a couple of rubbery-looking pillows, and a kitchenette set into the right-hand corner with a small round table and two chairs tucked into the corner between two windows. In the left-hand corner a slightly open door showed a fold of shower curtain. To the left of the door sat a chest freezer. Odds and ends of lumber and fishing gear were stacked in the space between the wall and the freezer.

"Sorry about that," Tina said. "This used to be the garage attic, where we pitched all the stuff we had replaced but weren't ready to throw away. We had it finished off so my daughter would have a little privacy when she came home on leave. I meant to clear it out, but..." She gestured vaguely. "I just haven't gotten around to it yet."

"Your daughter is in the service?" Kate said, because it was the only natural response.

"She was." Tina went to a cupboard and assembled a load of sheets, blankets, and a pillow. She walked to the bed and put them down, and it seemed to Kate she moved somewhat slowly, as if something weighed her down. It wasn't age. Grief, maybe?

She was a woman of moderate height, whose youthful leanness had been pared by life into something that approached gaunt. Her skin was pale and finely wrinkled. Brown eyes were deep set over hollowed-out cheeks. Her mouth was a still, controlled line that didn't look like it had relaxed into a smile in recent memory. She wore her grayish brown hair in a careless tumble cut just below her ears, more convenient than stylish. Her jeans were older than Kate's, and the original cream color of her hand-knit Aran sweater had faded to a dirty yellowish white. It was also unraveling at neck, hem, and one wrist.

"Towels in the cupboard, too," she said. "And—" She gestured at the stackable washer and dryer next to the bathroom.

"Nicer than I expected to find," Kate said. "I'll take it, if I can afford the rent."

"Five hundred a month?" Tina said.

"Everything included?"

Tina nodded.

"Cheaper than I expected, too," Kate said. "Is there a key?"

"On the wall next to the door."

"Okay," Kate said. "Would you like the rent up front?"

"That would be great, uh..."

"Kate," Kate said. "Kate Saracoff."

"Sorry," Tina said. "I've been a little ... distracted lately. Lot going on."

"No problem," Kate said, reaching for her wallet. She counted five one-hundred-dollar bills into Tina's hand.

"You always walk around with this much cash on you?"

"I cleaned out my bank account when I left Togiak," Kate said. "Is that a problem?"

Tina's eyes lingered on Kate's scar, and drew her own conclusions. "No, no problem. I can use the cash. Well. If you need anything, I'm in the house next door." She paused. "How were you going to get back to Bill's?"

"Walk," Kate said. "It's only, what, a mile or so."

"I've got a spare four-wheeler," Tina said. "Extra hundred a month. You pay for gas."

"Deal," Kate said, and handed over another hundred. Campbell's front money was down to fifty bucks and change.

"It's the red Honda in the garage. The side door is open."

"Okay," Kate said, "thanks."

Tina nodded and left, her footsteps sounding slow and heavy on the stairs.

Kate took a moment to marvel at her luck. Not only had she found a clean place to stay with hot and cold running water—she checked the kitchen sink and shower faucets and flushed the toilet to be sure—she was staying right next door to the prime suspects in Campbell's case.

If there was, in fact, a case.

She unpacked her daypack, scattering stuff around to show anyone who might be interested that she had moved in. "Stay," she said to Mutt, who flopped back down, pouting.

She stuck her head outside, listening. Apart from the distant hum of a small plane and some muted truck traffic on the main road, all was quiet. She went swiftly and silently downstairs and peeked around the corner of the garage.

The house next to it was large enough to house a family of eight and everyone's ancestors on both sides of the family all the way back to the gold rush. Two stories, white siding, two rows of tall, rectangular windows, each with its own fake wooden shutters, a front porch sheltered by an antebellum overhang held up by two fluted white columns. The front doors were etched glass with heavy brass handles, and on the second floor a pair of French doors over the porch opened into a half-circle deck, upon which at any moment Jefferson Davis would step out to make his presidential acceptance speech.

In short, a style of architecture one did not expect to see in a town the size of Newenham, especially a town that far from road and rail and slave cabins. Kate didn't have a clue what hints the exterior gave to the interior, but so far as she could tell, no one was looking out the dozen or so windows that faced the garage. She wondered briefly if Tina's daughter Irene had had a say in the construction of her apartment, and if so, if she had demanded that no window be on the facing wall of the apartment upstairs. Not much privacy otherwise from that battery of glass.

Kate pulled her head back and sidled around the garage in the other direction until she reached the door in the side. Another quick look at the house assured her that she remained unobserved for the moment, and she slipped inside. The red Honda ATV was squeezed into the only available space near the overhead door. As in most Alaskan garages, parking any vehicle inside it was way down on the list of purposes for which it had been built. She saw two snow machines on a trailer, a bench the length of the garage laden with parts and black grease in roughly equal measure, three red metal toolboxes made of stacking drawers that were each taller than Kate, a motorcycle missing its front fork, and various and sundry engines in various states of disrepair, some of which might have come out of airplanes. There were tundra tires sitting on top of a pair of wheel skis on one corner. The floats Kate had already seen out back. A metal skiff hung from the ceiling, as did a homemade framework of two-by-fours that held more lumber, two-by-fours, four-by-fours, and two-by-twelves, along with a lot of odd lengths of various kinds of molding.

No wonder they'd left the chest freezer upstairs.

The side door had a push-button lock. She pushed it and pulled the door closed and tried the handle. Locked.

She sidled back around the building and up the stairs and took a shower, dried her hair, and put on clean clothes, including her tightest T-shirt. She knew that much about bartending.

"Okay," she said to Mutt. "Time to go to work."

Mutt scrambled to her feet from the braided rug in the middle of the room she had staked out as her own and wagged her tail hard enough to beat out the rhythm for "In-A-Gadda-Da-Vida."

They left the apartment and walked around the garage, where Kate tried the door. It was locked. "Damn," she said out loud but not loudly. She looked over her shoulder at the house and tried the handle again, making it obvious. Nobody looking.

They walked around to the front of the house and went up the front steps, Kate feeling a distinct lack of crinoline about her person. She knocked on the door before she saw the bell pull, an ornate brass lion's paw, which she then pulled. There came a tolling inside reminiscent of Quasimodo in the belfry at Notre Dame. "Transylvania Six-Five Thousand," she said to Mutt.

She heard footsteps and the door opened, surprisingly with nary a creak nor a groan. Behind it was the young man from the booth at the bar. "Hi," Kate said. "Looking for Tina?"

He eyed her without favor. "What for?"

She smiled at him. It had no effect, which was not what she was accustomed to. She heard voices from the back of the house, and raised her own voice enough to be heard there. "I just rented the apartment over the garage, and Tina said I could rent her spare ATV, too."

"Who is it, Oren?" Tina came up behind him. "Oh, hello, Kate."

"Hi," Kate said, looking behind her.

Another woman and the older man from the booth came into the hall behind Tina. He was of medium height and built like a wrestler, with thick dark eyebrows, a broad nose that had been flattened a time or two, and a swarthy, frowning countenance. She was petite, trim, with cornflower blue eyes and blond hair the color of a particularly fine pale ale that hung to her waist in an absolutely straight silken swath. Her manner said she was Tina's age, but her looks were holding steady at forty.

"Oh," Tina said, "of course, I'm sorry." She didn't sound sorry; she just sounded tired. "Kate, this is my friend Jeannie Penney. She's our local librarian. And this is my husband's brother, Fred Grant. This is Kate Saracoff. She just moved into Irene's apartment."

Fred put a casual hand on Tina's shoulder. Just as casually, Tina slid from beneath it. "Is there a problem?" He eyed Mutt. Mutt eyed him back with interest. Jeannie Penney might have been hiding a smile behind her hand.

"I'm sorry," Kate said to Tina, "I was going to take the ATV back to Bill's, but the garage door is locked."

"Locked?" Tina looked bewildered. "That door's never locked."

Kate gave an apologetic shrug.

"Well, come on in, I'll try to find the key," Tina said, which was exactly what Kate had been hoping for. "Oh, Kate, this is my son, Oren. Oren, this is Kate Saracoff."

She disappeared back down the hall, followed by Fred and Jeannie.

Kate and Oren nodded at each other. Mutt, standing a little behind Kate, regarded him with bored indifference. Mutt's asshole detector was every bit the equal of Kate's bullshit detector, and Kate filed Mutt's reaction away for future reference.

There was a lot of family resemblance between Oren Grant and his mother, but it was all one step removed, as if he were the last copy made before the cartridge ran out of ink. He seemed somehow faded, almost in places even missing. He was tall but not so tall as his mother, had less hair with more gray in it, was the same kind of lean except that his lean looked flabby. His eyes were a little less brown, his cheekbones not so high, his jaw not so firm. He wore khakis and a white oxford shirt under a sweater vest, everything clean and neatly pressed, and somehow it all added up to his mother being the real deal while he tagged along behind, a wannabe, almost, maybe even an impostor.

Kate had met men like him before, the children of wildly successful parents. Usually no one had ever told them no, and later had never failed to buy them out of whatever trouble they'd gotten themselves into. If they didn't cut themselves loose young and start staking out their own lives, and they almost never did, the lure of a bought-and-paid-for lifestyle too strong, they grew older existing in their parents' shadows, becoming steadily more dissatisfied and increasingly whinier with each passing year.

Oren Grant looked like the whiny type.

Kate smiled at him. He frowned back at her. She decided to push it. "Is there a problem? Or you just don't like Natives?"

He flushed darkly, and called after his mother, "I can get the garage door opener in the car, Mom."

Her voice reached them from the back of the house. "But then she won't be able to get back in when she comes home after work." Her voice dropped then, but Kate heard her say, "I should probably start getting rid of some keys in this drawer."

The words sounded exhausted, and there was a murmur in a feminine voice.

"Wait here," Oren said, like Kate might start casing the joint the moment she was left alone.

Well, she had every intention of doing so. She smiled at him with all her teeth, the full treatment. He frowned back and went into a door on the right. Kate looked beyond him and saw a living room furnished with what looked like real leather couches and a seventy-inch flat-screen television on the wall over a rock fireplace. The door closed in her face and there was the immediate sound of an announcer calling an NBA basketball game from behind it.

She was standing in a hall whose ceiling reached up into the second story. A wide staircase with a very nice stained wooden bannister curved down one side of the room. The walls above it were covered with Alaska artwork, everything from Fred Machetanz to Anuktuvuk face masks, and what might be an original Sydney Laurence painting. A life-size sea otter carved from whale vertebrae leaned on his thick tail in one corner, and the beak of an eagle protruded a good six inches from an Alvin Amason painting in another. That beak had kid-size disaster written all over it. At a guess, Tina didn't have any grandchildren.

A corner table stood between the front door and the TV room. An oval mirror in a gilt frame leaned into the corner. On the shelf below was a wide wicker basket full of knit hats and leather gloves and a single lime green YakTrax. On the table itself was a small blue pottery bowl with two rings of keys in it.

A photograph sat next to the bowl, of a young woman in uniform, U.S. Army, Kate thought, although she wasn't that ept with the armed forces. The young woman wore a maroon beret with a black band and stood in front of an American flag with her hands clasped behind her. She wore no makeup and what hair she had was tucked behind her ears, but there was no hiding her essential femininity or the fact that she was her mother's daughter. The lines of her face, her wide brow, her small, straight nose, her firm jaw were all clearly defined. She met the camera's lens squarely, no shrinking or flinching. This copy was as fresh and crisp as the original.

The photograph wasn't draped in black, no badges or wings or other soldier's mementos, no burning candles. Nothing of the shrine about this photograph. It spoke for itself.

This would be the eldest daughter, Irene. Killed in November in Afghanistan.

The Grants really were having a lousy year, and Kate felt a twinge of conscience that she was very probably about to add to it.

But only a twinge. She stepped back from the photograph and looked around. Bedrooms upstairs, kitchen in back from what she could see. There was a closed door on her left. She opened it. It faced west, maybe a little west by south, which meant it would get all the light there was during the winter and all the light there ever would be the rest of the year. It was a craft room, filled with baskets of yarn and beads in clear plastic parts drawers and half-finished bracelets and stranded tams spread across the surface of three long folding tables. A thirteen-inch television–DVD player combo stood on the corner of one table, and a bookcase on the wall in back of it was filled with DVDs and pattern books. A recliner covered in brown corduroy worn smooth stood next to a floor lamp, a pile of paperbacks on the floor next to it. Kate tilted her head to read the spines. Susan Elizabeth Phillips, David Weber, Lindsey Davis, Charlaine Harris. Eclectic escapism. If those authors couldn't pull you out of the life you were living, you were well and truly stuck.

Tina's room, if she had to guess. Kate liked it.

She pulled the door closed again and moved softly to the next room. The door opened silently onto the office, which held a large desk and two filing cabinets and bookshelves against each wall.

Bingo.

She took note of the two sash-weight windows on the exterior wall before pulling the door closed again. When Tina returned to the hall alone, Kate was standing in exactly the spot she had been when Tina left her, Mutt sitting next to her, both of them the very picture of innocence. She looked up from the photograph of the woman in uniform when Tina reappeared. "Your daughter?" she said.

Tina's expression didn't change. "Yes."

"The resemblance is very strong."

"Yes."

The TV room door opened and Oren reappeared. He followed their gaze to the photograph of his sister. "I told her that beret made her look like Che Guevara." He laughed.

His mother did not. "Let's try this," she said, holding up a key. "It's marked garage, but who knows."

Kate followed Tina outside and around the house to the garage. The key worked and Tina said, "Put it on the ring with the house key." She showed Kate the button for the garage door. "There are two gas stations, one across from the AC and the other on the road to the airport. The airport one is cheaper. Outside the city limits, so no city tax."

"Thanks," Kate said with perfect truth. "I appreciate it."

Tina made a dismissive gesture and returned to Tara.

The ATV was either new or had been kept in extremely good condition. Kate unscrewed the gas cap and rocked it back and forth. Low on gas, but enough to get her to work with a stop to fill up on the way.

9

JANUARY 18, THAT EVENING

Newenham

IT WAS ALMOST SEVEN by the time she got back to Bill's. It was a Tuesday night and the crowd amounted to the same guy asleep on the same stool at the bar and two younger men playing cribbage in a booth, who stopped pegging long enough to examine Kate with interest. She put her jacket in Bill's office, Mutt took up station at the end of the bar, and Bill indoctrinated her into the mysteries of waitressing. "All people want is the right drink fast. Try to keep the orders straight and you'll be fine." Bill looked her over. "You'll probably get your share of come-ons from the customers. Don't take any crap. If someone persists in giving it—"

"If I can't take care of it, and I can," Kate said, "don't forget I brought my own personal bouncer." They both looked at Mutt.

Bill looked back at Kate, a latent twinkle in her blue eyes. "You'll do," she said.

There were never more than twenty-five customers at one time that evening, but Kate had never worked so hard in her life. She was constantly in motion physically and constantly on the alert mentally to the wave of a hand, a call for a round, keeping straight who ordered what at what table or booth, adding up a tab, figuring out change. There was a knack to carrying the tray, which strangely enough felt equally heavy loaded with full glasses as with empty ones. Most of the bar's patrons were regulars, they knew what they wanted and they knew the menu, and they were patient with Kate only up to a point. And then there were the passes, covert and overt, the oh-so-accidental brush of a hand against her hip, the inadvertent brush of a head against her breast.

Kate was accustomed to being underestimated where her reputation did not precede her. She was short, she was a woman, and she was a Native. Now she was a waitress, too, and evidently waitress was not only a job regarded with automatic disdain, it was also a job with a pheromone signature that flagged down every male between the ages of seven and seventy. It added an extra layer of distraction to a job she already didn't know how to do, but she gritted her teeth and smiled and remembered Jim's orders. *Just try to wrap it up in a week, otherwise I might have to come down there and clear it myself.* The thought of Sergeant Jim Chopin walking in the door in all his blue-and-gold glory made her smile a lot more genuine, which went some way toward increasing her tips, too.

She could have slacked off—it wasn't like she was going to be slinging beer to off-season fishermen forever—but it wasn't in her to do a job badly, so she found a moment to be grateful there was no smoking at Bill's and dug into it as if it were going to be her life's work.

At eight o'clock a short, plump blonde with sharp green eyes and curly blond hair came in with Liam Campbell and Wyanet Chouinard, and the three of them settled into a booth. Campbell was in civilian clothes, and looked just as devastatingly attractive in them as he did in his uniform.

Chouinard smiled and said, "Hi, Kate. I see Bill put you to

work." She'd changed out of her bibs into a blouse and slacks, and her hair had been freed from its ponytail to tumble gloriously over her shoulders.

"That she did," Kate said. "Thanks for the tip."

"This is Kate Saracoff," Chouinard told her companions. "She flew in from Togiak with me this afternoon. I heard Laura Nanalook took off again and Bill was short-staffed, so I sent her here. Kate, this is my husband, Liam Campbell, and my friend, Jo Dunaway."

Campbell nodded, as if to a stranger. The blonde kept looking at her, a frown spreading across her face. "What can I get you?" Kate said.

No one at the table looked at the menus she offered. "Jalapeño burger with onion rings, and an iced tea," Chouinard said.

"Who were you thinking of sleeping with tonight, again?" Campbell said. "Cheeseburger and fries, and two fingers of Glenmorangie."

The blonde was still staring at Kate.

"Jo?" Chouinard said. "You hungry?"

"Patty melt, green salad, blue cheese on the side, and a margarita, blended, with salt."

Kate could feel the blonde's eyes boring into her back as she went to deliver the order. They ate and drank and didn't linger.

By nine o'clock most of the booths were filled and a drunken couple was trying and failing to keep up with the Black Eyed Peas' "I Gotta Feeling" blaring out from the sound system. Up till then, the drink orders had been mostly beer. When the women drinkers showed up, the orders for Cosmos, Island Breezes, and Appletinis started coming. Whatever happened to a nice glass of chardonnay? In Niniltna, the height of drinking sophistication was the Middle Finger, and you had to earn one by climbing Big Bump. Like getting fifteen thousand feet straight up in the air all by itself wasn't enough of a high.

In Newenham, apparently palates were more refined.

At ten o'clock the blonde came back in. She went to the bar, acquired a stool from an inebriated fisherman ten years her junior with a hip bump and a dazzling smile, and ordered a beer, which she proceeded to nurse. A few minutes later, Bill told Kate to take fifteen minutes in her office with her feet up, handed her a fizzing glass of Fresca and ice, and pushed her in that direction.

Kate had just sat down in Bill's chair and put her feet up on Bill's desk when Dunaway came in behind her and closed the door. She stood there, hand on the doorknob, watching Mutt sit down next to Kate and rest her head on Kate's thigh. "Hello, Kate," she said. "I don't remember the dog."

Kate took a big swallow of her drink. The bubbles tickled pleasantly at the back of her throat.

"Wy says your last name is Saracoff, but it isn't. It's Shugak." Kate remained silent, and the blonde said, "You don't remember me."

It was a statement, not a question, so Kate didn't say anything.

"Anchorage," the other woman said, sitting down across from Kate and putting her own feet up. She'd brought her beer with her and it rested on her belly, clasped between her hands. "Eight years ago. You were testifying at the inquest of the death of Cornelius Bradley, the guy who cut your throat." She looked at it. "The scar's faded a lot."

In lieu of reaching up to touch the scar, a tell she'd thought she had rid herself of, Kate took a drink.

"It was the only court case I ever reported on," the blonde said.

Kate stopped with her drink halfway to her mouth. "Joan Dunaway."

"Jo," the other woman said. "Just Jo is fine. Did you see the story?"

"I saw it."

"The city editor butchered it before it went to print."

"Always the editor's fault," Kate said, and smiled without humor. "At least that's what every reporter I've ever met says."

"Edna Buchanan says there are three rules for the rookie journalist," Joan Dunaway said. "One, never trust an editor. Two, never trust an editor." Her smile was bleak. "Bet you can guess the third one."

"Bet I can," Kate said. "You still a reporter?"

"You still a private investigator?"

So she knew that much. Kate raised her glass and sipped. Her lower back ached from all the bending and lifting. Her own personal masseur, alas, was at present somewhat east of her current location.

"Are you working, here in Newenham, on a case?" Dunaway asked.

"Are you working, here in Newenham, on a story?" Kate asked.

They stared at each other some more. Mutt's ears flicked at the back and forth, but she left her head on Kate's knee.

"Because," Dunaway said, "I doubt very much that you've left your home, your adopted son, and your state trooper roommate to take up the profession of bartending six hundred miles away."

She'd done her homework, damn her for being a good reporter. "I doubt very much that you flew three hundred miles into the Alaskan Bush in January just to visit friends."

"Depends on the friend." Dunaway took a sip of her beer. "Does your case have anything to do with Eagle Air?"

Kate didn't flinch, but it was a near thing. "Does your story have anything to do with Eagle Air?"

Silence.

Kate took another drink. The Fresca was getting pretty low in the glass. She craned her neck to look at the clock on the wall. "I've got ten minutes left on my break. I was thinking of taking a little nap."

"I'm not going anywhere," Dunaway said.

Kate put some steel into her voice. "Sure you are. You're leaving this room."

"I'm not done asking questions."

"Tonight you are." Kate put her now-empty glass on the desk, let her head fall back against the chair, and closed her eyes. Probably what she should have done when Dunaway walked in.

After a moment Dunaway's chair creaked, and the door opened and closed again, shutting out the noise of the bar.

Kate opened her eyes and looked down at Mutt. "Another fine mess I've gotten us into, did you say?"

Mutt's wise yellow eyes blinked up at her.

"Don't you just hate being right all the time?" Kate said.

Dunaway had left the bar when she came out of Bill's office, and Kate went back to work. She kept the bar clean, washed glasses, ran food and tickets, and made countless rounds with a loaded tray and an ingratiating smile, which might have been the most difficult part of the whole job. Her ass was patted, slapped, and pinched, and one of the two young men playing cribbage made repeated attempts to see her later. "I'm old enough to be your mother," she told him.

Well, maybe only his much older sister. His enthusiasm, if anything, increased. *Cougar Town.*

At the end of the evening her back ached, her feet hurt, she smelled of soured beer and her own sweat, and she'd earned enough in tips to recoup the ATV rental, plus.

She had against all expectation picked up some potentially useful local information. A lot of people were sleeping with a lot of other people, none of whom she knew. The mayor and the town council were on a cost-cutting frenzy, and a lot of their employees were busy drinking down their savings before they got laid off. The logic of that escaped Kate, but then she didn't drink herself. Finn Grant's recent demise was toasted over more than a few of the tables she waited on. Some were more celebratory than others, and those Kate paid special attention to, flirting if it would let her linger as the conversation played out.

The consensus appeared to be that Finn Grant was as great a pilot as he was execrable a human being. One man did wonder out loud how an aircraft that somebody like Finn Grant flew every day could possibly have broken in flight, but he was very nearly laughed out of his chair and the conversation immediately degenerated into a round robin of stories of every time anyone at the table had been on a flight with mechanical difficulties. All of them, it appeared, most of them being Alaskans born and bred. Kate could have contributed a few stories of her own.

"You heard about the fight, didn't you? Finn going head-to-head with Wy Chouinard? I hear she threatened to kill him."

The speaker was a short thickset man with one gnarled hand wrapped around a bottle and the other a possessive presence on the knee of the woman seated next to him. Everyone at his table leaned in, and he gave a sage nod and burped for emphasis. "Fact. Day before he died. Mac McCormick was there, he heard it all."

"Who hasn't threatened to kill Finn Grant?" another man said, and a third, leaning over the back of the booth who appeared more sober than the rest, said, "Consider the source. Never knew Mac not to dress up a story."

The first man, angry at having his story stepped on and probably unhappy at being made to look no-account in front of his girl, said, "Wasn't the first argument they ever had, and she's a pilot, and she's in and out of Newenham airport every day."

Only too true, Kate thought.

The speaker glared at her, and she aimed a bland smile at the table. "How's everything, folks?" before giving the table an unnecessary swipe with a bar rag and moving on.

So Campbell hadn't been an alarmist when he said the town was talking about his wife's very public and most unfortunately timed fight with Finn Grant. Of course, this was winter, in rural Alaska, and that was always the time and place when the most outrageous stories were made up of whole cloth, and when the bloodiest fights started over the most ridiculous causes. Cabin fever was as real a condition as it was pernicious and pervasive. Months of unrelenting dark and cold would do that to a community. The smaller and more isolated the community, the worse the symptoms.

When Bill closed and locked the door behind the last customer, she cocked an eyebrow in Kate's direction. "Well?"

Kate stretched. "It's one way to get to know the community fast, I'll say that."

"Better than you ever wanted to," Bill said, going back around behind the bar. "One for the road?"

Kate looked at the clock. A little after midnight. Not near enough time for everyone back at massa's house to be settled down snug in their beds. "Sure," she said. She went into Bill's office and got her cell phone out of her jacket pocket. There were a couple of missed calls, one from Jim with no message and another from Annie Mike with voice mail, asking her to call back whenever Kate got the message. She didn't say why, but she sounded tense.

Kate deleted the message instead.

A tall cool glass filled with ice and Fresca waited for her at the bar. On the other side, Bill had pulled up a stool and uncapped a bottle of Alaskan Amber. "It's good that you don't drink," she said. "Have you ever?"

Kate shook her head, inhaling half her glass in one gulp. On your feet for six hours straight was a dehydrating experience.

"Why not?"

Kate looked up and met Bill's eyes. In Bush Alaska, you didn't ask people about their past prior to their arrival in your community. If they volunteered, well and good, but you didn't outright ask. It was not considered good manners, especially when much of the time the new arrival was leaving something behind that did not bear close examination, like an angry spouse, or the law.

On the other hand, Bill had given Kate a job at first sight, no questions asked. "Both my parents were alcoholics," Kate said, "so I've got the gene. Always been terrified that it would get hold of me."

"But it's more about control," Bill said.

It wasn't a question. Kate's smile was wry. "Partly." She shrugged. "Maybe mostly." She laughed a little. "Plus the stuff doesn't even pass the nose test with me. Can't stand the smell."

Bill's laugh was big and belly-shaking, if she'd had a belly. "And you're working in a bar."

"I needed a job."

Something in the quality of the silence that followed her words made her look up, to find that Bill was giving her a steady, assessing look. "Did you?" she said. "Because you're not a village girl on the run from an abusive family life."

Crap, Kate thought, but the time for dissimulation was apparently over. "What gave me away?"

Bill snorted. "Well, for one thing you're not a girl, you're a woman, and the only scar you've got is old. For another, you're way too articulate and self-assured." She nodded at the bar. "Nothing out there threw you, not even when Teddy grabbed your thigh. I've had a lot of waitstaff, and that alone would have any one of them either in tears or lying down and seeing how wide they could spread their legs."

She was being deliberately crude, eyes on Kate to see how she took it. Kate neither blushed nor took offense. She knew only too well the tendency of village girls—and boys—alone for the first time in the big city to embrace victimhood as a matter of survival.

"And you're not from Togiak, either," Bill said. "At a guess, I'd say ... Cordova? Prince William Sound, anyway."

And Bill was the Newenham magistrate, which meant she had her own bullshit detector all broken in and oiled up and ready to engage gears. Well, local authorities were never happy when they discovered they had been left out of the loop. "I used to work for the Anchorage DA," Kate said. "Nine years ago I moved into private practice."

"A PI, huh?" Bill said. "That fits. And you're in Newenham because—?"

So, off with the cape and the mask. Kate had known she

would be found out; she just hadn't figured it to be within twenty-four hours of hitting town. She made a mental note to be careful in her dealings with the magistrate slash bar owner from that moment on. "Liam Campbell hired me to look into Finn Grant's death."

"Did he." Bill Billington took a long, meditative pull at her beer. "Any particular reason I wasn't told?"

"You'd have to ask him," Kate said, which both of them thought was a little craven of her. She covered by adding in a brisk, businesslike voice, "So let me ask you some questions. Do you think Finn Grant was murdered?"

Bill slid the bar rag up and down the wooden surface of the bar. "I don't know," she said slowly. "I do know that practically everyone who knew him wanted the bastard dead. With the possible exception of Hugh Reid."

Kate conjured up the image of the eagerish middle-aged guy in the safari suit fawning over Gabe McGuire at Eagle Air. "Grant's partner."

"Yeah."

"What about the wife?"

"Tina?" The temperature in the bar dropped perceptibly.

Kate refused to be intimidated. "We always look first at the spouse. And not without cause, as you well know. Being the magistrate and all."

For a split second Bill looked angry, and in the next moment she laughed. "Yeah. Well, not this time. I've known Tina since I landed in Disneyham, and a saner person never lived. She's not capable of murdering someone, let alone her husband. However much she—"

"However much she what?"

Bill hesitated, then grimaced. "Ah, shit. He screwed around on her with every woman between Unalaska and Kaktovik who was dumb enough to fall for his lame line. He damn near bankrupted her family fortune half a dozen times, and he had to have been the world's worst father, neglectful, abusive—hell, downright oblivious." Bill sighed. "No, not a lot of love lost between Finn and Tina. But she didn't kill him."

"Did she know how to?"

Bill got down from her stool and pitched their empties in the trash. "Find me someone within a thousand miles who didn't."

Means, motive, and opportunity. In Kate's line of work, that was called three strikes. Prudently, she did not say so. "Who else looks good?"

"Not Wy Chouinard, for damn sure," Bill said.

Mutt, snoozing at Kate's feet, woke up with a snort at the snap in Bill's voice. "I didn't ask you who you thought didn't do it," Kate said, her own voice calm. "I'm asking who you think did. If anyone."

"Oh, hell," Bill said. "I'm sorry." She moved her shoulders as if she were trying to shake something off. "Hard when it comes that close to home."

Kate looked down to meet Mutt's great yellow eyes and remembered the last time someone had taken a shot at her and hit her dog instead. "Yeah."

"Christ, if it comes to that, I had motive myself. Half of Southwest Alaska came here to drink off their mad after he screwed them over, and half of them showed up in my court the next morning. I have a lot more leisure time now that Finn Grant is good and dead." Her laugh was more of a bark.

"Was Grant really that irresistible?" Kate said.

Bill shrugged, ashamed of her flash of temper. "I never saw the attraction myself, but I watched him operate over this bar for the last twenty years. He was a big man, big voice, big spender. When he wanted something, he went at it a hundred and ten percent." Her brow creased. "He was always a dog, but the last two years it was like his appetite doubled right across the board. There weren't enough women for him to lay, enough businesses he could gobble up, enough money he could spend on his new toy out at Chinook."

"You said he nearly bankrupted his wife's family," Kate said. "If that's the case, where did he get the money to upgrade to something like that FBO out at Chinook?"

"You've seen it, have you?"

"We stopped there on the way here, Chouinard had a mail drop. Even met a movie star."

Bill's head came up. "Gabe McGuire?"

Kate, surprised, said, "You know him?"

Bill tipped her head back and let loose with a long, reverential whistle.

Kate's laugh was a little forced. "Yeah, I guess."

"You guess? What's wrong with you, you gay or a man in disguise? The guy's a walking, talking incitement to riot."

Kate remembered McGuire on the Chinook tarmac that morning and thought again how much he reminded her of Jack. "How long has he been coming to Newenham?"

"Gabe?" Bill thought. "About five years, I think. Give or take."

"'Gabe'?" Kate said, one eyebrow going up.

"Yes, Gabe," Bill said. "We're by way of being friends now, but as you can guess, the man likes his privacy when he comes north. We don't mention him much to outsiders. Anyway, to answer your question, Finn has—had been hauling him out to Outuchiwanet Lodge ever since Gabe made it big enough to afford it. He hides out there for anywhere from a couple of days to a couple of weeks, hunting, fishing. Sleeping and reading, mostly, he told me once. No radios, no TV, no phones, no Internet access, just a lake and mountains and the lodge." Bill smiled. "About as pissed off as I've ever seen Gabe was when Finn told him that GCI was expanding cell coverage to the Bush communities north of here."

"What kind of hunting and fishing is he going to do in January?" Kate said.

"Like I said," Bill said with emphasis, "mostly he's hiding out. Take a pretty rabid fan to get to Outouchiwanet from Newenham without a plane, and nobody around here, including Finn Grant, has ever ratted him out. Or will," she added. "They all know Moses would eviscerate them if they did."

"Who's Moses?" Kate said.

"Moses Alakuyak," Bill said with an inscrutable smile. "He's, ah, what you could call the city father."

"Haven't met him," Kate said.

"Believe me, you will."

The clear day had segued into a clear night, with a sky full of stars and no moon. Kate held the four-wheeler to a medium speed to keep down the noise. Most of the houses and all the businesses she passed were dark, the Newenhamers all snug in their beds.

She pulled in next to the garage, parked under the stairs up to her apartment, and killed the engine. She peeked around the corner and cursed beneath her breath. The only lights on in the plantation house, on in any house within a mile radius were in the corner room with the television. Through a gap in the drapes, she could see the flicker of the television screen reflected against the glass of the windows.

She slipped upstairs and doffed boots and jacket. The clock read a quarter to two. What the hell was Oren watching at a quarter to two in the goddamn morning? Kate hated satellite television, not least because it kept people up past their normal bedtime.

She decided to wait an hour, and laid down for a nap.

At 3 A.M. she was back at the foot of the stairs, peering around the corner at the house. The television was still on. Fuck this. She went around the back of the garage, crept across the open space between the buildings, and slid along the wall to where she could inch up and hoist an eyeball over the windowsill. Behind her, Mutt was a gray ghost drifting over the snow.

The television was on, all right, and Oren was in the room, but he was out, head lolling against the back of the couch, mouth open in a snore she could hear through the glass. His legs were crossed on the coffee table in front of the couch, knocking over one of the six empty bottles of Bud Light sitting on the tabletop. Tall black men chased a basketball across the television screen. While she watched, one of them launched a court-length pass worthy of the Kanuyaq Kings.

She dropped back down and duck-walked around the back of the house. The office window was dark. She forced herself to wait and watch for five very long minutes. No lights, no movement. She hadn't seen a dog or any other pets when she'd been inside the house yesterday afternoon, and she was hoping there weren't any.

She tested the window. It was a vinyl sash-weight, as new as the rest of the house. True to form, it wasn't locked and slid up soundlessly at a touch. She told herself that she really should feel guilty about abusing Tina's innocent hospitality in this way.

She really should. "Stay," she whispered to Mutt. "And for god's sake give us a shout if you hear anything."

Mutt measured the distance between the ground and the windowsill. "Stay," Kate whispered again, with more force this time. "I mean it, Mutt. Guard."

As she turned to pull herself up through the window, she heard Mutt's butt hit the snow with a disgruntled sound.

She eeled inside, walking forward on her hands until she could get a foot beneath her, and crouched beneath the window, one hand on the sill, listening. The sound of the television came dimly through the walls but that was all. She rose and stood to one side of the window looking out at the unmoving neighborhood. Silent still, silent all. She went softly across to the door. Should she lock it, or no? If she woke Tina or Oren, a locked door would slow them down and give her time to escape, her caped crusader identity intact. But if she locked it, they would know someone had been there when they couldn't get in. She left it unlocked. Best-case scenario, no one ever knew she was here, and Mutt was all the DEW Line she would ever need.

She pulled out a pencil flashlight and went to the computer on the desk. Password protected. She tried Tina's birthday, her children's birthdays, Finn Grant's birthday, which information she had provided herself with before she left the Park. None of them worked, which raised her opinion of Tina's intelligence a notch.

Which meant Kate did things the hard way. Never mind the Paperwork Reduction Act, the paperless society had not yet truly arrived, so she could. She turned to the first filing cabinet.

One thing being chair of the Niniltna Native Association had taught her was how to read legal and financial documents.

Until three years ago, Finn Grant had been the sole owner and proprietor of his business, until then known as Bristol

Bay Air. Bristol Bay Air had a rotating list of assets, most of these airplanes, everything from a Piper Super Cub on wheel-skis to a Single Otter turbo on floats. There was a hangar at Newenham airport, until two years ago mortgaged to the hilt, at that time paid off in one lump sum, and today free and clear. There was a new deed to it with no listed lien holder, dated eighteen months before.

The only paper she could find on the house she was standing in was a tax assessment from the Bristol Bay borough. Her lips pursed in a silent whistle. A million five in a town the size of Newenham was a pretty hefty chunk of the tax base. Grant must have slept with the borough assessor's wife, too.

She could find no mortgage paperwork, no liens, no lines of credit. Could Finn Grant really have paid cash to build this Tara-wannabe three hundred plus miles off the road system? It wasn't like he was spending a lot of time in his own bed, if everything she'd heard so far was true. Still, if a career in criminal investigation had taught Kate anything, it was that trophies came in all shapes and sizes.

She closed the first drawer and opened the second. This one was dedicated to Eagle Air, a corporation that had evidently sprung into being full grown from the brow of Grant two years before. Hugh Reid was a partner in and also vice president of Eagle Air LLC. There were other partners and investors, about a dozen of them, with generic names like Northwest Partners, Pacific Capital, and Arctic Investments, most of whose business addresses were post office boxes in Lucerne, or Las Vegas.

There was a deed of sale for Chinook Air Force Base, seller, the federal government, buyer, EAI, for a cool five million dollars, cash.

Kate raised her eyes from the file and stared at the wall.

Five million seemed pretty low for an air base as nicely appointed as the one she'd seen yesterday. She doubted five million would buy fifty feet of paved runway anywhere in Bush Alaska.

There was a fat file of invoices and receipts for the remodel and furnishings of the FBO, all of them marked PAID IN FULL, including a dozen queen-sized Tempur-Pedic mattresses from the Cloud Collection at $3,600 a pop, shipped air freight from Sadler's in Anchorage.

Jesus Christ, she almost said out loud, and raised her head to listen, just in case she had. The television in the room across the hall was still broadcasting a muted roar from the crowd. There was no sound from the floor above. She put the folder back in the drawer, closed it, and found the income tax returns.

Finn Grant kept good records, she'd say that for him: the drawer held tax returns going back twenty years. She pulled one out at random and looked at the signature. Prepared by Clementina T. Grant, and signed by her for him, too.

So Tina kept the books.

Kate had another thought and opened up last year's return. This one had been prepared by an accounting firm in Anchorage.

She checked. So had the two years before.

So Tina had retired from family bookkeeping. Kate wondered if her retirement had been voluntary.

One thing was certain, Grant's income had jumped considerably over the past two, no, three years. She compared returns. The year before he bought Chinook Air Force Base was when the rise in income had begun. He'd filed extensions for eleven out of the past twenty years, but not in the last three.

The third drawer was the catchall for everything else, receipts, statements, deeds, bills of sale, organized by businesses. A couple of fishing charters, a guiding business, an air taxi. She flipped through the folders. There was nothing on the day-to-day expenses of Eagle Air. Those must be kept on the computer or out at the base itself.

Tucked into the deed file she found a transfer of title for Outouchiwanet Mountain Lodge and the 160 surrounding acres from Bristol Bay Air, Inc., to Gabriel McGuire Enterprises Ltd., for the sum of "one dollar and other valuable considerations."

That was interesting.

Outouchiwanet Lodge must have been a homestead in its first incarnation, 160 acres being the standard parcel granted by the federal government under the Homestead Act. No matter how rustic or remote, one dollar seemed pretty cheap. The other considerations would have had to be pretty valuable, indeed.

She closed the file, replaced it in the drawer, and slid the drawer home.

The light from the pencil flash caught the corner of a file folder on top of the filing cabinet. She opened it, and found herself reading the letter Tina's daughter Irene's commanding officer had written to Finn and Tina following her death.

> Irene was a good soldier and a damn fine pilot who backed up a ton of natural ability with a fierce dedication to training. She was well liked by her crew and trusted absolutely by every man and woman who rode with her, myself included.

He was a good writer, he stuck to the facts and he didn't

sentimentalize. The letter didn't sound rote, and a real sense of loss came up from the page.

There was another letter tucked in behind the first. This one wasn't on letterhead stationery and the typing had not been proofed, but it was even more poignant than the first.

November 23
Dear Mrs. Grant,

I'm not real good at this kind of thing, ma'am, but I wanted to rite to let you know that I flew with your daughter a lot of times during my tour in Afghanistan. She was a reel good pilot we all felt safe with her. Some pilots you don't even want to get anywhere near there aircraft but she dint take no chances with us or her aircraft. Its bad enough she died its how she died thats got us all down. Its just wrong the enemy is using our own weapons against us. I know I wont ever be able to use an M4 again without thinking of her. I'm so sorry for your loss, ma'am. And for ours.

Sincerely yours,
SPC GS Waichowski

Sobered, Kate closed the folder and set it back on top of the filing cabinet, understanding a little better the debilitating and ill-concealed despair that colored Tina Grant's general attitude. She herself couldn't imagine reading a letter like that about Johnny and not being at the very least suicidal after the fact.

Sound from the television room stopped, and she heard movement. She shut off the penlight. A door opened and unsteady footsteps sounded in the hall. Outside the window she heard Mutt get to her feet and tried to send her a telepathic message to make no sound.

The footsteps went past the office door and up the stairs. Kate heard a door closing, and turned the penlight back on to scan the room for any other clues. The arc of light caught something against the wall behind the door that made her pause. She moved in for a closer look.

It was a gun safe of a size to hold enough arms for a squad of marines. She opened the door, which was of course unlocked, and beheld a virtual armory of collector's items. Kate was no expert, but she was pretty sure the thin light of her flash passed over a pair of Purdey shotguns, what looked a little like a blunderbuss, and ... She looked closer. An AK-47? It sure looked like it belonged on the cover of a book by Robert Ludlum.

The weapon next to it looked like something Sigourney Weaver would use to kill the aliens who were trying to impregnate her adopted daughter. It didn't look like anything you could shoot a moose with. Not if you wanted to eat any of the moose afterwards.

Kate was not a member of the gun culture. For her, weapons were a tool, not a toy, and the mere existence of a weapon like the alien-killer in the gun safe was not by itself reason enough for her to want to have one of her own, or to shoot it, or even to hold it. She tolerated the gun culture in which she had been raised, but she'd never really understood it. Abel Int-Hout had been a collector, with a wall full of over-under rifles chased in silver and so individually heavy that Kate as a child hadn't even been able to pick them up, let alone raise one to her shoulder. Conversely, Old Sam had owned one bolt-action rifle, period. Said any job couldn't be done with a Model 70

Winchester didn't need doing, and the man who couldn't feed his family on the strength of it was no kind of a man.

She owned two firearms herself, a .30-06 rifle and a 12-gauge pump action shotgun. Both were used for hunting food for the freezer: the rifle for mammals, the shotgun for birds. She was a good shot, not a great one, mostly because she took her time and didn't get excited. Her father, Abel, and Old Sam had all three emphasized the need for placing the first bullet in the right place. Spoil the meat with a bad shot and you had to keep hunting. Put the moose down the first time and everybody got to go home. And eat.

Eating was her prime motivation for hunting, and if she thought about it, probably a little pride in continuing a family tradition that went back generations. She liked knowing that the meat on her plate had been romping around the Park twenty-four hours before, stripping the leaves from a diamond willow and eyeing up a likely cow browsing in the next copse over. Meat that came shrink-wrapped at Costco had spent its life in a warehouse with its head locked over a feed trough, never to see the sun.

She understood admiration for fine workmanship. She understood the need for accurate, efficient weaponry with which to win a war. She did not understand the need to have bigger guns and more of them than the next guy. It felt superficial, blustering, vain. The firearms in the gun safe weren't tools. They weren't even toys. They were trophies, and the man with the most of them when he died won.

Which seemed like a pretty good description of Finn Grant.

She closed the safe, and the pencil flash caught a framed photograph on the wall. She recognized Fred Grant, next to a man probably his brother, the late, unlamented Finn. Hugh Reid was there, his safari suit this time accented with a

Winchester ball cap, and so was Gabe McGuire. They were all holding alien-killers like the ones in the safe. McGuire was the only one who didn't have a huge grin all over his face, she'd give him that much.

Upstairs, a toilet flushed and water ran. There was a ghost of a whine from outside the window. Mutt was right, time to go.

She dropped out the window, next to a Mutt who had *About time* written all over her. Kate pulled the window closed and they sidled around the house and the garage and up the stairs to the apartment. Kate was in the lead and stepped through the door first.

It was possible that getting away clean from tossing Grant's office had led her to feel a tad overconfident. It was also possible that she was focused far more intently on getting home than she was on any dangers inherent in tracking down a putative murderer who had got away with it. It was further possible that she'd never taken the job seriously to begin with, had indeed seen it less as a job and more as a convenient means of absence from the Park at what she considered to be a propitious time.

Whatever. For one of the few times in her life, Kate Shugak was taken completely and utterly by surprise. Mutt might have been a little more on the ball, but Mutt was a step and a half behind her. The door was jerked out of Kate's hand and kicked shut in Mutt's face. Simultaneously, someone threw a bag over Kate's head and pulled it all the way down to her hips. She kicked backwards but didn't connect, and didn't get another chance, because she was lifted from her feet, tossed through the air, crashed into something hard that banged into the wall when she hit it, and landed hard. Something slammed shut over her head.

She kicked out and connected painfully with a solid surface. She fought with the bag. It was made of some heavy material, duck or canvas, and wet-proofed, a slick surface her fingernails could only scrabble against.

The top of her prison was opened and Mutt was thrown in on top of her. She knew it was Mutt from the language, which was deafening, and from the claw marks she could feel on her belly and shoulders even through the bag.

The top of the box slammed shut again, squishing Mutt on top of Kate. Kate and Mutt both snarled, to no avail.

They were locked in.

10

JANUARY 18

The Park

MEANWHILE, BACK IN NINILTNA, Jim had his own problems.

It was January. They were gaining daylight at the rate of half an hour a week, and to make matters worse, they'd had a long stretch of clear weather.

To the inexperienced eye, this would not seem to create insurmountable problems for local law enforcement, but clear weather plus days that were five minutes longer than the ones before them seduced Park rats into thinking that spring had arrived, never mind what the calendar said or the thermometer read. There was a honking big high hanging out over the Mother of Storms that showed every sign of staying there until July. Jim haunted the NWS online forecast and swore to himself every morning when it predicted more of the same. What he wouldn't give for a hurricane-force Arctic Express that would drive everyone indoors for a week, and keep them busy digging themselves out for another week.

Because for spring, think breakup, and for breakup, think trouble with a capital *T* and that rhymed with C and that stood for an outburst of criminal activity in its most tiresome form. There hadn't been a murder in a while (he refused to draw a connection between that happy nonoccurence and

Kate's absence from the Park) but there had been everything else on the books, up to and including assault of every kind and degree, robbery, burglary, and far too many nuisance calls via cell phone. Mary Kompkoff, for chrissake, had called in from her set net site on Alaganik Bay to report she'd caught Martin Shugak and an unidentified coconspirator (probably Howie Katelnikof) coming out of her gear shed with their arms full of her chain saw and various other power tools. Time was she would have handled the situation her own damn self, with the barrel of double-aught or a seal club, which before the advent of cell phones she had been known to do, with an enthusiasm that resulted in more than one medevac.

Now, in direct contravention of what Jim had always considered to be the fine libertarian spirit of the Park, she was dialing 911. And she wasn't alone. At closing time the night before, two drunk Suulutaq miners had absconded from the Roadhouse on Andy Gordaoff's ATV. Somehow they'd gotten off the road, which by this time of year was well packed down with high berms on both sides and virtually impossible to lose even in a whiteout. They'd wound up on Squaw Candy Creek, crashed through the ice, staggered out soaking wet into a wind chill that Jim after the fact conservatively estimated at thirty below, and somehow managed to crawl up the driveway to Bobby Clark's A-frame. Which they then entered without invitation. Bobby—naturally—called 911 and by the time Jim got there, Dinah was up making coffee for everyone and Katya was demanding the miners play Barbies with her.

Yesterday afternoon Cindy Bingley called in some excitement to report an assault on the front steps of her grocery store, and Jim arrived at the scene to find Alicia Malchoff, age fifty, whaling on her son, Lee, age twenty. It turned out Lee had impregnated one Julie Swenson, age seventeen, currently a senior at Niniltna High. When Jim understood the full story, his first impulse was to leave Lee to the tender mercies of his mother, and later, what everyone involved knew would be the even less tender mercies of Swede Swenson, Julie's father. Instead, he charged Alicia with assault, interviewed a tearful Julie, charged Lee with sexual assault of a minor since Julia had been sixteen at the time, and sent everyone home (Alicia), to work (Lee, at the Suulutaq) or back to school (Julie).

Less amusing was a 911 call from Bernie. Susie Kompkoff had shown up at the Roadhouse after one of her ex-boyfriends used a crowbar to teach her a lesson. A lesson in what, Susie didn't know or wouldn't say. Alcohol was involved, as it almost invariably was in these cases, and Jim had gone hotfoot to the ex-boyfriend's cabin, taken him into custody, and shipped him direct to Ahtna for arraignment before Judge Singh. Susie was given a remedial patch-up at the Grosdidier brothers' clinic and was now headed to Anchorage for appointments, in order, with the orthopedic surgeon, the dentist, the orthodontist, and the optometrist if she didn't want to lose all sight in her left eye.

There had been three other Assaults-DVR, three wrecks on the Ahtna road, the villages of Kushtaka and Kuskulana were getting an early start on their annual pissing contest, and one of Ranger Dan's people had confided in Dan that she was wanted for assault and attempted murder in Nuckolls County, Nebraska. Dan called Jim and Jim got online and sure enough, Virginia Ellen Perkerson, age thirty-six, had warrants for attempted murder in the first degree, two counts of assault in the second degree, assault in the third degree, and a petition to revoke probation. Dan brought Perkerson down from the

Step and as a matter of curiosity Jim asked her why she had confessed to charges that were five years old and three thousand miles away.

"I'm tired of Alaskan winters," she said.

So Jim sent her off to Ahtna with Susie's ex. It didn't help that Maggie was spending all her time commuting between Niniltna and Ahtna, which left Jim to answer the phone.

Harvey Meganack had been driving home from a Costco run to Ahtna and passed some guy in a Suburban who was pulled over by the side of the road. The guy hopped back in his car, forced Harvey off the road, and yelled at him while Harvey, locked inside his Eddie Bauer Ford Explorer, dialed—naturally—911. The guy, who it turned out was pulled over while making a call on his cell when Harvey passed him, was on his way to Niniltna, looking for a job at the Suulutaq. He said Harvey had nearly sideswiped his vehicle and all he wanted to do was call Harvey to account for his reckless driving. Turned out the guy had a warrant out on him for violating a DVRO in Anchorage. He was now a guest of the trooper post, in company with a Suulutaq miner who'd been caught in the act of liberating Herbie Topkok's Arctic Cat snow machine, and Herbie Topkok, who had remonstrated with said burglar with a little too much enthusiasm, and who Jim hoped would cool down after a night spent in a cell.

He hadn't even made it home last night, not that the bed there was any less cold or lonely than the one in the crash pad he maintained in town at Auntie Vi's B&B. Sergei O'Leary had gone off his medication and started shooting at the attacking pink grizzly bears again. Jim had been called to the scene—naturally—where after a lively thirty minutes dodging bullets until the clip ran out on Sergei's Kalashnikov, Jim had restrained Sergei and remanded him to the custody of the

Grosdidier brothers. Jim had the distinct recollection that he had left Sergei cuffed to one of the two beds they maintained in the Niniltna Health Clinic, complete with IV drip replenishing his meds. Sergei had other ideas, and twenty minutes after Jim had finally been able to put his head down for a few hours' well-earned rest, his phone went off. Matt Grosdidier, calling to say Sergei had yanked out his IV, somehow managed to haul himself and his hospital bed through the door of his room, down the hall to the connecting door to the brothers' house, and to the gun rack in their living room. There, he had liberated Mark's .357, which was loaded—naturally—and proceeded to shoot out all the windows.

"I know we took oaths to first do no harm, Jim," Matt said with what Jim considered remarkable restraint, "but if you don't get that asshole out of here, we're going to tackle the sumbitch and load him up with enough morphine to send him into his next life." Adding, a little unrealistically, Jim thought, "Where maybe the higher order of angels will have a better handle on controlling him."

By the time Jim got back into his uniform and down to the clinic, Sergei had run the .357 out of ammo and was waving around Luke's .30-06, most fortunately empty. Demetri Totemoff and Auntie Edna, who lived next door and across Riverside Drive, respectively, were waiting for him. Auntie Edna in particular had plenty to say about stray bullets being fired within city limits, especially when one of them went through the wall over her bed.

Demetri eyed the trooper with a considering gaze, but all he said was, "Think you might need a little help?"

Jim didn't think Demetri meant in tackling Sergei for the second time in less than twenty-four hours.

He also thought Demetri might be right.

Never more so than when he had walked into the post that morning. The phone was ringing. With a long-suffering expression, Maggie answered it. He stood with his hand on the doorknob, watching her face.

"What?" she said.

A minute later, she said, "*What?*"

This couldn't be good, and it wasn't, either. She hung up the phone and looked at him.

Maybe he should have gone to Newenham with Kate. "What," he said.

"Someone just tried to drive off with Suulutaq's Gulfstream."

"*What?*"

Ten minutes later he wished he had gone to Newenham with Kate, because when he walked up the air stairs to the jet, he found Erland Bannister sitting on one of the plushy seats, holding a cup of coffee and chatting with Vern Truax on the latest price per ounce of gold.

Vern Truax was the superintendent of Suulutaq Mine. Next to him sat Axenia Shugak Mathisen.

"Hey, Jim," Vern said.

"Vern," Jim said. He looked at Axenia. "Axenia."

A cool nod was her response.

"This is Erland Bannister," Vern said. "Erland, this is our local trooper, Sergeant Jim Chopin. But maybe you've already met."

"Not personally, no," Jim said evenly. "But Mr. Bannister is well known to the Alaskan law enforcement community."

Truax looked uncomfortable, as though Jim had mentioned something in questionable taste in polite company.

Erland Bannister was a contemporary of Old Sam Dementieff. Jim looked for the shrunken fragility common to most people in their early eighties, the beginning stoop, the grizzled jaw, the rheumatic hands, and found none of it. A tall man, lean and fit, Bannister still had all his hair. He had a strong nose, a stronger jaw, and a charming smile, if you ignored the calculating glint in his hard blue eyes. He was dressed casually, in slacks and a blazer over an open-necked shirt, but no one seeing him that morning would have doubted for one moment that every item on his body had been tailored to fit, including his gleaming leather shoes and his silk diamond-patterned socks.

What Erland Bannister hadn't inherited from his stampeder ancestors, he had earned, bought, and stolen himself. He was one of the biggest entrepreneurs in Alaska, into banking, transportation, and natural resources. He had also tried to kill Kate Shugak when she got a little too close for comfort to certain family secrets, and he had been put away at Spring Creek Correctional Facility in Seward for what everyone assumed would be the rest of his life.

It is always a mistake, however, to underestimate the power of money. Erland had hired a firm of the very best criminal lawyers to work on throwing out his conviction. It had taken them two years and Jim could only imagine how many billable hours, but they'd gotten it done. Erland was out, on the loose, the verdict set aside on a technicality and key evidence disqualified. The state made noises like they were going to retry him, but Brendan McCord had told Jim and Kate privately that absent new evidence, it just wasn't going to happen.

So Bannister was once again on the loose. And in the Park. And the management of the Suulutaq Mine, at least, probably in exchange for Bannister's vast wealth and admittedly extensive connections in the natural resource extraction world, seemed prepared to forget and forgive all his past transgressions.

Chopper Jim Chopin was not.

Bannister offered him a bland smile and did not extend his hand, a perspicacious decision on his part because Jim would certainly have refused to take it. "I hear good things about you from Vern, Sergeant Chopin. We're lucky to have a strong law enforcement presence so close to the operation. As we know to our cost—" He gave Truax a conspiratorial glance. "—that is not always the case in rural Alaska."

"'We'?" Jim said.

"Erland is one of our newest partners," Truax said.

"Really," Jim said. He looked at Axenia, who was watching her coffee cup like it might make a break for it.

Erland leaned forward to give Axenia a pat on the knee. "Axenia's here to hold a watching brief, aren't you, Axenia? After all, the Niniltna Native Association is the governing body of the largest group of people affected by the Suulutaq Mine, and we want to be good neighbors."

Jim looked at Truax. "I got a call that someone tried to drive off with your jet?"

The mine superintendent squirmed a little. "Yeah, it was one of my boys, had a little too much to drink, muscled his way on board and damn near got into the cockpit. Fortunately, one of Erland's pilots spotted him from the hangar. I told George not to call it in." He offered an apologetic smile. "I know how busy you are. I didn't mean to call you out for nothing."

Jim looked back at Bannister, whose smile became if possible even more bland. "Talk to you for a minute, Axenia?" he said.

Neither of the other two men made any objection, and

Axenia followed him outside to stand on the frozen ground and squint at him against the sun. "You know who Erland Bannister is, right?" he said. "You know he tried to kill your cousin?"

Her lips tightened. "I know he has been released, and not recharged, and from what I hear not likely to be," she said. "And I know he is a wealthy and influential man, who is now a partner in a concern that is going to have a great deal to do with the Park and the NNA shareholders for the next twenty years, if not longer. As a member of the board of directors, due diligence requires that I develop a relationship with him and with the other owner-partners in GHRI."

He looked her over head to toe, a slow, deliberate glance that called to mind one of his first memories of Axenia Shugak, an unkempt, desperate little teenager, who at first sight of the new trooper in the Roadhouse had tried to seduce him into getting her away from a hated Niniltna and an even more despised Park.

Her eyes darkened and he knew she had picked up on his thought, as he had meant her to, but she didn't say anything. "You've come a ways," he said. "Just not all the way back to the Park unless it's on a private jet, evidently."

Again, she refused to be drawn.

"So you're just going to fuck her over from a distance, is that it?" he said.

Axenia turned and marched back to the jet without another word.

When she got to the air stairs, Erland was there to hand her into the plane. Over her shoulder he said to Jim, "You tell Kate I said hello, won't you?" He smiled another bland smile. "Tell her if she needs some help, there are people in Newenham who would be happy to help out a friend of mine."

Inside his vehicle, Jim paused with his hand on the keys,

staring at the sleek white jet sitting so incongruously on the forty-eight-hundred-foot strip carved out of a mountainside in the Alaskan wilderness. Along with a new coat of pavement, Suulutaq had financed a grader and fronted training and a salary for a grader operator. As Jim sat there, Eknaty Kvasnikof fired the grader up and moved out onto the strip to scrape off those last few fugitive streaks of ice and snow that had escaped notice the day before. Jim was glad Eknaty had gotten the job—he had a family to feed and no money coming in until the salmon hit fresh water this summer—but Jim was sorry to see the gravel strip go. It seemed such a great leap forward, from Bush life to downtown.

Maybe at eighteen hundred an ounce Erland Bannister just thought the Suulutaq mine was a good investment for Arctic Investments, the new venture capital firm he had started upon his release.

Jim's eyes narrowed, and the expression on his face made Eknaty, high up in the grader's cab, wonder what he'd done to deserve that.

No one had tried to drive off with the Suulutaq jet. Bannister wanted Jim to know that he was now a partner in the mine, and he had gotten Vern to make up a story to get Jim on that jet.

Because Jim now knew Erland Bannister had a finger in the biggest pie in the region, the biggest pie in Kate Shugak's backyard.

And by letting Jim know, Kate knew.

It didn't help that last October Kate had learned that Erland Bannister was by way of being a shirttail relative.

With this gloomy thought, he started the engine and drove around to the other side of the airstrip and parked in front of the post office. There was a line of people waiting for packages, half of them on their cells. Auntie Joy was texting somebody.

Auntie Joy, texting. In a way, that felt even worse than the Suulutaq jet sitting on the Niniltna airstrip with Erland Bannister on board.

He checked Kate's box first, not that the woman ever got any mail. He checked his own box second, where he found a letter from his father's attorney.

He waited until he got back to the post, in his office with the door closed, before he opened it. It was a summary of his father's estate, with a bottom-line number that made him a little dizzy. Even after dividing assets with his mother, there were just as many zeros in the amount that was coming his way as there had been when he went to California last year after his father died.

Jim had never lived all that high on the hog, not even when he was averaging a new girlfriend every six to twelve months. In Tok, he'd lived in a rented house and driven a used pickup. He cooked at home more than he'd eaten out, largely because he firmly believed that the first step in any decent seduction was a good, home-cooked meal served with a good wine. That and a Dave Koz CD pretty much got the job done.

Then he'd moved to the Park and the state had subsidized his room and board at Auntie Vi's and the fuel for his state vehicle, until, he still didn't know quite how it had happened, he had moved in with Kate Shugak and Johnny Morgan. Kate owned her house and land free and clear and they shared the food and fuel bills. His biggest personal expenses were buying books, good beer, and replacing new uniforms when the old ones wore out. Out of uniform he wore jeans.

Through the years, he had earned a good salary, most of which went into savings and his retirement account. He just wasn't a big-ticket-item kinda guy.

He looked at the zeros on the account sheet again, and did some figures with a paper and pencil. He could quit his job tomorrow if he wanted to and never miss the paycheck. He could buy some land and build his own house. He could travel, and not last class, either. If he wanted to, he could leave policing the Park to the next trooper in line, could leave behind the Ulanie Anahonaks and their culture wars, the Harvey Meganacks and their get-rich-quick schemes, the Howie Katelnikofs and their everlasting search for that one illegal score that would set them up for life, no matter how many people they hurt along the way. If he wanted to, he could let someone else deal with the bootleggers and the drug dealers that sprang up wherever young men with money flourished, and the Erland Bannisters, the men with money who never had enough, who always wanted more.

If he wanted to. He turned to prop his feet on the sill and look out his window at the dense growth of evergreens elbowing one another to peer in over his shoulder. Three moose were laying on the snow below his window, waiting out the cold before they got up again to forage. As he watched, an arctic fox trotted by, nose to the snow. She took no notice of the moose and they none of her. Through the trees he could make out a few Niniltnan roofs, and some flashes of white where the frozen surface of the Kanuyaq River announced its omnipresence. As he watched, he saw a snowmobile dash down the river, followed by a dog team, Chick Noyukpuk on a training run probably, and a pickup truck.

Mrs. Doogan had assigned each of the Niniltna High seniors a poet, to be read and studied and reported on throughout their last year. Johnny's was Robert Frost. Jim didn't do poetry, ordinarily, but the *Collected Works* was sitting on the back of the toilet one morning and nothing else was in reach. The book opened naturally to a poem that read more like a story, about some guy splitting wood interrupted by a couple of other guys who were itinerant lumberjacks and who wanted to split the wood and get paid for it. The first guy loved splitting wood but they needed the work.

Personally, Jim was glad that Kate liked splitting wood herself, but this morning for some reason lines from the last verse teased at Jim's mind, something about love and need being one. He liked being a trooper. The showman in him reveled at the might and majesty of the law his uniform inferred. He enjoyed the instantaneous hush that fell when he appeared at any scene, the law itself on blue-and-gold legs. His passion wasn't necessarily for justice, per se, but he liked helping people in trouble, in leaving their lives a little better when he was done. Say then that the work satisfied the do-gooder in him, the civil and criminal wrongs, if not righted, at least alleviated. He was curious about what made people tick, as well as vastly amused by the incredible messes they got themselves into on either an amateur or professional basis. Law enforcement certainly gave him a front-row seat.

Love, then. He dropped his feet and turned back to his desk to look at the attorney's letter sitting there. If not need.

The next time Jim talked to Kate, he'd better have his seat belt fastened. It was going to be a bumpy conversation.

She preempted that decision by calling him way too early the following morning.

11

JANUARY 19, VERY EARLY IN THE MORNING

Newenham

MOSTLY, KATE WAS PISSED off.

Stuffed in a bag, for chrissake, and dumped into a very small space, and then her dog dumped in on top of her. It was downright embarrassing, was what it was. What would Spenser say?

"Mutt," she said, because Mutt's howling was starting to hurt her ears. The bag muffled her voice. "Mutt! Shut up!"

The howl died to a low, menacing growl.

"Knock it off," Kate said.

The growl stopped, possibly because Kate's growl was meaner than Mutt's.

Possibly. Or possibly because Mutt was just biding her time until they got out of another fine mess Kate had gotten them into to speak her mind fully.

Kate took stock. She was in a bag. A stuff bag? No, too big. A gear bag, used to stow lines and nets and fishing gear of every kind, more likely.

The top of her head was jammed against a flat surface, and she could feel the opposite surface against the toes of her sneakers. Her knees were bent to fit. She had a little wriggle room from side to side but not much, especially not when Mutt was factored in.

All 140 pounds of the half wolf-half husky were lying on top of her, and it was starting to get hot and stuffy inside the gear bag. Kate nudged Mutt. "Can you scootch over just a bit, girl? Come on, just a little bit."

She pushed and cajoled and bullied and finally got her fingers beneath the edge of the bag and managed to struggle free. Her face was pressed up against Mutt's, to the point that she was breathing in Mutt's exhale.

The pencil flash was still in her pocket. She fished it out and turned it on.

Quarters were too close for her to get her arm up but she could shine it around the inside of their cell with her hand held down at her hip. At first all she could see was gray hair, bared teeth, and one enormous yellow eye. Beyond that were flat white plastic surfaces intersecting at right angles. They were inside a rectangular box of some kind.

Mutt whined. It was an interrogatory whine, but it was also uncharacteristically tentative. Mutt was unhappy.

"It's okay, girl," Kate said, although she wasn't entirely sure that it was. She was also pretty sure that she shouldn't waste oxygen talking.

Because if she was right, they were inside the chest freezer in the apartment over the garage, and it wouldn't be long before they ran out of air.

She wriggled around some more, with some yelps of protest from Mutt when Kate's knee hit a soft spot or Kate's foot stepped on her toes, but eventually Kate got her legs together to kick at what gravity informed her was the lid of the freezer.

It bounced open a crack and held, which was a great relief in some respects—they wouldn't run out of air so long as her legs had the strength to hold the door open—but depressing in others—whoever had bagged them must have propped something against the lid to hold it down.

Damn lucky there had been no lock on this freezer. Kate had one on hers at home because it sat out on the back porch, and anyone—read Willard Shugak—could saunter by and make off with a moose backstrap or a king salmon filet. Kate did not hold with that, especially when she had done the catching and cleaning and butchering and packing.

She pulled herself up with a jerk. No time to let her mind wander. What was keeping the lid shut? She thought about what else was in the apartment. Bed, chairs, end table. They could have piled some furniture on the lid, weighing it down. But they would have slid when she popped the lid, and she hadn't heard the sound of anything sliding.

Wait a minute. In the space between the end of the freezer and the wall there had been some lengths of two-by-fours. Left over from the remodel, Tina had said. Of course. Easy enough for someone to slam down the lid and jam one of the two-by-fours between the wall and the lid of the freezer.

She kicked the lid again. Again a brief, blessed bit of fresh air, again the lid snapped right back down.

Had they had time to nail the ends down? Things had gotten a little confused there for a bit. Kate had no real recollection of the sounds of a hammer. Maybe there had been nails already in the two-by-four. Convenient.

Kate was pretty strong, but she might not be strong enough to kick loose a two-by-four.

What was she strong enough for?

Her cell phone was in the pocket of her jeans. With more wriggling, yelping, and cursing, she managed to get it out, the whole time mortally afraid she would drop it. It was so hot in the small enclosed space that she was sweating freely, and both she and Mutt were breathing too fast. She braced her butt against the bottom of the freezer and jammed both feet against the freezer lid, cracking it open that fraction of an inch. It was awkward and her muscles strained at the effort because she didn't have enough room to straighten her legs and lock her knees. The resulting tiny bit of air was more than worth it, though.

She wedged her arm up to where she could see the face of her phone, and pressed the ON button.

One bar. Figured. Could have been NO SERVICE, though. She pressed *1*.

By a miracle the phone at the other end rang, and rang again.

The third ring was interrupted by an angry male in full cry. "Maggie, whoever went in the ditch at this hour can fucking well wait until I've had some more sleep!"

"It's me," Kate said.

"Oh." A brief pause. "Sorry."

"Lots of 911 calls?"

"You could say that." She heard him roll over and yawn. "What's up?"

"Oh, you know, the usual," Kate said. "I'm locked inside a chest freezer."

A brief silence. "I beg your pardon?"

Kate repeated herself, and waited.

When next he spoke, Jim sounded resigned. "You're not kidding, are you."

"Alas," Kate said, "no, I am not." It was getting hot inside the freezer. Next to her, Mutt, hearing the voice of her personal god, whined loudly enough to be heard in Niniltna without benefit of phone.

"Anybody in there with you?"

"Just Mutt," she said.

"You really aren't kidding," he said. "How long have you been in there?"

"Hard to tell," Kate said, "things got somewhat confused. Maybe five minutes."

"Really," Jim said. "How is it you are still breathing?"

"I've managed to crack the lid," Kate said. "As long as my gluteus maximus holds up we're okay."

"Several responses fairly leap to mind."

"You may compliment me on my very fine ass when I get home."

"Deal. Shall I call Newenham 911? Believe me, I'd enjoy that."

"No, I got a plan."

"What kind of a plan?"

"An effective one, I hope. But if I don't call back in five minutes, send in the marines."

She turned off the phone and wriggled around until she could get it back into her pocket. She put her arms around Mutt and pulled her as close as possible. Mutt gave something approaching a squeal. "Hang on, girl," she said, and started rocking the two of them back and forth. After a couple of rocks she got some momentum going and they started hitting the sides of the freezer hard.

At first the freezer barely moved, and Kate despaired. Freezers weren't that heavy, an airtight plastic container and some refrigeration coils, this shouldn't be that hard.

She kept it up. The rocking motion gathered its own momentum. Pretty soon, the chest freezer began to rock, too.

Mutt didn't fight her but she wasn't happy, either, and she said so by yipping in Kate's ear, conveniently located right next to Mutt's muzzle and making Kate's head ring most unpleasantly. She held on and kept rocking, working up her very own personal free surface effect, until the two of them were slamming into the sides of the freezer, THUD-thud, THUD-thud, THUD-thud.

After what seemed like an hour but was probably only sixty seconds, the freezer lifted up just a tiny bit, only to fall back when its back feet hit the wall. But Kate had felt it and she redoubled their efforts, slamming against the side of the freezer harder and harder and harder, walking the freezer across the floor of the apartment, away from the wall a micrometer at a time, until the freezer was far enough away from the wall that the back feet cleared it when their combined weights slammed into the side and it toppled over on its side with a resounding crash.

Kate and Mutt spilled out between where the open lid of the freezer was propped open against the floor and the freezer itself, and lay prone for some moments, taking in air in great, thankful gulps.

When she felt like she could make it all the way there, Kate crawled to the pole lamp next to the recliner and turned it on. She took her first close look at the chest freezer. Their rocking had walked it away from the wall a good twelve inches before the bottom back of the freezer had cleared the wall. The Sheetrock on the wall showed multiple horizontal impressions where the freezer had struck.

"Good thing Tina didn't make me pay a security deposit," Kate said, a little light-headed.

Mutt got to her feet and shook herself all over, rearranging every hair back into its proper place. She looked outraged and indignant, and she looked at Kate as if to say, *Well?*

"Thank god there was linoleum on the floor," Kate told

her. “We’d never have done it on wall-to-wall carpeting.”

Mutt did not feel that this was an adequate response.

Kate called Jim. “We’re out, we’re okay, stand down.”

She hung up and surveyed the mess, her right shoulder and hip and knee warning of spectacular bruises on their way.

She investigated and sure enough found a length of two-by-four on the floor between the wall and the freezer. No nails, but there was a corresponding dimple on the lid of the freezer, and another on the wall in back of the freezer, enough to keep the two-by-four from skidding. Or maybe she just hadn’t kicked hard enough.

“We haven’t even been here twenty-four hours,” she said. “That’s a record for inciting someone into assault and battery.”

The once spare, neat apartment now looked like a disaster area. The bed had been ripped apart, the mattress lying catawampus, half on the box springs, half on the floor. All the cabinets in the little kitchen stood open, everything in them scattered across the counter, the table, and the floor. Kate’s bag had been opened and dumped, and her belongings were everywhere.

“Even for us,” Kate said a little plaintively.

For a toss of this magnitude, taking a knife to the mattress and the recliner would have been at minimum the logical next step, but perhaps her walking in the door had interrupted them.

She looked at her phone. It was a little after 4 A.M. At a rough estimate, she and Mutt had been in the freezer for ten, fifteen minutes at most.

She looked around the apartment. This had taken longer than fifteen minutes. Which meant she and Mutt had walked in in mid-rampage, and that said rampagers had fled immediately after said rampagers’ attempt to turn Kate and Mutt into next winter’s entrées.

She heard a whine and looked around. Mutt was standing at the door, her nose pressed up against the crack. "They're long gone, girl," she said, but she opened the door. Mutt was out of it like an arrow, shooting down the stairs and quartering the area around the garage. If there was any scent to be picked up, at least Mutt would recognize it again. Kate propped the door open a crack against Mutt's return and started cleaning up.

It was well past five when she was done, and in the process she had had some interesting thoughts, although it was early days for any conclusions.

She hadn't been in town for twenty-four hours. It seemed unlikely that she'd been made in that short a time. Not impossible, but unlikely. She—and Mutt—were fairly well known in other parts of Alaska.

There were three people in town who did know who she was. Liam Campbell. Jo Dunaway. Bill Billington.

Campbell and Billington she discounted immediately. Dunaway took a little longer, but for the life of her she couldn't imagine Dunaway hiring a couple of toughs even to satisfy her reporter's curiosity as to what Kate was doing in town.

If all three of them were out, then either someone else had made her, or ...

She paused in the act of sweeping creamer into the dustpan.

Or this toss had nothing to do with her.

If it wasn't about her, who was it about?

She boiled water and made some chamomile tea sweetened with honey, both found in the cupboard. The tea tasted just about as bad as one might expect of herbs steeped in hot water. She wondered if Newenham had a coffee roaster, or an espresso stand, or at the very least imported Kaladi Brothers from Anchorage. It was probably too much to hope for Captain's Coffee from Homer. She added more honey on the theory that it couldn't make it any worse and sat down in the recliner. She put up the footrest. She thought she deserved it.

This apartment, according to Tina Grant, had been built for the oldest daughter of the house, Irene, the woman in the photograph on the hall table. The soldier killed in action in Afghanistan. What was it Tina had said? *We had it finished off so my daughter would have a little privacy when she came home on leave.*

Had Irene ever stayed in this apartment? Kate thought not. It had seemed such a sterile place when she first walked in—no plants, no photos, no personal possessions of any kind. She wouldn't have been surprised to find the toilet seat sealed with a paper band.

But the garage itself had been around for a while, longer than that model of the antebellum South next door, certainly. Someone else could have hidden something here, and perhaps have failed to recover it before the space was remodeled into the apartment.

Kate put down her tea and spent the next half hour going over every surface in the room, checking for hidden squares in the linoleum floor, hollow spaces in the walls, movable tiles in the ceiling that might lift up and reveal something squirreled away. She looked inside all the cupboards, knocking against the bottoms and sides, and checked the bottoms of all the drawers. She checked to see if the medicine cabinet in the bathroom came out of the wall, a dodge she'd seen on the job in Anchorage with the DA's office many years ago.

Nothing.

Which was irritating. Almost as much so as the fact that someone had got the drop on her, and even on Mutt. They must have heard the two of them coming up the stairs, grabbed her, and slammed the door against Mutt while they bagged her and tossed her in the freezer. Mutt would have launched herself in the door at the first sign of a crack. They'd probably caught her in midair and used the momentum of her forward velocity to sling her in on top of Kate.

Probably two people, then. Probably two men, too, or two really ballsy women.

What had they been looking for?

If they'd been checking up on her, they'd come up empty. All she had by way of identification was a forged Alaska driver's license in the name of Kate Saracoff, home address a post office box in Anchorage, and her cell phone, and both of those she kept on her person.

She wondered if they had expected to find the apartment empty. It seemed likely, but she had a grudging respect for someone who had dealt so effectively with such an unpleasant surprise.

Mutt came in.

Two unpleasant surprises.

Kate got Mutt a bowl of water. Mutt gave a few laps to be polite and then collapsed on the braided rug with a disgruntled air.

"Didn't find anything to sink your teeth into?" Kate said, sympathetic. "Don't feel bad. Me, either."

She undressed, remembered to plug in her cell phone, and rolled into bed.

12

JANUARY 19

Newenham

It felt as if Kate had barely closed her eyes when someone started banging on her door. She blinked up at the ceiling, befuddled and disbelieving. The thump at the door came again, more demanding this time, and she yelled, "Wait a sec," got into her jeans mostly by feel, and shrugged into her jacket on the way to the door in bare feet. Mutt was already there, growling and snapping a warm welcome. She unlocked and opened the door a crack. A gnarled brown hand shoved the door wide, and she dodged back before it clipped her on the chin. Mutt gave a full-throated bark with bass notes that should have raised Cliff Lee Burton right out of his grave.

The dyspeptic little man on the other side of the door glared down at Mutt. His face was as brown and gnarled as his hand, his dark eyes deep set and piercing. He wore a short-sleeved white T-shirt beneath a pair of denim bibs that looked like they'd been bought new in 1889, and a ball cap with a New Orleans Mardi Gras logo on it. "Shut your mouth, you big moron, don't you know a friend when you see one?"

Mutt, astonishingly, shut her mouth.

He looked at Kate. "Get your ass dressed and downstairs."

Kate gaped at him for a second, and then the red started to

rise up the back of her neck. She shut her mouth, too. She also shut the door in his face, locked it, and went back to bed.

She was not allowed to go back to sleep, however, because the next sound was his foot hitting the door. This time she didn't bother with jeans; she stalked to the door in her underwear and T-shirt and flung it open. "Listen, old man—"

"Listen my ass, you got about sixty seconds to get dressed and get your ass down here or you can walk to Liam and Wy's."

"I'm not going anywhere at this hour"—the light had barely touched the southeastern horizon, and the night before had been long and hard—"and I haven't had three hours' sleep, and who the hell are you, anyway?"

"Name's Moses. I'll be waiting for you downstairs." He pulled the door closed and she heard footsteps pattering briskly down the stairs.

"Moses," she said out loud. She looked around and found Mutt, not exactly cowering, no, but certainly she had withdrawn to the opposite corner of the apartment, sitting half inside the bathroom, as far away as she could get from the front door and still be above the Grant garage. "Moses the sort-of mayor of Newenham? Or no, what was it she said, the city father? You think there's only one?"

Mutt's wide yellow eyes gave Kate to understand that she sincerely hoped so.

Kate's eyes felt full of sand and her mouth tasted of rotten eggs. She never afterwards understood why but such was the force of the little man's personality that she found herself staggering into the bathroom, brushing her teeth, washing her face, dressing and presenting herself and her dog in front of a red Nissan longbed with a white canopy. The red had faded a little pink and the white a little gray, but the cab was warm when Kate and Mutt climbed in. Mutt insisted on Kate getting in first.

"Hi," Kate said, "I'm Kate Saracoff. Who are you, again?"

"Moses." The longbed spun around on a dime and charged off down the road like a maiden lady goosed by a lecherous roué. Mutt gave a smothered yelp and pressed against Kate's side.

"Moses Alakuyak."

"Are you the Moses Bill Billington mentioned to me last night?"

He threw his head back with a loud cackle. "I'd by god better be."

"Where are we going?"

"What, are you simple or something? I told you, we're going to Wy and Liam's."

"The pilot and the trooper?"

"You know any other Wys or Liams in Newenham?" Kate didn't know hardly anyone in Newenham, but before she could say so Moses took another turn at speed and the longbed settled into a long, death-defying skid that barely held them on to the road. If the ground hadn't been frozen, he would have kicked gravel all the way to the Nushugak.

The buildings of Newenham passed in rapid review, cars, trucks, dogs, and pedestrians diving out of the way of the oncoming juggernaut, and then they were out of town again and on a road following the river south. Far too late in Kate's estimation, the old man slammed on the brakes and threw the pickup into another long skid and stomped on the gas just in time to gun them up a road heading straight into the trees. Any comparisons to Kate's recent snow machine trip from Niniltna to the homestead were disregarded because she wasn't driving this time, and she hung on like grim death to the edge of the bench seat.

The trees thinned out in time, barely, to make way for the truck, and they bumped down the road more in the air than on the ground, before slamming to a halt. They were on a small bit of gravel before an old white clapboard house and an equally old white clapboard garage, beyond both of which could be seen a vast expanse of swift-moving river. Moses slammed the longbed into first and killed the engine. He was out of the truck and around the back to grab a bag before Kate had her door open. By the time she and Mutt were on the ground he was in the house.

"I guess we go in, too," she said to Mutt.

Mutt dropped her head and looked shifty and cast meaningful glances at the forest of spruce and alder that crowded around the house. "Coward," Kate said. Mutt vanished into the trees without so much as a backward glance.

Kate walked into the saliva-inducing smell of pancakes on the griddle and the homey sight of Campbell, dressed in sweats with a spatula in his hand. Kate couldn't make up her mind which looked better, the man or the pancakes.

Chouinard was seated at a computer. There was a window open with a man's face looking out of it. She glanced over her shoulder to give Kate a welcoming smile and turned back to say, "Five o'clock sounds fine, Ephraim, I'll see you then." She signed out and removed her headset. "Don't know how I ever ran the business without the Internet. Morning, Kate."

"Morning."

The phone rang and Chouinard answered it. "Nushugak Air Taxi. Hey, Brad."

Under cover of the subsequent one-sided conversation, in a low voice Kate said to Liam, "Mind telling me what I'm doing here?"

Before Liam could answer, Chouinard said, "Sure," into her headset. "I've got a five o'clock flight scheduled for Silver Horn, I can pick him up right after. Say six o'clock? Great."

She hung up and the old man came out of the bathroom dressed in some kind of black costume that made him look like a ninja, without the mask. "Well," he said testily, "let's get to it."

Campbell turned off the grill, put the plate of pancakes into a warm oven, and removed his apron. He and Wy both donned rope-soled slip-on shoes and followed Moses out onto the deck, which seemed to float over a bank that dropped about a hundred feet to an ice-encrusted gravel beach below. Kate hadn't eaten since the burger the day before and she made an instinctive move for the oven, only to be bellowed at from the deck. "Get your ass out here, Saracoff, goddammit!"

There was something awfully familiar in the echo of that bellow.

She got her ass out there to find Moses facing Chouinard and Campbell, the three of them standing with their knees bent and their arms bent at the elbow, hands cupped with the palms facing each other. Moses was glaring at her. It seemed to be his default expression.

Maybe her defenses were down due to starvation and sleep deprivation. Maybe the old man reminded her too much of Old Sam, in attitude if not in stature. Maybe it was cultural, she just couldn't go up against an elder. Whatever the reason, Kate found herself planting her feet, bending her knees and elbows and raising her arms to cup her hands. When they started to move, she followed along as best she could, succeeding in tying herself into several spectacular knots and one time stepping momentarily off the edge of the deck. Luckily there was a railing, or next stop Dutch Harbor.

Kate did not believe organized exercise was necessary. She led an active life, and chopping enough wood to keep the fireplace in business through the winter was all by itself enough to keep a three-toed sloth fit for a gold medal in any Olympic sport you cared to name. She cross-country skied when she wanted to get somewhere without the aid of an internal combustion engine, she hunted out the back door of her house when she was hungry, and she'd taken her turn water-skiing on deck boards during Fourth of July celebrations on Alaganik Bay. There was the occasional run in Anchorage when she was restless and Mutt needed to shake out the urban fidgets, but she didn't skip rope or do yoga or dance around in leotards to synthesized music with a bunch of other robots in the Niniltna gym on Monday and Wednesday evenings.

This was something else entirely. The cranky little demon seemed to be suspended on wires, his limbs manipulated by an invisible puppet master with, she had to admit, a considerable amount of grace and style. It looked easy. It wasn't. For one thing, you didn't stop until you got all the way through the exercise, and it had thirty-six separate movements. For another, you didn't get to straighten your legs until you were done.

Moses named the movements as he performed them, which to Kate was the most ridiculous part of the exercise. Stork Spreads Its Wings? Turn and White Snake Puts Out Tongue? Shoot a Tiger with Bow? None of them made any sense, and half the time the movements had her looking the wrong way anyway, so she couldn't see what she was supposed to be doing.

Moses was not content with having her follow along, oh no, he was constantly in her face, pushing her arms into position, pulling her shoulders back, kicking her feet apart, poking at the backs of her knees. This was accompanied by a steady stream of running commentary. "Bend those knees!" "Extend that arm!" "Root from below, suspend from above!" "Jesus, you look like you're about to mate with a porcupine!"

She was so glad Mutt hadn't followed her inside.

As they worked, the light increased across the horizon, highlighting the far bank of the river. The Kanuyaq River was not a small river, navigable at least by small boats all the way to Ahtna in summer. This river was immense by comparison, kingly even. It looked like cold molten rock, thick and roiling with gray glacial silt, moving in slow and stately fashion steadily downstream. The occasional glint from the rising sun sparkled from the small pieces of brash ice bobbing in its current.

On the left, upriver, mountains emerged from the night sky, shorter than her own but just as sharp edged and menacing. At first white ghosts against the dawn, with the rising of the sun they turned a slow, pale magenta, the brief glorious alpenglow of sunrise and sunset on a clear arctic day, before coalescing into the icy, ravenous peaks and ridges of their everyday clothes.

"You wanna do form or you wanna admire the view?" Moses said, glaring when he caught her not looking at him.

"I want to eat breakfast," Kate said, glaring back.

He kept them at it for an hour, barking corrections to what he called everyone's "form," before snorting out a contemptuous, "Well, I guess that'll have to do. Practice, practice, practice." He brought his right fist into his left palm and bowed. Wy and Liam did the same in return, and Kate did her poor best to imitate them. When she straightened up again, painfully, he'd already gone back inside the house.

"What the hell were we just doing out here?" Kate said, massaging her thighs, trembling in their own personal earthquake. One way and another, she'd taken a hell of a beating over the last twenty-four hours. "And who the hell is that guy?"

Chouinard and Campbell exchanged a glance, and Kate couldn't help but notice that both had barely broken a sweat, whereas her T-shirt was soaked through. "Beelzebub," Campbell said. "Lucifer. Satan. He is called by many names."

"Liam!" Chouinard said. To Kate she said, "He's my grandfather. He, ah, takes some getting used to."

"No shit," Campbell said, and gave Kate a sympathetic look.

"I don't understand why he brought me here," Kate said. "I don't even know how he knew I was here at all. Bill mentioned something about a Moses Alakuyak at work last night but he didn't come into the bar. Did you tell him about me, or what?"

"Moses picks his own students," Chouinard said.

"You mean victims," Campbell said not quite beneath his breath.

"Liam!" To Kate, Chouinard said, "No telling with my grandfather. He—" She hesitated. "He knows things."

Kate gave it up and limped back inside and Moses slammed out of the bathroom, his ninja costume back in the bag and himself dressed once more in his denim bibs. "What's a man gotta do to get fed around this dump?"

They ate pancakes slathered in butter and maple syrup, the real stuff from Canada—"I've got a friend in the Mounties," Campbell said—and link sausage on the side.

Kate had a chance to look around between bites, and liked what she saw. A small house, and an old one, with comfortable mismatched chairs, each with its own reading light, and books sitting on every available horizontal surface. The largest focal point on the wall was a map of Southwest Alaska, much annotated with ruled route lines and pinholes and pencil scribbles. There were a few family photographs. A stubby little potbellied woodstove stood next to the Nushugak Air Taxi office. There was a television but it wasn't the focal point of the room, instead tucked into a corner on a triangular three-wheeled cart, looking as if it had been there for a while and might be there awhile longer.

The living room was separated from the kitchen by a counter with stools. Behind the kitchen a hallway led to bathroom and bedrooms.

There were no curtains on the windows, which all faced east, toward the glorious view of the river, the opposite bank, and the rising sun.

Moses mopped up the last of his syrup, pushed his plate back, and stood up. "Not bad. Little heavy-handed there on the buttermilk, Campbell. You."

Kate looked up to see Moses fixing her with that glare. "You know he didn't do it, right?" It was more of an accusation than a statement, and he didn't wait for an answer, grabbing his bag and slamming out of the house. The engine of the longbed started up and receded into the distance.

"Don't worry, I can drop you off at Tina's on my way to the airport," Chouinard said.

Great, Kate thought, *one of the chief suspects in this non-murder giving me rides home. Not to mention her grandfather picking me up.*

She caught Campbell's eye, and knew he was thinking the same thing. "I'll drive you," he said.

Not that it was going to be any better for her cover to be seen in the local trooper's company. Surely no one would notice that, either.

Campbell grinned. "We could always phony you up a record. GBH, maybe. I can think of at least one likely victim."

"Very funny," Chouinard said, thinking that Kate was naturally reluctant to be seen getting driven home by the state trooper, and probably not happy about the rumors that would spark about her husband, either. As Campbell went to change into his uniform, she said, "Or we could make you my cousin. We probably are cousins, anyway."

"Are you Native?" Kate said in surprise.

"A quarter Yupik, from Moses." Chouinard smiled. "And aren't all Alaska Natives related?"

Kate laughed.

"What's the joke?" Campbell said, coming back into the room, immaculate in his uniform, which had to have been tailored to fit, because it fit so very well. What was on the inside of it didn't necessarily need embellishment, but packaging in this case didn't hurt the contents one bit. Until this moment Kate had believed that Jim Chopin lacked any competition for poster model for the Alaska State Troopers.

She realized she was staring and gave herself a mental kick. It didn't help when she saw that Chouinard had a sly smile on her face. *You should see my trooper,* she thought, and smiled back. They both laughed, albeit at different things.

This time Campbell didn't bother asking, although Kate was sure anyone who spent that much time on their appearance had to be at least minimally aware of its impact. At least he didn't preen.

"Time for me to go make a living." Chouinard grabbed a daypack, kissed Campbell, raised a hand to Kate, and was gone.

"How much does she know?" Kate said.

"Nothing," he said. "Why? She say something to you?"

"No, but I wondered when we stopped at Eagle Air on the way here. Seemed, well, convenient."

He shook his head. "She's got the first-class mail contract for these parts. Eagle Air's on her route. And the less she knows about what you're doing in town, the better, at least up front."

"Agreed," Kate said. "However, Bill Billington pretty much figured it out for herself. She braced me about it after work last night. I told her the truth."

If anything, he looked relieved. "Good. I was willing to keep it on the lowdown but she really would have been pissed if you'd lied and she found out about it. Pissed at me," he said, clarifying matters. "Really don't care if she's pissed at you."

Kate laughed. "Understood."

"So what's up?" Liam refilled their mugs and they drew up stools on either side of the counter. He spilled a little coffee when she told him about last night's attack. "Jesus Christ," he said, mopping up.

"What I said," Kate said.

"You haven't been in town a day," he said, shaking his head. "Is this what Jim meant when he said you'd shake things up?"

"Maybe," Kate said. "Maybe not. I haven't spent any time in the Southwest, but I worked almost six years in Anchorage and I've been to enough AFN conventions. Someone here could have recognized me, and could be aware of what I do for a living. Could even have been someone I've testified against. You're a trooper, you know every time you bag a bad guy, you make an enemy. But..."

"But what?"

"But I'm wondering if the attack didn't have more to do with the place than the person staying in it." She explained why.

"Okay," he said when she finished, "but if that's so, why wait until the space was occupied before searching it?"

"Could be they didn't know it was occupied." She smiled. "After all, I haven't been here a day." Her smiled faded. "All I've got on me traceable back to Kate Shugak is my cell phone, and I was carrying that, so I haven't been outed yet, that I know of. They made a hell of a mess of the place, but I think I surprised them before they could start ripping up floorboards. It had that kind of feel to it. You know?"

He did. "You keep saying *they*. Was there more than one?"

"I'm pretty sure it would have taken two people working together to tackle Mutt."

They both looked at Mutt, who had infiltrated cautiously into the house when the diminutive demon left. She blinked back at them, ears up at the sound of her name.

"I see what you mean," Campbell said. He earned Mutt's undying devotion by putting down the plate holding the last of the sausages.

"Something else," Kate said.

"What?"

"Why I was so late getting back to the apartment. I, ah, got access to some of Grant's records last night."

"Did you," Campbell said, and took a fortifying gulp of coffee. "Notice I do not ask how."

Kate grinned. "The books are in order, so far as I can tell, but I still don't see where the money is coming from. He was spending it like water before he died, and now Tina's acting glad to get cash to rent out her garage apartment. Doesn't make any sense."

"Ah," Campbell said.

Kate raised her eyebrows and waited.

"Yeah," Campbell said, "it may be I have a line on where

Finn was getting his money." He explained Jo Dunaway's theory.

"If Finn Grant got his hands on any part of Alexandra Hardin's inheritance," Kate said, "he could afford to overthrow the government of Taiwan if he wanted."

"As was explained to me," Liam said, his grimness matching her own.

"Who explained it?"

"Ah, yeah," he said, an expression consisting of one part helpless fury and one part acute misery passing over his handsome countenance. "Ever heard of a reporter named Jo Dunaway?"

Her mug set itself down on the counter of its own volition. "What about her?"

"I see that you have," he said, misery increasing. He sighed. "She was my wife's college roommate. And her lifelong best friend. She has bigger ears than anyone else in the entire state and she may—" He ran a finger around the inside of his collar. "—she *may* have heard a rumor that Finn Grant's death was less than accidental, and that Wy was a possible suspect."

"That's why she's here," Kate said without thinking.

His head came up like a hound's on the scent. "You've seen her?"

"She reported on a case I testified in back a ways," Kate said. "She recognized me when you brought her in the bar last night."

He sat up straighter. "You've talked to her?"

"I wouldn't call it talking, exactly," Kate said. "She accused me, I insulted her. Honors were about even, I thought."

"And you were going to tell me this when?" he said.

"Any minute now," Kate said.

"Uh-huh," he said.

They sat in mutual gloom for a few moments.

"However," he said, cheering slightly, "no one has come looking for that money yet, and until they do, I am less concerned about how he paid for anything than in how Finn Grant died."

"Money is a powerful motive," Kate said. "Especially a lot of money."

"Uh, yeah," Campbell said, "about motive," and explained about how the local Native association might be interested in acquiring Grant's FBO.

She looked at him. "And you were going to tell me this when?" Her tone of voice was enough to pull Mutt straight up off the floor. She gave Campbell an accusing glance.

He patted the air at both of them. "I didn't hear about it until the day I got back, and we haven't had a moment to talk until now."

She was steaming. "So not only do we have a reporter dogging us, the suspect list might just have increased by a couple of hundred shareholders? Especially if Grant was steamrolling over them the way he did everyone else?"

He winced. "That's about the size of it, yes."

She tapped out a tattoo with her fingernails, thinking. "Is Tina Grant looking to sell?"

"I don't know," Campbell said. "She's been tried pretty hard over the past two months. I don't know that she has plans to do anything about anything yet."

Not quite at random, Kate said, "I met Gabe McGuire at Eagle Air yesterday."

"Really? I didn't know Gabe was back."

"Why," Kate said with what she felt was pardonable annoyance, "does everybody in Newenham call Gabriel McGuire, movie star, number one box office draw, and Oscar nominee, by his first name?"

Campbell looked taken aback. "I don't know, I—he's been vacationing here regularly for the last four years or so. He's pretty well known locally." He reflected. "He spends a lot of money here, which naturally endears him to the business community. And—"

"What?"

Campbell met her eyes squarely. "He's a good guy, Kate." He held up a hand. "I know, I know, you don't think of someone you've seen on the cover of *People* magazine as a regular guy, and okay, he isn't. Obviously. But he doesn't walk around like his shit don't stink, either. He doesn't expect people to kowtow, he doesn't screw all the women within a hundred-mile radius, he keeps his posse in line. So far as I know, he doesn't import illegal substances into the borough, for either resale or recreational use, although I admit I haven't visited him at Outouchiwanet. Pretty upstanding citizen, at least on the face of it."

"Outouchiwanet. That like Outouchiwanet Mountain Lodge?"

He nodded. "Why?"

"Because in those records I, ah, acquired?"

He looked pained, but said encouragingly, "Yes?"

"There is a transfer of title for Outouchiwanet Mountain Lodge, made out from one Dagfin Arneson 'Finn' Grant to one Gabriel McGuire. Fee, one dollar, and other valuable considerations."

"One dollar? Really?"

"Really."

"Dated when?"

"Within a month of the formation of the corporation that owns Eagle Air, Inc."

Campbell thought it over. "I did get the feeling that Gabe wanted to buy the lodge. He spends almost all his time there when he comes up. Stops in town to buy supplies and grab a burger at Bill's, or he did before Finn moved operations out to Chinook. Then it's straight out to the lodge." He looked down at his mug, swirling the now cold coffee in it meditatively. "Understandable. The suck-uppery must be pretty advanced at his level. He's put a premium on privacy. Unless a fan was rabid enough—and rich enough—to charter his own private plane, Outouchiwanet Mountain Lodge would be out of reach of most of them."

"Privacy would be worth more than a buck to him, what you're saying?"

Campbell nodded. "It's a pretty nice lodge, and there's some property attached to it, too."

"A hundred sixty acres," Kate said.

He tried not to cringe at the thought of how she knew that. "Originally a homestead?"

"Be my guess."

"Those aren't thick on the ground anymore, and fewer than that unsubdivided. Nor is any significant amount of privately owned acreage anywhere in the state. Yeah, worth a lot more than a dollar."

"So I'm thinking Finn held him up for a partnership stake in the company in exchange for the publicity McGuire would bring to Eagle Air," Kate said.

"You said he was here?"

She nodded.

"Want me to get Wy to fly me out to Outouchiwanet and ask him?"

He made the offer like Indiana Jones volunteering to jump into a pit full of snakes and given his fear of flying, he should have. Hadn't someone defined courage as being shit-scared of it and doing it anyway, whatever it was? If that was true, Campbell had to have balls the size of cantaloupes.

Kate was appreciative of the sacrifice, if not also a little suspicious. Campbell, not to mention everyone else she'd met in Newenham, seemed a little too close to Gabe McGuire for her taste.

She ignored the niggling little feeling at the back of her mind that said she was looking too hard for reasons to dislike McGuire, and said, "Hold off on that. Let me poke around a little more first."

"Where?"

She beamed a smile at him that left him visibly shaken, married man and all. "I'm thinking about dropping in on Eagle Air next. Unannounced, of course."

Liam gazed at her with a kind of fascinated horror. "Jim was right," he said. "You really never did meet a rule of evidence you like."

"Well," Kate said with modesty unbecoming, "they do tend to get rather in my way."

13

JANUARY 19

Newenham

LIAM DROPPED KATE AND Mutt in town in a discreet alley next to what he informed her was the only hotel in town. It was just about this time of year that everyone in Alaska tired of chewing over the same old scandals and started looking for something new. She got a hard look from an older woman looking out the window of the lobby, which relaxed a little when she saw Mutt. Something about a dog was just naturally disarming.

"You're a regular Get Out of Jail Free card, you are," Kate said, and Mutt wagged her tail in agreement. "Although best not to test the theory, okay?"

They made it back to the apartment in due time and opened the door, which she had locked on the way out this time, with some caution. It was as she had left it, and she showered and changed and went back outside to throw a leg over the four-wheeler. Mutt hopped up behind and they headed out the road to the Newenham airport.

Unlike the Park road, unlike most any road not on the Railbelt in Alaska, this one was paved, the winter's ice melting into soupy puddles as the sun warmed the black macadam. ATV slash snowmobile trails paralleled it on both sides, and Kate took every opportunity available to her, diving off first one side of the road and then the other, kicking snow halfway up the utility poles fenceposting the trails. There wasn't a lot of traffic and she took advantage of it. She frightened the life out of a two-year-old moose who had just been kicked out by his mama and so was prone to nervousness, scattered a roost of magpies into a protesting cloud, and raced an arctic hare and won, or would have if the hare hadn't recognized the better part of valor and veered off into the underbrush.

It occurred to Kate that there was cause to rejoice in investigating a case in which she was related to no one involved.

Chouinard's voice rang in her ears. *Aren't all Alaska Natives related?* She laughed out loud and hit the gas.

The road followed the river north of town for a little over a mile and then veered west and inland. Directly ahead, the Wood River Mountains formed a sharp, white outline against the pale blue horizon. The road widened into a broad turn that followed a row of buildings next to a long paved airstrip and finished up in the parking lot of what was obviously a terminal. A small plane was taking off from the strip. She pulled to one side, killed the engine, and watched it climb, circle back, land, and take off again. Somebody doing touch and goes, a student pilot, maybe, or maybe a commercial pilot doing their mandatory three full stops a month requirement to maintain their license to carry passengers. Or maybe that was at night? She kind of thought taildragger versus tricycle gear figured in there somewhere, too, which wasn't surprising, given the number of times new pilots (and sometimes old ones who should know better) pranged a plane on landing because they forgot or never learned the difference.

She wasn't a pilot. All she knew about flying was what she picked up riding shotgun next to George and Jim.

Why had she never learned to fly? God knows she spent

enough time on airplanes. Her parents hadn't flown and neither had Old Sam, but Abel Int-Hout had been a pilot. He'd been busy teaching his own sons, though, and by the time he got Ethan in the air he was probably tired of teaching, or she was off at school. At any rate, the subject had never come up.

Be fair. She had never asked, and now never could. As always, there was that sharp, remembered pain at the memory of the old homesteader. As always, she acknowledged the pain, accepted it, didn't try to deny it. It was the least she owed the old man. He'd given her her home back when her parents died, in defiance of none other than Ekaterina Shugak, not to mention the conventional wisdom of the Park that said no grade-school girl should be allowed to say where she would live. So what if he hadn't taught her to fly.

She could still learn if she wanted to. Plenty of people learned later in life, mostly when they got to where they could afford it. Which she couldn't, so she put the thought firmly from her mind, in spite of the enticing image of herself in the left seat, lifting off an airstrip bulldozed down the center of that flat piece of property to the east of her house, gaining the sky in her very own ... what? What would she want to fly herself? Something that could get in and out of everywhere, on and off beaches, low and slow so she could beachcomb. Probably a Super Cub. Be nice to have a vehicle that could carry one and three-quarters of a ton of freight, and deliver it to a location less than a mile from her house.

Which brought her full circle, because last time she checked, a Super Cub was going for $130,000, and they weren't building any more of them.

Aviation was as much a part of the Alaskan identity, zeitgeist, whatever you wanted to call it, as was oil production, gold mining, dog mushing, king salmon, and king crab. All of which, come to think of it, were made possible by aviation. What was the statistic Jim had quoted, something like one out of thirty-seven Alaskans had a pilot's license? Kate still knew Park rats who had pilot licenses but not driver's licenses. Admittedly, much of the time that was because the long arm of the law wasn't that long in Alaska. Three hundred and eighty troopers stretched only so far, especially over a land mass twice the size of Texas, most it without roads. Which was why the Alaska State Troopers recruited as many pilots as they could get their hands on.

There were tie-downs for small planes on both sides of the runway. There were several small shacks behind some of the tie-downs, including one with a sign suspended from the roof, which read NUSHUGAK AIR TAXI. There was what Kate thought was a Piper Super Cub—she couldn't see the tail—tied down in front of it, red and white, tail number 78 Zulu.

Chouinard had picked her up in Togiak in a Cessna 180. So she was a two-plane operation, and Kate knew from Chouinard's conversation with McGuire the day before that Chouinard was rated in other aircraft.

Jo Dunaway's pugnacious face swam into mind. If a reporter as experienced and as hard-nosed as Dunaway was worried enough about her best friend to fly down to Newenham in January, Chouinard might have more motive in the matter of the alleged murder of Finn Grant than Liam Campbell was letting on.

Like any cop, public or private, Kate was experienced at having people lie to her, even clients.

She found the access road and followed it to the other side of the runway. She got off the ATV and walked around Grant's old hangar, to anyone watching looking for a place to take a leak.

The back door was locked. The side window wasn't, although she'd bet large it hadn't been opened since it was installed, as witness the nearly impenetrable thicket of alders that had been allowed to grow in front of it. Dirt and dead mosquitoes filled in the track and the slider squeaked and groaned in protest as she wrestled it open. She hoisted herself over the sill and into a cavernous space in which her every step echoed. It hadn't been gutted, but it had been abandoned, nothing left but some indeterminate litter, an almost-empty spool of half-inch polypro, and one red metal, many-drawered tool chest. A door in the wall led into a utilitarian office, with army surplus desk and filing cabinets, all empty.

She went to the tool chest and opened a drawer at random, another. Socket wrenches in both inches and metric, tin snips, screwdrivers. She closed the last drawer and remembered similar tool chests in the garage below her apartment. No room for another tool chest there. Or someone was still using this hangar to work on aircraft.

She heard an engine approaching, and looked out the window to see Fred Grant pull up in a dark blue Dodge pickup that looked brand new. She was across the hangar and on the outside of the window and around the building thirty seconds later, where she walked toward the four-wheeler, ostentatiously buttoning up her jeans.

Fred Grant paused with his hand on the hangar office door.

Kate pretended she saw him for the first time. "Hey," she said.

"What are you doing here?"

Kate nodded at the alders beside the hangar. "Couldn't find a bathroom."

His eyes narrowed. "Wait, you're—"

"Kate Saracoff," she said. "You're Tina's brother-in-law. Met you yesterday afternoon at Tina's house, right? Frank?"

"Fred," he said. "Fred Grant." He looked from her to the hangar and back again. "What're you doing out here?"

Kate shrugged. "Out for a ride. Getting acquainted with Newenham." She climbed on the four-wheeler and started the engine and Mutt, who had been scouting the underbrush for a snack, trotted back to assume the position.

"Ready?" Kate said. Mutt took a mouthful of jacket by way of reply. "Okay, let's go! See you around, Felix."

She felt Fred Grant's eyes on her all the way to the road.

She went back the way they had come, again with as much time off the road as on. For one thing, the road was wetter now after another hour of sun beating down on and heating up the black pavement beneath the snow and ice to make nice big puddles everywhere. For another, it'd been a while since she'd done any off-roading and a tune-up of ATV skills wouldn't hurt, especially with what she had planned for later.

She navigated decorously through town—Campbell was getting in his vehicle in front of the trooper post and she avoided eye contact as assiduously as any shifty-eyed miscreant would—and opened up the throttle a bit on the road past the turnoff to Chouinard's house, heading south down the west side of the Nushugak River.

When Chinook Air Force Base was built, the first barges had landed at Newenham to offload. They'd brought heavy equipment with them, backhoes, bulldozers, graders, loaders and shovels and dump trucks, everything they needed to build a road to the property twenty-five miles south, where the base would be constructed. At the head of the list was a stopgap runway long enough to handle planes big enough to carry any heavy equipment they needed, which they then used to build the two permanent runways and started airlifting everything in.

The air force stopped barging things to Newenham after that, but the road between the town and the base remained. When the base was commissioned, it soon became obvious that the major benefit the town of Newenham accrued from Chinook AFB was a higher rate of sexually transmitted diseases, not to mention a steadily increasing number of unintended pregnancies among high school girls. The town council got together with the base commander and agreed to plow up the road on both ends to stop the free flow of traffic between the two communities.

It never quite stopped it, of course, the hormonal drive to seek out new life and new civilizations and lay them being an irresistible force for young men far from home. The young women of Newenham were no less strongly influenced, but if the plowing up of the road didn't make it impossible for the two to meet, it at least made it difficult.

The previous day Chouinard had IFR'd the remnants of that road, and had pointed it out to Kate and told her the story behind it. For someone unacquainted with the area, the only thing that could have been better was a ten-foot billboard with a bright red arrow marked THIS WAY TO EAGLE AIR! Kate appreciated the assistance. Better than AAA.

To all intents and purposes, Kate looked like any other Newenhamer that afternoon, out for a joyride with her dog on a sunny day. She was not the only one on the road, having passed a dozen others on ATVs, although most of them had plastic milk crates filled with groceries bungeed onto the rack in back. The few women ignored her. Every man gave her a second and sometimes a third glance, especially after they got a look at Mutt. "Biggest dude magnet on the planet," Kate said over her shoulder, and Mutt looked as smug as she could with a mouthful of Kate's jacket.

The road ended in a large cleared area that sloped down to the frozen edge of a wide creek that emptied into the Nushugak. The land and the water were both frozen over but it looked like a large gravel deposit had been discovered on the creek and thoroughly exploited, leaving behind a dozen deep bowls that looked from the multiple lines of tracks as if they were now being used to launch snow machines into orbit. Beyond the creek the landscape was a series of snow-covered tussocks and hillocks anywhere from five to a hundred feet high, Kate guessed made from the alluvial deposits first of glaciers and then from rivers, silted over in time and self-seeded with thick stands of alder and birch and cottonwood and willow.

At one time there must have been a bridge over the creek. Today, there was a nice track packed down from a winter's-worth of four-wheeler and snow machine traffic that led up the near side of the creek. Kate turned right and followed it upstream. Just when the underbrush started making forward motion difficult, the track veered left across the creek, which had narrowed to four feet in width. It was accessed by a short but very steep drop, and the side opposite looked even steeper.

"Hop off, Mutt!" she said. There was a muffled but by no means unexcited "Woof!" from behind her and she heard a thump when Mutt hit the ground. She gunned the engine and let up on the brake. The ATV damn near popped a wheelie and launched itself down the slope with reckless abandon. There was a bump at the bottom just before the creek's edge and later Kate had reason to suspect that it had been built there on purpose, because they hit the bump at full throttle and sailed into the air. She wasn't sure they even touched the ice on the creek before landing with a hell of a thump on the other side. She stood on the pedals and leaned forward and kept the throttle firmly down, and the sturdy little ATV sped up the opposite bank.

She burst over the top to hit another bump and go airborne again. She whooped and hit the brake and pulled the handlebars around and threw her weight over, skidding to a picture perfect hockey stop that would have turned Wayne Gretzky a pale green with envy.

Mutt came over the top of the creek bank like she'd been launched from a catapult. "Mutt, don't you dare!" Kate just had time to say before Mutt cannoned into her, knocking her off the four-wheeler and ass over teakettle into the scrub brush, where she showed no mercy.

It was fifteen minutes before Kate managed to regain the vertical and shake most of the snow out of her clothes. "You," she told Mutt severely, "are a menace to society and civilization and forward motion of any kind."

"Woof!" Mutt said, tongue lolling out in a lupine laugh.

Kate laughed back at her. "Okay, enough horseplay, let's get back to work."

Mutt followed her back to the four-wheeler, managing to catch the hem of Kate's jeans in her teeth and dump her on her ass one more time. Mutt always had to have the last word.

Kate stood on the seat of the ATV to reconnoiter. The massive buildings of Eagle Air loomed to the south, and the nearer, smaller buildings of Newenham to the north. Behind Newenham rose the white peaks of the Wood River Mountains. "Not as high as ours," Kate said to Mutt. "But not bad."

Mutt, less tolerant of competition, sneezed.

On their east was the wide expanse of the Nushugak River, its leaden surface on a cold boil into Bristol Bay. It had to be ten times as wide as the Kanuyaq at this point, and much deeper. The Kanuyaq's mouth was braided with islands and sandbars built from glacial silt, splitting the Kanuyaq's current into diffuse streams. The mouth of the Nushugak by comparison was like a fire hose, steep sides concentrating the collected outflows of all the upriver creeks and streams into a single determined cataract. It was low because it was winter, but Kate could see previous high-water marks on the opposite bank. All rivers were entities deserving of respect. This one, Kate suspected, was a monster to be feared.

There was a small settlement of some kind on the opposite shore, impossible to tell at this distance if it was inhabited or abandoned. A long level area spoke of the possibility of an airstrip, but then wherever there were or had been people in Alaska, there was an airstrip.

The remains of the road to the air force base were very clear. The taiga took a long time to recover from the traffic of man. The same held true for muskeg, and farther north, tundra. So long as the permafrost beneath remained insulated from seasonal changes of temperatures, all was well, but strip any thickness of that protective layer away and the permafrost would melt, resulting in wounds that were not easily or quickly healed. Kate remembered flying to the North Slope five years before and looking down from the airplane to see the long straight tracks of the Cat trains of the fifties and sixties, left behind by teams of geologists looking for mineral deposits, the laying of communications lines, survey crews headed for the site of the proposed Rampart Dam, yet another of Edward Teller's less-than-bright and thankfully tabled ideas. The remnants of all those trails had been a sobering reminder of just how sensitive the arctic landscape was.

Kate grinned to herself. She also remembered the old fart

who had said, "For a thousand years it was a frozen wasteland. Now all of a sudden it's the goddamn delicate tundra."

She followed the track into the thick brush with her eyes. The trees and shrubs were mostly free of snow, although the ground was still covered with a thick layer that had melted over time into a frozen rind. She squinted at the horizon. It looked clear all the way to Unimak Pass and likely to remain so. Tonight the moon was half full, which was good and bad. She wanted to be able to see where she was going, but she didn't want to be seen getting there.

She pulled out her cell and looked at the time. It was right at noon. She had to be at work in four hours. There was time for a little more reconnaissance.

She climbed on the four-wheeler and restarted the engine. She raised an eyebrow at Mutt. "You coming?"

Mutt leaped up to the back in one graceful jump, nipped Kate's shoulder, and took up station with a mouthful of jacket.

What was left of the road between Newenham and the onetime air base had been crisscrossed by many vehicles intersecting it at many angles on their way into and out of the thick underbrush. ATVs large and small, snow machines of every persuasion, Kate even saw the parallel tracks of cross-country skis. Near enough to the creek she'd just vaulted was a large frozen pond with clear signs of a hockey game, the marks of blades dug in deep and the giveaway of drops of blood sprinkled across the ice. It would seem that the land between Newenham and Eagle Air constituted a recreational area for the local population. Again, this was good in that who would look for her among so many. Again, it was bad in that there would be that many more witnesses for a night raid.

As she drew nearer the air base she looked for signs of the crash that had killed Finn Grant, but the investigation and the subsequent cleanup in December had been prompt and thorough. She'd already checked and there had been two major storms since then, too. Off the end of the air base's north–south runway she found what might have been a flattened area on top of a hillock, but that was all.

From this perspective, the air base appeared to have been constructed on an immense gravel pad that pushed it ten feet up in elevation. She climbed up on the apron north of the hangar where Chouinard had parked the Cessna the day before, pulled up at the side, and walked around to the front. The hangar door was cracked and she applied her eyeball and saw that McGuire's jet was parked inside.

Wouldn't do to let the movie star's feet get cold on takeoff.

She passed on to the office. "Stay," she said to Mutt, and went in.

Chouinard had not exaggerated. The reception area was lush, with bamboo flooring polished to a rich sheen (Kate wouldn't have known it for what it was if Iris Meganack hadn't made such a big deal out of her new kitchen floor), some kind of textured silk wallpaper in a subdued ivory, a sleek teak desk facing the door with a telephone that looked straight out of *The Jetsons* sitting on it and nothing else. Behind it sat the young woman, Tasha Anayuk, who had attended the arrival of Gabriel McGuire and Co. the day before. She was wearing her Eagle Air uniform. "Yes? May I help you?" she said.

Kate peeked beneath the desk. And her Eagle Air four-inch heels. Jesus. "Hi," Kate said with an ingratiating smile. "We met yesterday, I was a passenger with Wy Chouinard."

Tasha's expression of professional politeness eased into a more natural giggly breathlessness. "Sure! I remember." She gave a rapturous sigh. "You were here when Gabe came." It sounded like Tasha was reporting the Second Coming.

"Uh-huh," Kate said. "I've been four-wheeling around town this afternoon and I guess I kind of overshot. I know this is private property, but—" She dropped her voice to a conspiratorial whisper "—I wonder if I could use the bathroom?"

She made a rueful face, and Tasha laughed. "Sure!" she said again, pointing. "It's right over there."

When Kate came out again, Tina Grant was standing next to Tasha's desk.

"Oh," Kate said, trying to look surprised. After all, she wasn't supposed to know anything about her landlady. "Hi, Tina."

"Hello, Kate. What are you doing out here?"

Kate waved an airy hand. "Exploring. It's such a nice day, so warm for this time of year, I didn't want to be stuck inside." She put on an anxious look. "I hope you don't mind my taking the ATV off road?"

Tina almost smiled, although Kate wouldn't have seen it if she hadn't been observing closely. "It's what they're built for," she said.

Kate made a show of looking around. "This is really something," she said. "We stopped here yesterday on the way from Togiak, but I didn't get a chance to see the inside."

Tina responded to the unspoken prompt. "Would you like a tour?"

"Oh no, I don't mean to intrude."

"We're not that busy at the moment," Tina said, and beckoned Kate to follow her.

It turned out that Chouinard had grossly understated the luxurious appointments of Eagle Air Fixed Base of Operations. No expense had been spared, from the thick carpet underfoot to the designer comforters on the beds. Kate copped a surreptitious feel of one of the mattresses. It felt like $3,600 worth of mattress, all right.

The ready room was full of overstuffed leather furniture, a wall-mounted television screen the size of a wooden pallet, and at the end of the tour Tina even gave Kate a slice of crème brûlée cheesecake, served on a white bone china saucer with the Eagle Air logo in the center and what Kate was pretty sure was a real silver fork, also with the Eagle Air logo on the handle.

The pie was terrific, and she said so. "Glad you enjoyed it," Tina said, and seemed to sigh. Kate raised her eyebrows slightly, in an inquiry polite enough either to ignore or respond to.

She did not have high hopes, but surprisingly, Tina chose the latter. "We've got a lot of it on hand, and we need to get rid of it before it spoils."

Kate grinned. "I'll be happy to choke down any or all of it before it goes off."

In answer, Tina opened the refrigerator door. It was stuffed with luxury comestibles, not least among which were three entire cheesecakes.

"Wow," Kate said. "Wealth beyond dreams of avarice."

"Yes," Tina said wearily, "my husband believed you could never have too much of a good thing. I tried to stop delivery but the gourmet food company in Anchorage said he'd paid through the end of March, so it just keeps coming until the money runs out. I've been giving most of it away in Newenham."

Kate waited hopefully.

Tina waved a hand. "This was his big idea. You know what an FBO is?"

Kate thought it best to dissimulate. "Ah, sort of an airport?"

Tina nodded. "Only for private planes." A pause. "Finn had a lot of big dreams."

"'Had'?" Kate said delicately.

Without a change of expression, Tina said, "He died last month."

"Oh," Kate said. "I'm sorry."

Tina looked at her with a little more attention than she had before. "You must have heard about it. Bill's is better than Google for getting the news out."

"How did he die?"

"He went down in his Super Cub."

"Oh," Kate said, "I think I did hear people saying something. I didn't realize that was your husband. I'm so sorry."

Tina's face was unreadable. "Thanks."

Kate, treading carefully, said, "Do they know what caused the crash?"

"A part came off the engine in flight," Tina said.

"Who maintained his plane?"

"He maintained this one."

"Ouch," Kate said, and saw that Tina appreciated the lack of sentimentality. It encouraged her to probe. "He was alone?"

Tina nodded. "He was coming to work." She waved a hand, encompassing Eagle Air FBO's snazzy surroundings. "He commuted from town daily in the Cub."

Kate nodded, letting the silence gather. "You work out here, too?"

Tina had allowed her head to fall against the back of the black leather couch. Her eyes were closed, which somehow made her look infinitely older. "Me?" she said without opening her eyes. "No. I mean, I do now, of course, but before I worked at the hangar in Newenham."

She didn't sound grief stricken, only exhausted. "Family

business," Kate said, keeping her voice soft and monotone, as inoffensive and unobtrusive and inconspicuous as she could make it and still be talking out loud.

Tina sighed. "Yes. We all worked for Finn, one way or another."

"Your son," Kate said. "Oren."

"Yes. And my daughter Evelyn."

"You're all pilots?"

"I used to be. Evelyn still is. Oren, no. Oren works in the office."

So all three of them had opportunity if they'd been at work that day, and two of them would certainly know about the nut on that oil filter. But Oren had been raised and worked around planes himself, and if he had an ounce of curiosity, he could very well have known about it as well. "Wow," Kate said. "Are you all mechanics, like your husband?"

"Evelyn is."

Kate took a chance. "Is Evelyn the daughter in the photograph? The soldier?"

Tina's eyes opened at that. "No," she said, sitting up. "That was my other daughter, Irene."

"Oh," Kate said, and wondered if she should risk it. It was her job to prod the sore spots, but she didn't want to alienate Tina, at least not until she absolutely had to. "I'm sorry. You said 'was'?"

Tina took a deep breath and let it out slowly. She looked up to meet Kate's eyes, and Kate wondered if it had been such a good idea to leave Mutt outside. The only thing that kept her in her chair was that Tina's rage was not directed at her. "She was killed. In Afghanistan."

"Oh," Kate said. "Oh, hell. I am so very sorry. I shouldn't have asked."

She was almost sincere. Kate had recently had a great deal to do with other members of Alaskan royalty, none of whom had improved on acquaintance. Children of privilege, infused with a sense of entitlement, and she doubted any of them had ever struggled to make the rent. If Oren was dropped into the Park without a babysitter, he wouldn't last five minutes. The woman sitting across from her might be worn down by recent tragedy, but she was still one of them by birth, and by marriage, if that ersatz Tara in Newenham was any indication. Kate wasn't so hard-hearted that she didn't feel some sympathy for Tina's recent multiple losses, but she would still swing the sledgehammer that brought down the house of Grant if the situation warranted it, and she was beginning to think it did. "I'm so sorry," she said again.

"It's okay." Tina took another deep breath. "No, it's not okay, but it's real, it happened, I have to get used to it." She smiled, the first time Kate had ever seen her do so, and it was a travesty. "She was killed by a sniper bullet. Some anonymous Taliban guy, they said, shooting at anything in an American uniform."

They sat in silence. "Never have understood exactly what we're supposed to be doing over there," Tina said at last. "They call it nation building. In her letters home, Irene said there was no nation to be built. Just a bunch of tribes that have been squeezed into the single most inhospitable part of central Asia by surrounding nations, to keep them out of their hair."

"How did it happen?"

"She was a helicopter pilot."

"Oh, no," Kate said.

Tina shook her head. "Not another crash, no, or not until she was shot out of the air. I read about it online, afterwards.

There was a sniper hiding one hill over from what they call a forward operating base, waiting for the next helicopter to land. The next helicopter just happened to be hers. Killed her and five other people." She shook her head. "And I keep thinking, for what?"

Her mouth twisted. "Finn didn't agree, of course. He was ex-army himself, and he was all about duty, honor, country. Well, he said he was." She smiled again, although this time it was more like a grimace. "It's why Irene joined. Finn's approval was the single most important thing in her life."

They sat in silence for a few moments. Tina looked at Kate. "I don't know why I'm telling you all this. I barely know you."

"Sometimes it's easier to talk to strangers," Kate said.

"I guess." Tina let her head fall back against the couch again. "God, I'm tired."

"I can see why," Kate said. She made a show of standing up and brushing crumbs from her jeans. "You have to be busy. I should get going anyway, I don't want to be late for work." She smiled. "I'm a little afraid of Bill."

Tina stood up, too. "She's good people."

"I got that," Kate said. She followed Tina out into the lobby. Tina paused and said, "You're Native, aren't you?"

Alarm bells went off, but Kate nodded. "Aleut." It was always best when undercover to stick to the truth as much as possible.

"But not from the village."

"Alaska's largest Native village," Kate said, by which she meant Anchorage.

Tina nodded. "I thought so. What brought you to Newenham?"

Kate grimaced. "It's a long story. There was this guy." Also true.

"When isn't there," Tina said. Her gaze lingered on the scar on Kate's throat.

Sometimes the scar had its uses.

Kate fussed with the zipper of her jacket until she saw Tina go through a door behind Tasha's desk. There was a brief glimpse of filing cabinets and a paper-covered desk before it closed.

Bingo.

She spent the journey back to Newenham with the pleasant taste of crème brûlée cheesecake on her tongue and an even stronger itch to know why Tina had been so glad to get five hundred in cash for the apartment over the garage.

And if getting tossed into a chest freezer had anything to do with it.

14

JANUARY 19

Newenham

KATE WALKED INTO BILL'S Bar and Grill at 3:59 P.M., doffed her coat, and waded in. It had been a long time since she'd worked regular hours. It had the charm of novelty.

Bill's was much more crowded this evening, with people standing around with their drinks in their hands waiting for an empty chair or booth. The music was loud and nonstop, and people were dancing anywhere they could find a vacant square foot of linoleum. Kate remarked on it during a refill run to the bar and Bill, unloading and reloading Kate's tray with practiced speed, said, "Yeah, looks like the dividend was pretty good this year."

Meaning, Kate soon learned, the annual dividend from the local Native association. The Roadhouse was always crowded after NNA issued a dividend, too, although theirs went out quarterly.

"Still don't know why it took them so long to get it to us," one man muttered into his beer, one of many, it would seem.

"Sure you do!" Another man slapped him on the back and guffawed. "They have to take their cut first!"

Kate delivered empties to the bar. "Local Native corporation dividend come out today?"

Bill nodded. "They made a killing on an 8(a) contract. Some three-way deal with a cell phone provider and the federal government to provide rural access for mobile phones, and then AT&T bought them out."

Kate nodded. She was familiar with 8(a) contracts from her time on the Niniltna Native Association board. They'd always seemed to be something of a swindle to her, but it offered a legal advantage to Native-owned corporations in bidding on federal contracts and Alaska Native corporations and associations and tribes had not turned up their noses at the opportunity. "How big was the payout?"

"About thirty thousand. Per shareholder."

Kate pursed her lips in a soundless whistle as Bill loaded her tray. "That ain't chump change."

Bill's expression was sour. "Yeah, and it's burning a hole in their pockets. They're snow-machining and four-wheeling and flying in from Togiak and Manokotak and loading up on groceries and spare parts and new trucks." She nodded at the room. "And booze."

Kate hoisted the tray. "You don't seem very happy about it. Money in the bank for you."

"I can see three TRO violations in the making without turning my head." Bill gave a gloomy nod. "It'll be a late night tonight at the bar, and an early morning tomorrow in court."

In spite of the larger crowd, Kate was hitting her stride as Bill's new barmaid. She got fewer drinks mixed up, she lost Bill less money making change, she didn't drop any glasses, and when Mac McCormick and John Kvichak, who had tried to make time with her the night before and who, born optimists, renewed their suit this evening, instead of calling up Mutt she laughed at them. This made everyone else at their table laugh, too, and her tips went up accordingly.

She just had to pick Mutt's fights, she told herself smugly on her way back to the bar. While she'd been busy at the tables, Oren Grant had come in and taken up residence in a back booth. By the time she brought him his manhattan, he had been joined by a woman a little younger than he was and with enough of a likeness between him and Tina and the photograph in the hall that Kate identified her as Evelyn, the youngest daughter of Finn and Tina Grant. She waved Kate down and ordered a beer. Delivery interrupted a low-voiced argument. Oren's face was flushed, Evelyn's like stone. As Kate approached the table, she heard Evelyn say, "There's nothing we can do about it, Oren. It's her decision. She's the wife, she's the heir, she gets to say."

"Don't you get it, Evelyn?" he said. "Jesus, you want to have to earn your own living?"

"At least I can," she said, her voice rising.

Kate set the beer and the glass down and beamed around the table. "May I get you anything else?"

Oren looked away, red faced. Evelyn shook her head, expression smooth. "No, thanks, we're fine."

Kate smiled back, taking a quick, assessing look at the other woman. About Tina's height, same lean build, same strong jaw. She wore jeans and a dark green sweatshirt advertising ALASKA SHIP SUPPLY in Dutch Harbor.

Kate had one of those, too, from another undercover job on a crabber out of Dutch that had nearly gotten her killed, not to mention eaten by king crab. Getting tossed in a chest freezer was an amateur effort, by comparison.

When she got back to the bar, the little demon from this morning's workout had arrived, and judging by the lip-lock he laid on Bill, they were in something of a relationship. Evidently they hadn't received the memo on no sex after sixty.

He pulled back and looked down at Bill's face and growled deep in his throat.

"Jesus, Moses," the young fisherman sitting on the nearest barstool said, "get a room."

Moses looked at him and grinned, and it was an evil, dirty, low-down, nasty kind of grin. "When's the last time you got laid, Teddy?" The kid turned brick red. Moses booted him off his stool and took his place. A beer appeared magically in front of him and he drained it in one long swallow. Another appeared. Same. A third.

Kate, fascinated, paused in loading her tray to watch. He slammed the third empty down on the bar and looked at her. "You know he didn't do it, right?"

It was the same thing he'd said to her this morning, and she didn't know what it meant now any more than she had then. "Who didn't do what?" she said.

He looked disgusted and didn't answer.

She boosted her laden tray and made for the farther corners of the bar. If she stayed out of reach, maybe Mein Führer wouldn't force her to do ninja stuff again.

Somehow she knew that was a forlorn hope.

This tray went to a crowd of people in their twenties who were getting louder with every round. Kate spotted Tasha Anayuk in the mix, flushed, heavy eyed, barely able to sit upright. The lout sitting next to her probably wasn't a lout when he was sober, but he wasn't sober now and he was all over Tasha, putting his hands in places that, Kate firmly believed, shouldn't see the light of day unless said places were behind closed doors or on the Playboy channel.

But Tasha was of age, and she didn't even recognize Kate when Kate set her beer down in front of her. The night went later, more people came in and got louder and drunker, and there were a couple of incipient fights that broke up when Kate called Mutt in to consult. One look from those intent yellow eyes, and the immediate leak of testosterone through the combatants' pores was almost visible. That look helped close the bar down, too, when Bill called for closing time and nobody wanted to go home. When the door shut behind the last of them, Bill said to Kate, "That dog alone is worth every dime I'm paying you."

"You're paying me?" Kate said before she remembered that Moses was still at the bar, not anywhere near as under the weather as he should have been, given his astonishing rate of consumption. He did have his head on the bar, though, cradled in his arms, and his eyes were closed. Maybe he had finally passed out.

"Don't worry," Bill said, "he already knows."

"Did you tell him?" Kate was disapproving.

"No, I didn't tell him," Bill said. "He knew anyway."

Moses raised his head. His eyes were dark and deep and infinitely knowing, and Kate had the feeling that they could see right through her.

"You know he didn't do it, right?" he said for the third time.

They got back to the apartment over the garage a little after midnight, Kate opening the door and standing back to let Mutt go in first. All clear, and she went inside and stripped down to her skin and took a long, hot shower. Waiting tables was a lot more physical than she had ever guessed. No way was she rubbing that smell off on the sheets, no matter how short a nap she was allowing herself.

Which was two hours. At 3 A.M. her internal clock kicked in and she woke instantly, her eyes wide open, aware of who and where she was and what happened next. It was a great gift and she knew it, especially after waking up next to Jim Chopin off and on for the last three years. Jim was not a morning person. He still had a hard time remembering who she was at first sight, at least until the first quart of coffee went down. The first six or twelve times she'd taken offense, until she realized that, in the immortal phrase of Robin Williams, Jim just wasn't in his body yet.

She allowed herself five seconds' worth of regret that she was alone in her monastic little twin bed, and then she got up and dressed, long johns, lined jeans, and three layers on top with her jacket over all. Chemical warmers went under her toes and inside her gloves, and she broke out the balaclava. If Moses, that cryptic little bastard, was going to make her dance around like a goddamn ninja, she might as well look like one, too. She pulled her headlamp on over the balaclava and adjusted the wide woven elastic band around her head until it felt marginally more comfortable than a bustier.

You know he didn't do it, right? His face had twisted every time he said it, as if it was painful to get the words out, and that thousand-mile stare of his made her uneasy every time he turned it on her. She wished she knew what the hell he meant.

No, she didn't, she told herself firmly. She had a job to do, a pro bono one, true, but a job nonetheless. Time to get on with it. "Ready?"

Mutt danced in place. Ready.

There was a lot more traffic out on the streets of Newenham than there had been that day, or even the night before, everything well lit by the half moon hanging overhead, light reflecting off the snow with enough wattage to read the newspaper by. Evidently the party hadn't stopped when Bill closed the bar, and now, at three o'clock, things weren't even beginning to wind down. Pickups, ATVs, snow machines with belts kicking up sparks on patches of intermittent pavement, it was a city-size traffic jam. A ring of vehicles sat on an empty corner, noses pointed at a crowd around a burn barrel, which contained a blazing fire. A boom box was blaring out, if Kate was not mistaken, the last cast album from *Glee*. Well, at least it wasn't rap. Bottles were being freely passed and Kate caught a whiff of the noxious evil killer weed as she went by.

She might also have caught a glimpse of a white Chevy pickup parked discreetly around a corner, and approved. No point in causing a fuss unless Campbell absolutely had to, but also no point in not being on or near the spot if trouble did break out. There were a lot of people in town with a lot of money to blow and many of them were young people, always a 911 call in the making. She remembered yet another undercover case in the oil fields of the North Slope of Alaska, where she'd watched a game of check poker, the hand of poker the check number, seven players and winner take all. Each check had been about twelve hundred dollars, a week's work at that time. And the losers had groaned and drunk some more.

She wondered if any of that was going on in Newenham this evening. Not even the most dedicated drinker could put away thirty thousand dollars of alcohol in one evening, but one bet and he could wake up as broke as he'd been the previous morning. Without much conviction, she hoped that the local Native association, having given so freely with one hand, might also be patrolling for abuses in connection with that giving with the other. But she didn't see any sign of it.

She went through town, repressing her Protector of the Small reflex every time she saw someone too drunk to walk, maintaining a decorous pace so as to attract no undue attention. Bundled up as she was, she doubted she even looked female, which in present circumstances she thought a very good thing. At the stop sign to the river road, another four-wheeler shot out of nowhere, precipitating a drastic swerve that dumped Mutt off the back of Kate's ATV, and vanished at speed up the street. From the fleeting glimpse she caught, Kate could find it in her heart to forgive the young man's erratic driving, given the young woman straddling him and all. A young woman who was not wearing an amount of clothing adequate for the ambient temperature, in Kate's opinion, but it was none of her business. Mutt, ruffled, spoke her mind in their receding direction, and jumped up in back of Kate again.

The hinterlands dividing Newenham and Eagle Air's operation were also much more lively this morning. There were a couple of bonfires with people gathered around, more couples in clinches in what shadows the half moon allowed, and a couple of sporting events, one a race between an ATV and a snow machine. The snow machine won, but only because the ATV disappeared into the ice of a small pond that was part of the course. Kate slowed down, but rescuers appeared and hauled him out, stripped off his soaking pants and parka then and there, and repackaged him in various volunteered articles of clothing. After which they all returned to the bonfire for another round.

The good news was that no one paid any attention to her. She was just another shareholder rejoicing in her dividend. She was a little concerned that the revelry might extend to Eagle Air, that she might arrive to the sight of a shivaree in progress, but when they poked a cautious nose up over the edge of the gravel pad, all was calm. Security lights shone from every corner of hangar and office, but no lights from any of the hangar or office windows. She circumnavigated the gravel pad once just in case, before leaving the four-wheeler at the base of the pad in back of the hangar.

She pulled out an enormous pair of heavy gray wool socks and pulled them over her boots so her soles wouldn't squeak on the snow. The edge of the pad was about twenty yards from the hangar's back wall. She and Mutt crept up over the edge onto the pad and inveigled themselves across the hard-packed snow and into the shadow of the building.

Kate leaned against the metal siding, waiting for a siren to go off or someone to shout "Halt, who goes there?" When nothing happened she tried the back door, a windowless metal slab of formidable solidity. It was locked. No reason it should be that easy. She and Mutt apparitioned around the building to the front door. Amazingly, like Tina's front door, like Tina's office window, like Tina's garage, like the old hangar at the Newenham airport, like Kate's apartment, it was unlocked. It seemed to be something of a meme. "Mutt," Kate said, her voice the barest whisper, "guard."

Mutt's "Whoof!" was the bare minimum of sound. She floated soundlessly over the tarmac to where the base office intersected the hangar, where the edge of the roof and the location of the moon allowed a corner of gray shadow almost exactly the color of Mutt's coat, and took up station. If you didn't know she was there, you would never have seen her. Kate's hand stilled on the doorknob, watching, and she thought that if Mutt's IQ got any higher, Kate might have to abdicate as the senior partner of the firm. She laughed beneath her baclava and eased inside.

There was a night-light on the wall, a tiny bulb behind a small, elegantly wrought glass leaf. She waited, listening. There was no sound. She went around the edge of the room, the better to avoid creaks in the floor, just in case. She opened the door she had seen Tina go through the previous afternoon, and stepped inside, pulling the door closed behind her. It was a heavy wooden door with heavy brass fittings and a lever handle, precision machined, and it slid shut with barely a click. There was a great deal to be said for sparing no expense on construction, especially from the burglar's point of view.

She leaned against the door and played her pencil flash around the room. No chest freezers. It did have corner windows, the one behind the desk facing the hangar. She went softly around the desk to investigate. The windows were vinyl sliders, with two locks, top and bottom. They unlocked as smoothly and as silently as the window opened.

No alarm whooped. She waited. There was the faintest of rustles in the shadow opposite, followed by the drift of a lupine specter in her direction. "Guard," Kate whispered. She didn't hear anything but she knew Mutt had assumed the picket position beneath the window.

She turned and surveyed the room. The desk was right in front of her so she put away the pencil flash and clicked on her headlamp and started there, coming up empty for the most part, finding only office supplies, pads, pens and pencils, a half-empty box of printer paper. There was a handful of the small Swiss Army knives in various colors scattered in the top drawer, the ones everyone in Alaska used to have in their pockets before 9/11 and TSA put a stop to it. These had been embossed on one side with the Eagle Air logo. Giveaways, no doubt. There was a box of .30-06 cartridges, six missing, and a ziplock bag holding some commemorative coins, their tarnish proclaiming them either pure silver or fake gold. There was a desk diary for that year that she opened hopefully, only to find it blank. Well, Finn had died on December 11.

A power cable came up through a hole in the desk but there was no computer. The computer in the office of Grant's house had been a laptop. Tina probably brought it back and forth.

The bank of file drawers against the wall were the inevitable next step, and revealed a day-to-day record of operations of Eagle Air, Inc., going back over two years, dating from shortly after the purchase of the air base. One entire set of drawers was devoted to computer printouts of flight plans that went back thirty years, back when Eagle Air was Bristol Bay Air and, before that, Arctic Air Express. Kate flipped through them rapidly. They were organized into monthly logs. The early logs were filled in laboriously—and for the most part illegibly—by hand, the Bristol Bay Air flights printed out on—Kate squinted in the light of her headlamp—what she thought might have been a dot matrix printer. It made her eyes hurt just to look at them. Eagle Air logs were crisp and professional spreadsheets, printed out on eight-and-a-half-by-eleven pieces of paper, every number neatly centered in its column, each column equidistant from its neighbor, all columns neatly centered on the sheet. Kate gave a silent cheer to Hewlett-Packard and the invention of the ink cartridge.

She concentrated on Eagle Air, Inc. and the last three years. Flights incoming listed a preponderance of company jets registered in names even Kate recognized, most of them right off the *Forbes* and *Fortune* 500 lists. Kate's lips pursed in a silent whistle. Finn Grant may have had some cause for Eagle Air's luxurious furnishings and gourmet foodstuffs. You couldn't expect the boards of directors of Exxon Mobil and Berkshire Hathaway to sleep in bunk beds with no mattresses and eat out-of-date MREs bought in odd lots on the Internet. It was how many Alaska outfitters treated their clients. Not that they charged them any less.

She passed the membership of the board of directors of the Niniltna Native Association in quick mental review, and an involuntary grin tugged at her lips. She'd like to see someone serve Harvey Meganack First Strike Rations.

The flight plans out listed three main locations as destinations: Zion River Lodge, Four Lake Lodge, and Outouchiwanet Mountain Lodge. The records for Outouchiwanet Mountain Lodge stopped abruptly two years before, which would have been when McGuire invested in Eagle Air in exchange for deed and title to Outouchiwanet.

She closed the drawer and looked around for a map. It was on the wall next to the door, a big USGS 1:63,360 topographical map, reproduced, Kate discovered, on a metallic sheet set in a heavy wooden frame mounted directly on the wall. A cluster of magnets clung to one corner, and two bright blue plastic metal circles marked the locations of the two lodges Finn Grant had still been operating at the time of his death. The two remaining lodges and Eagle Air, Inc., formed a sort of scalene triangle stood on its longest point, with Eagle Air at the bottom and Zion River and Four Lake at top left and top right, respectively. She looked for Outouchiwanet Lodge and found it tucked into a bight in the side of Three Lake. Judging by the elevation markers on the contour lines surrounding the bight, Outouchiwanet had some spectacular view, always assuming sunlight ever got down in there to illuminate anything.

Interesting country north of Newenham, four long lakes, named, imaginatively, One, Two, Three, and Four south to north, each running east–west, stacked parallel one on top of the other. The mountains between them formed a formidable ridge between the Nushugak River delta and the Yukon–Kuskokwim River delta. Anyone who spent his adult life flying in and out of that kind of terrain, with all the attendant terrors of schizophrenic Alaskan weather thrown in, without incident until his untimely death, had seriously mad skills in the air. She remembered the guy in the bar comparing Finn Grant's personality to his flying ability.

Which made his overlooking even so little a thing as a loose nut on the oil filter of his Cub that much less likely, she thought. There are old pilots, and there are bold pilots. There are no old, bold pilots. Chaos theory be damned, old pilots got old by not making mistakes like that.

For the first time, the possibility that she really was investigating a murder in the first degree took solid root.

She went back to the file drawers. Many of them were taken up by paperwork that made up the lifeblood of the Federal Aviation Administration: aircraft registration forms, pilot check rides, aircraft history and maintenance status along with engine annuals. Kate wasn't able to wade into all of it—she would have needed a month longer than she had—but it appeared to her untrained eye that Finn Grant had bought a third single Otter and three Cessna Caravans in the last year alone. There was also the necessary ream of paperwork backing up the most recent Otter's conversion to a turbine engine, dated the previous August.

That did give her pause, because she remembered George Perry in Niniltna telling her a story only last year about flying most of the way around the world in pursuit of just one single Otter so he could keep up with Niniltna business as usual and at the same time meet the demands of custom from the Suulutaq Mine. If he didn't, mine management would find someone else to ferry their employees to and from work. George had the monopoly and wanted to keep it. He'd found his Otter somewhere in Africa—had it been Ivory Coast?—

and brought it home in triumph by way of Vancouver, BC, where he'd had the piston engine pulled and a turbine engine installed at a cost of a cool $1.5 million.

The point being, George said, was that you couldn't find single Otters nowadays, it was too good an aircraft and they were all working, not sitting around with FOR SALE signs in the window.

A single Otter, turbo conversion, and three brand-new Cessna Caravans. Kate shook her head and wondered just how much Finn Grant had overcharged Gabriel McGuire for Outouchiwanet Mountain Lodge. Although she supposed there were limits to the wallet of even the world's biggest box office draw.

Again with the snide, she thought, exasperated. Why did the man rub her so much the wrong way? She'd met him one time, she hadn't exchanged more than a couple dozen words with him. Enough.

She closed the drawer with unnecessary force, catching it at the last minute before it banged shut and casting a guilty look over her shoulder. She moved down to the last of the cabinets, all of which were made from the same polished teak as Tasha's desk in the outer office and the desk in this office as well, and slid the first drawer out.

She surfaced half an hour later, her brow creased.

As expected, the tourist business at Eagle Air slowed during the winter months, when the creeks froze up and the bears went to sleep. There were some December and January caribou hunts up around Mulchatna and some four-day board retreats that didn't involve hunting or fishing. There were a lot of those in the summer as well, but from the copies of the king salmon punch cards she found, most retreats were conducted rod in hand.

Most independent air taxies in Alaska took up the slack in tourism in winter by flying locals between villages and towns and towns and Anchorage. From the evidence in these drawers, Eagle Air, Inc., had instead moved exclusively into air freight.

The cargo manifests went back eighteen months, or the hard copies did, the ones the loadmaster, often Grant, and the pilot, a rotating group of half a dozen names, had signed. The contents were listed variously as *electric apparatus, testing instruments,* and *electronics*. The destination for all of them was the airport code ADK. ADK, ADK.

As in Adak, Alaska?

Kate went back to the map. Adak was an Aleutian island about twelve hundred miles south-southwest of Anchorage, which would put it, what, about nine hundred miles from Newenham, give or take. Adak had been a naval air station before BRAC shut it down, just like BRAC shut down Chinook.

Kate frowned. Adak had been a topic of conversation at Native gatherings for some years. The regional Native corporation in the area had negotiated a deal for the existing buildings and facilities, which included a very nice airport, indeed, and an extensive harbor with docks. The docks were capable of supporting a healthy commercial fishing industry and cargo in sufficient quantity to sustain a population of six thousand people, including USAF personnel and their dependents. The airport was large enough and modern enough to support a naval air squadron, and the corporation had intended to develop Adak for tourism. It was a wild, beautiful place, an obvious choice for adventure and ecotourism, until the Middle East decided to embrace regime change as a regional activity and the price per barrel of oil went up over a hundred dollars.

It had cost Kate six hundred dollars to fly home from Dutch Harbor, one way, and that was five years before. Adak was twice as far down the Chain. She didn't want to think what a round-trip ticket Anchorage–Adak–Anchorage would cost, and no tourist would, either, especially after they had already shelled out for the round-trip ticket to Anchorage for themselves, their spouse, and their two and a half children.

The docks and boat harbor were large enough to tempt an Outside investor to build a fish plant on Adak to process crab and Pacific cod, but it was currently in the throes of a bankruptcy battle between the Native corporation and a large number of angry creditors. At the mercy of weather and vandalism, the unoccupied portion of the base, also known as most of it, was rumored to be in a state of disintegration.

What the hell was Finn Grant doing shipping cargo to Adak? At last count, the population was around three hundred, and the Native corporation was scrambling to keep its investment from heading straight into the fiscal toilet.

She closed the drawer and looked at the clock on the wall. She'd been here almost an hour. Outside the window, the bright moon stretched long shadows on the tarmac. Through the crack in the window she could hear the distant sounds of four-wheelers and snow machines, and now and then a faint scream of laughter, or just a scream. Surprising that so far she had heard no gunshots. Surprising, too, that none of the revelers had come to Eagle Air to avail themselves of two long straight stretches of pavement for drag racing.

She turned and her headlamp caught a gun rack on the wall. One of the many firearms it held was a dark, familiar shape, and she stepped closer.

It was another AK-47, she thought the same model she'd seen in Grant's home office. Again with the moose-inappropriate firearm, but by all accounts from many wars a simple, effective, reliable weapon, designed to kill as many people as possible without jamming. The weapon, so Bobby Clark said, that had won the Vietnam War. He had one on his wall, too, although Bobby's had a wooden stock and hand grip.

She'd been curious after Bobby showed her his, so she'd looked it up. A weapon that had been reproduced by nations from Albania to Yugoslavia, over a hundred million of them had been manufactured worldwide. It or a local variation thereof was the weapon of choice in every dirty little insurrection in every backwoods little nation on every continent since the first one had been stamped out in the USSR, right through to today. General Kalashnikov must have been so proud. Although he'd had more than a little help from the German weapons developers the USSR had relocated safely on their side of the border following World War II.

Next down was a single-barreled pump-action shotgun. She checked. A Remington Model 870, same as hers. Next was another pump-action shotgun, this one in a camo finish, a Benelli. It looked newer than the Remington, and the weapon below it was the twin of the alien-killer she'd seen in the gun safe back at the house.

It appeared that Finn Grant hadn't limited his spending on mansions and remodels and high-end furnishings and gourmet snacks. She wondered if his FBO investors knew.

She also wondered if the presence of this much firepower might have something to do with the dividend shindig maintaining a discreet distance.

She turned and surveyed the office. She'd been through the desk, through the files, and absent a computer she was just about out of ideas. Nothing on the coffee table, nothing under the cushions of the two chairs near it. The map was screwed to the wall, and the framed duck stamp hanging on another wall lifted easily and revealed nothing but more wall.

She went over to the desk and went through it one more time. Pens, pencils, knives, diary, coins.

Ammunition.

Perhaps sensitized by the weaponry on the walls of both offices, she spilled the box of cartridges across the top of the desk.

One of those things was not like the other.

The brass of the casings shone in the light of her headlamp, but one did not reflect as much light. Further, he was a portly little fellow, broad in the beam, with a much blunter nose. She picked it up, and then picked another up to compare weights. The fake cartridge weighed much less than the real one. She put down the real cartridge to examine the fake one more closely. It was plastic. There was a crack between the bullet and casing. She inserted a fingernail, and the bullet pulled out of the case to reveal a thumb drive.

Oh, hell yes.

A soft whine through the crack in the window brought her head up. The engine of a small vehicle sounded much closer than it ought to have. In one continuous movement she stuffed the thumb drive in a pocket and swept the cartridges and the box back in the drawer and closed it. A snow machine, she thought, an Arctic Cat maybe, one of the new ones, coming fast. Probably one of the party-hearty crowd from Newenham.

But just in case it wasn't, Kate said, "Stay," and then had to repeat herself firmly. "Stay, Mutt."

She switched off her headlamp and made for the bathroom she'd used that afternoon as the sound of the snow machine roared up to the front door. She was barely inside the bathroom before the door to the office opened. Applying her eye to the crack of the bathroom door, she saw someone zipped into a formfitting snowmobile suit, black with neon green stripes. They pulled off a visored helmet and headed for the office.

It was too dark for Kate to see who it was, but she was pretty sure it was a woman. Tina? But why come by night, by what was presumably stealth, when she had the run of the place during the day?

Tasha? From what she'd seen at Bill's earlier in the evening, by now Tasha was passed out cold, Kate hoped alone and in what Kate hoped was her own bed.

The light in the office went on, and drawers opened and closed. Whoever was in there wasn't being quite so stealthy as Kate, or saw no need to be.

Maybe she should just tiptoe out. Maybe that corner between office and hangar was still dark and she could wait there until whoever this was left and she might get a look at them, and maybe even follow them.

She put her hand on the doorknob and someone else drove up, this person on an ATV, running a little rough. The engine stopped and she heard the squeak of boots on snow coming toward the door.

She sure hoped nobody had to pee.

And that Mutt wasn't getting too restless with all the traffic going in and out.

Noise in the office had stopped abruptly when the ATV pulled up. The door to the office opened again and Kate, peering once more through the crack, saw someone much larger than the first person come through. A man this time, who either wasn't wearing or who had already doffed his helmet outside. She couldn't make out his features but he seemed middling tall and either beefy or muscular, and his stride was long and solid, making the floor tremble just that little bit when his feet hit the ground. He made straight for the office, opened the door, and went in.

A voice spoke, too low for Kate to catch the words. Another voice answered, a man's voice.

The first voice raised in volume. Definitely a woman. "There's nothing here."

"Let it be," the man's voice said. "There's nothing you can do now. Just go on home and leave it behind you."

"You found it, didn't you? And you took it. Damn you! You'll beggar us, don't you get that? I won't let that happen!"

The man's voice changed. "Hey! What the hell do you think you're doing! Give me that!"

There was the thud of flesh on flesh and footsteps staggering back and forth.

And then, there was a gunshot.

15

JANUARY 19

Newenham

THERE WERE IN FACT several, three or four in a row very fast, as if someone were ripping off a series of really loud farts. Kate knew again that horrible conviction of mortality everyone always feels in the presence of flying bullets, and teleported herself into the very small space between the toilet and the wall, arms wrapped around her head. In the very short space of time she was allowed for clear thought she hoped that the interior construction of Eagle Air FBO was as high in quality as the exterior.

The shots stopped as abruptly as they had begun when something large and metallic hit the floor. "Fuck!" the man yelled.

From outside the building, Mutt half barked, half howled. Before the sound had died away, Kate was on her feet with her hand on the knob when heavy footsteps moving fast went out the front door and a moment later the ATV started up and moved away in high gear.

Kate came out of the bathroom at the same time Mutt crashed through the front door. "I'm fine, you moron, go get the guy! Mutt! *Fetch!*" Mutt growled, turned on a dime, and launched.

Kate ran to the office.

The overhead light illuminated the scene inside to vivid and horrible effect. Sprawled on the perfectly waxed bamboo floor, Evelyn Grant lay in her own blood, a rich, darkly red pool that rapidly increased in size as Kate, momentarily paralyzed, watched. The alien-killer was a few feet from her right hand.

"Fuck is right," Kate said, and ran to the bathroom to grab the hand towels. She ran back to the office, dropped to her knees, and slid the rest of the way over the slick bamboo floor to the injured woman. She folded one towel in fourths and pressed it against the side all the blood seemed to be coming from. "Evelyn," she said. "Evelyn?"

"What the hell is going on here?" a voice said from the door.

She looked up to see Gabe McGuire standing in the doorway, dressed in gray sweatpants and brandishing a paint-splattered wooden yardstick like it was a broadsword.

"Oh, just what I don't need," Kate said. "What did you think you were going to do with that?"

He looked at the yardstick. "I don't know. It was standing in the corner of the room. I just grabbed it when the noise woke me up." Hair standing on end in a way it had never been allowed to on film, McGuire looked from the yardstick to Kate to the woman on the floor. "Jesus Christ," he said blankly.

Kate looked down and saw that the first towel was showing signs of red. She swore and looked up. "Hey." McGuire was still gaping at Evelyn. "Hey, you, shit-for-brains!"

McGuire looked up, his expression dazed.

"Yeah, you," she said, "get over here."

He stared at her for a long moment, before crossing the floor to kneel at her side. "Press here," she said.

When he replaced her hands with his, she folded the second towel. "Here, use this, too. No, right here, can't you feel the hole? Hard. Harder, damn it, if you don't want her to bleed out right under your hands."

"I know what I'm doing," he snapped, and indeed, he seemed to, sliding the second towel beneath his hands without releasing pressure on the wound. Evelyn's eyelids fluttered and she moaned, a pitiful sound. Her pulse was rapid and her skin was pale and clammy. The trash can next to the desk was small and rectangular. Kate dumped it, raised Evelyn's feet and put the trash can beneath them.

She pulled out her cell and hit the speed dial. Campbell answered on the first ring. "It's Kate Shu—Saracoff," she said. "We need a paramedic at Eagle Air immediately. Evelyn Grant has been shot and she's doing her damnedest to bleed out."

"On my way." *Click*.

"Love a cop who's on the ball," Kate said, thumbing the phone off. "You got her?"

"I got her," McGuire said grimly. "I think the wound must be clotting. The blood flow is slowing down."

"Don't let up on the pressure."

"I know what I'm doing," he said again. He looked up, eyes fierce. "Mind telling me what the hell's going on?"

"First you tell me what you're doing here," she said.

He jerked his chin toward the ceiling. "I'm sacking out in one of the bedrooms, or I was. What are you doing here?"

"Why are you spending the night here?"

"I flew in from the lodge to take a video conference tomorrow." He glanced at the clock on the wall. "This morning."

"You don't have Internet access at the lodge?"

He looked at her as if she were insane. "Are you kidding

me? We've got a satellite phone for emergencies. That's it."

She remembered the phone call Chouinard got when they were waiting for Satan to get into his ninja togs. "Brad one of your posse?"

He blinked. "Brad Severson, yeah, he's my PA."

"What time did you get here?"

"Oh, dark thirty." He misinterpreted her expression. "Sunset or thereabouts. Wy Chouinard flew me over."

"Was there anyone here when you got in?"

His eyes narrowed. "Just Tasha, and she took off right after I arrived. Something about a big party in town. You know, you're starting to sound an awful lot like a cop."

"How would you know?" Kate said. "No one else has been around since you got here?"

"Except for you? Except for her?" Indicating the woman whose side he was holding together with bloodstained hands. "Except for whoever shot her, which I assume wasn't you? No."

"You didn't hear anything?"

"Until I heard someone shoot off an M4 fifty feet from the pillow my head was resting on? No."

"How did you know what kind of a weapon was used?"

He nodded at the rifle on the floor. "I'm not blind."

"How do you know it's an M4?" Kate said.

He looked as exasperated as a nearly naked man doing compression on an open wound could. "I carried one every day for a month and a half last year." She stared at him, uncomprehending and suspicious, and he said, "*No Retreat*. My last film."

"Oh." She looked over his shoulder, finding a nice safe place on the wall to stare at. There was entirely too much skin showing on altogether the wrong man.

Mutt crashed through the office door and skidded to a halt, her toenails scraping across the wood floor as she danced for purchase. She took in the situation at a glance. Her hackles rose and a low growl issued from somewhere around her sternum.

"You lost him?" Kate said.

Mutt ignored her, continuing to growl at McGuire, as if to prove she was good for something.

"Officially now a perfect evening," McGuire said, not nearly so terrified as he should have been. "What should we do for a second date?"

Kate was horrified when she almost laughed. "Mutt. Mutt! It's okay, stand down, babe." She got to her feet.

"Where are you going?"

"Upstairs to get more towels," Kate said.

One of the bedroom doors was open. There was a pile of clothes on the chair, shoes and a daypack next to it. The bedclothes were thrown back, a pair of glasses and a paperback novel open on the nightstand. She grabbed a towel out of the bathroom and went back downstairs.

Mutt had taken up station before the desk, where she could keep an eye on the door and on McGuire at the same time. "Good girl," Kate said.

McGuire looked up. "The bleeding has almost stopped."

"Good. Maybe I can find some tape."

"I can hold it until the EMTs get here."

"Don't know how long they'll be," Kate said. "Best to have a plan."

She was investigating the drawers of Tasha's desk when she heard an ATV approaching. She went to the window, hoping it wasn't the guy who'd shot Evelyn coming back.

It wasn't, it was Campbell, who killed the engine and came

in, long legs eating up the ground. "Where?" he said when she met him at the door.

"In here." She pointed at the office and stood back to let him go in first.

McGuire looked up. "Hey, Liam."

Campbell was stern, if not accusatory. "What are you doing here, Gabe?"

McGuire looked at Kate, standing a little in back of Campbell. "Just like a cop." He looked back at the trooper. "Got a conference call in the morning. Wy flew me in early yesterday evening, ask her, I was probably her last trip of the day. How long before the EMTs get here?"

"There's only one. I called him and he wasn't on another call, so he said he'd be right out. Probably five, ten minutes behind me."

"I wasn't here," Kate said, looking hard at Campbell.

"What?" McGuire said.

Campbell looked hard right back, and then they both turned to look hard at McGuire. "Gabe, I don't expect you to understand this," the trooper said, "but as a personal favor to me, I'm asking you to keep Kate's presence here quiet. For now, anyway."

McGuire started to say something, and stopped. For a man dressed only in sweatpants, his knees and hands now liberally stained with blood, he looked remarkably composed. "I found the body?" he said.

Campbell nodded. "You heard the shot, you came down and found the body, you called me."

Amazingly, McGuire gave a wry smile. "Do I need to call a lawyer?"

Campbell looked at Kate, and Kate shook her head. "Kate says no," Campbell said.

"And what Kate says, goes?" McGuire shook his head. "Okay. But as payback I get the full story, and before very long." He stared at Kate. "Including who you are and what you're really doing here in Newenham. You're no barmaid."

"How did you know I was working at Bill's?" Kate said.

"Just exactly like a cop," McGuire said. "Wy told me on the flight over. Yes, I asked. What, did you think I had special powers?" His eyes narrowed. "Or just guilty knowledge?"

Kate let go of the very loose grip she had on subtlety to begin with and said bluntly, "You're a partner in Eagle Air."

McGuire looked surprised, as well he might by this new attack on a different front, but his turn to rally. "Yeah. So?"

"How did that happen?"

"I fail to see what that has—"

"Gabe." Campbell's voice was dark and deep, and in spite of herself, Kate gave an internal shiver. It would have taken a stronger woman than she was for every feminine instinct not to moan in response to the double dose of masculine beauty and full-on testosterone filling up this room. Mutt was not unaffected, either, head swiveling between the two of them, with what Kate could only describe as a pretty lascivious pant going on.

McGuire's mouth shut in a taut line. "Fine," he said curtly. "Finn wanted a big name for his start-up. I wanted Outouchiwanet. He wouldn't sell it to me outright, but he would if I'd let him use my name. If I bought in, others would. So I did, and he deeded it over. End of story."

"That's it?" Kate said.

"What else is there?" McGuire said. Kate watched the realization dawn slowly in his eyes, and he looked around the office again, more slowly this time, without ever letting up on

Evelyn's wound. "What else is there?" he said again, with more pointed emphasis.

"Not your concern," she said.

"Like hell it isn't," he growled. "If the jackals in the press get hold of this story, whatever is going on here will be splashed across the front page of the *National Enquirer,* starring me. I'm not Mel or Arnold, but believe me when I tell you it'll draw a lot of attention I doubt any of us wants."

"Tell them the truth," Kate said. "You were sleeping upstairs, you heard a shot, you came down and found her bleeding on the floor. You applied pressure and called 911. You saved her life. You're a hero." She smiled, and it wasn't a very nice smile. "Have to be used to that."

He grimaced, but all he said was, "I left my cell upstairs."

"And brought a yardstick instead to beat off the bad guys with," Kate said, and shook her head. "I'll get it."

She washed the blood from her hands first. His cell was in his jacket pocket, the very nice bomber jacket he had been wearing when she met him, made from very soft brown leather, worn enough to be supple and creased. There was a wallet in his other pocket, containing his driver's license—she wondered if a movie star had to stand in line at the DMV with the rest of the Great Unwashed—amazingly in the name of Gabriel McGuire. It was Kate's understanding that movie stars were invariably burdened at birth with names like Gedaliah Shuttlecock or Aloysius Entbuch, which names were then changed the instant they hit Hollywood. His pilot's license was in the same name.

McGuire had two credit cards—both of which bore the complacent air of being able to accommodate the price of a Boeing 747—and a thousand in cash in hundred-dollar bills.

Walking-around money for the movie star. She put the wallet back in his pocket, took the cell and went back downstairs. "Does 911 ring directly to your phone?" she said to Campbell.

He shook his head. "We've still got dispatchers."

"Is anyone going to check his phone to see if he dialed 911?"

"That would be me." He took McGuire's phone, turned it on, and dialed 911. Someone answered and he responded briefly and hung up.

Kate smiled for the first time in what felt like forever. "My kinda cop. Mutt, let's go."

Campbell walked her out. "Where's your transportation?"

"Yeah, don't mind me," McGuire said behind them, "I'm just the guy trying to keep someone from bleeding to death."

"Parked out back."

Outside the door, Mutt's ears went up and Campbell cocked his head. "I can hear someone coming. Talk fast."

She talked fast, telling him about everything except the thumb drive, which was burning a hole in her pocket. She also told him about the argument she had seen between Oren and Evelyn at Bill's the night before. When she was done, he said, very thoughtfully, "Shit."

"Yeah. If I'm right, this is a much bigger can of worms than you thought. You still want me on this job? Because I'm thinking, and I can't even believe I'm saying this, you might do well to call in the feds."

He looked at her, his eyes hard. "If something has been going down on my patch, I need to know about it. If I call in the feds too soon, I never will. Damn straight you stay." The sound of the approaching ATV got louder. "You better get out of here."

"All right. I'll touch base tomorrow."

Campbell went back inside and Kate started around the building, before she remembered something and trotted back in to stick her head inside the door of the office. "Be best if you don't print the shotgun. The Remington."

Campbell followed her pointing finger, swore out loud when he realized what she meant, and looked as if he'd have said a lot more, barring present company.

McGuire actually laughed.

"Sorry," she said, a little shame-faced. "What can I say, I've got an older one just like it at home."

"Get out of here before I put the cuffs on you myself," Campbell said.

She got, and she and Mutt were sliding down the ice-covered edge of the gravel berm when the oncoming ATV approached the hangar on the other side. She timed the starter from the moment he killed his engine, waited until she heard the door open, and then left it in low gear at a very slow speed until they were well away.

The air was still and cold, and as they headed north to town Kate saw a swirl of aurora on the northern horizon, a pale, neon green in a single graceful, dancing arc. The parties were winding down and Kate took it sedately through town with no near misses, approached the garage in stealth mode, and parked beneath the stairs. When she unlocked the door, she stood back and let Mutt go in first.

The apartment was as empty as they'd left it. She went to the window facing Grant's house and peeped through the blind.

Grant's house had light blazing from three windows. As she watched, she saw Tina and Oren come down the front stairs and climb into the pickup parked in front. The engine started, the headlights came on, and they drove off.

She let the blind fall back and waited long enough for them to be out of sight before she turned on the lights in the apartment. She showered and changed into sweats and T-shirt. She was tired but still revved from the evening's events, so she made herself a cup of the ghastly chamomile tea, dosed it liberally with the Sweet'N Low she found in a drawer (right next to the Coffee-mate, gah), and curled up in the recliner. Mutt had flopped down on the rag rug and was snoring. She must have given the guy a run for his money, but Kate was now regretting sending her after him. Mutt was a pretty distinctive individual. If she'd been seen in pursuit, she would be easy to identify later, which would blow Kate's own cover sky high. If she hadn't already.

Kate put the tea down and looked for a phone book. She found it in one of the kitchenette drawers, a slim volume that included all the communities between Naknek and Port Molar and Platinum and Pilot Point. There was even a page for "Our Yup'ik Friends." Kate stuck to English.

She put back the phone book, poured the rest of the tea in the sink, and stood looking out the window. Streetlights shone near and stars shone far, and in front of her the leaden expanse of the Nushugak River moved steadily southward.

Somewhere out there, Evelyn Grant fought for her life, while Tina Grant prayed for the survival of her one remaining daughter, and Oren Grant, one hoped, for the survival of his one remaining sister.

Kate thought about calling Jim, but she really didn't want to have to explain what she was doing up at this hour of the morning the second night in a row. She went to bed, and was almost instantly asleep.

16

JANUARY 19

The Park

JIM WORRIED AT THE problem of Erland Bannister all the next day, with a small side preoccupation with Axenia Shugak Mathisen, just to cover all four major food groups.

Not that Bannister was his problem yet, per se, but he would be when Kate got back from Newenham. She was not going to take kindly to a partnership between a sworn enemy of the State of Shugak and the association of which she was a prominent shareholder and immediate past chair.

Axenia was another matter entirely. Axenia was Kate's cousin, she was family, she was a tribal member and a shareholder of the Niniltna Native Association and a member of its board. She wasn't even a Park rat anymore, and so not anyone he was responsible for. On every front she was untouchable by his white, state, sleeping-with-Kate hands. Which would in no way alleviate the shitstorm he saw coming his way when Kate found out he had not told her immediately of Axenia's presence on the same jet as Erland Bannister.

He avoided thinking about it by flying out to the Kruzensterns' homestead to arrest that notorious ladies' man Lars Kruzenstern for sexual assault of a minor, although Holly Kvasnikof most emphatically did not look like a minor, and hadn't appeared all that interested in filing charges. There seemed to be a lot of that going around this January. Her mother had been very interested, to the point of hitting Jim with flying spit from where she was seated on the other side of her kitchen table. Lars, on the other hand, seemed philosophical about the whole deal. "I figured she was lying about her age when she told me she was eighteen, but I figured her for twenty-five, not sixteen." His smile was blissful. "Whatever happens, it was worth it."

Jim filed his report and flew Lars to Ahtna, where he abandoned him to the tender mercies of the Alaska judicial system. It was not Lars's first encounter with the law, and it was not Judge Roberta Singh's first encounter with Lars. He flew back to Niniltna in the expectation of seeing Lars ROR in the Park within the day, if he could hitch a ride home in that time, and drove to the scene of an accident between a four-wheeler driven by Davy John and a Dodge pickup driven by Howie Katelnikof. There was disagreement as to who had caused the accident, which had been called in—naturally—by a Park rat on his cell phone. Davy had taken a tumble but amazingly he'd been wearing a helmet and was unhurt. Howie had no registration for the Dodge, and no proof of insurance. Jim smiled at Howie and pulled out his ticket book, the day having become suddenly brighter all around.

Afterwards he continued out to the Roadhouse to check in with Bernie, the ponytailed, draft-dodging ex-hippie owner of the only bar between Niniltna and Cordova. Emigrating back into the United States after Carter's pardon, Bernie drifted up to Alaska, where he bought the remains of an old roadhouse on an old mining road from an old-timer whose daughter he married to grease the wheels of the deal. He'd remodeled it, added a house to live in and some one-room cabins to rent, and settled in to become the bartender of choice for the Park. Also the only bartender in the Park, or the only professional one, but he did live up to the higher standards of his profession, and for that Jim was profoundly thankful. Bernie wouldn't serve drunks or pregnant mothers, he'd removed car keys at the point of the baseball bat he kept behind the bar from the grasp of anyone he deemed too drunk to drive, and his establishment had become the drinking hole for any thirsty Park rat or Suulutaq miner with a bend toward sociability.

He was also the repository of more Park gossip than all four aunties put together, and a useful source of information, when he was of a mind to share.

It was a little after noon when Jim pulled into the parking lot, and he was lucky enough to catch Bernie alone. The tall, thin man, growing steadily more solemn and cadaverous with each passing year, looked up from behind the bar when the door opened. "Hey, Jim."

"Bernie." Jim hooked his ball cap and jacket on the coatrack beside the door and took a stool. "Where is everybody?"

Bernie paused in the act of polishing a glass. "You know, I've never been able to figure out what the deal is with Tuesday mornings. Nobody's ever here on Tuesdays until after noon." He put the glass down. "What can I get you?"

"I'm on duty."

Bernie shook his head sadly. "Poor bastard." He got a can of Diet Coke from the refrigerator beneath the bar and poured it over a glass of ice. Jim stood up on the rungs of the stool and kyped a couple of lime wedges from the container behind the counter and squeezed them in. He sipped, thinking longingly of an Alaskan Amber, but sticking manfully to his duty.

"You really are pitiful," Bernie said, watching him.

Jim set his glass down and sighed. "I know."

"Why do I have the honor? Not that it's not nice to see you without your sidearm drawn, but..."

Jim looked up, affronted. "When have I ever drawn my weapon in the Roadhouse?"

Bernie grinned. "Well, there was that time those two pipeliners showed up on the Alyeska bulldozer...."

Jim was indignant. "What was that, six years ago? Seven?" He reflected. "Besides, that wasn't my sidearm, it was his."

"Whatever." Bernie polished the bar, did he but know it, in almost the exact same massaging movement Bill Billington was lavishing on her own bar six hundred miles south-southwest. Some things are universal. "Hear Kate's out of town."

Jim toyed with the ice in his glass. "Yeah. Got a job."

Bernie grunted. "Can you say where?"

"Rather not." He'd rather not think about it, come to that. With every day that passed, Liam Campbell grew more handsome and more charming in his memory, and Jim wasn't even gay.

"You lonely?" Jim looked up to see a smile curling the corners of Bernie's mouth. "There's a new girl out at—"

"I'm fine," Jim said, with probably a little more emphasis than necessary. "What do you hear from out the mine?"

Bernie shrugged. "Same old. They keep drilling and the mine keeps getting bigger, and meantime the price of gold keeps going up. Looks like it's here to stay." He raised his head to look around the barnlike room that under his stewardship had hosted belly dancers, Big Bumpers, Baptist congregations, quilting circles, Kanuyaq 300 Trail Committee meetings, at least one shoot-out with live ammunition, and enough just plain elbow benders to turn a healthy profit. The Suulutaq miners hadn't changed the ambience all that much, although his women customers from twenty to fifty had never been so swamped with attention. He was pretty sure a couple of them were selling it in one of his cabins out back, one throw at a time. Well, what the hell. Lots of goodwill and maybe one small thrill, wasn't that how the song went? And everyone stopped in for a drink afterwards. "It hasn't been bad for business, that I can tell you."

Jim grunted. "Mine, either." He drank. "Anybody from the mine management side of things drop in? Truax? Like that?"

Bernie stopped massaging the bar. "I figured this was more than a social call. What specifically is it you're after, Jim?"

Jim examined the bottom of his glass, avoiding Bernie's eyes. "I heard they've been acquiring some new investors."

"Yeah?"

Jim nodded.

"Well, I woulda thought they already had all the investment money they needed," Bernie said, "but that's a decision way above my pay grade." At Jim's look he said, "Sure, I bought some Global Harvest stock. You didn't?"

Jim shook his head.

"Well, you should. For one thing, you'd get an annual report, which would answer a lot of questions."

Jim thought of the list of securities that had come with his portion of his father's estate. He wondered if he, too, would now be receiving annual reports. The prospect was depressing.

"In fact," Bernie said, watching him, "I just got the latest GHRI annual report in the mail."

"You did?" Jim sat up. "Could I take a look?"

The afternoon was taken up with a break-in at Camp Teddy's ("It's not the theft, Jim," a mightily pissed Ruthe Bauman told him, "I can replace what's stolen. It's the damages. Who rips a toilet out of the wall?"), a late lunch of moose tongue sandwiches at Bobby and Dinah's, a show-and-tell at the end of Career Day at Niniltna High, and a domestic dispute between Alma and Derendy Shugak, which resulted in the arrest of her ex-husband for Assault 2, Assault 3, Assault 4, and Criminal Mischief 3. Jim deposited Derendy in a cell at the post and left Alma at the Grosdidier brothers' clinic.

He was halfway home and looking forward to dinner ready when he walked in the door—it was Johnny's turn to cook—when a phone call diverted him back to Niniltna and a report of vandalism at the high school. It wasn't anything that hadn't happened a hundred times before the introduction of cell phones into the Park, that hadn't been previously handled capably by its principal every single one of those times. Jim wrote up a report and drove home thinking with longing of those halcyon cell-free days—Jesus, were they only a month ago?

He thought about calling Kate, but she'd been up pretty late the night before and he really didn't want to wake her up in the middle of her first real sleep since she'd got to Newenham.

News of the partnership between Erland Bannister and Axenia Shugak Mathisen could always wait.

17

JANUARY 20

Newenham

Six hundred miles to the south-southwest, Liam Campbell was up all night dealing with the Evelyn Grant shooting. She was in the local hospital, which was the regional hospital for Southwest Alaska so the care was of a pretty sophisticated standard for the Bush. The opinion of the doctor on call that evening was that the prognosis was good and that so long as Evelyn woke up soon, there should be no fears for her eventual full recovery. The bullet had by some miracle ricocheted off her eleventh floating rib through the intercostal space between the eleventh and twelfth floating ribs and lodged just under the skin on her lower back. "Bizarre things bullets do inside bodies," the doc said. He sounded admiring.

"You'll let me know as soon as she wakes up?"

"I will," Doc Stanford replied. "Is it true that Gabe McGuire was the one who found her?"

Liam hadn't mentioned Gabe's presence at the scene to anyone, and he was dead certain Kate hadn't said anything to anyone at all. The Bush telegraph never ceased to amaze him with its speed and accuracy.

The doc waved a hand. "All I meant was, good work on his

part, applying consistent, firm pressure to the wound until Joe got there."

"Yeah," Liam said, "good work."

"I haven't met him yet," the doc said a little wistfully. "Hear he's a good guy."

"Yeah," Liam said, "a good guy."

"I hear he bought a lodge on one of the Four Lakes."

"Yeah," Liam said, "on one of the lakes."

"My sister would love an autographed picture," the doc said. "For that matter, so would my mother."

And so would the doc (not for nothing was Liam an experienced law enforcement officer). "Yeah," Liam said, "I'll pass that on. You got the round?"

The doc handed over the spent, squashed piece of metal in a small ziplock bag. Liam had the doc sign and date the bag, and then he extricated himself from the clutches of Gabe McGuire's newest adoring fan and went to the waiting room.

As he approached the door, he heard a low voice muttering in furious tones. He slowed his steps. "What does it matter why she was there, or how late it was? Someone attacked her, Mom, someone shot her!"

"Liam said—"

"Liam said! Jesus, Mom, you can't trust anything he says! He was sent here as punishment for screwing up on the job. They always transfer the deadbeats to Newenham, the worst teachers, the worst doctors, the worst cops, it's always been that way—"

"That's enough, Oren." Tina's voice sounded tired, as if she had been remonstrating with her son for a lot longer than the time they'd spent in the waiting room.

It wasn't enough for Oren. "Okay, fine, Mom, I know you think the sun shines out of his ass. Think about this instead, then: How much is Evelyn's little trip to the hospital going to cost us? Will we be able to pay for it after you sell off or give away everything Dad built?"

Oren's question had the sound of something having been said before, many times.

Tina's voice was sharper this time. "We're not going to go hungry, Oren."

"Right, Mom, and who was it who just rented the apartment over the garage because we couldn't pay this month's light bill because you refuse to touch any money in the Eagle Air bank account?"

Tina didn't answer.

Oren lowered his voice to where Liam had to strain to hear it. "You have to drop this ridiculous idea of paying back everyone Dad ripped off, Mom. He screwed them, okay, no question there, but he's dead, and we're alive."

This was followed by silence.

Over his shoulder Liam said in a voice meant to carry, "Yeah, Doc, I'll let you know." Louise Prewett, a heavyset nurse's aide in her fifties, dressed in a flowered pink uniform, appeared at that unfortunate moment, looked from him to the empty corridor, and took a wide detour around him.

Liam couldn't wait for that story to make the rounds. He walked into the waiting room. Tina and Oren were sitting in chairs across a low table, Oren slumped and sulking, Tina looking as tired as she sounded and about twenty years older than the last time Liam had seen her. First Irene, then Finn, now Evelyn. The way Tina looked, if she were going to survive, Evelyn had to.

"Tina," he said. "Oren. Is there anything more I can do?"

"Sit with me for a bit, Liam, if you would," Tina said.

Liam sat in a chair equidistant from both Tina and Oren.

He wasn't about to take sides, not even in body language. An interested observer, on the other hand, might pick up a clue or two as to what was going on between mother and son, and if it had anything to do with what had gone down at Eagle Air earlier this morning.

"Liam," Tina said, "what you said before. How you think Evelyn got hurt."

Oren's snort of disgust was badly concealed. He stood up. "I'm going to get some coffee, if there is such a thing in this bad excuse for a real hospital."

Tina closed her eyes briefly when Oren stamped out.

Liam waited. Without opening her eyes Tina said, "You said before that you thought it was an accident. That it looked like Evelyn and whoever it was struggled over the gun and that it just went off. That it was probably one of the partiers from last night's blowout who drove out to Chinook and broke into the office."

"Well," Liam said, very carefully indeed, "as you know, Gabe McGuire heard shouting." McGuire hadn't, but absent the presence of Kate Shugak, this was their all new and improved story and they were sticking to it for now. "He heard what he thought was a struggle, followed by a shot, several shots. The weapon was one of Finn's, hanging right there on the wall for anyone to grab. It certainly sounds like it might have been an accident."

"But it was a man."

"Yes." One point upon which Liam felt he need not quibble.

She opened her eyes. "And you still have no idea who it might have been?"

Liam shook his head. "There has been too much traffic between here and the base to tell which vehicle might have been the one he was driving. He was driving away by the time

Gabe got downstairs. And when Gabe saw Evelyn..."

"Yes." She leaned forward to touch his arm. "When you see Gabe again, please tell him how very grateful I am for his actions. Dr. Stanford said he saved Evelyn's life."

There were tears in her eyes, and the ghosts of Irene and Finn were very much present in the room. "I will," he said, although he wouldn't, because Gabe might rip his head off and stuff it up his own ass if he did. And he wouldn't be able to find it in himself to blame Gabe much, either. "Tina, now isn't the time, I know, but when you get around to it, you might want to lock up all those guns Finn had on display in the office. At the very least, you should unload them."

There was a flare of emotion in her eyes that he couldn't quite read. "I'm going to throw the whole boiling lot of them into the Nushugak."

There was a savage undertone to her voice that he'd never heard from Tina Grant before. "Some of them might be valuable," he said, and felt that it was a weak response.

"I don't care," she said. "I wouldn't touch a dime that was associated with those guns."

Which didn't exactly accord with the picture forming of Tina Grant hurting for money.

Liam went from the hospital to the post, where he wrote up an incident report that owed a great deal to years of experience and a fertile imagination, and prayed no one would ever know. He filed Gabe's statement and added a note that it had been taken at the scene and in what circumstances. Gabe had displayed an unexpected talent for screenwriting, and it had taken some persuading to tone down the "rapid rasps" of Evelyn's breathing and the "glutenous carmine" of her blood, not to mention the "acrid smell of spent powder" and "the immediate arrival on the scene of Newenham's finest."

Although Liam did wonder just how much Gabe was trying it on, as a way of exacting a little revenge.

He got home just in time to kiss Wy good-bye on her way to work, when the phone rang. It was Tim, calling from Anchorage, to say hello and ask for money. Which was of course immediately promised to him.

"Sucker," Liam said, holding her from behind, all the better to nuzzle her neck.

"I swear, it's in the job description of kids in school, they have to call home for money once a week," Wy said, hanging up.

"How is he?" Liam said, still nuzzling.

Wy sighed, tilting her head to give Liam better access. "Fine. I heard a girl's voice in the background."

"God help him." With even more feeling he added, "God help us."

"He doesn't have a lot of luck in the sweetheart department, true."

Liam picked her up and turned her around and sat her on the counter. He smiled down into her eyes, parting her legs so he could step between them. "Fortunately, I do."

He loved the kid, he really did, but this kind of seduction was a lot easier with him three hundred miles away. He had a secret, traitorous thought that Tim would have to repeat some subject so he'd have to stay longer, and then Wy slid her hands into his hair and he forgot Tim's very existence.

"The door is unlocked," she said when he pulled her T-shirt out of her jeans and slid his hand up to the catch of her bra. Her breasts were warm silken weights in his palms.

"Liiiiiiaaaaaaaaaam," she said when he bent his head to suckle nipples already hard through the fabric of her shirt.

"The curtains are open," she said, her head falling back

when his hands came around to cup her ass and snug his erection into the sweet spot between her legs.

“So we’ll make anybody watching reeeaally jealous,” he said in a thick voice.

“I have to get to work,” she said weakly, when he reached for the snap of her jeans.

“And you will,” he said. “Later.”

18

JANUARY 20

Newenham

KATE WOKE ALONE, NOT that there was room in that narrow twin for anyone else but her. She had become unaccustomed to sleeping alone for any length of time, and it was next to impossible not to wake up and feel for the warm body next to her. Jim was always remarkably accommodating in the matter of morning wood, too. Whether he knew who was reaching for it or not.

An image of Gabe McGuire's bare chest slid before her closed eyes.

With an oath, she sat up, swinging her legs over the side, and yelped when her feet touched the cold floor. Mutt, happily chasing rabbits in her sleep, jumped up and barked and growled in four different directions at once.

"Sorry, girl." Kate pulled on socks and let an indignant Mutt outside.

Moses Alakuyak was standing on the stairs.

"No," Kate said, even as he pushed past her into the room.

"Yeah," he said, "this'll have to do, we don't want to walk in on the kids this morning," and started shoving all the furniture against the walls. When he'd redecorated to his satisfaction, he went into the bathroom and came out in his ninja outfit. "You know he didn't do it, right?"

"I don't know what the hell you're talking about." Maybe it came out more forcefully than she had intended.

The Old Nick ninja snorted. "On your feet, girl."

No doubt about it, he sounded more like Old Sam every time she saw him.

Ninety minutes later he went into the bathroom and came out in his civilian clothes. Kate was sitting on the bed, head hanging, sweat dripping from her nose, the muscles of her thighs vibrating beneath her elbows. "I thought you'd be in better shape than this," he said.

She managed to raise her head long enough to give him a killing glare.

The little son of a bitch laughed all the way down the stairs when he left.

"How do I keep letting him do this to me?" she asked the room. The room wisely returned no answer. Kate was no pushover, but Moses Alakuyak was another order of magnitude of tyranny entirely, and she and the room both knew it.

Meantime, the sweat had dried on her body and she realized how cold it was in the apartment. The garage beneath was unheated, while the apartment itself had electric radiators. Her landlady was picking up all utilities, it was true, but Kate was enough of an Alaskan to be appalled at the potential heating bill to leave them on low overnight. She turned them up pretty quick now, though, and went to stand beneath some hot water while the apartment heated up.

Dry and dressed, she was warmer but no less horny. The only marginally effective substitute for horniness was food, preferably good food. The kitchen had one frying pan and one saucepan, but no toaster. She couldn't find a spatula for love or money. There was one fork, four spoons, and a table knife. Fortunately Kate had her Swiss Army knife, which amazingly she'd remembered to put in her checked luggage when she'd had to go through TSA in Anchorage on the way to St. Paul. There was one plate, three glasses, and one chipped ceramic mug with the handle broken off.

She'd bought some groceries on the way back from Eagle Air yesterday afternoon, including eggs, sausage, and a rustic loaf. She poured a little oil into the frying pan set on high heat, and when it began to smoke tossed in a piece of bread sliced into cubes. She put water on to boil in the saucepan, and fit the single-cup plastic coffee filter she'd bought the day before with a folded paper towel and filled it with coffee, the real stuff this time, her first purchase the day before. When the bread was brown and crisp, she crumbled in some sausage, and when it was browned, she poured in two eggs beaten in one of the glasses. Salt and pepper, and a handleless mug of coffee, liberally dosed with half and half, she took her breakfast to the postage stamp sized table in the corner overlooking the river and sat down to tuck in. Done in short order—this was the hungriest job she'd ever worked—she pushed the plate back and crossed her legs on the table to sip her coffee.

It was another gloriously clear day. There had to be a honking big high pressure system hanging over Bristol Bay that hadn't moved an isobar in any direction in the last twenty-four hours. Okay by her. Made an investigation all that much easier if she didn't have to fight the weather, too. Of course, there was indubitably a low building up its own pressure in back of that high that would bring in one hell of a blow when it finally pushed the high out of the way. "Let's be gone by then," she said.

There was an admonitory yip from the other side of the door, and she went to let Mutt in. She'd bought food for Mutt the day before as well, at which Mutt turned up her nose. Kate took a closer look and saw a suspicious bit of white fur caught in Mutt's teeth. She only hoped it was an arctic hare and not someone's cat.

It was an hour before the library opened. She got out her copy of *Team of Rivals* and opened it where she'd left off reading it in the Park, page 581. Thus far, despite unwitting and often deliberate provocation on the part of each and every member of his cabinet, Lincoln had resisted blowing up at anyone except for the army meteorologist. Everybody always got mad at the weather guy. She read twenty pages and quit, because she was on the wrong side of the middle of this book. Lincoln was just too good a guy and she wasn't in any hurry to get to Ford's Theater.

Under the phone book was a sales flyer for the local gear shop. A Ruger nine-millimeter automatic for $350. A Taurus Judge Magnum for $470. At least the Ruger was made in the U.S., but it wasn't like you could take either handgun hunting and bring home anything to eat. Her eyes dropped to the bottom of the page. A Honda thousand-watt generator, good for ten hours on a gallon of gas, nine hundred dollars. It was the size of a suitcase, and even had a handle. She was about to tear out the ad when she noticed the date was May of the previous year.

She washed the dishes and called Campbell at the post. He sounded very mellow this morning. "How's Evelyn Grant?" Kate said.

Campbell switched gears from mellow to business. "Conscious."

"And talking?"

"Says she can't remember anything at all during the time we most need her to."

"Really," Kate said. "She say why she was there?"

"Not very convincingly, she says she remembered some unspecified paperwork of her father's that she needed. Can't remember much about that, either."

"She say why she waited until four in the morning to come looking for it?"

"No."

"So," Kate said, drawing out the word, "not your star witness in the case of the State of Alaska versus John Doe, in the little matter of aggravated assault, firearm involved."

"Not at the moment." He paused. "I heard a bit of a hoohaw between Tina and Oren in the hospital waiting room, before they saw me coming. Oren's pissed at Tina over money."

"Put that together with the argument I saw between Oren and Evelyn," Kate said. "My professional estimation would be that that was mostly Oren, too, and my professional estimation of his character would I'd guess match yours. He has all the personal charm of a dung beetle. To be fair, though, we have to remember that in the space of, what, two months, Tina and Oren have lost a daughter and a sister and a husband and a father, and last night they almost lost another daughter and another sister." She touched the scar on her throat. "No one ever shows to advantage after that kind of personal trauma."

"Yeah."

Campbell didn't sound convinced, and he didn't sound happy. Kate had heard that exact same tone in Jim's voice when he knew he was going to have to bust someone he liked, or maybe just someone he knew. Price you paid when you policed a small community. Propinquity was hell on a law enforcement officer. One of the reasons why the divorce rate was so high in the profession.

And Campbell didn't tell Kate to stand down, either.

The Newenham Public Library was laboring beneath the same kinds of budget cuts as starving libraries all over the nation, to the point that they'd cut back their hours to thirty a week. It was a pretty draconian measure for a Bush Alaska institution that, quite apart from being the sole-source provider of reading and reference material for three hundred miles, provided a refuge for residents who just wanted to get out of the house occasionally. If the library closed entirely, nondrinkers would fall back on the school gym, while everyone else would be at Bill's. Sergeant Campbell's workload would rise accordingly, which wouldn't make him happy.

The librarian was Jeannie Penney, whom Tina Grant had introduced to Kate two days before. Kate was not the first library patron that morning, and was also less preoccupied with casing the library for a late-night burglary, so she paused to take a little time to run a mental make on Tina Grant's best friend.

Jeannie Penney was a vibrant sixty-something who looked a lithe, well-packaged forty. She had long straight blond hair all the way down to her ass, electric blue eyes peeping shrewdly out from behind artfully tousled bangs, and skin like cream velvet. She dressed plainly, in pressed jeans and a snug cream-colored turtleneck, and wore the simple clothes better than anyone Kate had ever met. She moved rapidly around her one-room-in-a-strip-mall domain, scooping up books discarded by patrons and reshelving them in one continuous graceful movement, checking out a copy of David Wiesner's *Tuesday* to a four-year-old who could barely see over the edge of her desk, his amused mother allowing him to do it himself, after which she helped a high school student find Vic Fischer's book on the Alaska constitutional convention for a term paper.

What was on the shelves looked ready-made for a rural Alaskan community. A full bookshelf was given over to Chilton manuals, another entire shelf was packed with books about guns, including *Shooter's Bible*s that went back twenty years, and one entire aisle was dedicated to handcrafts and DIY. The fiction section consisted mostly of popular fiction going back to Nevil Shute and Georgette Heyer and forward to Stephen King and Nora Roberts, all of them looking well thumbed.

"Sure we have a computer," Jeannie said, tossing her hair back like a filly who was ready for the race. "Back in the corner there, see? Internet access? Of course! The city council and I had words about it, but we've got it." The steel behind her smile was plain for anyone with the wit to see it. "And on a one-meg DSL line, too, none of this dial-up nonsense."

Jeannie told Mutt she could wait outside, and Mutt went back outside and waited. Jeannie demanded Kate's driver's license and got it. "I will hold this hostage until you log off. Sign here." One well-manicured finger pointed at a register, and Kate signed obediently. "You get half an hour. After that, if no one is waiting, you can have another half an hour."

"Thank you," Kate said, as it seemed like that was all she was going to be allowed to say. Jeannie Penney gave her a bright smile displaying perfect teeth and turned to her next patrons, an old Yupik man and his granddaughter who wanted help accessing the National Archives because he didn't have a birth certificate and those—here was spoken a terrible-sounding word in Yupik—people in Social Security wouldn't believe he had been born in his own village. Jeannie had the phone number of the right person to call at her fingertips and she dialed it for them then and there.

Kate admired efficiency in any endeavor and she had a soft spot for librarians and teachers anyway. She was, however, a little breathless as she made for the computer in the corner and logged on with the password Jeannie had given her. When she opened the cap on the thumb drive she saw that it had 256 gigabytes of memory, which seemed like a lot, until she plugged it in and a folder marked, originally, "Finn's Notes" popped up. There was no demand for a password. She crossed mental fingers and clicked on it. It opened.

The only security she had encountered thus far in Newenham was the password-protected laptop on Tina Grant's desk. It made her wonder what was on it.

The files on the thumb drive were folders, numbered and listed chronologically, the most recent items saved listed first. The folders held mostly Word documents, but there were also some audio files and the most recently saved folder contained a video file dated October of the previous fall. She found the volume control on the computer and turned it down as far as possible before hunching over the computer and clicking PLAY.

Ten minutes later she sat back and blew a long, silent whistle.

The video's audio quality was poor and the camerawork left a great deal to be desired, but when you got past those you were left with unmistakably court-worthy evidence of an Alaskan big game guide not only flying and shooting the same day, but violating the wanton waste law when he and his client took only the trophy rack, leaving the moose carcass to rot. The camera even managed to capture the tail numbers on the Beaver sitting on a lake in the background.

Kate had seen videos like this before, shot by undercover Fish and Game agents on illegal hunts. Shortly thereafter the guide would show up in court, and upon conviction to be stripped of license, airplane, a large chunk of change, and considerable free time. And they were always convicted. Never mind voir dire, Alaska juries always had at least one member who hunted for personal use who had stumbled over one of those carcasses themselves.

Kate got online and Googled the guide's name, Leon Coopchiak. It didn't pop up in any court cases, federal or state. It did find a website on AlaskaHuntingGuidesDirectory.com, Jackknife Pass Outfitters, based in Newenham, where he was listed as one of three guides. It wasn't a very sophisticated site, one page with a photograph of grizzly bears fishing for salmon in a small waterfall, with a two-button menu bar, RESERVATIONS and CONTACT US. Kate clicked on RESERVATIONS, and her eyebrows twitched together when the website for Eagle Air, Inc., Newenham, Alaska, popped up.

This was a much ritzier, multi-page website, with a gallery of photographs, a page of videos, a choice of lodge or camping adventures, full outfitting ("We carry only the highest-rated camping, hunting, and fishing equipment"), a list of the different trips offered ("You only shoot with a camera? We have nature tours from a day to a week, guaranteed to put you nose to nose with Alaskan wildlife from grizzly bears fishing for salmon to bull moose in rut to migrating caribou herds twenty-five thousand strong!") and a picture of the chef ("The best gourmet camp food you will ever eat!").

Kate had spent most of her life avoiding a nose-to-nose confrontation with any of the above, but one man's meat. She backed out of the Eagle Air website to Jackknife Pass Outfitters and clicked on CONTACT US. The website for Eagle Air, Inc., Newenham, Alaska, appeared again.

She felt someone hovering behind her, and turned to look.

A dark-haired man of medium height stood in front of the magazine shelf, nose in a copy of *Ms.* magazine. My, wasn't he evolved.

She turned back to the computer. So Finn Grant had video evidence of an Alaska big game guide committing two of the highest penalty offenses you can commit as a hunter, either one of which was guaranteed to lose a guide his license. And the website of the guide caught committing these crimes on camera was now automatically forwarded to the Eagle Air website.

Kate clicked on the folder again and counted.

There were eleven separate files.

Campbell's voice echoed in her ears. *He strong-armed a lot of the businesses he bought out. Bought up their debt and foreclosed. Bought the buildings they were doing their business out of and raised the rent on them, or just booted them out. Bought out their competitors and lowered prices to drive them out of business.*

The dates on the documents went back more than fifteen years, so this was not an activity Grant had begun recently. She clicked through the files, one at a time, with a steadily increasing feeling of incredulity, and disgust. Infidelity, wife abuse, child abuse, prostitution, driving while drunk, flying while drunk, same flying and shooting, cheating on taxes federal, state, borough, and local, fishing inside the markers, fishing in a closed area, and fishing with illegal gear. Grant even had evidence of the Newenham postmaster refusing to give someone their mail because that someone refused to attend the postmaster's church. It was the only other video file in the folder. It looked like Grant had worn a hidden camera when he went in to pick up his mail.

Interfering with the mail was a federal offense, for which you could do federal time. Kate wondered what Grant had gotten from the postmaster in question in return for keeping quiet about it.

Most of the documents had been created by Grant, but every instance had corresponding evidence, a date, a place, a time, copies of documents and faxes, sometimes a statement by a corroborating witness. In the case of the post office video, there were half a dozen witnesses, and most of them had signed statements. Kate wondered what they had received in return. Finn Grant looked to her like a quid pro quo kinda guy.

There was nothing nastier, nothing dirtier, nothing more soul destroying than blackmail. She longed violently for a shower, a hot, scouring shower, preferably with a Clorox rinse. She wanted to return to the apartment, pack up her gear, and even if she had to walk to the airport get on the first plane going anywhere, just away from here.

Being tossed into the chest freezer now seemed more like a reasonable reaction to outrageous provocation than personal assault. Any one of Grant's victims would be frantic to recover the evidence Grant had held over their heads all these years. They would start on the outbuildings, the shop, the garage apartment. She made a mental note to ask Campbell if there had been any reports of break-ins at Grant's house, Grant's Newenham hangar, or out at the Eagle Air base.

Well. Other than the one of which he had personal evidence right at the scene. Currently occupying a bed in the Newenham hospital.

She glanced at the clock on the wall and went grimly to work. Each folder was dedicated to one person. There was no indication as to how Finn Grant had started his little hobby, just a steady accumulation of information over the years. An item in a tax cheat's folder read

Last night at Bill's WW said he hadn't paid income taxes in twenty years. Terry Ballard said today that WW's been high boat for herring spotting the last three years. Have to find out how much that comes to. Ten percent of that, plus interest and penalties, is a pretty good stick. Might even be worth turning WW in myself.

A note in an adulterer's folder read

Got in from Jackknife late last night, crashed at the hangar, on the way home this morning saw Chris Bevens backing out of Tasha Anayuk's driveway. Think Chris' wife Annika is the one with the money, have to check.

Another note read

Saw Father Tom with Sergei Watson's little boy. Wasn't the archbishop at that Chamber of Commerce meeting in Anchorage in June?

By the time she got to the last folder she wanted to throw up. When she clicked on it and saw the name there, she was sure she was going to.

Jeannie had granted her a stay when her first thirty minutes were up, but half an hour later she looked over her shoulder at the librarian's desk and Jeannie spread her hands and mouthed *Sorry* and nodded at a man pretending to read a newspaper. It was the same man she'd seen earlier reading *Ms*. His left hand was missing the top half of its middle finger. Another fisherman who hadn't moved fast enough to get his hand off a running line between a winch and his cork line.

She wasn't sorry to close out the folder and pull the thumb

drive. She stuck it in her pocket and hoped it didn't smell. When she stood up, the man with the newspaper hustled over and elbowed her aside to get in front of the computer before anyone else could.

The library had filled up over the past hour. All the seats at the two tables were filled and there was someone browsing at each of the six bookshelves. The library had been arranged so that anyone sitting at the desk could see straight down the rows of shelves. Kate was pretty sure she knew who had made certain of that. Jeannie Penney was seated at her desk and Kate stopped on her way out to thank her for the extra half hour.

Jeannie waved her off. "It's there to be used. Some people—" She cast a dark blue look at the man who had taken Kate's place. "—think they can park on it all day, so I had to make rules so everyone would get a chance."

"Is there a fee?" Kate said. "I'm happy to pay it."

"This is a public library," Jeannie said firmly, "and by definition is a free service for all citizens." She grinned and shoved forward a large glass jar with a punctured plastic lid, half full of bills and coins. "Far be it from us to discourage anyone from supporting their local public library, however." She watched with approval as Kate stuffed a five-dollar bill into the jar.

"How long have you lived in Newenham?" Kate said on impulse.

"Honey, I was born here."

"You're local?" Kate hadn't meant to sound so startled, and Jeannie flashed an appreciative smile.

"You think I'm a little too high end for a Newenham librarian? Honey, that's so nice of you." Jeannie twinkled. If Kate had been a man, she would have gone down like ninepins. "My parents were BIA teachers. I grew up hating every living thing in this town and in the entire state, too. I married young and well, a high boater from Anacortes, and moved us Outside first chance I got. We were happy there for over thirty years. And then my children grew up and moved out, and he died and left me more than enough money to spend every winter in Hawaii, so I started looking around for something useful to do with myself." She shook her head. "Don't ask me how I ended up back here, because I don't know myself. It is not my favorite place in the world, but someone has to look out for these people. They were going to let the library close, can you imagine?" She cocked her head. "You?"

For the first time on this job, Kate was sorry she had to lie. "Kate Saracoff. I'm not from around here."

Jeannie laughed. "Honey, I'd know you if you were." She looked expectant.

"Anchorage," Kate said, "at one time, anyway. I got to Newenham by way of a man." It had worked before.

Jeannie looked wise. "And you wouldn't be the first to do so. You got a job yet?"

Kate nodded. "Waiting tables at Bill's."

Jeannie nodded approvingly. "Bill's a good person, she'll look out for you." She added, "So long as you can abide that drunk shaman she's landed herself with. Anyone who would invite drinking and prognostication into their lives in one package must have some kind of death wish."

"Prognostication?" Kate said.

Jeannie rolled her eyes. "He's supposed to be some kind of seer."

"Seer?"

"You know, predict the future, or know if you're telling lies, or talk to the dead." Jeannie rolled her eyes again. "Personally, I think it's the box checked 'None of the above,' but the locals, especially the Yupik locals, think he's the real deal."

"He kidnapped me my first morning and made me do something he called form."

Jeannie's eyes sharpened. "Really. Interesting."

"Why?"

"They say the last time he did that was when Liam Campbell got here."

"Wow," Kate said, making a joke out of it or trying to, "I'm so special."

You know he didn't do it, right? Who didn't do what? Finn Grant didn't blackmail all those people? Didn't kill himself in his own airplane? Finn Grant's death was why she was in Newenham, why Liam Campbell had asked her to come, he was the only *he* Moses could mean.

"You going back to the apartment?" When Kate nodded, Jeannie said, "Oh good, then you can drop these off at Tina's," and handed her a couple of books, the latest by Laurie King and T. Jefferson Parker and a reprint of a Manning Coles novel Kate herself was interested to see. "She's a huge crime fiction fan, is our Tina," Jeannie said. "To tell the truth, which I shouldn't and almost never do, I always bump Tina up to the top of the waiting list when a new Laurie King comes in." She looked down at her desk and said in a less audible voice, "She has had little enough joy in her life, poor thing."

"She just lost her husband," Kate said, testing.

"No big loss, there," Jeannie said. "But she lost her daughter, too, last year."

"The photograph of the soldier I saw in her hallway."

Jeannie nodded, still looking at her desk.

"She's not having her best year," Kate said.

Jeannie started to say something, and stopped. Kate

decided to push a little. "I flew in from Togiak," she said. "We stopped at Eagle Air on the way. It was her husband's, right? I wondered why..."

Jeannie looked up, the friendliness in her eyes on the wane. "Wondered why what?"

Kate reminded herself that she was on the job. "Tina seemed glad to get my rent in cash. And then she rented me her ATV, for cash. It just—" She shrugged. "—seemed odd for the owner of a ritzy operation like Eagle Air to act broke."

Jeannie's eyes narrowed, and Kate knew immediately that she had asked one question too many. All confidences were at an end.

At least for the moment. Jeannie Penney seemed like a source worth cultivating.

19

JANUARY 20

The Park

"You look like hell," Johnny said.

Jim stared morosely into his coffee cup. "Like to see what you would look like after a night like I've had."

"I heard you come in," Johnny said, flipping a slice of French toast. "What was it, 4 A.M.?"

"More like three."

"What was it this time? Or should I say, who?"

Jim drank coffee. "Darryl Kvasnikof got high and broke into his parents' house."

Johnny was annoyingly blasé. "That all? Darryl finally draw down on his dad?"

"If that had been all, I would have been home a lot earlier," Jim said.

Johnny either did not notice or ignored Jim's testiness. "So what else was going on while I was getting my eight hours of uninterrupted sleep?"

Jim made a rhetorical suggestion as to what Johnny could do with his eight hours of uninterrupted sleep. Johnny laughed. "He broke in with a chain saw."

"Oh."

"And then he resisted arrest."

"Uh-oh."

"And then after I took him in he busted out the cell light, pissed on the floors, took a dump and smeared his shit on the walls, and lit the cot on fire."

"Wow," Johnny said, awed.

"I understand him being mad at his dad, but it would have been nice if he'd managed to exercise his rage on his dad's house instead of my post."

"Probably knew you wouldn't shoot him."

"And none of which I would have known about until this morning if I'd been able to come straight home after I jugged him."

"Why weren't you able to?"

It wasn't as if Johnny wouldn't hear all about it at school. "There was a rape last month, at a Christmas party. The girl's underage and there was more than one guy involved. Little fuckers took pictures with their cell phones and put them online, and one of the girl's friends saw them and told her parents, who finally told the vic's parents last night. The vic didn't want to come forward. It took her parents until midnight to convince her. Or just about the time I was coming home from jugging the Darrylinator."

"Jesus," Johnny said, shaken.

Jim raised his head from his hands. "You hear something? Did Van?"

Johnny shook his head, looking a little green around the gills. "Nobody ever tells us anything. They know I live with Kate, and that you do, too, and that Van and I are, you know."

A few moments later, a plate loaded with thick French toast and spicy moose sausage patties appeared in front of Jim, along with a jug of real maple syrup.

Food is love. And he was starving. He picked up his fork and dug in.

Johnny sat down with his own plate. He knew better than to ask the victim's name, but there was something he had to know. "Tell me it wasn't guys at the school."

Niniltna Public School, grades kindergarten through high school, had a student population of less than eighty. Jim appreciated Johnny's apprehension. "All three were Suulutaq miners, is the bad news. The worse news is two of them are locals. And no, none of them were your classmates."

By contractual agreement, the Suulutaq Mine was required at least in the early exploratory stages to have Alaska residents as 50 percent of their employees, and they were further required to recruit first from the Park. Most of the locals employed at the Suulutaq were earning more money in a month than they had in any previous year of their lives. The younger they were, the less wisely they spent it. "Alcohol involved?"

"When isn't it."

"Shit," Johnny said, face pulling into a scowl. "I don't get that. Sex by force. I just—" He shrugged, baffled. "Drunk or sober, high or straight, I just don't see the attraction."

"It's not the sex, per se, it's the power."

"I know that. I still don't get it."

"I hope you never do," Jim said. "The worst news is, one of them's her cousin. Or second cousin. Something like that, a family relative, anyway. Somebody she thought she could trust when he invited her to a party. Turned out she was the party."

"How is she?"

"As of last night? Beginning to get really, really angry."

"No wonder you're fried." Johnny stared down at his plate, his appetite gone. "You should have stayed in town."

Jim would rather have been hanged, drawn, and quartered than admit that he wanted to be home in the bed he shared with Kate, whether Kate was in it with him or not, rather than in his crash pad bed at Auntie Vi's. "Yeah. After I rounded up the perps and, uh, restrained Darryl and got him and his cell cleaned up, I was on autopilot. Next thing I knew I was home."

"You should have slept in."

"Can't. Things to do, places to go." He gave a close approximation of the old shark's grin. "People to see."

"Right." They finished their breakfast but their hearts weren't in it.

Suited up to head out, Jim paused. "Hey."

Johnny looked up from stuffing his daypack. Jim thought he saw a box of condoms disappear inside but he didn't say so, remembering all too well age seventeen. "How pissed off will Kate be if I hold off telling her something until she gets back? Something not good, something she's going to want to know, but something she most likely can't do anything about?"

Johnny frowned down at his pack, relieved that Jim had missed the condoms and that this wasn't going to be one of those conversations. "Is it something that in and of itself will piss her off?"

"On a scale of mild simmer to full boil?" Jim sighed. "We're talking Mt. Redoubt on a five-eruption day."

Johnny was impressed. "We could sell tickets."

"We could, although I'd rather be selling them from Beta Centauri. I haven't told her yet. Obviously."

"Obviously," Johnny said. "Wanna tell me?"

"No."

Johnny thought about it. "If you tell her now, while she's

on a case, she'll be pissed off at the situation and pissed off she can't do anything about it, and just generally pissed off at the messenger. That'd be you. If you wait to tell her when she gets home, she'll only be pissed off at the situation, pissed off she can't do anything about it, and pissed off at you for not telling her."

Jim sighed again. "So she's pissed off whether I tell her or not."

"Good luck with that," Johnny said.

Jim flipped him off and left.

• • •

When he got to town he continued past the trooper post to the Niniltna Native Association building. Annie Mike walked to work every day, come rain or whiteout, so he couldn't tell if she was at work yet. He went inside, where he found Phyllis Lestinkof holding down the front desk. Phyllis looked neat and crisp in blue slacks and a white long-sleeved shirt open at the throat to display a tiny sparkling pendant on a nearly nonexistent chain, with matching earrings cupped inside a stylish haircut. "Hey, Phyllis," he said. "Looking good."

She gave him an efficient nod and an impersonal smile. "How may I help you, Sergeant Chopin?"

"I'd like to talk to Annie Mike, if she can spare a moment," he said. He could do formal when the occasion warranted, and evidently Phyllis had decided her first week on the job did.

"I'll see if she's in," Phyllis said, and waited pointedly until he wandered over to the other side of the lobby.

Annie was in and she would see him. Although he knew the way perfectly well, Phyllis escorted him to Annie's door, knocked in a restrained fashion, waited to be bidden to enter, and announced him before she'd let him inside.

The door closed behind him with a discreet click and he said, "I feel like I was just ushered into the Oval Office."

"Good," Annie said. "About time we showed a little professionalism around here."

It was a nice office, eggshell paint on the walls, cherrywood furniture, a seating area, a console with a large framed print of the Niniltna Native Association logo hung above it. The wall-to-wall carpeting was an institutional gray but there was a nice area rug on top of it, and plants were thriving in the corners and on the desk.

Behind it sat the new-minted chair of the Niniltna Native Association. She was still Annie Mike, widow, mother, secretary-in-perpetuity of the Niniltna Native Association, plump and capable, if a little harried. But in spite of that tension, she seemed taller, somehow, as if the authority and responsibility invested in her by Kate and the shareholders had given her added physical as well as mental, emotional, and corporational stature. It wasn't entirely unexpected, and he wondered if it would have happened so quickly if Kate hadn't gotten out of town as fast as possible immediately after Annie's election. Kate had been right about that.

This morning Annie wore a bright pink polyester pantsuit with a paisley shirt underneath, but the cheerful color was not reflected in her expression. There were deep shadows beneath her eyes, as if she had been taking a lot of calls way too far into the night. Shareholders leaning on her, he thought, wanting her to fill the vacuum Kate left behind. "You look pretty in pink," he said, and was rewarded when her face relaxed into a smile.

"Stop trying to flirt with me or I'll tell your girlfriend," she said, and came around her desk to sit in one of the two armchairs.

Kate hadn't spent one more minute than was absolutely necessary in this office. Annie, by contrast, looked at home.

"Is Kate around?" she said, reading his mind.

"Uh, no," he said. "She's out of town on a job."

"Oh." She frowned. "I left her a message on her voice mail. She hasn't called back."

"Well. You know." He gave a vague gesture and hoped he hadn't broken a sweat. "Cell phones. Lose messages all the time."

"Mine never does," Annie said a little grimly, and Jim thought of the phone ringing off the hook at the post. Annie was right about that.

"Speaking of Kate," he said. "I need your advice. A piece of information has come my way. I know it's going to send Kate into orbit. I don't know how you'll feel about it, either."

"Tell me," Annie said.

"Erland Bannister has bought into the Suulutaq Mine."

Annie was silent for so long, he began to wonder if he'd shocked her into speechlessness. "I see," she said at last. "And you know this how?"

He told her.

"I see," she said again, and brushed at a bit of nonexistent fluff on her hot pink pants leg. "I did not know this, Jim." She didn't look happy about it, either.

"It sounded to me like it happened recently. Bannister seemed ... more than usually pleased with himself."

"The word you are looking for is *smug,*" Annie said dryly.

Jim gave a short laugh. "I suppose so. Yes, all right, the bastard seemed pretty damn smug."

Annie looked introspective. "I wonder which is more important to him, a good return on his investment, or rubbing Kate's nose in his participation in it?"

"About equal, be my guess," Jim said. He felt weary, and did not attribute it solely to next to no sleep the night before.

"I think you're wrong," Annie said after a moment. "I think it has much more to do with Kate." Her eyes met his. "She put him in jail."

"He tried to kill her," Jim said, exasperated. "After conspiring to conceal another murder, and colluding to send his sister to prison for life for a crime she didn't commit."

"That's not the way he sees it," Annie said. "She put him in jail, it took him two years to get out, and he wants revenge. One of the best ways to do that is to invest in something that will bring him to the Park on a regular basis. Kate's Park. He's out of the family business, did you know?"

"Heard something about that," Jim said. "Nothing specific."

"It was kept very quiet," Annie said, "but you can take it from me that Erland Bannister is no longer in any way connected to Bannister Enterprises or to the Bannister Foundation. Victoria Muravieff made sure the word went forth."

Jim looked at her, fascinated. The quiet little mouse taking notes in the corner was all kinds of gone, replaced by this mogul with sources all over the Alaska power structure. The Return of Ekaterina Shugak. He wondered if Kate understood the magnitude of what she had wrought. "Did she buy him off?"

"Victoria?" Annie considered. "That wasn't the feeling I got. There was more a sense of ... duress, shall we say."

"Erland didn't go willingly."

"No. And another reason to be angry with Kate."

Jim remembered a conversation he'd had last year with Kate about Erland's antecedents, and had a pretty good idea what Victoria had used to pry Erland's hands off the family business. By now, Erland would know who had handed Victoria that pry bar. Arrogant, power-hungry, homicidal Bannister might be, but nobody ever said he didn't have his finger on the pulse of the state. Information was power, he knew it, he collected it, and he used it.

Annie was looking at him, eyebrows raised, so he straightened out his face and said, "So he'll be looking for new investments. New Alaskan pies to stick his fingers in."

Annie nodded. "And if one of those pies is in the backyard of the woman who orchestrated his downfall, so much the better."

"Great," Jim said heavily.

A moment of mutually shared gloom ticked past before Jim got to his feet. "Well, thanks, Annie, for not making my day."

"Sorry, Jim." She offered him a sympathetic smile. "And, Jim?"

He paused at the door, looking at her over his shoulder.

Her round face was serious and her gaze bored into his, demanding his attention. "Know your enemy."

He hadn't told her about Axenia being on the jet with Erland. He would tell Kate, and Kate could tell her. Niniltna Native Association business was not his business, other than on an individual, civil, and/or criminal basis.

He was almost running by the time he hit the front door.

At the post, Maggie was on the phone, explaining why she would not dispatch an Alaska state trooper to mediate a dispute over the sale of a secondhand snow machine. She hung up and glowered at him. "You need help. We need help."

"I know." He thought of the state budget, and of how thin the troopers were already spread. He thought of Liam

Campbell on his own in Newenham, with seven times the population of Niniltna and without even any local cops for support. With the kind of money the Suulutaq was going to bring into the state, he'd bet half his salary that the Niniltna post would get help before the Newenham post did.

Which didn't necessarily mean he'd turn it down.

"You look tired," she said. "Anything to do with the four assholes in back?"

"Everything to do with them," he said. "You read the reports?"

She nodded grimly.

"You up to taking them to Ahtna in the van?"

She brightened. "You'll handle the calls?"

His shoulders slumped. "I'll handle the calls."

She was up out of her chair and halfway out the door before he'd finished his sentence.

He logged on and read through yesterday's daily trooper dispatches. He couldn't say with any truth things were any worse in the Park than they were anywhere else in the state, unfortunately.

Maggie pulled the van out of the impound lot in back of the post and Jim helped her cuff-and-stuff the three rapists and the Darrylinator in the back. "Got your pepper spray?" She nodded. He looked at the sky, low and gray, kind of how he was feeling. "Okay, be on your way, and if it looks worse by the time you turn 'em over to Kenny, stay the night, okay?"

She flashed him a smile. "You don't have to ask me twice."

He knew without asking that she'd already called her husband, and that she would be stopping at their house to pick him up, and that the reservation had already been made at the Ahtna Lodge. At least someone would be getting laid tonight.

There were, mercifully, few nuisance calls the rest of the morning. At noon, he caught up on his paperwork and went down to the Riverside Café for lunch in a slightly better frame of mind. He sat at the counter, the better to be fussed over by proprietor Laurel Meganack, a pocket Venus in T-shirt and leggings, her smartly cut black hair flopping flirtatiously in bright brown eyes that took in his hunger and his fatigue at a glance. There was a large mug of coffee in front of him before he had his jacket off, and she began assembling a canned salmon salad sandwich with onions and sweet pickles and mayo on sourdough bread before he ordered. He got himself on the outside of that and got a refill on his coffee and started to feel something approaching human.

He looked around. The café was surprisingly only half full. Before they'd started exploring the Suulutaq, the Riverside had been a Park rat hangout. Afterwards, it was eternally full of young McMiners, dog-dirty and loaded for bear. Today was a welcome respite.

He nodded at the man two stools down. "Demetri."

"How you doing, Jim."

"Busy," Jim said.

"I bet." A rare smile lit the other man's square, serious face. Echoing Jim's thoughts, he said, "Nice to be in here without the rabble rousers bringing the roof down."

"Isn't it, though."

"You see this?" Demetri handed him something that proved to be a trifold brochure, with the name GAEA next to a circular logo of a woman with long dark hair cradling the earth in her arms. The distinct outline of Alaska was visible.

"I've seen it."

"Looks professional."

"That it does. And that was some hatchet job they did on

the head of Suulutaq Exploration's love life."

"Forced him to resign, I hear," Demetri said.

Jim nodded. "They've got someone with money backing them for sure." He scanned it. "Same message as the last one. Suulutaq, baaaa-aad." He refolded the brochure and handed it back.

"You don't agree?" Demetri said.

"You do?" Jim said, his coffee mug arrested halfway to his mouth.

Demetri shrugged and tossed the brochure farther down the counter. "I do sometimes wonder if the world needs another gold mine."

"Have you checked the price of gold lately?" Jim drained his mug and paid his bill. "There's no stopping the mine now, Demetri."

"I suppose not." Demetri didn't sound convinced.

As the owner of a high-end, extremely lucrative hunting and fishing lodge in the Quilak foothills, Jim supposed Demetri Totemoff had reason to regret the discovery of the world's second largest gold deposit on Park land. But at eighteen hundred an ounce, there were just too many people who were going to want to get it out of the ground.

"I don't love it, Demetri. I doubt you can find a Park rat who does, no matter how much money they're making off it." Least of all Kate Shugak, he thought, and when she finds out the Suulutaq brought Erland Bannister into her Park, she's going to love it even less. "About the most we can hope for is the economy comes back gangbusters fast and the price of gold goes back in the toilet." Jim shrugged into his jacket and slapped Demetri on the shoulder. "Later."

He did a routine patrol out on the road as far as the turnoff to the Roadhouse, and then up to the Step. The natives were not restless. The Natives weren't, either. He went back to the post and caught up on his paperwork, of which there seemed to be more every day.

Off and on, he wondered what Kate was doing.

Wondered if there'd been any more close encounters of the chest freezer kind.

Wondered if the bed she was sleeping in felt as empty as the bed he was sleeping in.

Wondered if Liam was having the same effect on Kate that he did on any other double-X human being.

Wondered if he should call her and tell her the news about Erland Bannister.

Know your enemy.

He reached for the phone and called Anchorage instead. One ring and it picked up on the other end. "Brendan? Jim Chopin in Niniltna."

"Jim!" The fruity voice, an Americanized Rumpole, rolled out of the receiver. "Tell me that luscious little cupcake of a Shugak has finally left you for a better man. Namely *moi*. Even now she wings her way west into my gentle but manly arms—"

"In your dreams," Jim said. "I need a favor."

The voice sobered. "Name it." As annoying as Anchorage Assistant District Attorney Brendan McCord could be on the subject of Kate Shugak, he was one of any Alaska state trooper's best assets on the job.

"I need a look at a cold case."

"Name?"

"I mean a really cold case, Brendan."

"How cold are we talking here? North Pole?"

"Try Saturn."

"Name?"

"Emil Bannister."

There was a long silence. "Erland Bannister's father?"

"Yeah."

"You're the second person in the last four months to ask for a look at that file, Jim."

"I know," Jim said.

20

JANUARY 20

Newenham

Kate and Mutt had been waiting only ten minutes when Wy Chouinard landed at Newenham airport. She waved at the two of them and taxied to the Nushugak Air Taxi tie-down. Kate helped her push the Cessna back into its parking space. The last two rows of seats had been removed and the back of the airplane was filled with packages and boxes and brown canvas mailbags. Chouinard backed her pickup to the cargo door and began loading. Kate helped.

"Thanks," the pilot said, giving her a quizzical glance.

"Tell me about your grandfather," Kate said.

Chouinard raised an eyebrow. "I, ah, haven't seen him today."

"I have," Kate said with feeling. "Way too early."

Chouinard tried unsuccessfully to turn a laugh into a cough. "Better you than me."

"He keeps telling me, 'He didn't do it.' You heard him yesterday morning. Do you know what he means by that?"

Chouinard shrugged, pulling another mailbag out of the tail of the plane. "No one ever knows what Moses means." In a lower voice Kate was pretty sure she wasn't meant to hear, Chouinard added, "Not until it's too late, anyway."

"Jeannie Penney down at the library? She says he's some kind of seer."

"Does she?" Chouinard said, noncommittal. She pitched a mailbag into the back of the truck and turned with a determined smile. "I wouldn't worry about it. He's been around a long time, he's probably confused you with someone else."

Kate had known another old man who was never confused about anything, but she let it go. Moses had only been her toe in the door. The two women worked in silence to empty the plane, and Chouinard buttoned it up as Kate closed the tailgate on the pickup. They turned to face each other at the same moment.

"But you didn't come here to talk about Moses," his granddaughter said.

Kate took in the other woman with a measuring glance, and liked what she saw. Chouinard's gaze was direct and unflinching, her hands and clothes showed she worked for a living, her airplanes were spotless, and Kate had personal experience that the engine on at least one of them purred like a baby in the air. Kate had flown a lot of miles and she knew a lot of pilots, and she was aware that love had a lot to do with the care and feeding of aircraft. It was obvious to the meanest observer that Chouinard loved hers, and that she loved flying.

Of course, to all reports, so had Finn Grant.

Kate made up her mind. "No, I didn't."

The pilot folded her arms and leaned against the Cessna. Kate folded her arms and leaned against the truck. Mutt looked from one woman to the other, made a conscious decision not to referee this power play, and trotted off into the scrub brush to scare up a snack.

"Cyril Wolfe," Kate said.

Chouinard's eyes flickered.

"You were spotting for two different herring seiners during the same season about four years back, a honking big no-no that if it became known to the fishing community would have blackballed you from ever spotting for anyone again. It might even have destroyed your air taxi business, given that most of your customers have to be either fishermen themselves, or fishing-related family, friends, and businesses."

Chouinard waited, outwardly calm, but Kate saw her fingers bite into her arms.

"I found the file Grant kept on you," Kate said. "I've seen the evidence, including notes on separate statements he got from deckhands working for both of the fishermen you were spotting for. Bastard even managed to get a copy of the bank statement, transferring funds from Wolfe's account to yours."

Chouinard's eyes narrowed. "Who the hell are you?"

"He was blackmailing you," Kate said. "What did he want? To buy your business for pennies on the dollar?"

"Who the hell are you?" Chouinard said again.

"What did he want?" Kate said.

There was a brief, sizzling silence.

Chouinard gave a short laugh. "Maybe he wanted to buy me out, but that was only for starters. I don't think once Finn got his hooks into you that he ever stopped wanting more."

Their eyes met in perfect comprehension for at least one moment.

"He could have had the business," Chouinard said. She shrugged. "Hell, he might even could have had me, I might have gone that far. Then."

"Why?"

At first Kate thought Chouinard wasn't going to answer.

Then her gaze fell and she shifted where she stood. When she spoke again her voice was hard but not defensive. "I have a son. Tim. He's adopted. The adoption process costs a lot of money. I went looking for it. I found it. Finn found out somehow." She shook her head. "It would have hurt my reputation, no question, but by then it was all far enough in the past that I don't think it would have put me out of business completely. Alaskans have forgiven a lot worse." Her mouth tightened into a thin line. "Besides, there's no law against spotting for two different fishermen. It's not very ethical, if you don't tell them about it. I'm not proud of it, but I wasn't going to go to jail for it and I knew it." Her eyes narrowed. "And I sure as hell wasn't going to sell my soul to Finn fucking Grant to keep a secret we both knew he'd blab all over Southwest the first time he felt like it." She looked Kate straight in the eye. "So, no. He wasn't blackmailing me. Not that he didn't try."

Kate was almost certain she believed her.

"What's this about?" Chouinard said. "Really?"

The ability to lie, lie off the cuff, and lie well was an essential skill in any undercover investigator's toolbox, but Kate had already lied once that day to a woman she'd liked at first sight. She went with her gut. "There is a possibility that Finn Grant was murdered."

Chouinard stiffened. "You mean..."

"Someone may have sabotaged his plane, in the hope it would crash and kill him, yes." The thumb drive with motive enough to murder ten men burned a hole in the pocket of her jeans.

Chouinard thought. "Finn was an execrable human being, but he was a damn good pilot. I found it real hard to believe at the time that he would have taken off in an aircraft with the nut backing off the oil screen." She looked up. "Do blackmailers ever blackmail only one person?"

"Not if they are successful the first time they try it, no. Liam tell you about the oil screen?"

Chouinard nodded. "The NTSB guy called him at home."

"Were you around, the morning Grant took off?"

"I was in town," Chouinard said. "I sleep with the local state trooper, however, so..." Her eyes widened and her voice trailed away.

Uh-oh, Kate thought.

"Liam," Chouinard said through her teeth. "Liam!"

She marched around the truck and got in. Kate barely got vertical before Chouinard hit the gas, and if the pavement had been dry, she would have left a twenty-five-foot strip of rubber behind. As it was, the ass end of the pickup skidded around nearly 180 degrees before the wheels found purchase and the truck launched itself forward on a ferocious course Kate was only too sure of.

Mutt bounded out of the underbrush, a ptarmigan feather hanging from the corner of her mouth and an expression of wild surmise on her face.

"I think we better head on over to the trooper post," Kate told her.

• • •

Sure enough, Chouinard's pickup was in front of the aging but neat little building. Kate parked the four-wheeler and went to the pickup, pulled it all the way into the parking space, and turned off the key. With the engine off, the shouting from inside the post was much louder. She looked at Mutt. "We who are about to die, salute you." She went up the steps and looked over her shoulder. Mutt was still standing next to the ATV. "Come on, you little coward. Once more into the breach. Into the valley of death and all that."

Mutt squared heroic shoulders, went up on tiptoe in that half-sidling, half-gliding step that instantly labeled her lupine ancestry, and followed Kate warily inside.

Where the shouting had come to a halt. Chouinard and Campbell were glaring at each other over Campbell's desk.

"Uh," Kate said.

They both whipped around to fix her with furious stares. Mutt gave out with something between a sneeze and a whimper, but she remained loyally at Kate's side. Besides, the door was closed and she didn't think the situation had deteriorated to the point where she had to go through a window. Yet.

"You had to tell her," Campbell said.

"I didn't have to tell her anything," Kate said. "She figured it out on her own."

"What's this about Finn Grant and blackmail?"

Kate pulled the thumb drive from her pocket and tossed it. Campbell caught it by reflex. "A bullet? No, wait, what?"

"It's a thumb drive," Kate said at the same moment Campbell pulled off the cap to display the USB connector. "It was in the box of ammo in Finn Grant's desk drawer."

His head whipped up, and the dangerous look in her eye made her hope that the Get Out of Jail Free card Jim had given her still worked. "On it," she said, "you will find a folder labeled 'Finn's Notes.' Inside 'Finn's Notes,' you will find evidence which would lead any rational person to believe that over the years Finn Grant collected a fair bit of information on eleven different people, and that he used that information to, ah, influence them." Kate shrugged. "You said he had pressured a lot of businesses into selling to him. I figured he didn't do that strictly from charm of manner. I looked for what he did do."

"When did Liam say that?" Chouinard said, still glaring at her husband.

"The only name I recognized was your wife's," Kate said, not looking at Chouinard, "so it seemed logical to talk to her first." She paused. "You also said, back in Niniltna, that you thought Finn Grant's death was suspect." She nodded at the thumb drive. "You're holding what I'd call serious motive for eleven different killers right there in your hand."

"You hired her to look into Finn's death," Chouinard said. She was very nearly giving off sparks. "Goddammit, Liam, why didn't you tell me?"

"Goddammit, Wy," Campbell said in a near bellow, "why didn't you tell me!"

"You knew about the spotting!"

"I didn't know Finn was blackmailing you!"

"He wasn't!"

The door opened and everyone turned around to see who it was.

Jo Dunaway walked in.

"Jo," Chouinard said, surprised.

"Fuck," Campbell said, not.

Kate said nothing at all, but Mutt caught the vibe, and a rumble started deep in her breast.

"What are you doing here?" Dunaway said to Kate.

"What are you?" Kate said.

"None of your goddamn business," Dunaway said.

"Backatcha," Kate said.

Mutt growled some more.

"Yeah," Dunaway said to her, "we've met. Put a sock in it, why don't you?"

Kate almost smiled. "Mutt," she said.

The growl petered off, although Mutt kept in practice by

giving Dunaway the beady yellow eye, which would have been enough to back down a lesser woman.

"You know who she is?" Dunaway said to Campbell, pointing at Kate. "She used to work for the Anchorage DA. Until she killed a perp in a knife fight. What, you never wondered how she got that scar? Nowadays, I would venture to say understandably, she's a PI." She looked from Campbell to Chouinard and back again. Her brow darkened. "So you did know."

"Some of us knew sooner than others," Chouinard said, and turned back to Campbell. "Liam, I had nothing to do with Finn Grant's death."

"I know that, Wy." Campbell now looked about as wretched as a human being could.

"I knew it!" Dunaway's voice went up an entire octave.

"Knew what?" Chouinard said.

Dunaway leveled a finger at Campbell. "Knew he had you down as a suspect!"

Campbell ignored her, speaking directly to Chouinard. "You never got along. You had a big fight with him the day before he died, in front of about six upstanding citizens of the city of Newenham. No one's been talking about anything since, and you know it. I had to do something, or the rumors and the innuendo would have run us out of here. You want to move?"

Chouinard bit her lip and looked away.

"'Cause I don't," he said. "When I went up to Anchorage to testify in the Berdoll case, I made a side trip to see Jim Chopin. Remember I told you about him? One of my training officers. I told him the story. He recommended Kate, and she agreed to look into it."

"Why didn't you tell me?"

"Because the fewer people who know about something like that, the longer an undercover investigator has before people find out and things start to unravel. And I was right. Already she's turned up this." He held up the thumb drive, although he directed an unfriendly look in Kate's direction that promised she hadn't heard the last of her delay in handing it over.

She met the look without flinching, and he was first to lower his eyes. He knew as well as she did that it was fatal to play favorites in any investigation, and when Kate arrived in Newenham, she had had no proof of Chouinard's lack of involvement in the crime. She didn't now, come to that, but at this point the suspects were so thick on the ground she was happy to let her gut dictate the removal of at least one of them.

Kate could see his sudden realization that while he was explaining himself to his wife, there was a reporter in the room. He said to Dunaway, "All of this is off the record, Jo. You don't write about it. You don't talk about it." He pointed at Kate. "You don't tell anyone about her, either, are we clear on that? Or I will charge you with interfering with an ongoing investigation."

Dunaway gave him a look that would have smelted a man of inferior steel. "I've known Wyanet Chouinard a lot longer than you have, Liam Campbell. She's my oldest and dearest friend and I would never do anything that might hurt her." She turned on her heel and went out the door, slamming it hard behind her.

Kate waited for the echoes of that slam to die away. "Uh, I've got to get to work."

Liam looked at her, back down at the bullet thumb drive, and over at his wife. Clearly, there was much he wanted to say, and equally clearly, much he would not say in front of Chouinard.

"We'll talk later," Kate said, and made good her escape.

Or so she thought, because Dunaway was lying in wait outside. She planted herself in Kate's path, ignoring Mutt's menacing growl with more sangfroid than anyone who had ever heard it before, and said not quite through her teeth, "Wyanet Chouinard is in everything but blood my sister. I don't know exactly what you're doing here, but if whatever it is you're doing hurts her in any way, I will feel a strong need to do a lengthy investigative report on the life and times of one Kate Shugak. Do you understand me?"

Kate walked around her and got on the ATV.

Dunaway walked over and stood in front of them. "Do you understand me?"

Mutt jumped up behind and Kate started the engine and put it in gear. She thumbed the throttle, focused somewhere beyond Dunaway's right shoulder. The right front tire was about to run over Dunaway's foot when she stepped out of the way. Kate did not look back.

Dunaway cursed, long and fluently, and stared after them in frustrated speculation.

She'd spent the last two days nosing around Newenham, pretending she was doing a story on a reality television show said to begin filming in the area the following summer, featuring the wild and hairy salmon fishing season. Her ploy had opened virtually every door she had knocked on—who doesn't want to be on TV—but she had discovered very little more about Eagle Air FBO and Finn Grant than she already knew. No one had heard the name of Alexandra Hardin, or not in conjunction with Grant, not even the local banker, and no one knew where Finn was getting all his spending money.

Her face cleared and she pulled out her cell phone.

She had just remembered that she knew an FBI agent.

21

JANUARY 20

Newenham

She and Mutt were half an hour late to work.

Bill got there half an hour later. At Kate's look she said, "Don't even start. As I suspected, last night's festivities led to a long day in court. Hold down the fort, I'm taking a nap." She marched back to her office and closed the door firmly behind her.

Five minutes later, Moses Alakuyak walked in, marched past Kate without so much as a by-your-leave, and let himself into the office. That time, Kate heard the lock click.

Her shift started out slow and continued that way. A few people showed up for the hair of the dog, grumpy and silent. She saw the man who had taken her place at the library. He seemed to be avoiding her eye. Later he was joined by another man, short, black-browed, heavyset, and balding. At six o'clock Chouinard and Campbell came in and took the booth in the back. Kate took a tray over. "What'll you have, folks?"

Chouinard looked amused, Campbell annoyed and maybe a little embarrassed. At least they were no longer at each other's throats. "Beer and a burger," he said.

"Same," Chouinard said.

Makeup food. Kate took the order to the pass-through,

where stolid Dottie the cook and happy-go-lucky Paul, her son and aide-de-camp, looked happy to have something to do. The order was up in record time, and Kate delivered it with a pleasant smile. "Anything else?"

"No thanks," Chouinard said.

"Did you see everything on that thumb drive?" Campbell said.

"Yes," Kate said. "Like I told you, the only name that meant anything to me was hers."

She waited, but he bit into his burger, probably as a means of avoiding further conversation.

She was behind the bar, washing glasses, when Gabe McGuire walked in. Even the hungover looked up at that, and then looked away again deliberately, trying so hard to pretend he was just another guy that it was instantly obvious he wasn't. He ignored it, looked around, spotted Campbell and Chouinard, and joined them. Kate took a deep and she hoped unobtrusive breath, picked up her tray like it was a buckler, and arrived at the booth with a smile fixed to her face.

McGuire looked up at her without surprise. "Kate," he said lazily.

"What can I get for you?" Kate said.

"Dottie frying chicken tonight?"

"I can ask."

"If the answer is yes, please tell her all dark, and green salad with oil and vinegar."

"Anything to drink?"

"Iced tea."

"Chicken? Wednesday isn't a chicken night." Dottie looked through the pass-through. McGuire gave her a little wave, and dour Dottie actually smiled. "Coming right up."

Bill and Moses emerged from Bill's office, rumpled and

radiating an air of sleek satisfaction. "I hate you both," Kate said to Bill in passing.

Bill laughed out loud.

"And your shirt's buttoned up crooked," Kate said, and did a round. The run on Bloody Marys continued. When she brought McGuire his chicken, he said, "Take a break, why don't you."

She got a drink. By the time she got back to the booth, Chouinard and Campbell were leaving. "We'll be talking," Campbell growled in her ear. They left and she wasn't fast enough on her feet to get out of it, so she slid in opposite McGuire. There was a sardonic look in his eye, as if he were fully aware of her feelings, but he wasn't going to offer her an easy out, and then Mutt came over. She rested her chin on the table and blinked sad yellow eyes up at McGuire. He looked at Kate and raised an eyebrow.

"Her middle name is Iron Gut," Kate said.

McGuire liberated a thigh from the mountain-high pile—Kate wondered if Bill knew how extravagant Dottie could be with Bill's chicken, given the right incentive—and offered it. Mutt took it delicately between her teeth and retired to enjoy the largesse.

McGuire craned his neck to watch. "Sure she's okay with chicken bones?"

"If she was going to choke on a bird bone, believe me, she would have done it years ago."

"She makes me feel like Little Red Riding Hood. She's not a wolf, is she?"

"Only half," Kate said.

It surprised a laugh out of him. The sound of it surprised a smile out of her, and he stopped and gave her an appraising look. "You should do that more often."

"I have to get back to work," she said.

"Really," he said, biting into a drumstick. He had strong, even teeth. She wondered how much they'd cost him. "Which work is that?"

"Sorry, what?" She left off admiring his teeth long enough to meet his eyes. They were very nice eyes, dark, steady. She pulled herself together. This was an actor, for chrissake, someone who at the first sign of a wrinkle ran screaming for the plastic surgeon. "Work," she said. "Right now, I've got a job bartending and I'd best get back to it."

"You haven't been sitting here for five minutes, Bill's not yelling at you, and no one's hollering for a refill. Relax."

For whatever reason, she sat down again.

"So," he said, "what's your sign?"

This time she laughed out loud. He grinned. "Well, if you won't tell me what your day job is..." He gestured with a wing. "How did you get that scar?"

"What are you doing here, anyway?" she said.

"Is it why your voice is so rough? Not that it sounds bad, I hasten to say." He met and held her eyes. "Sounds kinda sexy. Somewhere between a cat's purr and..." He smiled, long and slow. "A buzz saw."

"Shouldn't you be back out at your lodge?" Kate said. "Won't your posse be looking for you?"

"You're good at avoidance," he said, forking up a bite of salad. "Shows me something." He chewed and swallowed, in no hurry. She recognized the certainty that came from spending most of a working day as the focus of a camera lens, a cast and crew of hundreds and an audience of millions. It wasn't vanity, exactly, or even arrogance. Call it habit.

"So why are you still here?" she said. *And why am I still sitting here?* she thought.

"Always the cop," he said in a long-suffering voice. She refused to respond to the goad, and he looked up with a grin. "I had a more than usually interesting night," he said. "I thought if I hung around a little longer, I might find out why."

"Ask the trooper," Kate said.

"I did."

"And?"

"And he changed the subject." He paused. "He said the woman who was shot is going to be okay."

"Yes."

"She say who shot her?"

"I haven't heard," Kate said.

He snorted.

"How'd you get in from Eagle Air?" she said.

"Tasha gave me a ride."

"Ah. You spent the day out there?"

He nodded. "I was in conference most of the day."

Was that what they were calling it nowadays, she thought, and was immediately ashamed of herself, on Tasha's behalf, if not McGuire's.

"Lining up the dough for a new project." He cocked an eyebrow. "Want to know what project?"

"Not especially," Kate said.

He laughed again. Heads turned toward them. Moses, on his customary stool at the bar, swiveled all the way around to give them a long, hard look. "How about I tell you anyway? It's a film about the gold rush. And we're going to shoot it in Alaska."

"Good plan," Kate said. "A lot of it happened here."

"Don't you want to know if there's a part in it for you?"

"I'm not an actress," Kate said.

"You got that right," he said, laughter gone. "Thank god."

One appreciative look from a handsome man didn't usually send a shiver down her spine. She wondered if that quality was the little bit extra that got him top billing, a personality that made every man want to be like him and every woman fall in love with him, a personality that the camera only enhanced and magnified for mass consumption. Such stuff were dreams made of.

Not hers, she told herself. "Who are you playing? No, wait, let me guess. Jack London."

His eyes mocked her change of subject. *Chicken,* they seemed to be saying, and they weren't referring to what was on his plate. She met his gaze with as much blandness as she could muster, and raised an eyebrow of her own.

He shrugged and leaned back. *Okay, I'll play.* "I don't think Jack London made it as far as Nome."

"Nome," Kate said. "Oh, then, of course it has to be Wyatt Earp." She tried really, really hard not to imagine how sexy Gabe McGuire would look wearing a six-shooter slung low on his hip.

He raised an eyebrow yet again at her tone. "You have an objection?"

She raised a shoulder, let it drop. "Haven't there been enough movies made about Wyatt Earp?"

"About Wyatt Earp in Tombstone, yes," he said. "Not about Wyatt Earp in Nome."

She looked around the bar. At any other time, three guys would be shouting out for a refill. Now, silent still, silent all. Couldn't anybody see she was going down for the third time here? Grasping at straws, she said, "You really don't have a satellite dish at Outouchiwanet?"

His smile was too fucking knowing. "There was one. I took it down the same day Finn signed over the deed. With my own two hands." He regarded said hands with satisfaction.

"Can't say I blame you," she said, thinking of the havoc cell towers were wreaking on her Park at this very moment. "Pretty quiet out at the base today?"

"Something you wanted to know?" he said. "If there is, stop pussyfooting around and spit it out."

Kate's eyes narrowed. "Okay. Any traffic today?"

He shrugged. "That Cessna came through again, the Cargomaster. Seems like there's one of those every day. The air freight business must be good. Oh, and Reid came back. I'm guessing either Campbell or Tina Grant called him. He was flapping around like a seagull, squawking about how terrible it was, what happened to Evelyn, and he assured me nothing like it had ever happened before, it was an aberration, he knew just how I felt, coming up here for a private vacation and then this happens, dreadful, he'd do everything in his power to see my name didn't come into it, yadda yadda."

"You don't like him."

McGuire shrugged. "He's a suck-up and a starfucker. I never would have put my name to anything to do with Eagle Air if it had been only Reid involved, I don't care how bad I wanted Outouchiwanet. Finn was the brains in that outfit." He paused, as if he were deciding whether to tell her what came next. "Reid offered to buy me out."

"Did he."

He gave her a small smile, turning his glass of iced tea round and round in his fingers. "Seemed to think I would like to be shut out of the whole thing." He drank. "He was right, too. I wouldn't have bought in if Finn hadn't been holding Outouchiwanet hostage."

"Finn want you as partner for the star power?"

He nodded. "Wouldn't be the first time."

"How did you meet him? Finn Grant?"

"A mutual acquaintance. Although I don't know how a first-string guy like Erland ever got hooked up with a wannabe like Finn. Still." He shrugged. "I guess we were all wannabes at some point." He drained his glass and grinned at her. "I certainly was."

Kate felt a distant roaring in her ears. "Erland?" she said, in a voice not her own. Next to her, Mutt's ears pricked and she looked up at Kate.

He looked at her curiously. "Yeah, Erland Bannister."

"Oh," someone else said, and in some distant portion of her mind noted how weak the response was.

"You know him?"

"Yes," that other person said.

He misunderstood. "Yeah, I found out after the fact, he's a pretty big mover and shaker up here."

The roaring in her eyes died down, and she felt herself return to her body. "How did you meet him?" she said, carefully casual.

His brow puckered—he should be more careful about wrinkles—but she could see him decide that it wasn't a state secret, after all. "I'd just hit it big with the Cook bio, and I got offered *Kandahar*."

"I saw that," she said.

"Yeah? No actor should ever ask, but I'll risk it: Did you like it?"

She paid him the respect of thinking about it. Also because it gave her more time to adjust to the sudden and unwelcome appearance of a specter at the feast. "I don't know that anyone with any truth in them could say they liked it. I couldn't look away from the screen." She looked at him and told the truth. "I couldn't look away from you."

He looked—was it displeased? "It was an incredible script."

"Yes," she said. "But it is all about that one character, that one year in Afghanistan filtered through him. His squad is assigned to take and keep one tiny little valley in southeastern Afghanistan, he gets shot at, he gets dehydrated from the heat, he shoots some people, he gets bit by a tarantula, he gets shot at again and shoots some more people, two of his buddies get shot dead in one firefight, he gets wounded and his best friend dies, his fiancée Dear Johns him from back in the world, he gets shot at some more and shoots some more people, he makes friends with an Afghani kid who gets shot by his own for fraternizing with the enemy, he shoots some more people, and after a year, after losing half his squad, the army abandons the valley. It's all about him."

Surprised, and showing it, he said, "He's your way into the story."

"Yeah, well, I don't know that I wanted a way into that story," she said.

"You against the war?"

She shrugged. "As much as I ever pay attention to national politics. Seems like every president needs his little war."

He made a come-ahead motion with his hand, and since according to the Oscars he was a Motion Picture Academy-certified good actor, she believed he wanted to hear more. "I watched *Kandahar* with a friend who lost both legs below the knee in Vietnam. When the movie was over he told me, "'I left my legs in Vietnam to keep South Vietnam free of the red menace, to keep the dominoes from falling. Now it's all one big happy country, our best friend in Southeast Asia, and a luxury tourist destination. What was the point?'"

"So, he didn't like it," McGuire said. "But you did."

She laughed in spite of herself, and shook her head. "The

film was amazing." She thought, and added, "It'd make an unbeliever out of you."

His turn to laugh. "So you are against the war."

"Wars," she said.

"All wars?"

"Unless they're coming across our borders in tanks?" She thought it over. "Yeah. Well, okay, Hitler had to be stopped, no question. But since then? Has anyone really threatened our borders? Korea? Vietnam? Iraq? Afghanistan?"

"You don't think 9/11 was a good reason for going to war?"

"In Afghanistan?" She snorted. "A hundred thousand of our guys on the ground for ten years, and who takes him down? A seventy-nine-man SEAL team. In Pakistan." She thought of Irene Grant, dead of a sniper shot less than three months before, and grieved for the waste of a woman she had never known.

He made that same come-ahead motion with his hand, which must have had some kind of power of hypnosis in it. Or maybe she just needed more breathing space between her and the name he'd just dropped oh so casually into their conversation. She said, parsing the words out carefully, "I think what I really object to is the deification of the warrior." She leaned her head back against the booth. "We send them off to marching bands and waving flags and tears, we bury the dead at places like Arlington with more marching bands and waving flags and tears, we honor them with parades and speeches and more marching bands and more waving flags and more tears on Memorial Day and Veterans Day. I can't help but think that all of it is at least in part a cynical attempt by the nation—any nation—to convince young, impressionable people to volunteer to be cannon fodder. Which in and of itself guarantees the continuation of war. No cannon fodder, no war. It's not like any Bush ever personally challenges any Saddam to a duel." She shook her head and looked down at her drink, swirling the melting ice around in the glass. "Like Bobby said. For what? Does anyone really think Iraq is going to become the fifty-first state? They can't even keep the lights on in Baghdad twenty-four/seven."

"Wow," he said. "I didn't know we were telling the truth."

She smiled, a little mocking in her turn. "Be careful what you ask for, little boy." The shock had worn off, leaving her cool and clear-eyed, mistress of the now familiar fury simmering just below the surface. If Erland Bannister was in the house, she wanted to know how he had got there, and what he was up to. "You were telling me about buying your jet."

He had an obvious inner debate over whether to let her change the subject, and gave in. "After *Captain Cook* and *Kandahar,* I could finally afford my own transportation, so I went shopping for a plane. I met Erland Bannister at a Gulfstream dealership. We got to talking, he mentioned he was from Alaska, I told him I was looking for a hideout along with the airplane to get me there, and he told me about Finn's operation."

Deliberately casual, she said, "You and Erland Bannister best friends now?"

McGuire shook his head. "It was the only time I met him. It was a good tip, though, I owe him. Finn was just Bristol Bay Air then, an outfitter running hunting and fishing and flightseeing trips out of Niniltna. I remembered how much I'd liked it up here when I was a kid working in Akutan. So I came up, and I've been up at least a couple of times a year ever since." He smiled at her. "I make enough money to pay for gas and groceries. Someday I just might make it a one-way trip."

"Spend a winter here first," she said. "A lot of people can't handle the cold, let alone the dark."

"I'm from Montana, remember?"

"I never knew where you were from in the first place," she said, and got to her feet and began collecting his dirty dishes. "You all done here?"

"Yeah, but, hey, where you going?"

"Back to work. See you around."

Or not. She delivered the dishes to the pass-through and made another round of the bar, which had filled up a little, but was nowhere near as full as it had been the night before, which was just as well, because someone else was filling drink orders and making change. She saw McGuire come to the bar to pay his tab, stand chatting to Bill and Moses for a while, and then, giving her a long, unfathomable look, take his leave. She made sure she was on the opposite side of the room until he did so.

Erland fucking Bannister. Was there any pie in the entire state of Alaska he didn't have a finger in?

She went blindly about her job, taking orders, bussing tables, washing glasses, conscious that Bill and Moses both were watching her. So was Mutt, all of them wary, as if waiting for a delayed fuse on a bomb to tick down to detonation. She made an effort to contain her rage, so it didn't spill all over Bill's Bar and Grill and frighten the customers. She owed Bill that much.

The last week had been a nice respite from the memory of Old Sam's death and the scavenger hunt he had sent her on the month following it, which revealed more about him and her family than she had ever wanted to know. Erland fucking Bannister had played a big part in those revelations, and he had never been on her dance card to begin with. Not the least attractive part of Sergeant Liam Campbell's proposition was that the job took place six hundred miles away. Any rational person would have thought it a safe distance. Out of sight, out of mind, and all that.

Not.

Although why was she so surprised? Why wouldn't Erland Bannister know Finn Grant? What could be more natural? Thick as thieves, wasn't that how the old saying went? Took one to know one. Finn Grant would incline in Erland Bannister's direction the way water ran downhill.

She made an effort and smiled at the half dozen men sitting at the table she was currently tending. To a man, in a group fight-or-flight reaction they shoved their chairs back, so as to get the table out of the way if either became necessary. One of them even bolted to his feet.

Her rage did not cloud her powers of observation so that she didn't notice the sideways looks, the elbow nudges, the flurry of attempts to chat her up, at least until they saw her smile. If Gabe McGuire was interested in Kate Saracoff, she must really be something. Even Bill said invitingly, "You and Gabe seemed to be having an interesting conversation."

"He thought so," Kate said, and moved off.

Bill called for last drinks at eleven thirty and closed the bar promptly at midnight. "I got this," Kate said.

"Good," Bill said, "since it's your job."

Kate gave her a grin that was almost real. "Go home."

Bill thanked her and she and Moses left.

Kate washed down the tables and swept the floor, still on autopilot. Mutt plunked herself down next to the front door, indicating her willingness to head for the barn immediately, if not sooner. Kate wasn't the only one who'd been up most of the last two nights. "At least Moses didn't tie you into a pretzel for an hour and a half," Kate told her. "Don't worry, I wouldn't mind an early night myself."

She bagged the garbage and took it through the kitchen to the back door. She flipped the wall switch to turn on the light over the stairs but she didn't see it come on through the window in the door. Crap. She opened the door, straining to see in the darkness, and felt her way down the stairs and over to the Dumpster. The door swung closed behind her.

Maybe it was mention of Erland Bannister that had shaken her out of her usual caution, but really there was no excuse after the chest freezer incident for her not to be on her guard.

They rushed her as she was lifting the lid of the Dumpster. There were two of them, and they hit her at the same time, knocking her chest-first hard into the edge of the Dumpster.

All the breath was forced from her body in a single *whoosh*.

"Can't see a fucking thing!" she heard someone say from a great distance as she tried to breathe in and couldn't. Her lungs, her chest felt paralyzed.

"Have you got her?"

"I think so!" They caught her hands and held them behind her. "Can you find her pockets? Check her pockets!" A hand groped her breast and somebody laughed, a high, thin giggle stretched to the edge of terror.

Not professionals, someone thought somewhere in the deep recesses of an oxygen-depleted brain. Little white lights were sparking in front of her eyes. Her diaphragm would not extend no matter how hard she pushed at it. She heard a thud like a distant cannon going off, and then the sound of claws scrabbling on wood. She heard deep-throated, growling barks that promised much. She kicked out feebly, no strength behind it, because she couldn't draw any air into her lungs.

"Find her fucking pockets before that fucking dog of hers breaks out and rips us a fucking new one!"

Hands forced their way into her pockets, one after the other. "It's not here! Goddammit, I thought you said she had it!"

"I saw her put it in her jeans at the library, goddammit!"

"Shit! Did you check her watch pocket?"

Both speakers were male. One seemed to be the boss and the other a whiner.

Another ominous thud coincided with the definite sound of splintering wood.

"It's not on her, goddammit! What the fuck do we do now?"

"Come on, help me!"

"Oh, man, gross!"

"If she's in here, the dog won't chase us! Help me, goddammit!"

Hands grabbed her shoulders and her feet. She swung back and then forward and the hands let go at the end of the forward arc and she sailed through the air and gravity kicked in and she landed in the Dumpster with a disgusting, squashy-sounding splat.

The lid slammed down on top of her. Footsteps, running very fast. The distant sound of an engine starting and moving away in first gear with the gas pedal all the way down.

Kate wasn't in any shape to pay attention. She landed hard, which jolted her diaphragm out of its stasis. She inhaled, an enormous gulp of air, feeding her starved alveoli.

That was good.

But along with the air came the smell of three days'-worth of garbage, the remnants of burgers and fries and shakes and uneaten maraschino cherries, everything out of the bar, kitchen and bathroom garbage cans, paper towels and used Kleenex, not to mention used condoms from assignations consummated in the parking lot, all of it sitting there beneath her, fermenting.

She sucked it all in, for the moment just grateful to be breathing again.

22

JANUARY 21

Newenham

THE LID FLEW BACK. "Climbing out of there any time soon?" an irascible voice said. "Or were you thinking of spending the night?"

For a split second she thought she was hearing the voice of Old Sam.

"Gimmee."

She focused and saw a hand stretched out to her in the darkness. Mustering up the initiative from somewhere she grasped it. It pulled her over on her front and began a steady tug, sliding her through and over wine boxes, squashed beer cans, slimy lettuce leaves, and rotting tomato tops until she could reach the side of the Dumpster with her other hand. Between the two of them they got her out and on the ground.

"You're lucky they didn't toss you into the bottle bin," Moses said beside her.

There was another ominous thud and even more ominous crunching sound from the back door of the bar, accompanied by a continuous growling, slavering, threatening howl that Kate realized hadn't stopped since she'd gone in the Dumpster.

"Tell that dog of yours to cease and desist before the Newenham magistrate has her up on charges," Moses said.

Kate took another, cleaner breath of air and called up the requisite energy. "Mutt! It's okay! I'm all right!"

The howling stopped but there was another thud against the door, and even in the darkness Kate thought she saw it sag slightly in defeat. She grabbed the railing and hauled herself up the steps. It wasn't fully functional after Mutt's battering, but she pulled and swore at it and finally got it open. "I'm okay, girl, stand down."

Mutt, crouched to go airborne, poised in mid-launch. Her lips pulled back from her teeth, she went up on tiptoe and in reverse in the same movement, and the sound she made then would have been indistinguishable from "Eeeeee*yeeeeeew*!" in any other language.

"Nice," Kate said, "thanks, I appreciate your sympathy and support." She turned around to see Moses still on the bottom step. "What?"

"You planning on standing out here all night?" he said.

"I'm locking up, going home, and taking a shower," she said shortly. "Do you know who those two guys were?"

"Too dark to get a good look at them," he said.

"Not what I asked," she said.

"You're welcome, by the way," he said.

She stopped the futile attempt at brushing herself off and glared. "I hear tell you're supposed to be some kind of soothsayer. You couldn't have gotten here five minutes earlier? Maybe your crystal ball broke down?"

"For people in real danger, maybe," he said. "For you, no."

She watched him vanish around the corner of the building, and thanked whatever powers there were that he hadn't decided it was a good time to do form.

Whatever the hell that was.

Mutt politely declined the invitation to hop on back of the

ATV, instead loping beside Kate all the way back to the apartment over the garage. The mood Kate was in, it was a good thing it was empty.

The next morning her cell phone rang way too early. She groped for it with her eyes closed. "Make it good," she said.

"Don't start with me," Jim said, "I'm not even of this world yet."

She woke up. "Hey."

"Hey, your own damn self. Seen the inside of any chest freezers lately?"

From fast asleep on the braided rug Mutt woke and came all upstanding at the sound of her love god's voice. She padded over and nosed the cell phone. Kate shoved her aside. "Get your own guy." To Jim she said, "Dumpsters okay with you?"

A brief silence. "I don't even want to know, do I."

"You really don't. But I had a shower. I'm all, you know, cleaned and pressed. Wanna have phone sex?"

"Sure," he said automatically, because he was a man and any question with the word *sex* in it automatically elicited an answer in the affirmative. "Wait," he said, "what?"

She laughed, a husky, intimate sound. "You awake now?"

He cleared his throat. She imagined him shifting to ease the fit of his pants, and smiled to herself. "So, what were you doing in the Dumpster?"

"Coward," she said softly.

"The kid's right here," he said, or maybe he hissed.

She laughed again.

"Dumpster," he said. "I'm assuming you didn't climb in of your own free will." He paused. "Unless you did."

"I didn't," she said, laughter failing, and ran a hand through her hair to make sure no bits of eggshell lingered there.

Wouldn't hurt to shower again this morning, just to be sure. "Much as it humiliates me to admit it, I got thrown in."

"Where was Mutt?"

"On the other side of the door."

"That's never stopped her before."

"Wouldn't have stopped her this time if they hadn't run off and I got out in time to calm her down. As it is, I think I have to pay for a new one."

"Who did it? Or maybe that question should be, why?" There was the sound of another voice, and she heard Jim say, "Somebody threw your esteemed guardian into a Dumpster."

"Really?" she heard Johnny say. "Did anybody get pictures?"

"So?" Jim said into the phone. "Whodunnit?"

I saw her put it in her jeans at the library.

"I've got it down to around ten or so," she said.

"Oh," he said. "Well, at least you're narrowing the field. What the hell's going on down there, anyway?"

"If anything," she said, stretching, "Campbell grossly underestimated the amount of enemies his vic had. And get this."

"What?"

She shoved the covers aside and sat up. Mutt leaned against her bare legs and yearned toward the phone. "Erland Bannister is connected to Finn Grant somehow."

There was a long and, Kate sensed, somehow fraught silence. "How?" Jim said eventually.

"I don't know, exactly," Kate said. "He, ah, made an introduction to someone I met down here."

"Someone involved with the case?"

"Sort of, although not really."

"Thanks for clearing that up." Another odd silence.

"What?" Kate said.

"It'll keep till you get back," he said. "What next?"

She looked out the window. Dawn was drawing a thin light on the horizon. "I think I'm going to hitch a ride," she said. Before he could ask what she meant, she said, "What's going on at home?"

A momentary silence, to let her know he noticed she had changed the subject. "A lot of the usual, a couple of the not so usual."

"Such as?"

"Don't clutch, everyone's alive," he said, "but Frank Echuck got his hands on his dad's three-fifty-seven, and he shot his brother David with it." Hearing the intake of Kate's breath, he said more loudly this time, "Remember, everyone's alive. David got off with a grazed forearm. Pretty big graze, and his ears are still ringing, but a lot better than it could have been."

"Don't tell me Nick just left that cannon sitting around loaded!"

"Okay, I won't," Jim said, "but he did. He told the kids never to touch any of his firearms unless he, Nick, was present. That might work when the kids are younger, but once they hit their teens, it's all about pushing the limits. Like I said, David was mostly scared, and the boys at the clinic patched him up. In the meantime, I'm not sure Frank's ever going to be able to sit down again. I might have stepped in, were I a better person, but let the punishment fit the crime and all that."

Kate waited for her heart to slow down. "Nick needs a gun safe," she said.

Jim snorted. "Oh hell, Kate, you know better than that. Nobody outside of Anchorage owns a gun safe. A gun rack over the door is the best we can hope for, maybe, and I told

Nick so. By the time I left, he'd stopped whaling on the kid and was getting out his tools." A pause. "I told him he could start locking up his liquor, too."

"They'd got into his booze?"

She could almost hear his shrug. "They're fourteen, their mother split, when they're not at school they're home alone."

"This is happening too damn often," Kate said.

"Over the entire state," Jim said. "I'm just glad this time I didn't need a body bag. Listen, Kate..."

"I'm listening."

"You know Frank and David are Annie Mike's nephews."

"Yes," Kate said.

"She's pretty shook by this, as you might imagine. And..."

"And?"

"And, just looking at it from the outside in, you understand, not being a shareholder and all..." It didn't take telepathy to hear him thinking, *And thank god for that.*

"Yes?" Kate said, although again telepathy wasn't required to guess what was coming next.

"Yeah, well, I think the board's giving her first days as chair a rough ride. Things I hear indirectly, you know, and she looked pretty frazzled even before I told her about the twins. She could probably use a phone call about now."

"No," Kate said.

"Ah, come on, Kate—"

"No," Kate said, even more firmly. "I took this job for this exact reason, so she couldn't lean on me and so the shareholders couldn't end-run around her to me and undercut her authority. I know it's tough, but she has to learn, and she can only learn by doing. And everybody else has to learn to go to her, not come to me."

"Yeah, well, there's been some of that, too," he said grimly.

"Johnny and I should have left town with you."

Someone hammered on the door. She knew instantly who it was. "Shit," she said, with feeling.

"What?" he said. "What now?"

"Just a little gnat I have to swat," she said. "Call you later."

She hung up, pulled on her sweats, and went to the door.

"Get your ass in gear," Moses said, "I ain't got all goddamn day."

Mutt didn't exactly whimper, but she did retreat again to the far side of the room. "Look at that, you even scare the dogs." Kate started to close the door in Moses' face.

"Fry bread," he said.

The door halted in midswing.

"With nagoonberry jelly."

The door opened again. "I really do hate your living guts," she said.

At least he hadn't been lying about breakfast. Only ninety minutes of torture later and Kate had a heaping plate set before her. "How come Bill doesn't have to do whatever the hell it is?"

"Tai chi," Chouinard said.

"Yang style," Campbell said.

"I could really give a shit," Kate said.

Both of them snickered. Moses ignored all three of them, head down in his own plate. His table manners were neat but efficient and he was done before the rest of them were halfway through. He grabbed the bag holding his ninja outfit and gave Kate a hard stare. "Some people can fly no hands, you know," he said, and marched out.

Kate meditated on the door. "I don't understand why he feels the need to speak at me in tongues," she said.

Campbell and Chouinard exchanged a glance and kept their mouths full.

"I got tossed into a Dumpster last night," she said.

Campbell choked on his fry bread and only narrowly missed spitting nagoonberry jelly down the front of his pristine uniform. "Really," he said, coughing, his eyes watering.

"Really," she said, and told him about it.

When she was done he said thoughtfully, "Describe the guy at the library."

"Mid-forties, medium, medium, brown, brown," she said. "I'd say there was a little Native going on there, maybe Yupik as his torso seemed a little longer than his legs." She thought. "Oh yeah, and he was missing a finger on his left hand. Or part of one, the top half of his middle finger."

"Artie Diedrickson," Campbell and Chouinard said at the same time. "And the other guy was probably his boon companion, best friend, and co-conspirator, Leon Coopchiak," Campbell said.

"The guy in the video," Kate said.

"Okay," Campbell said, brightening in much the same way Jim Chopin did whenever he had a clear line on a perp. "Let's go find Artie."

Kate shook her head. "I've got other plans."

He knew her MO well enough now to be immediately suspicious. "Other plans? What kind of other plans?"

She shrugged, noncommittal. "Might be another lead. Might not be. Want to check it out."

"Another lead?" Campbell looked at Chouinard. "Ten—eleven if we're being strictly fair—blackmail victims not enough motive for murder for you?"

She spread her hands. "I got an itch. I want to scratch it. It's likely nothing. If it's something, I'll let you know. In the meantime, you'll run down the perps off that list?"

"Which, absent a confession, cannot be admitted in court," he pointed out. "Since I can take no official cognizance of how it came into my possession."

"Then get a confession," Kate said, and smiled at him.

He looked at her, and she looked back, the picture of innocence, if a cobra with its hood extended could be called innocent. He shook his head. "Jim didn't tell me the half of it, did he."

"Where would be the fun in that?" she said sweetly.

He looked wary, as well he might, but he didn't ask and she didn't tell. He left and Kate and Chouinard cleaned up the kitchen. On the wall Kate saw a photograph of Chouinard and Campbell and a teenage boy. "Who's the kid?"

"My son," Chouinard said, looking over her shoulder. "Adopted."

"Oh, yeah, I remember," Kate said. "As it happens, I've got one of those myself. How old?"

"Sixteen."

"Mine's seventeen. Going to graduate high school this year. Where's yours?"

"At AVTEC at the University of Alaska in Anchorage, getting his A&P certificate and, I hope, a degree."

Kate raised her brows. "At sixteen."

At first she thought Chouinard wasn't going to answer. "He had a pretty hairy childhood. After I, ah, found him, he got into some trouble. Liam got him out of it, and I thought he was going to be okay. Then he lost a girlfriend. As in, she died."

"I think I read something about it."

Chouinard gave a short laugh. "You and everyone else in the state of Alaska."

The series of articles on Clayton Gheen had short-listed Jo Dunaway for a bunch of prizes, and maybe even a Pulitzer, if Kate remembered rightly. It didn't make her think any better of the reporter, of course. "Teenagers are already one gigantic hormone banging off the walls. Couldn't have helped to have his life put under a microscope for everyone to see."

"Jo kept him out of it as much as she could, but..." Chouinard shrugged. "He wanted to talk to her. Wanted to talk about Amelia. And Christine, another of Gheen's victims that Tim knew. So I let him. Maybe it was a mistake, I don't know." She shook her head and tried for a smile. "Remorse is the ultimate in self-abuse. Who said that?"

"Travis McGee. Well, John D. Macdonald did, channeling McGee."

Chouinard smiled, a real one this time. "Right. Anyway. Tim tried to go back to school, but it just wasn't working for him. He'd grown up too much, too fast. He came home one day and told me all the other kids were fuckups and fuckoffs—his words—and he wanted to get his GED and learn a trade. I'd already been teaching him to fly, so I pulled some strings and got him into AVTEC. When he gets his degree, he says he's coming back to work for me." Chouinard smiled, looking out the window at the river. "I'd like that. I'd like it a lot, but two years in the big city might change his mind." She turned to Kate. "How about your boy? He have plans?"

Kate laughed. "He's either going to be a wildlife biologist, the next Bill Gates, or married and the father of five before he's old enough to drink."

"Yikes," Chouinard said. "You have the talk with him?"

"Yep. You?"

They shuddered simultaneously, and laughed together.

"You should call me Wy," Chouinard said.

"You should call me Kate, Wy," Kate said.

They shook on it.

Thighs aching, stomach full, strangely at peace, Kate, with Mutt perched behind, headed out once more to Eagle Air.

In her strange exalted mood, she was unsurprised to see a Cessna Caravan Cargomaster touching down on the runway as she crested the edge of the gravel berm. She pulled correctly around to the front, every inch the legitimate visitor, and to any interested observer was just about to go inside when Tasha Anayuk came trotting out on her four-inch heels. She flashed Kate a smile and said in her perpetually breathless voice, "Hi! Be right with you!"

"No problem," Kate said, "take your time."

The Cessna pulled up to the fuel tanks. The engine stopped and the pilot climbed out. He was a balding, middle-aged man dressed in plaid shirt and blue jeans, a small paunch bulging over a wide leather belt with a flashy brass buckle.

Tasha pushed over a ladder on wheels. He said something and Kate heard her giggle. She started back toward the office and pivoted to say, "Don't forget to come in and sign your invoice, Boyd!" She arched her back so as to show off her admittedly lush figure to the pilot, who fully appreciated it. He was no Gabe McGuire, but maybe Tasha had a nervous tic that caused her to flaunt the merchandise before any male standing in line of sight.

"Now, how may I help you?" she said to Kate. "Oh wait, I remember. Kathy?"

"Kate. And you're Tasha," Kate said.

"Well, come on in, Kate," Tasha said.

"Thanks," Kate said, but she paused briefly after Tasha had gone inside. There was a stick on the ground near the door, and she picked it up and threw it to land next to the

Cessna. "Mutt," she said in a low voice. "Go make friends with the nice pilot."

Mutt gave her a quizzical look, but she headed for the stick. Kate went inside.

"Is that your dog?" Tasha said when Kate came in. "Gosh, she's just beautiful. She looks like a wolf."

"Only half," Kate said.

"'Only,'" Tasha said, giggling. "Well, that's okay, then. I guess she won't eat Boyd alive."

I wouldn't be too sure of that, Kate thought.

"So what are you doing out here?" Tasha said, bustling around in back of her desk.

"I told Wy Chouinard I was looking for work, and she mentioned Eagle Air might be looking for another girl."

"I heard Bill gave you a job," Tasha said.

Tasha was evidently too blotto to remember Kate bringing her a beer on dividend night. "Everyone in Newenham knows everyone's business, I guess."

"It's not that big a town," Tasha said with an engaging twinkle.

"No, and I really appreciated being able to go to work as soon as I hit dirt, but I don't go to work at Bill's until four in the afternoon. Maybe you need some morning help?"

"I could use it," Tasha said, sighing. "This one-woman-operation thing is getting old fast. I don't get hardly any time off. Finn was going to hire four of us, and then ... well."

"He died, I heard. Who's running things now?"

"Mrs. Grant, sort of, but mostly Mr. Reid. He was here the first time you came through."

"Oh yeah, I remember, skinny guy, safari suit, seemed like the nervous type. Where does he live?"

"Anchorage. He's been back and forth like a Ping-Pong

ball, though, ever since Finn died." Tasha nodded to herself. "I'll have to talk to him, see if he'll let me hire you. He has to know that if we're going to keep this operation going, we have to have some more people on the ground. I'm already taking reservations for bear hunts in the spring, and then it'll be the fishermen, and all those everlasting board retreats, and the ecotourists, and on top of that we've got all these cargo contracts that Finn signed that we have to honor if we don't want to give them all their money back." She looked worried. "Plus Mr. Reid thinks they could sue."

Kate nodded in the general direction of the Cargomaster. "You've got enough people in the air, I take it."

Tasha nodded again, vigorously. "Gosh, yes, that's the first people Finn and Mr. Reid hired. Well, they bought all those planes as soon as we moved out here, and as Finn says—excuse me, used to say—they weren't earning money if they weren't in the air. And with the new, bigger planes coming in—"

"Bigger planes?" Kate said.

Tasha shrugged. "Finn was talking about buying some big cargo plane. Like buying it from the Greeks."

Kate had been unaware until then that Boeing and Airbus had competition, especially in the land of Hermes. "Greeks?"

Tasha frowned. "Maybe it had a Greek name?"

"Hercules?" Kate said.

Tasha brightened. "That's it!"

A few years back Kate had worked for an air taxi outfit out of Bethel with a Herc on the equipment list. A venerable aircraft that had been around for almost sixty years, the Lockheed C-130 Hercules aircraft was a four-engine clamshell with a three-hundred-mile-per-hour cruising speed and a two-thousand-mile-plus range. It had been originally designed as a troop and weapons carrier for short takeoffs and landings in combat zones. What was far more interesting to Kate was that the Herc could carry up to thirty-six tons of freight, but before she could ask Tasha what she thought Finn Grant was planning on carrying thirty-six tons of, the door opened and Boyd walked in.

He was closer to sixty than fifty, and whatever salary he was earning wasn't going for clothes or grooming. He was a little out of breath. Mutt shouldered in between him and the door and went to stand next to Kate.

"Your dog?" Boyd said.

She nodded.

"Thought she was a wolf when I looked down from the ladder and saw her sitting there."

Kate opened her mouth. "Only half," Tasha said.

"She's gorgeous, whatever her heritage, and she teaches a pretty good game of fetch." He looked at Tasha. "Figured I'd put my feet up in the break room for a bit. Reid around?"

Tasha shook her head.

"Good." He looked at Kate and gave her a once-over. "Buy you a drink?"

The smile that spread across Kate's face was one part predator to two parts siren. "Sure," she said, and she and Mutt followed him into the luxurious ready room Tina had hosted her in.

"Want a beer?" Boyd said, already at the refrigerator. "I'm flying, I can't."

"Diet anything works."

"Ice?"

"Sure, if there is some."

"Whatever you want, we've got it."

Kate noticed the possessive. "Are you a partner in the business?"

He nodded, his back to her as he filled two glasses with ice and split a Diet Coke between them. "All the pilots are." He found a lime and cut it into wedges and squeezed in one each. He turned. "Sit, sit," he said. "Boyd Levinson. What's your name?"

"Kate," she said. "Kate Saracoff. And this is Mutt."

Boyd gave Mutt's head a good scratching, which she appreciated, tail thumping the floor hard enough to set up a symphonic resonance with the glassware in the cupboard. *Slut,* Kate thought. "Where are you flying to this afternoon?" she said.

"Adak," he said.

"Wow," she said. "That's way the hell and gone out the Chain."

"Eight hundred sixty-four miles," he said, and toasted her, giving her another once-over that was appreciative without giving offense.

If he'd been twenty years younger and fifty pounds lighter, it might even have elicited a positive response from any reasonable female, and may well have, once. But hope springs eternal in the male of any age or condition. It was one of those verities of life.

It was one of the surest bets you could make. Kate raised her glass in return to his toast and accompanied it with another of her very best smiles. Even Mutt's ears pricked up at that vast expanse of gleaming enamel. Boyd looked like he might thump his tail, too, if he had one.

"I've never been to Adak," Kate said.

23

JANUARY 21

Newenham

LIAM WENT FIRST TO Artie Diedrickson's home. His wife—soon to be ex, she informed Liam—didn't know where he was and didn't care, but if Liam really wanted to talk to Artie—she couldn't imagine why—he could frequently be found at the home of that useless asshole, Leon Coopchiak, if Leon's grandmothers hadn't finally gotten a clue and thrown Leon out on his own worthless ass.

He escaped with his life if not his ears intact and went from Artie's to Leon Coopchiak's. Leon wasn't married, not surprising when his establishment was home to two grandmothers, three uncles, his mother, four sisters, and assorted offspring. None of them knew or would admit to knowing where he was, and one of the sisters even said, "I don't know what you're talking about, Sergeant Campbell, we don't have a brother."

He was just as glad when she closed the door in his face. Hostility times that many people was more than he could take this early in the morning. The upside was nobody shot at him to help him on his way.

He decided to put Artie and Leon on hold for the moment, and started working his way down the list of other victims on

Finn Grant's thumb drive.

Lucy Nick opened the door, saw him, and started to cry. Feeling like an ogre, he followed her into the house, a small, painfully neat clapboard building on the edge of town. It was surrounded by trees, right up to the eaves, which darkened the interior but which undoubtably also made her clientele feel more secure, most of them being married.

"How did you find out?" she said, sinking down into a sunken couch. It was covered in a bright floral print that looked ordered out of the JCPenney catalog. She'd covered it in Visqueen to protect it from stains.

"Finn Grant," he said.

She put her face in her hands and rocked back and forth. "He promised," she said. "He promised he wouldn't tell if I just gave him what he wanted."

He chose a straight-backed chair, circa the same designer as the rest of the room, and balanced his cap on his knee, looking, he was sure, as uncomfortable as he felt. He was pretty sure she was still crying behind her hands. It just didn't get any worse than that.

"You probably think I'm a slut, don't you," she said.

"Lucy, I—"

"It wasn't like I planned it. I just ... slid into it."

"Lucy, I don't really care about—"

"Roddy died, and we weren't well off. I leased his boat and permit out to Norman and Dwayne, his two deckhands." She reached for a Kleenex.

"Lucy, I—"

"Dwayne stopped by, only offering to help, you know, and I was so lonely and so frightened, and one thing led to another, and he left some money behind, and then he told Norman, and Norman—" She blew her nose, a soggy, bubbling sound that added to the miasma of general misery in the room. Liam wanted to be anywhere but here.

"Lucy, really, that's not why—"

"It was so easy, you know? A lot of times men don't want the complications, and most of them are nice to me." And she added unexpectedly, "And I had no idea how much they were willing to pay for a half an hour of a woman's time."

"Lucy," he said loudly. She looked at him, startled, eyes red and swollen. "Finn Grant found out about you, uh, the business you were operating out of your house, didn't he?"

"Finn!" Her face darkened. "That bastard!"

"He found out, didn't he? And he was blackmailing you."

She called Grant some more names, some of which were new, even to Liam. "He said he'd tell my kids."

She was crying again, sobbing, even, this time more angry than pitiful. "My Cindi, and Roddy Jr.," she said, sobbing and rocking back and forth. "They're both in college, in Anchorage now." She glared at him through her tears. "How many parents in this town can say that?"

"Not many," Liam said, thinking of Tim at UAA, and as always when he did so sending up a little prayer that the kid was keeping his nose in his books and not up his ass.

"If I didn't give Finn what he wanted, he said he would tell them how I was paying for their education. They'd drop out, I know my Roddy would for sure. Cindi, she'd be so ashamed and embarrassed, but Roddy would come home to take care of me, and he'd be stuck in this goddamn deadhead of a town for the rest! of his! life!" She punctuated the words with her fist, slamming it into the cushion next to her.

"Lucy," Liam said, raising his voice again.

Her face was congested with fear and rage and her eyes were fierce. "What," she said, or maybe spat. "Just what do you want, Liam?" Her mouth twisted. "I've got plenty to offer if you'll just leave me alone."

With what he felt was truly commendable self-control, Liam said quietly, "All I want is to know what Finn Grant wanted from you."

"You mean besides the usual?" she said.

Liam closed his eyes briefly. Of course. Finn would have loved getting something for free that everyone else had to pay for. "Yes," he said, "besides the usual." Because no way would Grant be looking only for the occasional free lay.

"He wanted our spot in the small boat harbor," she said, sitting back against the couch, exhausted. "When the Corps of Engineers opened it, Roddy won first choice in the lottery. We got the first two spaces, A-1 and A-2, right at the bottom of A Ramp. Two parking spaces went with them, in the lot next to the A Ramp dock." Her lips trembled, and Liam was afraid she was going to start crying again, but she didn't. "They were the best, most convenient moorings in the whole harbor, and Roddy won them fair and square."

"Why did Finn want them?"

She gave him a look of utter contempt. "For his fishing charters, of course. He didn't want his wimpy little Outside clients to have to walk too far to get on board."

He looked up from his ball cap, which he was now twisting in his hands. "Lucy, were you in town the day Finn Grant died?"

She blinked at him. "I—what?"

"Were you in town the day Finn Grant died?"

She looked bewildered. "When was that? Last month?"

He nodded. "The eleventh."

"I don't know, Liam. Oh, wait. I went to Anchorage to visit the kids and look at a condo." Again with that sudden ferocity she said, "Because I've got enough saved now for at least a down payment. I signed the paperwork over Christmas, and as soon as I've got a for sale sign on this house, I'm getting out of here!"

"Good for you," he said. "So you weren't in town when Finn died."

She smiled, a fearsome sight with her red eyes and dripping nose and blotched cheeks. "I heard the news when I got off the plane. It's all anyone was talking about in the terminal." She clenched her hands. "I was glad," she said in a low, intense voice. "Glad, do you hear me? That bastard made my life a living hell. All I could think about was the kids finding out." She slumped. "And if everyone found out, the men would stop coming, and how could I ever make enough money to pay their school bills?"

Liam had had about as much as he could take. He stood up. "One last question, Lucy. Are you a pilot?"

"What?" she said. "No. God, no."

"You know anything about airplanes? Ever worked around them? Any family members pilots?"

"No, no, and no," she said. "All I know about airplanes is they get us places quicker. And tickets on them get more expensive every day. And you get felt up when you have to get on the big ones." Her mouth turned down. "And you don't get paid for it, either."

"Okay," Liam said, and made for the door.

"Wait!" she said, coming after him before he could get off the porch. "Liam, wait!"

He turned to see her standing in the doorway. "What are you going to do?"

"Do?" he said. "About you, you mean? Nothing. Nothing, Lucy," he added when she looked disbelieving. "Nothing at all. I've never had a call out here. So far as I know, you live a quiet life. Your, ah, social life is not a subject of police interest."

He was at his vehicle before she spoke again. "Liam?"

He paused with the door open.

She smiled at him, a pathetic effort. "You're welcome back," she said. "Anytime."

His next stop was Willie Wassillie's house, a large split-level ranch south of town with a two-car attached garage set on five acres on the river. Willie had a shop on a dock, with a boat ramp leading down to the river and a set of stairs leading up to the house. A dry dock on the edge of the beach would be accessible only at spring and fall high tides. He was a fisherman, the high boater Finn Grant had referred to in his files, and on the evidence of Liam's own eyes a very successful one.

His wife, Emily, answered the door. Liam was ready with a story of a minor altercation Willie might have witnessed down at the docks the previous summer, and she sent him down to the shop, where he found her husband mending nets in the loft.

Willie Wassillie was more Yupik than Lucy, short, bowlegged, thick chested, with a broad brown face, black hair in a buzz cut that hadn't changed since he'd gotten out of the marines, and a gaze that seldom met Liam's own, so he couldn't tell what color the eyes were. He would have been raised to believe that that was rude, and unlike Lucy, he spoke little, another village trait.

After Liam's last interview, this was something of a relief. He took advantage of Native custom and after sharing some of Willie's coffee and a few of the excellent sugar cookies Emily had sent to work with Willie that morning, came to the point. Willie Wassillie hadn't paid federal income taxes in his life, which amounted to at least forty years of income he was liable for. Finn Grant knew it, and now Liam knew it. "What did he want, Willie?"

Wassillie passed a worn flat mending needle made of what looked like ivory through the green line of the net he was mending, formed what to Liam's fascinated eyes was a complicated construction that when pulled tight resolved itself into a mesh opening exactly the size of the ones on either side of it, and knotted it off. He put down the needle and reached for his thick white porcelain mug.

Liam knew stalling when he saw it, Yupik or white. "If it makes you feel any better, you weren't the only one Finn was blackmailing."

Wassillie looked up. His eyes were an unexpected blue. "I know."

"How?" Liam said bluntly.

Wassillie shrugged. "Word got out. People talking to people they shouldn't. You hear about Joe Griggs?" At Liam's nod, he said, "No one ever knew if it was an accident, or suicide. Course, that trooper they had before you wasn't much use. But right after they buried Joe, Finn bought his business from Joe's wife."

"She still around?"

Wassillie shook his head. "Sold her house, left town. No one's heard from her since." He picked up his needle again.

"What did he want, Willie?"

Wassillie looked for the next hole in his net, taking his time. There was a potbellied woodstove on the first floor and all the heat from the fire within had migrated to the loft. Liam was in no hurry.

"My white grandfather homesteaded Jackknife Pass."

Liam waited.

"He left it to me."

Liam waited some more.

"Finn said if I sold it to him, he'd keep quiet about the taxes."

"What kind of a price?"

Wassillie admired a section of newly mended net. "Borough assessment."

Liam winced. Borough assessments were notoriously lower than fair market value. "Ouch. When was this?"

"Five years ago."

"You remember where you were, the day he died?"

Wassillie was a lot quicker on the uptake than Lucy Nick had been. "Why would I? Kept his word. Took the lodge and never told anyone what he knew. Never asked for anything more."

"Didn't answer my question," Liam said. "Do you remember where you were that day?"

The ivory mending needle went to work, creating a graceful pas de deux between twine and net. "It was your wife had the fight with him the day before he died."

Liam bit back the first, second, and third things he wanted to say. "Willie. Do you remember where you were that day?"

After a while, Wassillie answered. "Hawaii. Wife and the kids with me. We always go to Hawaii in January."

Being blackmailed out of his grandfather's fishing lodge notwithstanding, Wassillie was definitely a high boater, all right. Of course, if he wasn't paying federal taxes, he had more walking-around money than most.

"Mind if I check with Emily on the Hawaii trip?"

Shrug.

Time for Liam to go. "Thanks for the coffee," he said, and got to his feet.

"Hey." Liam paused at the top of the stairs, one hand on the railing.

"You gonna tell anyone?"

Liam pulled on his ball cap, settling it firmly over his head. "Tell who what? I'm a state officer, not a federal one. Although, personally, I think you're an idiot. The IRS doesn't fool around. You'll do federal time when they catch you."

There was the barest gleam of a smile on Wassillie's taciturn face. "They haven't yet."

Emily confirmed the Hawaii trip. She even showed him digital pictures, with date stamps. They had three kids and seven grandkids, a healthy-looking bunch with white teeth gleaming against tanned faces. Everyone looked happy and relaxed, standing in front of a bungalow with a screened porch that ran the full length of the house. "So nice to have the family together once a year," Emily said, looking fondly at the photographs. "Good that we built a place big enough to hold them all."

Liam drove away thinking that if Wassillie was dodging taxes, at least he was putting the money to good use elsewhere.

He spent the day checking the rest of the names on Finn Grant's thumb drive. One had died, the aforementioned Joe Griggs. Two had moved away, one five years before and the other two years before. A few of those who remained tried to deny the evidence, until Liam quoted them chapter and verse. No one could say Finn Grant wasn't thorough.

None of them made any bones over their relief at Finn Grant's death, and all of them were perfectly appalled at the idea that the local trooper had inherited Grant's files. A few of them, more wearily than resentfully, wanted to know what they had to do to keep him quiet.

And one and all, like Lucy Nick, like Willie Wassillie, were able to demonstrate conclusively that they hadn't been anywhere near Finn Grant's Super Cub during the time in question.

Liam drove back to the post. Tenth on the list was the priest. The local Catholic church was closed between visits by the priest who made the rounds of all the villages between and including Pilot Point, Newenham, and Togiak. Liam had met Father Dougal on occasion and had found him tolerable, for a member of an institution that hadn't had a new idea since Alfred the Great united the Saxons against the Danes. He called the Anchorage archdiocese and asked for him. Only three more phone calls and he tracked him down in Manokotak.

"Father Tom?" Father Dougal said, and Liam noted the drop in temperature from one sentence to the next. "What did you want to know about him?"

"First of all, where is he?"

"He's, ah, taken early retirement," Father Dougal said.

Unseen by Father Dougal, Liam's eyes hardened. *Early retirement* in terms of priestly vocation had lately come to mean only one thing. "You haven't answered my question, Father Dougal."

"You haven't told me why you're asking, Sergeant Campbell."

"His name came up in connection with a case."

Dread flattened the priest's voice. "What kind of case?"

"Murder," Liam said bluntly.

"Murder?"

Coming from anyone else, the relief in Father Dougal's voice would have sounded comic, but Liam was not amused. "I need to know when Father Tom was last in Newenham."

"Is he a witness?"

"I am not at liberty to say."

Father Dougal's tone sharpened. "Is he a suspect?"

"I may not comment on an ongoing investigation, Father Dougal," Liam said, rather enjoying himself. "Will you put me in touch with Father Tom, please?"

"Yes, well, I'm sorry, Sergeant Campbell, but Father Tom is on retreat."

"I thought you said he'd retired."

A good liar's most important asset was a good memory. Evidently, Father Dougal wasn't the first and lacked the second. It was the best thing Liam knew about him, so far. "Uh, yes. Of course."

"Which is it?" Liam said. "Retired, or on retreat? And regardless, I need to speak to him."

In that age-old refuge of those lower down the ladder, Father Dougal decided to pass the buck. "I'll forward your request to Father Tom's superiors."

"You do that," Liam said, and hung up.

He put his feet up and folded his hands over his belt buckle and regarded the toes of his boots with a gloomy expression. He didn't hold out a lot of hope that Father Tom was the perp in Grant's murder, but he sure as hell didn't mind trying to hang it on him, just for the sheer satisfaction of nailing him for something. He knew a trooper who had been an investigating officer on the case that had uncovered the ring of Catholic priests stationed in tiny parishes in the Yukon River district. It transpired that many of them had been transferred there from parishes in the Pacific Northwest, where they had been found to be molesting and raping altar boys. No measures had been taken to correct their conduct or to punish them for it, oh no, Liam's friend had said. They'd just been moved, to isolated communities of indigenous people that were too small to have running water, let alone a local cop.

Liam's friend had then gotten very, very drunk. Liam had helped him. Later, the friend had retired the day after he became eligible for retirement, and went to work as a guard on the Trans-Alaska Pipeline, where the worst he had to deal with was imported hookers, bootleggers, dope dealers, power thieves, and disappearing D9 Caterpillar tractors. The last time Liam had seen him, he had looked ten years younger.

He plugged the thumb drive back into his computer and scrolled down through the folders. Other than Father Tom, he had accounted for all the names on the list save Leon Coopchiak's.

The door opened and he looked up, only to be turned into a pillar of salt.

Ex-trooper Diana Prince, his onetime subordinate, was back.

And by the look of the medicine ball-sized belly that preceded her through the door, not alone.

"If it isn't the Wicked Stepmother," he said.

His cell phone rang, lately an unusual occurrence. Newenham's local populace had pretty much given up on expecting a uniformed response for anything less than murder.

But this time he knew who it was without even looking at the display. Eyes on Diana Prince, who looked untidy, overweight, irritable, and oddly out of uniform, he answered. "Hi, Dad," he said.

There was a rich chuckle in his ear. "Hey, son."

"Let me guess why you called," Liam said. "My status as an only child is about to change."

He hung up without waiting for a reply. "The last person I

expected to fall for my father's bullshit was you," he said.

Prince, a onetime lithe, black-haired beauty with electric blue eyes, waddled to a chair and didn't sit so much as fall into it. "Don't rub it in."

"Oh, I think I will," Liam said.

"I need a job, Liam," she said. "And a place to stay."

He drove back out to Leon's house. Nobody was home this time, which at least saved him from another beatdown by a Newenham woman, who seemed to be collectively honing their skills in the art today.

He sat in his truck, tapping out a rhythm on the steering wheel.

He'd dropped Diana off at home, where at least she'd have a comfortable chair with a place to put her feet up, which looked like they needed it. The sides of her shoes had been slit to allow for expansion. "Your feet look like they belong to Henry the Eighth."

She cast him a look of acute dislike.

He brought her a glass of ice-filled orange juice.

"Thanks," she said with real gratitude. She drank deeply and set the glass down, putting her head back and closing her eyes.

His strayed down to her massive belly. "You sure it's not twins?"

"I'm sure," she said without opening her eyes.

"Dad's thrilled, I'm sure," he said. "This time maybe he'll luck out and get a son who isn't afraid to fly."

"Maybe," she said, "except she's a girl."

"Oh."

She opened her eyes and looked up at him. "I'm sorry, Liam."

"You could have said good-bye," he said. "Hell, you could at least have resigned so I could have got someone in to take your place. John Barton kept saying you'd be back, there was no point in sending someone to fill your slot. The local cops resigned in a body when Jim Earl cut their pay again. It's been a little frantic out around these parts."

"I know. You're right. But your father—"

"Yeah, I know, Colonel Charles Campbell, USAF, not just a man but a god."

"He's a brigadier general now."

"Oh," he said for the second time.

He waited for more, but she had closed her eyes again, and she looked so exhausted that he forbore from further recriminations, at least for the moment. "You can have Tim's bedroom, second door on the right after the bathroom. Wy's in the air. I'll leave a message on her voice mail so she knows you're here."

"She going to be as happy to see me as you are?"

If he had stayed with Diana he was going to keep asking questions and she really didn't look up to giving him the answers, so he'd shelved family, for the moment, and gone back to work. After all, it wasn't like he wanted to talk about his father. Most of the time he worked at not even thinking about him.

Artie Diedrickson, now. Artie Diedrickson was a bit of a boob.

Boobs, like water, tend to find their own level. That level usually included alcohol.

He poked his head in at Bill's. She was there but he didn't see anyone else of interest. He waved and left.

He went by the other bar. No luck there, either.

At the liquor store next to the AC he went in to talk to the clerk, Sally. She was a fifty-five-year-old matron with a plump figure and a flirtatious eye, who appreciated being chatted up by a good-looking man in uniform. Liam leaned against the counter and smiled down at her. "Hey, Sal."

She fluffed up her tightly permed hair. "Hey, Liam."

"How's business?"

She fluttered her heavily mascaraed eyelashes. "Less boring, now that you've dropped by."

Liam had no problem with putting a little zing into someone's step, so long as everyone concerned understood that his wedding ring wasn't merely for show. Five minutes give-and-take and he was the happy possessor of the information that Teddy Engebretsen had come in around noon and paid cash for six cases of beer. "We make all that crowd pay cash now," Sally said, crossing her arms and leaning on the counter, so as to display her substantial bosom to effect.

"Wise decision," Liam said, and threw in an appreciative glance, just for extra.

Forget it, Liam, he thought, *it's Delinquentville.*

The tiny community huddled in a hollow between two small hills, off a road which was off another road which was off the road to the airport. The road had a name but no one remembered it, because the street sign marking the intersection never lasted more than twenty-four hours after the city put up a new one, and after a while the city decided to spend its money elsewhere. Delinquentville (so christened by Liam shortly after his arrival in Newenham) was a collection of ancient log cabins, broken-down trailers and gear shed lean-tos, awash in a sea of stuff that had been too good to throw away for a hundred years, which by now had deteriorated to junk that wasn't worth the effort of throwing away. It was a fine distinction, but it was one of the few the residents of Delinquentville were capable of making.

Pushki and alders threw up sprouts from piles of cement blocks and rusty car bodies. Scrub spruce clustered around the perimeter, leaning in over the jagged line of roofs as if to eavesdrop on the latest get-rich-quick schemes. Dogs chained to doghouses outside and house dogs inside set up a continuous howl that competed with the blaring of Coldplay, Lady Gaga, and Lil Wayne.

Here was gathered every Newenhamer who'd ever been thrown out by his wife, his mother, or his girlfriend. Herein dwelt the deadbeat dads, the incurable drunks, the serial adulterers, the petty thieves, the liars, the losers, and the louses, the unlucky, the unloved, and the unemployed. If your stepfather had harried you out of the house after he married your mother, if your girlfriend dumped you for another and vastly inferior guy, if the skipper had kicked you off your boat, not for showing up drunk but for your inability to do your job in that condition, you were sure to find a roof and a meal and sympathy in Delinquentville.

Delinquentvillers were overwhelmingly male in gender, although females were always welcome as visitors. One or two had tried it on a permanent basis, though not for long. Karl Marx would have approved, as Delinquentvillers practiced a communal lifestyle, albeit an involuntary one. Beer in particular was regarded as community property whoever brought it home.

On the whole, Liam was with Marx, although for different reasons. Delinquentville's existence meant he knew right where to go whenever Brewster Gibbons called to report that someone had tried to abscond with the Last Frontier Bank's ATM machine. It was a frequent enough occurrence that Liam was pretty sure Brewster had Liam's cell on speed dial.

Teddy Engebretsen had at one time been son-in-law to Mayor Jim Earl. A year after Liam's arrival on the scene, the mayor's daughter discovered that she had been deceived in her chosen spouse and had flounced out of Newenham on her father's dime. Jim Earl had evicted Teddy from the house he had bought the newlyweds, with an enthusiasm that had launched Teddy all the way to the tumbledown shack Liam was parked in front of now. And Teddy Engebretsen was one of Artie Diedrickson's many boon companions in downward mobility.

Liam got out of the truck and closed the door softly. As yet no one had looked out a window to see the trooper approaching the door. From behind it blared the sounds of Bon Jovi, which sort of surprised Liam, because that was almost like real music. He pulled his ball cap down tight on his head, shifted his belt so that his weapon was prominently displayed, although he did not unsnap the flap on the holster. There were plenty of weapons in Delinquentville but they were for the most part hunting rifles, and while Liam didn't delude himself that anyone was going to be happy to see him, he couldn't imagine a time when a Delinquentviller would draw down on him. Shiftless sad sacks they might be, but they were not in general predisposed to violence.

He knocked. He had to knock twice before anyone heard him over Bon Jovi's exhortations to keep the faith. "It's open! Wouldja just come the fuck in?"

He knocked a third time. "Jesus, you deaf? Just a fuckin' minute, wilya?" Footsteps tromped toward the door. Teddy opened it, and gaped at him, the trooper in his resplendent blue-and-gold uniform, perfectly tailored, excruciatingly tidy, a joy to behold.

Except, perhaps, for the occupants of Delinquentville. There was a single moment of electric silence, and then it was like the house exploded.

"It's the trooper!"

"Shit!"

"Run for it!"

"Get the fuck out of my way!"

Someone dived through a window without bothering to open it. Someone else kicked the boom box, and Bon Jovi scratched to an abrupt mid-wail halt. Liam heard a body crash against what had to be the back door. A toilet flushed, and someone screamed, "What the fuck do you think you're doing!"

"Jesus, are you deaf, man, it's Campbell!"

"Fuck!"

Teddy had vanished. Liam decided that even that hard-ass Fourth Amendment magistrate, Bill Billington, would say the open door qualified as an invitation to enter, and strolled inside. "Yoo-hoo," he said. "Anybody home?"

The main room of the cabin was totally trashed, empties all over the floor, *World of Warcraft* still running on the television, the sickeningly sweet smell of marijuana just beginning to dissipate. The furniture looked like Teddy had harvested it out of the municipal dump. Liam would not have subjected the seat of his immaculate uniform pants to that kind of abuse, not that he'd ever been invited to.

A movement caught the corner of his eye, and he turned to see Artie Diedrickson bolt toward the back door. Liam caught him by the scruff of the neck two steps shy, and had the cuffs on him when Leon Coopchiak slithered out of the kitchen in what he no doubt thought was unobtrusive fashion and made for the same back door. He was more successful than Artie, he made the door and was through it before Liam could catch him.

"Shit," Liam said. The last thing he wanted was a foot chase.

He went through the door, which was probably not his brightest move ever—What if one of these yo-yos did actually have a gun on him and was drunk enough to use it?—and stumbled into the obstacle course also known as Teddy's backyard. A smokehouse made from an old refrigerator tilted west with what might have been a homemade still tilting east next to it. Behind them was a greenhouse cobbled together of extremely used corrugated plastic, with a lot of green plants inside that he was certain were not tomatoes. He was fleetingly relieved not to see anything that resembled a meth cooker.

There were plastic paint buckets and empty Chevron fifty-five-gallon drums and a heap of broken-down chain saws and a dogsled in some indeterminate stage of repair. There were two snowmobiles and three ATVs and what might possibly have been the remains of an old U.S. Army jeep that Bill Mauldin had driven back from Italy after he won his Pulitzer in World War II. As many pieces as it was in, it could also once have been a Sherman tank, or possibly a baby carriage. Three dogs of indeterminate heritage were standing on top of the doghouses they were chained to, barking hysterically.

Leon was scrabbling over a rusty oil tank in a direction apparently chosen at random. The sun hadn't filtered through this mess in months and possibly years, and a nice thick layer of ice covered the ground. Liam in pursuit hit a patch of it at a dead run. It retaliated with concentrated malevolence and slid his feet right out from under him. Yelling and waving his arms, he slid into a pile of rotting lumber with nails sticking out of it, avoiding multiple impalements by inches, only upon recoil to kick over a burn barrel with a fire burning brightly inside it. It spilled in his direction and he jumped back and tripped over a pile of rusty rebar and angle iron and stepped into a bucket of white paint, open for some reason, covered with a thin layer of scum and pine needles. Kicking his foot free of the paint bucket he lost his balance and crashed into another barrel, this one with the top cut off. It was full of used oil. The edge was jagged and sharp so he threw both arms around it to catch his balance, just in time for it to rock back in his direction and slosh a gallon of the stuff in his face and down the front of his uniform.

He gave it a vigorous shove in the opposite direction and bent over, hands on his knees, coughing and hacking and heaving to get the oil out of his mouth and nose. He stood up and wiped his face on his jacket sleeve. He looked down at the length of his previously immaculate, superbly tailored self. His right foot was wet to the knee with white paint. The oil ran down his leg to join it.

Sally wouldn't have allowed him anywhere near her.

The dogs had stopped barking. In the subsequent stillness, a raven cawed, loud and mocking. He looked up and saw it sitting in the top of a spruce tree, peering down at him. It clucked and clicked its beak, conveying a vast and unmistakable amusement.

"All *right*," he said. "That is just about *enough*."

He turned on his heel and took off after Leon.

24

JANUARY 21

Adak

It wasn't until they were almost over Unimak Pass, the steaming cone of Mount Shishaldin passing on their left and the Aleutian Islands stretched out before them like a string of irregularly shaped pearls draped over a curve of deep blue velvet that Kate remembered the last time she had flown this same airspace, in an even smaller plane. Jack Morgan had been her pilot then, Jack Morgan, her onetime boss, her best friend, her lover, five years dead now.

The pain of her loss had once been so debilitating that she had had to leave the Park for a place that held no memories of him. That pain no longer brought her to her emotional knees, but she was conscious of his absence. She thought she always would be, and she thought it wasn't a bad epitaph.

Almost with his last breath he had commended his son into her care. She remembered Johnny's voice on the phone. *Did anybody get any pictures?* She turned her face to the window so Boyd wouldn't see her grin. Jack Morgan was gone, but he had left her wonderful memories, everlasting gratitude, and a made-to-order son.

She saw the faint outline of her own face in the Plexiglas and her grin faded.

It really bugged her that Gabe McGuire in person reminded her so much of Jack. Movie stars should stay up on the movie screen where they belonged, one giant step removed from anyone's real life.

It bugged her even more that McGuire could quote Jimmy Buffett verbatim.

"Great view, huh?" The voice over her headset crackled.

She resumed her most come-hither smile and turned back to Boyd. "I've never seen anything like it," she lied.

"Yeah, well." Boyd shrugged. "Lucky on the weather."

"No kidding," she said, "you can practically see over the horizon. I've spent a lot of time on boats—and planes—but I don't remember a time when the Earth seemed quite so round to me."

He looked at her, his expression appraising. He didn't say anything but Kate got the distinct impression that she'd passed some kind of test. Whatever happened to guys who just wanted a brainless bimbo for a one-night stand?

He'd passed his own test. She had enough experience in the air that she knew a good pilot when she saw one, and Boyd qualified. He was one of those people who didn't just climb into an aircraft, he put it on. The rudder pedals became an extension of his feet, flaps and ailerons extensions of his arms and hands. They had lifted off from Eagle Air with no unseemly amount of excess throttle, and when they reached altitude Boyd leveled off and throttled back and kept her there without seeming to think much about it. In spite of the fact that he had obvious hopes when he'd invited Kate for the ride-along, there was no slap-and-tickle or insinuating mention of the Mile-High Club once they were airborne. He was a pilot, he was on the job, and he could wait for the payoff until he got them safely down on the ground again.

Kate admired good pilots, partly because the histories of aviation and Alaska were so entwined, and partly because like most Alaskans she'd spent so much time sitting to the right of them. It was a pity, because every instinct she had told her that Boyd Levinson was as bent as they came.

"What are we hauling?" she'd asked him, looking over her shoulder at the lashed-down rubber totes as she climbed in.

"Spare parts for processors who deliver to Adak," he said glibly.

The distinct smell of machine oil in the air of the cabin was recognizable to anyone who had ever been forced to help Old Sam dismantle the kicker on the *Freya* before the fishing season started, so Kate was willing to believe there were moving metal parts in the sealed rubber totes. She smiled at him, and he smiled back and changed the subject. "What do you do?"

"Right now?" she said. "Bartend. Before? I worked on a processor ship out of St. Paul."

He looked over his shoulder at Mutt, and raised an eyebrow.

"She came later," Kate said.

"Tough job," he said, "fish processor. Especially for a woman."

Kate didn't take offense. He was right. "No kidding," she said. "It's mostly guys on the crew, and not very evolved guys at that. You were a bitch if you didn't and a whore if you did. Good money, I managed to build up a little stash, but I was glad to get off."

He smiled at her again. "I'm pretty evolved."

She smiled back. "I noticed."

His smile widened into a grin. So did hers, which, although he didn't know it yet, didn't mean quite the same thing.

Normally, he explained, he had an iPod hooked into the

airplane's sound system, and listened to podcasts like *Planet Money* and *Rush 24/7*. She understood the implication and endeavored to be at her wittiest and most sparkling. It wasn't that difficult, as again, like most pilots with that many hours, Boyd had led an interesting life. The army had taught him to fly, and he explained, he'd been career.

"So you retired?" she said, adding mendaciously, "I wouldn't have thought you were old enough."

He preened a little. "I retired, all right, just a lot earlier than I expected to."

"Why?"

He made a minute adjustment to the throttle. "I don't know. I guess if I had to put a finger on one thing, it'd be Iraq Two. But for real, it probably started with Afghanistan."

"You didn't ... approve?" Kate said delicately.

"Above my pay grade," he said. "I took an oath. Not up to me to approve or disapprove." He moved his shoulders, as if trying to shrug off the subject, and failed. "I'm all for making the world a tyrant-free zone, but really, what the hell was the point?" He shook his head, unconscious that he was repeating words said by another vet months before and hundreds of miles away.

There was an edge to Boyd's voice detectable even over the headphones. Kate wondered how much that edge had to do with the cargo in back, which with every passing mile she was becoming more certain was not spare parts for fish processors. "Buy boys big toys, they're going to find a way to play with them. Only solution is not buying the toys in the first place. I don't see that happening any time soon."

"No." He smiled at Kate. "You see the last *Star Trek* movie?"

They flew on, the conversation ranging from the relative

merits of *Star Trek: The Next Generation* and *Star Trek: Deep Space Nine* ("*DS-Nine* didn't really get rolling until the war with the Dominion started," Boyd said) to the best way to cook moose backstrap ("Sear it on all sides in a hot and I mean hot cast-iron frying pan," Kate said, "finish it off in the oven, and serve it with a raspberry vinegar sauce").

They had a bit of a headwind at altitude and it was almost four hours before they came around Cape Akuyan and descended over Kuluk Bay before touching down in Adak. It was a little after two in the afternoon. The thin, bright rays of the arctic sun outlined all the bays and bights that cut into the coastline of the island and lit up the lakes scattered haphazardly across its interior. Mountains rose up in an ice-clad spine. At the lower elevations, the snow cover was patchier than she'd imagined. There were no trees.

She wondered if the view was much changed from when Old Sam and One-Bucket McCullough had served here during World War II, first recruits for Castner's Cutthroats, and had to blink away unexpected tears.

The town of Adak was a revelation. For one thing, she couldn't believe how large it was, bigger than Cordova and Ahtna combined. Two runways, both two hundred feet wide and over seven thousand feet long, formed the western and northern boundaries, with a little spillover. From the air it looked like there were more miles of road on this one island than could be found in all the rest of Southwestern Alaska combined. Three massive docks extended into the water, each long enough to host an aircraft carrier. A line of equally massive warehouses extended shoreward from each dock, and each warehouse looked individually capable of storing supplies enough for several fleets. Which, Kate supposed, they had been designed to do. It had originally been a navy base.

The roads were for the most part empty of traffic, and very few of the uniformly prefabricated buildings looked occupied. Indeed, as the Cessna lost altitude and Kate got a closer look, many of them appeared one small step up from abandoned.

Understandable, she thought. Days like today had to be very rare at any time of the year, and short of the occasional birder in pursuit of a glimpse of the whiskered auklet, she couldn't see casual visitors contributing much to the island's economy. Especially when the airfare alone set you back a minimum of twelve hundred dollars round-trip. And nobody sane bought a ticket to Adak one-way, or anywhere on the Chain, for that matter.

Boyd put them down with nary a bump about halfway down runway 05 and taxied to the south end, coming to a stop in front of an enormous hangar. "I've had rougher elevator rides," Kate said, and his answering smile nearly outshone the sun. Pilots were so easy when you knew how.

He unbuckled his harness and opened the door as a man in a large truck with a canvas top on hoops that looked like it might have the Dirty Dozen in the back pulled around to the side of the plane. The driver got out as Boyd was climbing down to the pavement, a small, wiry man wearing Carhartts and a knit watch cap. His arms were so long, he looked like Reed Richards. He regarded Kate without favor. "Who's this?"

"A friend," Boyd said, "relax."

The man looked over his shoulder, and his face lost color. "And what the fuck is that?"

Boyd followed his gaze and shook his head. "I still can't believe I let you talk me into bringing her along."

Mutt shouldered past Kate and leaped down to the pavement. Kate gave Boyd a slow, up-from-under smile, not quite fluttering her eyelashes. Boyd swallowed, and even Mr.

Fantastic was not entirely unaffected. "Love me, love my dog."

She watched as they opened the cargo doors of the aircraft and began shifting the rubber totes from the plane to the back of the truck. They looked heavy. She offered to help and was turned down, brusquely by the simian and more graciously by Boyd. She and Mutt wandered around the corner of a nearby hangar and found a quiet corner to drop her jeans. Four hours on an airplane with no bathroom tested even the best bladders.

She came back around the building to peer through the cracks of the door on the immense hangar nearby. It was larger than the one at Eagle Air that currently housed Gabe McGuire's Gulfstream. It was also empty of anything but a stack of pallets, a couple of sets of block and tackle, a pile of bungee cords, and some coils of half-inch polypro, suitable for lashing down cargo.

"Kate!" She looked around and saw Boyd waving at her. "Want to take a look at the town?"

"Sure!"

Mr. Fantastic appeared to be arguing vociferously with Boyd, and broke off only when she and Mutt approached.

"Aw, relax, Shorty, wouldja?" Boyd said. "I told you, she's a friend. It's a long damn flight from Newenham, a man could stand some company once in a while." To Kate, Boyd said, "Mutt will have to ride in the back."

It was a struggle for Kate not to volunteer to ride in the back with Mutt, not to mention all those nice totes, whose lids were held on with duct tape. The Swiss Army knife in her pocket pressed against her hip in a meaningful way. She gave Boyd a sunny smile. "No problem. Mutt, up!"

Mutt took the tailgate in a single bound, Kate was escorted to the cab, there to take up the middle position between

Shorty at the wheel and Boyd on the window. Shorty started the engine, muttering darkly beneath his breath.

He knew two speeds, fast and stop. The roads were, astonishingly, paved, which made the ride smoother than it could have been. "That used to be the McDonald's," Boyd said, pointing. He thudded against the passenger-side window when Shorty yanked the truck around a corner. "And there, that's the bowling alley. They just rebuilt it a while ago, pretty good food. That used to be officers' country over there, see? The Native corporation rents out beds there. We've got a nice apartment on lease. Clean sheets, stocked refrigerator, hot shower."

Boyd smiled down at her. Kate smiled back. She may even have snuggled up against him, just a little, to keep hope alive. She was going to dash it soon enough.

They bounced off the road and through some buildings and emerged on the longest, widest continuous dock Kate had ever seen, connecting the three deep-sea docks she had seen from the air. Compared to the rest of the town, the dock was jumping. Three fish processors were in port, along with two hundred-foot crabbers and a U.S. Coast Guard cutter, *Munro,* a 378-foot white hull with a landing pad for a helicopter on the aft deck.

The ship they stopped next to was a rusty freezer trawler two hundred feet in length, with a crane mounted behind the house. The crew was on the alert for them, and moments after they'd arrived had the crane in motion and a pallet swung onto the dock. Boyd and Shorty stacked the tubs on the pallet and lashed them down and they were climbing back into the truck half an hour later. "Isn't there even any paperwork?" Kate said in an awed voice.

Boyd slung a casual arm around her shoulders. "All taken

care of in advance, Kate. Now, how about a well-earned drink at the end of a long day?"

They pulled up in front of the Aleutian Sports Bar and Grill, a long, low dive of a place that put Kate forcibly in mind of a bar she'd been in in Dutch Harbor, over six years ago now. That bar had been cut into the rusty hull of a beached trawler, but the clientele in Adak looked exactly the same. It was mostly men, young men, young fishermen to be exact, and very few women. The very few women, mostly locals, mostly Natives, were each virtually under siege by the many young men, none locals, none of them Native, and many of them Russian. One girl who didn't even look of age to Kate's critical eye had six drinks lined up in front of her. Another was starfished against a wall, serving as the beautiful assistant for a pair of knife-throwing fishermen. To Kate's relief, a harassed-looking bartender disarmed the fishermen before the first knife was thrown. Another girl occupied the middle of the dance floor, getting down and dirty to an ear-banging number by Katy Perry and Kanye West, of which alleged music Kate would have remained thankfully ignorant were it not for Johnny's dogged determination to bring her musical tastes into the twenty-first century. The girl stood at the center of six, no, seven fishermen, a big enough circle that she was managing to avoid full frontal contact with any of them. Safety in numbers. Smart girl.

A few hard-eyed white women, older than the locals (by older, Kate judged them to be in their late twenties), she identified as professionals. Kate got her own share of attention just by stepping in the door. The noise was earsplitting, the air was filled with cigarette smoke, and the floor was greasy underfoot. Mutt demonstrated her displeasure by laying her ears back. Feet that might have stepped on ordinary paws just naturally levitated out of her path.

Boyd steered Kate through the crowd to a table, acquired chairs by a feat of sheer legerdemain, and held hers for her with an inviting smile.

She smiled back. If she didn't get away from Boyd soon, it was going to wear out and she'd have to replace it. "Order me a beer and a burger?" she said. "I'm just going to go freshen up a little."

Boyd raised his voice to be heard over the crowd. "She going with you?"

Kate swiveled, saw Mutt a pace behind, and batted her eyelashes. "You know how us girls are. We can never go to the bathroom alone."

Boyd's laughter followed them into the john, a four-holer that showed the same attention to cleaning and maintenance as the bar. Of course there wasn't a back door.

Kate went into one of the stalls. There was a full roll of toilet paper. It was the best that could be said.

A pair of giggling girls came in as she emerged from the stall. Both of them reapplied their makeup while exchanging less than complimentary notes on the last five men who had propositioned them. She took her time drying her hands, and was rewarded when one of the bartenders came in. A stocky white woman of middle age, she had muscular arms and a firm belly beneath a knotted bar towel. "Hey," she said to Kate.

"Hey," Kate said.

"Nice dog."

"Thanks."

"Wolf?"

"Only half."

"Jesus," said the other woman with neither surprise nor fear, and without much emphasis, either. She went into a stall.

Kate waited. The bartender came back out and went to one of the sinks. She wore a T-shirt with three-quarter sleeves. When she reached for the soap, the sleeves pulled up enough for Kate to see bruises that looked as if they'd been left behind by someone grabbing her arms above the elbows.

The woman saw her looking and pulled her sleeves back down. She pushed the soap dispenser, squirting soap into her hands.

"What's your name?" Kate said.

"Jean."

"Hi, Jean, I'm Kate."

"Nice to meet you, Kate," although Jean didn't sound particularly excited.

"I wonder," Kate said. "Is there a back way out of here?"

An experienced bartender, Jean didn't ask why Kate needed a back door, especially with Mutt for a bodyguard. She turned off the faucets and reached for a towel. "Outside, go to your immediate left, follow the wall past the men's all the way to the back, right around the corner, left through the storeroom. There's a gray steel door. Should be unlocked."

Kate raised an eyebrow. "Not the first time you've given those directions."

"Won't be the last in this bar, either," Jean said. She pitched the crumpled towel in the garbage, and left.

Kate waited until there was a crowd of people between the restroom and the table where Boyd sat, and slipped out. Jean's directions were foolproof. A minute later they were on the outside of the storeroom door.

Kate grinned down at Mutt. "Solidarity, that's what I'm talking 'bout."

Mutt, just glad to be back on honest dirt, give an enthusiastic sneeze of agreement.

25

JANUARY 21

Adak

THE BAR WASN'T FAR from the docks. Kate and Mutt dodged a few forklifts and a couple of trucks, picking up a smattering of wolf whistles and not a few offers of marriage along the way. They passed a gear shop and Kate went in and bought a navy blue hoodie in men's large with an unobtrusive Adak Fisheries logo on one shoulder, and a pair of thick wool socks, also in men's large.

When she came out again the sun was sliding down the horizon, casting conveniently long shadows. Kate found one next to a tottering stack of battered wooden totes that smelled of fifty years'-worth of pollock. It was a peek around a corner from a full view of the freezer trawler where they'd dropped off the Cessna's cargo. Kate was relieved to find it still there.

She cast a quick glance around at the other docks. One of the processors was gone, and it looked like the cutter was preparing to get under way. Gigantic frozen bricks of processed seafood and shellfish were being unloaded from the other trawlers. They were settled on trailers and towed off to the warehouses, Kate guessed to wait on a container ship that would ship it to market.

She ducked back around the totes and pulled the hoodie

over her jacket and tied the hood around her face so that only her eyes and nose showed. It hung down to her knees, and she pulled the hem in a little, too. She looked down at herself, satisfied. With the bulk of jacket and jeans beneath it the hoodie was voluminous enough to totally desex her. In a town where gender alone brought more attention that the traffic would bear, the more people who didn't notice she had breasts, the better.

The large navy blue socks she pulled on over her boots. The cursory glance she had been allowed of the freezer trawler had told her that the crew wasn't all that keen on maintenance and she wanted to be sure of her footing on the slimy decks when she went aboard. The rough wool should take care of that nicely, as well as muffle her steps.

Her biggest fear was that Boyd would show up on the dock looking for her, but the sun dropped below the horizon with no sight of him. The tide was coming in, and she had watched the superstructure of the freezer trawler slowly rise next to its mooring. There were no lights on in the wheelhouse, but then there usually weren't, the watch saving its night vision for the depth and radar screens, electronic charts and the LED readouts packed into most bridges. If the ship had any kind of a responsible captain, there should be at least one person on watch 24/7, but if Kate were lucky, the rest of the crew was onshore. She might even have had her ass pinched by one of them on her way to the bathroom at the Aleutian Sports Bar and Grill.

She waited until it was full dark, huddled next to Mutt on a none-too-clean and not-very-thick pad of old cardboard boxes. Mutt, always and ever a direct-action kind of girl, was being very patient with all this lurking around. "Good girl," Kate said softly. She squeezed the arm around Mutt's neck.

"Stay," she said, and got to her feet.

Mutt got to her feet, too.

"No," Kate said, putting as much force into her voice as she could without raising it. "Stay, Mutt. Stay."

Even in the dark and in the shadow of the stack of totes, Mutt's yellow eyes took on a stubborn sheen. "I mean it, Mutt. Stay."

She waited until a forklift rumbled by and emerged from behind the totes in its wake. She walked down the dock—head down, brisk, assured stride—past the trawler. She didn't see another boat parked past the trawler, but she was counting on whoever was on watch on the trawler not to look twice at her if she didn't look like a girl and did look like she knew where she was going.

No one hailed her. She walked all the way down the dock to the end and found a ladder and started down it until her head was beneath the level of the dock. If someone was watching, with any luck they'd think her boat was too small to show, although if they'd thought about it for five seconds, they'd know it was high tide.

She counted to a hundred, one-Mississippi at a time, feet braced between a rung and the stringers. She'd pulled the hoodie's sleeves down over her hands but the steel felt cold through them and even through the soles of her boots, and the air was colder even just those few feet closer to the water.

No one yelled or came to peer over the edge of the dock where she had last been seen. When she finished her count, she climbed until just her head was just above the edge of the dock.

There was no movement on the trawler, no new lights. She climbed up the rest of the way and walked down the dock, keeping as close to its edge as she could without tripping on a cleat and pitching over the side. The last time she'd gone overboard in the Gulf of Alaska at this latitude she'd been wearing a survival suit. She didn't care to repeat the experience a second time, with or without one.

When she got to the ladder that led down to the trawler she stepped on it without looking around and made her way down without haste. She stepped over the gunnel and onto the deck and proceeded to the rear of the house, the place she figured she was least likely to be seen by the casual eye, either from the dock or the wraparound windows of the bridge. The harbor was almost flat calm. A mooring line rubbed against a piling, a block rattled as the deck shifted, and there was as always the soft sound of water slapping against the hull, but the seagulls had headed for the barn long since and the rest was silence. Kate was grateful for the forklifts and tugs on the docks. With more luck, they would cover any inadvertent noise she made.

Or not. She heard a thump and looked up to see Mutt's head peering inquisitively over the roof of the superstructure.

"Mutt!" she nearly shouted, and just barely didn't.

The head disappeared. There was another thud and Mutt's head peered over the aft deck of the house.

Kate was furious, in part because she couldn't vent it in the pile of language that was backing up behind her clenched teeth.

There was the merest echo of paws on steel grating stairs, a small pause, and Mutt's nose poked cautiously around the side of the house.

Kate glared at her.

Big yellow eyes blinked owlishly back.

There had been a moment late last fall when Kate and Mutt had had it out over who did what job in the partnership, and just how far backup went. Mutt had won that argument, with a pretty bold line drawn beneath it, too.

It appeared that she had not forgotten it.

And just how the fuck am I supposed to get you off this fucking boat again? she thought at Mutt.

Mutt gave a disdainful, albeit muted sneeze in reply.

The sooner she got what she came for, the sooner they'd be off this rusty bucket and away.

She took a cautious step toward the hold and a very loud car horn honked several times what felt like right behind her. When she got her heart back under control, she looked through the pilings of two docks to make out the hull of the Coast Guard cutter. A truck moving very fast ran out on the dock and behind the cutter's superstructure so she couldn't see what was going on. Somebody late for duty. She took a deep breath to steady her nerves and moved out of the shadow of the house once more.

A movable ladder set over the lip of the hatch led down into the hold and Kate made for it, Mutt padding behind. The ladder was cold and slimy and it was dark when she stepped off at the bottom. Her boots splashed in something. She was fumbling for her trusty penlight when she heard another heavy thump, followed by a scrabble of claws. She swore beneath her breath and cupped the end of the penlight before she turned it on.

It silhouetted Mutt like a movie star in a spotlight. She was standing on top of a twenty-foot freight container bolted to the back wall of the hold. It was set back beneath the edge of the deck and Kate couldn't imagine how Mutt had contorted her body to jump from the deck to the container.

She panned the light around. There was nothing else in the hold except an inch of water in the bilge, glittering iridescently in the penlight from all the oil that had been spilled over the years. The scent of twenty years'-worth of hauling fish and crab from fishing grounds to dock was strong enough to make her eyes water.

The door to the container was on the left end, and she made for it, hampered by the ribs of the steel hull, which interrupted anything like smooth progress. The third time she tripped she saved herself from falling only by catching the corner of the container.

There was a thump followed almost immediately by another and a third with a splash. A second later a cold nose pushed at her hand and she jumped and nearly slipped and nearly fell again. She brought the penlight around to look at her dog. "I just hope you're proud of yourself!" she said in a furious whisper. "How the hell do you think we're going to get you out of here?"

Mutt raised an unimpressed eyebrow.

Kate grabbed back everything she wanted to say at the decibel level she wanted to say it at and sloshed around to the door of the container. It was bolted but, as her karma seemed to be running lately, unlocked. It was a long bolt and a little rusty, like probably every other metal thing at this lat and long, and the hinges gave a long and, to Kate's stressed sensibilities, nerve-racking protest when she opened the door.

She shone the penlight around the inside. The pallet of rubber totes was lashed down in the back.

At least something was going right with this little B&E. She stepped inside and heard the *ticky-tack* of Mutt's toenails behind her.

She put the penlight in her mouth and had the knife out of her pocket and the blade extended three steps away. Loosening the lines, she got one of the totes free and ran the blade around the top beneath the lid. Duct tape, an Alaskan staple that stood up to almost anything, nevertheless bowed even its head to naked steel. Kate pulled the lid off the tote and stood staring down at what the penlight revealed.

Behind her Mutt let loose with a growl that could have been heard in Newenham. With no conscious thought, Kate spun on her heel and launched herself at the door. She and Mutt crashed into it together, just as it slammed shut on them both.

They tumbled to the floor. On the other side, above their heads, the bolt slid home with a malevolence that felt distinctly final.

In the same moment, the deck shook beneath their feet, followed by a low rumbling roar and a bubbling of water from the stern. Someone had started the trawler's engine.

"Well, shit," Kate said.

There was a shout from on deck, too muffled to understand, but Kate heard some non-Mutt thuds that she was pretty sure were lines hitting the deck, probably after they'd been let loose of the dock. They were casting off.

She pushed herself to her feet and shoved at the door. It moved enough to open a crack, which in itself only revealed the darkness inside the hold.

Mutt gave an interrogatory whine.

"Aren't you ashamed of yourself," Kate said severely, "letting them get the drop on us like that?"

"Wuff," Mutt said, which Kate correctly interpreted to mean, *You should talk.*

On the other hand, her suspicions as to at least one of Finn Grant's extracurricular activities with Eagle Air had been proven correct, and that was always gratifying.

The penlight showed her the way back to the tote. She put the lid back on it and sat down to think things over.

She was locked in a container in the hold of a freezer trawler in Adak. Unless she was mistaken, the freezer trawler was getting ready to get under way, destination unknown. And no one knew where she was.

Probably time to rectify that last while she was still in range of a cell tower. She pulled out her phone. Three whole bars. "Wow," she said, "better than downtown Anchorage," and hit the speed dial. Jim answered on the first ring. "It's me," Kate said.

"Hey," Jim said.

"What are you up to?"

"I'm at the post, just got back from Ahtna," Jim said. "Had to convince Judge Bobby that Art Beaver deserves time."

"And did you?"

"Of course," he said. "You know she's always had a little thing for me."

"Yeah," Kate said, "me and Kenny Hazen have talked about that."

He laughed, and she imagined him sitting at his desk, his feet up and that shark's grin on his face. God, he was an attractive man, smart, funny, good at his job. He read, he liked rock and roll, he was an exciting lover, and even a good cook. Looked like he was in Alaska to stay, something always iffy if someone hadn't been born in the country. There had to be a flaw, and she kept looking for it, assiduously, because no one package could be that right for her. It frightened her a little, how much she liked him. How much she enjoyed just talking to him on the phone.

And he didn't remind her a bit of Gabe McGuire.

Above, there was some more shouting and hurried footsteps.

"What's with all the noise?" he said.

"Why I'm calling," she said.

A smile in his voice. "Another Dumpster dive?"

"Actually," Kate said, "kind of a funny story."

"Another chest freezer?"

"Try a container."

Jim's momentary silence was less alarmed than long-suffering. "You mean like a freight container?"

"Yeah."

"You're inside a freight container."

"Yes. One of the small ones, one of the twenty-footers, I'd say."

Jim let out a long, controlled breath. "The dimensions are so important."

"I thought so."

"Are you in Newenham, Kate?"

"That's where the funny comes in," Kate said. "I'm in Adak. Well. I am for the moment."

"Adak?" Jim said. "As in, on the island of Adak?"

"Yes."

"Adak on the Aleutian Chain?"

"Yes," Kate said.

Hoping this time might get him a different answer, he said, "As in closer to Russia than the U.S.?"

"*Da*," Kate said.

Another brief silence. "Failing to find the funny here, Kate."

"I haven't got to the best part yet," she said. "You haven't asked me where the container is."

"Okay," he said, pretty patiently, she thought. "Where is it?"

"In the hold of a freezer trawler," she said.

Silence from the phone, while the engine revved, hydraulic gears clunked beneath the deck, and the hull swayed. "Which is just now pulling away from the dock."

Another silence. "Really," Jim said at last. "Where's it going?"

"No idea," she said.

"So," he said, "thinking this might be the time for me to activate my 911 reflex."

"Reluctantly," Kate said, "I agree."

"Is Mutt with you?"

Kate looked down at the 140-pound half wolf-half husky pressed against her leg. "She insisted."

"Well, thank god for that. Okay, I'll—"

She felt Mutt shift beneath her hand a moment before she heard the sound of an amplified voice. "Wait," she said, coming to her feet. She took the phone from her ear.

"Russian fishing vessel *Alexei Kosygin,* this is the United States Coast Guard. Return to the dock, I say again, return to the dock immediately and prepare to be boarded."

"The cavalry might have arrived," Kate said into the phone. "I'll call you back." She hung up on a protesting squawk.

A few minutes later she staggered against the distinctive bump of hull against piling. The engine shut down. Ten minutes later she heard voices in the hold. "Hey!" she shouted, banging on the door. "Hey, let me out!" Mutt added her voice to Kate's, and after a moment's stunned silence a scurry of footsteps approached the container. The bolt drew back and the doors swung open, each door attended by a Coastie with his sidearm drawn, behind which there was an entire Coast Guard boarding team with their weapons out. They all had very powerful flashlights, all of them trained in a single stream of blinding light on her and Mutt standing there, hands and teeth in plain sight.

"Hi, guys," she said, blinking. "Take me to your leader?"

26

JANUARY 21

Adak

ON CUTTER *MUNRO*, THE boarding team handed her over to their commander with a distinct air of relief. The Coastie captain was six-foot-six, his executive officer was six-foot-four, and Kate was five-foot-nothing. It was like standing between a couple of Sitka spruces. Further, they were clad in smart, clean uniforms and she most definitely was not. There was also the little problem of her trespassing on private property, not to mention what she had been apprehended in the same container with. She couldn't help but feel a little outnumbered.

Fortunately, Mutt made up in charm for what Kate lacked in height, and it wasn't long before both officers had unbent enough to make friends with the dog. This allowed the third man in the room, who was dressed in civilian clothes, to produce his credentials.

Kate looked at them and sighed. "Why didn't you just board the ship before it cast off?"

"Because I only just got here," said Federal Bureau of Investigation Special Agent James G. Mason, with an apologetic look at the two Coastie officers. Kate remembered the arrival of the honking truck just before she had gone below on the freezer trawler. "I wasn't on the ground here in Adak until an hour ago. I called from the airport, and the boarding team was suiting up when the bridge officer told the captain he'd just seen someone—" He looked at Mutt and his lips quirked. "—accompanied by a very large canine, board the *Kosygin* in a, ah, surreptitious manner."

Couldn't have been all that awful goddamn sneaky, Kate thought.

Reading her mind, Mason said, "They were watching the ship with, ah, night vision goggles, I believe."

"That makes me feel only marginally better," Kate said, "but thanks."

"I'd called ahead, so Captain Lloyd—" He nodded in the captain's direction. "—knew not to allow the *Kosygin* to leave port. So when the *Kosygin* started to, ah, make steam, Captain Lloyd launched the first boarding team on one of the OTHs to, ah, crowd them from the water side, and when they got the lines back on the pilings, the second boarding team hit them from the dock."

"There did seem to be an awful lot of them," Kate said.

"Lucky for you," the executive officer said.

"No question," she said, "you've definitely got the grateful thanks of the taxpayer tonight." She would have tried out her best smile to soften them up but something told her this was going to be a tough room.

"So," Mason said, still in that diffident manner that must have seduced an awful lot of witnesses into spilling their guts, "would you mind telling me, ah, exactly what you were doing on board?"

The answer was such a cliché, but only because it was true. "I'm a private investigator," she said. "I'm looking into what may not have been an accidental death. In the course of my investigation, some, ah, other facts came to light." She tried not to grin.

The four of them, and of course Mutt, were sitting in the captain's cabin, a nicely appointed suite with a bedroom, a bathroom, a tiny kitchen, and a living room with a couch and a pair of easy chairs grouped around a coffee table. Kate thought of the galley on the *Freya,* which was where most of its social life took place, and which consisted of cooking facilities opposite a long-rimmed table bolted to the deck in front of a long, hard bench. There was roughly a light-year's-worth of difference in comfort, and Kate gave a fleeting thought to her career choices at the age of eighteen.

But only a fleeting one. Mason cocked his head and raised his eyebrows invitingly. The agent looked to be in his mid-thirties, fit and slender, with dark hair razor-cut short in a style that wasn't far off Kate's own. He had a deep tan and his skin looked chapped, as if he'd recently been spending a lot of time outdoors in the sun and wind. He wore chinos and a button-down oxford shirt so neatly pressed, you knew he had just taken off his tie. Rimless glasses slid continuously down a long, thin nose, and he kept pushing them up again in a disarming habit that made him look like a nervous schoolboy. Disarming, Kate thought, as well as misleading. There was a sharpness about the gray eyes behind the glasses that told her Special Agent Mason didn't miss much. "Why don't we start with you telling me what you're doing here?" she said.

The two Coasties looked scandalized that a mere civilian would gainsay a special agent of the FBI, but Mason was more adaptable. "I belong to a task force that has been investigating an arms dealer who is shipping American arms stolen from armories across the nation, which are then smuggled into hot spots in Asia for resale to insurgents, guerrillas and terrorist groups." His mouth tightened. "Many of whom then turn them upon American troops stationed in the area."

He shifted in his seat and looked suddenly much older, the light picking out lines around eyes and mouth that Kate hadn't seen at first. "Over the last twelve to eighteen months, we've seen an increase in M203 grenade launchers, which are a modification of the M4 carbine. The M203's ammunition is what you might call versatile—tear gas, armor-piercing, fragmentation, buckshot, you name it, it can shoot it. They call it Barbie for men."

She didn't laugh. She didn't even smile. It seemed he didn't expect her to. At any rate, he continued to speak in the same slow, sober voice. "Quite apart from furnishing the enemy with reliable, accurate arms of the best manufacture and quality, you can imagine the kind of effect that has on some poor grunt whose ride home gets shot up with a weapon manufactured two states over from where he was born."

"Wouldn't do my morale any good," the captain said.

"Or the crew's," the exec said.

Something tickled at the back of Kate's mind. "What are you doing in Adak, Alaska?"

"I've been working out of Afghanistan," he said, "trying to trace the arms back along the route they were smuggled out by. There are other agents from all of the three-letter agencies working the case from this end. So far without much luck."

"Again, Adak," Kate said.

"I—it's a long story you don't need to hear, so I won't go into it," Mason said. "But a tip from an informant led to Petropavlovsk. In Russia?"

"Yes, on the Kamchatka Peninsula," Kate said with what she considered saintlike patience. "And?"

"And in Petropavlovsk another informant told us about a fishing trawler named the *Alexei Kosygin*"—Mason worked his eyebrows a little at the name—"which had been observed to be unloading more than fish when it made port. Said informant talked his way on board with a couple of bottles of vodka and got a look at the log. The *Kosygin*'s last ports of call before leaving the Bering Sea were always either Adak, Alaska, or Dutch Harbor, Alaska."

"It was my understanding that most Bering Sea fishing vessels stop in one place or the other to and from their home port to the fishing grounds, yes," Kate said.

Mason smiled. "You make a good devil's advocate, Ms. Saracoff. However, it's fair to say that the arms in the hold of the *Alexei Kosygin* were not honestly come by and were not going honestly anywhere, either. I'm sure their serial numbers, when they are traced, will bear that out."

Kate wondered if she was going to be able to get off the island before Mason's people used what she was sure were the excellent communications equipment on *Munro* to tell him her name wasn't Saracoff, which wouldn't lend her story any credibility. She wondered if *Munro* had a brig.

Mutt sprawled on the floor, happily gnawing on the jawbone of an ass that the captain had caused to materialize from the galley.

Kate didn't think the brig would have to be big enough for two.

Mason, whose interrogation skills included allowing a silence to draw out until it begged to be filled, merely waited, unmoving, leaning forward with his elbows on his knees, large hands dangling between them, watching her with an unblinking gaze from behind his rimless glasses.

"Those were M4s in the totes?" she said.

His gaze sharpened. "Yes. You recognized them?"

"Not by name," she said, "but I've seen two others like them in private possession in the past week." Chances were Mason's search for serial numbers would also find matches on the weapons she'd seen racked at Finn Grant's house and at Eagle Air. "It may be," she said, "that your arms smuggler and my maybe-not-accident victim are one and the same."

It took Mason a moment to get there. "You mean the guy I've been chasing is dead?"

"That may be the case," Kate said, not without sympathy, and watched as Mason slumped back against the chair.

After a moment he said, "My last duty assignment was Anchorage. I'm back here now solely to track down these specific arms, it was thought because I would be able to exploit any local contacts as necessary." He looked at Kate and his smile was rueful. "My boss is going to want a lot more information about this person of interest, dead or alive."

"Just because he's dead, doesn't mean the operation isn't ongoing," Kate said.

Mason's eyes narrowed. "Those weapons in the hold of the *Kosygin*?"

"Were shipped well after his death," Kate said. She remembered Shorty's remark at the airport. *You better hope the boss doesn't hear about it.*

Mason was quick. "So there is an ongoing operation?"

"Yes," Kate said. She hesitated. "A small operation with, I believe, the intention of becoming a larger one. Although..." She shook her head.

"Although what?"

She met his eyes. "Although I don't know how they thought they could get away with it."

"The buyers were paying a lot for these weapons, Ms.

Saracoff. It has been my observation that a lot of money has a way of clouding good judgment."

Kate nodded. It had been her observation as well.

"Now, Ms. Saracoff, pay up," Mason said. "Who are you working for?"

Client confidentiality was an inviolable tenet of the private investigator's creed. "The State of Alaska," she said. "Sort of."

His eyes narrowed. His bullshit detector must be pretty good, too. "Who at the State of Alaska?"

"Sergeant Liam Campbell," she said. "He's an—"

"Alaska state trooper," Mason said, "yes, I know, we've met."

All Kate could think of to say was, "You have?"

"Yes." His deferential, deprecatory *ahs* had disappeared, she noticed. "Is he still posted to Newenham?"

"Yes."

"Still with the pilot?"

"Wyanet Chouinard? Yes. She's why he hired me." If Campbell was pissed off at her for telling the truth, then he was pissed off at her. The hunt was on, her blood was up, and the case was breaking. Besides, finding out what had been really going on at Eagle Air would almost certainly reveal the motive for Finn Grant's murder, which was what he'd hired her for in the first place. She outlined her investigation for Mason, omitting any self-incriminating details.

He listened without interrupting, his mouth a compressed line. The Coasties listened, too, even more quietly, as if they were afraid that if they made a noise, Mason would remember they were there and send them from the room and they wouldn't get to hear the end of the story. Mutt chewed on her bone.

"So I was with them when they delivered the totes to the

ship. I ditched Boyd in a bar and came back, and the rest you know."

A slight smile relieved the agent's grim expression. "Tell me, Ms. Saracoff, just what would you have done if we hadn't, ah, ridden to your rescue?"

"Called in the marines," Kate said. She nodded at the captain and the exec. "Or in this case, the Coasties. I had my cell. I saw the cutter at the dock." She shifted a little in her chair. "There's something else you should know."

"I can hardly wait," the exec muttered.

"My name isn't Saracoff, it's Shugak," she said. "Kate Shugak. There is, or there used to be, an FBI agent in Anchorage by the name of Gamble. He'll vouch for me."

I hope, she thought.

27

JANUARY 22

Adak

THEY FED HER AND let her sleep in a vacant bunk—Mutt was allowed to spend the night in the captain's cabin, which Kate considered most unfair—and the next morning her identity and character had evidently been vouchsafed by someone because they let her have her cell phone back, which the XO had very kindly charged overnight. She gave him one of her very best smiles and he tripped over the door sill on the way out of the captain's cabin. Always nice to know you've still got it.

She called Jim first to let him know she was out of the container but in custody. She hung up on him when he started laughing.

Campbell she reached at home.

"Where the hell are you?" he said. "Bill was worried when you didn't show up for work yesterday."

"I'm in Adak." There might have been a slight element of sadistic glee in her voice when she added, "Oh, and I'm also in the custody of the U.S. Coast Guard. You know, just FYI."

"I'm sorry," he said, "I could have sworn you said you were in Adak."

"I did."

"And that you're in the custody of the Coast Guard."

"Them, too."

"The United States Coast Guard?" he said. "Wait, 'them, too'? May one ask who else you're in the custody of?"

"Is that even a sentence?" she said. "The FBI."

"The FBI?"

"Yes."

"The Federal Bureau of Investigation?"

"You know, this is fun and I'd love to keep playing, but I called because the Coasties found a pallet loaded with M4 carbines, along with, the weapons officer on *Munro* tells us, enough accessory kits to turn all of them into grenade launchers. The same weapons, not coincidentally, that I saw in the back of a Cargomaster that landed at Eagle Air yesterday afternoon, which I then hitched a ride on to Adak and saw said weapons delivered to a Russian fishing trawler. Which was where they were seized, along with the crew and the ship. And, you know, me."

A pregnant silence. "This seemed like such a nice, quiet little town when I was first posted here."

"The FBI agent is named James Mason. He says he knows you."

There was another brief silence. "Okay, yeah, a while ago, on another case, I met an agent named Mason."

"That's him. Meantime," Kate said, "I need a favor."

"What?"

"I need you to rustle me up a ride, or I won't get back to Newenham until Tuesday."

"Are you kidding me?" he said.

"Plus, if things go well, I'll need room for four."

"Four? Four passengers? This is nuts, and besides, even I know Wy doesn't have anything with the kind of range to—oh."

"What?"

"I got an idea," Campbell said. "You going to be on your cell?"

"Yeah, but it'll be off for the next hour or so."

"Why?"

Unseen by Campbell, Kate smiled. "Because the FBI's doing a bust, and I'm going along for the ride."

She ended the call, turned off the phone, and said to Mason, "Let's go."

In the end it was almost too easy. The captain whistled up a vehicle from the Coastie agent shoreside and they drove to the Aleutian Sports Bar and Grill. Kate went inside. It was too early for a crowd but not too early for Jean to be on duty. "Hey," she said.

Jean looked up from behind the bar. "Hey, yourself."

"You ever go home, or do they keep a little rollaway bed behind the bar just for you?"

Jean smiled. It did nice things to her face. "I see you made it out alive."

"Thanks to you," Kate said. "Anybody come looking for me?"

"Your ex-boyfriend was asking around."

"Wasn't with him long enough for him to be an ex," Kate said. "Was he mad?"

"Seemed more philosophical about it. Got the feeling it wasn't the first time he'd had ye old bathroom trick pulled on him." She opened the dishwasher and said, "And he didn't leave alone after all, either."

Kate laughed. "Sounds like what little I know about him. I need another favor, Jean."

Jean paused in the act of racking dirty mugs and glasses.

"Do you."

Kate nodded. "I do. I'm looking for some people, only I don't know my way around town. Any chance you could knock off for an hour, give me directions?"

Jean gave her a long look. "What's in it for me?"

"What do you want?" Kate said.

Jean gave a short laugh. "I want to get the hell off this rock, but I don't suppose that's something you can do."

"Well, I don't know," Kate said slowly.

The old officers' quarters for the Adak Naval Air Station was a pleasant row of split-level homes on tiny lots that might once have been well kept. It was obvious now that anyone who loved them enough to maintain them was long gone. Shingles were missing, shutters sagged, windows were broken out, the street was littered with debris from the last big blow, another one of which was always on its way in the Aleutians.

Mason, Kate, and Mutt left Jean in the car, parked around the corner. There was no sign of movement from inside the house. Before they split up to take the back and front doors, Mason drew his weapon. "I don't think that's necessary," Kate said. "I spent the whole afternoon with him yesterday. I don't think he's armed."

Mason looked from Kate to Mutt and back again. "And you aren't?"

Kate shook her head and went around to the back, where she found a door into the kitchen, unlocked. There was something about the entire southwest of Alaska that did not love a lock. She eased the door open and stepped inside, listening. The door closed as silently as it had opened, which given the neighborhood's general air of dissipation, surprised her. She slipped through the room, Mutt padding behind, and peeked around the corner, to see Mason coming in the front door. She pointed at the olive drab duffel bag sitting next to it, Boyd's name stenciled in bold black Marks-A-Lot on the side. He raised his eyebrows and she nodded.

The ground floor held kitchen, living room, dining area, and a half bath. Kate pointed at the stairs, and Mason nodded. They went noiselessly up the stairs and down the hall, checking one room after another. One empty bedroom, another, a bathroom.

At the end of the hall at the back of the house, Kate found Boyd asleep in the master bedroom, sprawled facedown on a king-size bed, snoring, a deep, larynx-rattling, window-chattering glottal roar. The woman on her back next to him was snoring louder than he was.

Kate stepped into the hall to signal to Mason and went back in the bedroom, putting herself on the same side of the bed as Boyd. She waited until Mason was on the woman's side.

He raised his eyebrows. She nodded. He grabbed the woman's hands and hauled her over on her side, away from Boyd.

"Wha—?" she just had time to say, before Kate said in a voice pitched to be heard back in Newenham, "Boyd, you faithless bastard. And here I thought it was true love between us."

Mutt, her tongue lolling out of an anticipatory lupine grin, punctuated Kate's statement with a very loud "*Woof!*"

His companion screamed. Boyd jerked awake with a snort.

Kate had either forgotten that Boyd was ex-military or had discounted it on the evidence of the paunch and the slightly dissipated air. Boyd levitated from the bed and came all upstanding in a single movement, landing on his feet with his knees flexed and his arms and hands curved and ready for attack. He grabbed the front of Kate's jacket and pulled.

Everything seemed to slow down, and someone seemed to have hit the mute button. Mason had his hands full with the woman, who was shrieking hysterically—Kate could tell because she had her mouth open—and fighting him tooth and claw. The blood from a long red scratch drooled down his cheek.

In her mind's eye, Kate had a distinct picture of Boyd getting his shoulder into her diaphragm, knocking the air out of her the same way it had been before she went into the Dumpster behind Bill's. She saw Boyd straightening his legs and back and the momentum launching her into the air. She saw herself hit the wall in a full-on body splat. She saw her unconscious body slide down to the floor, out for the count.

Only none of that happened. She was never able to fully account for it afterwards. It might have been that after having been tossed first into a chest freezer and then a Dumpster and after that locked inside a freight container, she was simply spoiling for a fight. It might have been that Moses Alakuyak, that archetypal little archfiend, was a better teacher than she had given him credit for. Whatever the reason, she felt her arms come up in horse stance position and she stepped into Boyd instead of away, as every instinct screamed that she should. She grabbed chest hair in both fists—he had a lot of it—and stepped back, keeping her arms in position and not coincidentally yanking on his chest hair.

His chest hair straightened and his skin tented over his chest. His eyes widened and his mouth opened. He must be shrieking, too. More to the point, his grip on her jacket loosened. She didn't let go, though, she kept pulling him forward until he was fully off balance and ready to fall on her. Pull Back. Press Forward.

At the last possible moment she stepped forward with her left foot, anchoring it behind his right one, and advanced another step with her right foot, bringing her center of gravity over her feet and past them and all the weight of her body with it. Push.

Boyd was rocked completely off balance. His arms flung wide and windmilled and he fell backwards, landing hard on the floor. It knocked the breath out of him and he gaped and gulped like a fish out of water.

Kate was intimately acquainted with the feeling. Real time returned in a rush, and she leaned down and tapped his diaphragm. The first thing she heard when her eardrums started working again was the *Whoosh!* of air returning to his lungs, a sound that reminded her all too painfully of her recent encounter with the Dumpster in back of Bill's.

She wished the demon ninja had been there to see.

The next sound she heard was the woman, sobbing, and Kate looked across the bed to see that Mason had finally gotten the cuffs on her and was dabbing at the scratch on his cheek with a handkerchief. "We can only hope she isn't rabid," he said with distaste.

Mutt had her jaw open and her tongue lolling out in a boisterous canine laugh.

Jean knew where Shorty lived, too. He wasn't near as much fun.

28

JANUARY 22

Adak

THEY STOPPED BY JEAN'S place so she could stuff her belongings into a daypack and a plastic grocery bag. There was no sign of whoever had left the bruises on Jean's arms, a good thing, because Kate was in no mood. They returned to *Munro* to grab some lunch, laid on for them in the captain's cabin.

"The crew of the trawler?" Mason said.

"All members secured and under guard," the captain said. His curiosity warred with his professionalism. His professionalism won, and he let them wolf their lunch in peace.

Campbell called as Kate was wedging the last bite of an excellent sliced beef sandwich into her mouth. "Be at the Adak airport in half an hour." He hung up before she could swallow and ask who was picking them up.

Hard to believe now that she had ever regarded cell phones with anything like misgiving. She passed the news to Mason, who looked at her with increasing respect. "You do get things done, Ms. Shugak."

"Call me Kate," she said. "I'm always on a first-name basis with my co-brawlers after I've been in a fight with them." She smiled at the captain. "It's a little rule I have."

The captain's eyes went to the scratch on Mason's cheek. The struggle to ask was almost visible. Again, admirably, Kate thought, professionalism won and he refrained.

"The trawler?" Mason said as they rose to their feet.

"Impounded," the captain said. "Engineering is running a quick-and-dirty check to see how seaworthy it is, after which I'll have a prize crew deliver it to Kodiak, along with its crew. Kodiak's expecting them, and will wait to hear what you want done with them."

"Send them to Anchorage, probably," Mason said, thinking out loud, "although they're bound to be little fish."

"The ship's ours," the captain said, glad to find some means to exercise his authority. "We seized it."

Mason waved an airy hand. "Nothing to do with me. Let's let that battle be fought on land, by the lawyers for our respective services." His smile had a soothing effect, and Kate bet he knew it.

The captain exerted executive privilege to drive them to the airport, mostly, Kate thought, because he was hoping to hear a little more of the story. In that he was disappointed, but when the Gulfstream landed and Gabe McGuire got out, he was well repaid if the dumbstruck expression on his face was any indication. At any rate, he stalled out the car twice before he drove away.

Kate herself was not best pleased on any number of fronts. "You're my ride?"

McGuire grinned down at her from his rarefied Olympian heights. A ray of sun found a way through the gathering clouds to gild his hair, darken his eyes from chocolate to espresso, and make his teeth that much whiter against his—probably sun bed—tan. "I am."

Boyd and Shorty gaped at him. Jean turned beet red and

looked like she'd swallowed her tongue. Mason was made of sterner stuff. "Special Agent Mason, Mr. McGuire. The FBI appreciates the assistance. If you'll give me a receipt, we can at least make a stab at getting you reimbursed for fuel."

"I appreciate the offer," McGuire said. "Av gas isn't cheap." He looked at Kate. "You ready?"

Kate had never been on a private jet before and it was difficult to remain unimpressed. The interior surprised her by its lack of ostentation. There were about a dozen overstuffed chairs and one plush couch and a lavatory that looked like any other bathroom on a plane. The windows were a little bigger than she was used to, the cabin a lot smaller, and there were no middle seats. Nothing looked new. "Where's the wet bar?" she said.

"Left it in L.A., along with the pole dancers," McGuire said, closing the hatch. "Lester?"

Up front, Lester leaned out of the left seat and looked down the aisle.

"Wind 'er up, we're good to go."

Lester nodded and leaned back. The engines, which had never been all the way shut down, began to whine louder.

"Welcome aboard," McGuire said. "Our flight time to Newenham will be one hour and forty minutes. We have six emergency exits, four window exits, the forward door and the aft baggage door." He pointed. "In the event of a loss of cabin pressure, oxygen masks will drop out of the overhead. Put yours on first before helping anyone else. There is a life vest under each seat and two life rafts under the couch. Please read the safety briefing cards." He pulled one out of a seat pocket and held it up. He made eye contact with each of his passengers, even the ones in handcuffs. "Everybody fasten your seat belts. It was a little bumpy coming in but nothing to worry about."

"Make one hell of a flight attendant," Kate said, not quite under her breath.

He ignored her, and nodded at Shorty and Boyd, already strapped into the last row, Mutt sitting guard between them. "We have any problems, you're responsible for getting them out," he said to Mason.

Mason nodded. "Understood." Mutt wagged her tail.

"You two," McGuire said to Shorty and Boyd. "You want to make a break for it, wait till we're back on the ground. Start anything in the air on my plane and I promise you you will have the privilege of personally experiencing downward velocity at thirty-two feet per second, without benefit of aircraft. Understood?"

Boyd and Shorty nodded, dazed expressions indicating they thought they might have somehow wandered into the middle of a major motion picture.

"Let me take that," McGuire said to Jean, and buckled her pitiful amount of luggage into an empty chair. Jean stared up at him, rapt. "Here, let me help you with that," he said, and buckled Jean in, too. He eyeballed everyone one more time and nodded. "You saw the head on the way in. I'll tell you when it's okay to use it. There are soft drinks in the cooler"—he pointed again—"help yourself."

"Sorry, how long to Newenham again?" Kate said.

"An hour and forty minutes."

She had to grin.

"What?"

She nodded at Boyd, who scowled. "Took us four hours in the other direction yesterday."

"Smaller plane?"

"Much."

He smiled. "Sometimes it's good to be king."

He went forward, and everyone in the passenger section craned their necks to watch him climb into the right seat, including Kate and Mutt. Except Mason, who was thumbing notes on his smartphone.

They taxied out onto the runway, the engines wound to a scream, and the craft lunged forward as if launched from a pad at Cape Canaveral. They were airborne and climbing steeply a few seconds later. Maybe it was the size of the plane that gave the illusion of excessive speed, but Kate felt she had never slipped the surly bonds of earth more rapidly. Through her window she watched Adak drop away.

She felt a touch on her elbow, and looked around.

"I didn't think I'd ever get out of that shithole," Jean said. "I owe you."

Kate shook her head. "Paid in full."

The other woman was still a little befuddled. "Doesn't seem like enough." She ran wondering hands over the cream leather arms of her chair. "I've never been on a plane before in my life."

Kate, that compleat Alaskan, was incredulous. "Where are you from, anyway?"

"Anacortes. I came up on a crab boat. The skipper, he seemed to think ... Anyway, I jumped ship in Adak." Her smile was more a grimace. "Been trying to get out ever since."

"How long were you stuck there?" Kate said.

"Eighteen months, thirteen days," Jean said. "And about twenty hours."

Kate took note of the averted eyes, the tightened mouth, and let it be. Jean hadn't struck Kate as the victim type, but then she'd met a lot of women in Jean's situation who fit that description, both personally and professionally. "I don't know that you'll like Newenham any better than Adak, but it's closer to Anchorage and cheaper to get out of." She paused, thinking. "If you feel like staying, I might have a job for you."

Jean looked around again at that. "You're kidding."

"No guarantees, but I think so. It's bartending, something you know how to do. Pay's not bad and the tips are good. Boss seems like a good person, a little cranky, but fair. Her boyfriend—" She rolled her eyes. "He's obnoxious but good entertainment value. No promises, but I might also know a place for you to stay, too."

Jean's eyes filled with tears, embarrassing them both. Kate turned in some haste and tapped Mason on the shoulder. When he looked around she jerked her thumb at the front row. He followed her and took the seat across from her, and they put their heads together. "A few things you should know," she said, and filled him in on the events of the past week, including two instances of B&E, which she thought was deserving of some praise for her candor, considering the Fifth Amendment and all.

The special agent did not appear to share her sentiments. "I don't even know where to start," he said.

"Then don't," she said. "I hear the rule on this aircraft is no fighting at forty-five thousand feet."

He was steaming. "You do understand fruit of the poisoned tree, right?"

"I'm a private investigator," she said. "It was mostly a favor for a friend of a friend, and all I did was follow my nose. I wasn't looking for an international arms-smuggling ring. It's just what I found."

"What about him?" He nodded toward the cockpit.

"Campbell wouldn't have sent him if he thought he was involved." Kate thought about it. "Or maybe he would. So what? We needed a ride. We got one."

29

JANUARY 22

Newenham

An hour and forty minutes to the second later, they touched down at the Newenham airport. Mason spent the first part of the flight trying to bring Kate to an appreciation of the error of her ways, and abandoned the attempt only when she pretended to doze off in her very comfortable chair. Mason sighed and moved to the rear of the cabin, where he played *Let's Make a Deal* with Boyd and Shorty.

She did fall asleep then, and didn't wake up until McGuire touched her shoulder.

"What?" She blinked around. "We're there? Wow. I didn't even feel us land."

McGuire's smile was beatific. Kate looked at Lester, standing behind McGuire, and said, "If I'd known you were going to let him fly, I'd have spent the entire flight holding the plane up in the air by the seat cushion."

"When you know Gabe better, you'll know nobody lets him do anything," Lester said.

"Sadly, I have no intention of getting to know him better," Kate said, and brushed past both Lester and the twinkle in his eye.

They were parked in front of Finn Grant's old hangar.

Campbell was waiting. So was the ninja master, with his truck, Kate hoped only for the necessary extra transportation services.

Kate heard the scraping sound of a hangar door opening, and turned to see Tina Grant standing in the opening, Oren Grant standing at her shoulder. She thought she saw a third figure in the shadows behind them, probably Fred. On the facing wall between the door and the roof, the Bristol Bay Air Freight logo was still faintly visible beneath the overlay of the more flamboyant Eagle Air's.

She nudged Mason. "Grant's wife and son. And brother back of them, I think."

Boyd and Shorty were being put into Campbell's vehicle. They didn't yell to Tina and Oren for help, and Tina and Oren didn't come bustling out to offer any.

Mason turned his back to the hangar and spoke to Campbell in a low voice. "You got anybody at the terminal will tell you if any of the Grants buy a ticket out of town? Or roll out an airplane, I hear nearly everyone in the family's a pilot."

"I can make a call," Campbell said. "But the only Grant pilot left is Evelyn, and she's in the hospital."

"What about Fred?" Kate said.

Both men looked around. "Finn's brother," Kate said.

Campbell looked chagrined. "Forgot about Fred." He shook his head. "Everybody always forgets about Fred."

"Look pretty foolish if the whole family was in on it and we let them get away."

Campbell sighed. "Okay. I'll make a call to Naknek, too, just to be on the safe side. Fred lives in Naknek, although he's been in Newenham every other day since his brother died. I know the trooper there pretty well, and he owes me a couple."

"Thanks, Liam."

"You two do know each other," Kate said. "How?"

They got into Liam's vehicle without answering and drove off.

"Irritating," McGuire said.

Kate jumped. "Could you at least clear your throat or something to let me know when you're standing right next to me?"

"How else am I supposed to find out anything, you being so forthcoming and all?" he said.

"Nothing you need to know," Kate said, and started for Moses' truck. Jean was already sitting in it, and Mutt was in the back.

McGuire caught her elbow, bringing her to a halt and, did he but know it, lucky to escape with his hand still attached. Kate did not take kindly to being manhandled. "I just let you thumb an eight-hundred-mile lift," he said mildly, although his eyes were beginning to spark. "I figure the least you can do is be civil to me."

"I am civil to you," Kate said.

It surprised a laugh out of him. "God help me if you ever start being rude."

"Mr. McGuire," Kate said, "I appreciate the ride, really, I do. We would have been stuck in Adak for four days waiting on the next commercial flight, or the next Coastie Herc, whichever came first, if you hadn't flown down to pick us up. Either way, it would have been a much slower and much less comfortable ride. But I'm not going to be here much longer, and there isn't much point in furthering a friendship that isn't going to last a day longer than necessary." She started toward the truck again.

McGuire caught up and stood in front of her, forcing her to a halt. "Okay," Kate said, glad to feel her temper flare, "just who the hell do you—?"

"You wanna know what I think?" McGuire said, leaning down so that their noses almost touched. "I think you're terrified. I think you're just as attracted to me as I am to you, and because you think of me as a face on a magazine cover, and in spite of that self-confidence you clank around in like a suit of armor, I think you don't know what to do about it. So you act hostile so I won't make any moves and you don't have to deal with it."

She looked him firmly in the eye and said what she should have found a way to insert into their first conversation. "Mr. McGuire, flattered as I am by your star-studded attention, as any red-blooded American female would be, I'm in a relationship."

His eyes stared into hers. She set her teeth and wouldn't blink no matter how much her eyes stung.

He straightened up but he didn't move away. "So you say," he said.

Nothing got Kate's back up faster than when she was accused of lying. Especially when she was telling the truth.

She was pretty sure.

She marched around him and over to Moses' pickup and wrenched open the passenger-side door. Mutt was already in the back. Jean took one look at Kate's set expression and scooted over to the middle of the seat, saying absolutely nothing that might direct any of that her way. Moses, looking his usual pissed off, said, "You done playing patty-cake with the movie star?"

30

JANUARY 22

Newenham

THEY TOOK JEAN TO Bill's, who raised an eyebrow at Kate. "Nice to see you alive."

"Yeah," Kate said, "sorry about that. Things, well, escalated. Also, I quit."

"Really," Bill said. "You're done here? That didn't take long."

"I think so," Kate said.

"You don't sound all that sure."

"I'm sure," Kate said firmly. "This is Jean, by the way. She's an experienced bartender, and she needs a job."

Bill looked Jean over. "You going to stick around a little longer than my last hired help?"

Jean blinked, and was hired.

"The bones are restless," Moses said, taking a stool.

Kate looked at him.

"The bones out of the grave," Moses said. "They're coming up the cellar stairs." Somewhere between the airport and Bill's, his usual irritable attitude had vanished, to be replaced by what appeared to be resignation.

Bill's cornflower blue, impossibly young eyes went wide. Jean was uncomprehending but frightened anyway. Even

Mutt's ruff went up a little at his words. Kate was the first to recover enough to speak. "I don't know what you mean, Uncle," she said, and only the two of them were conscious that this was the first time she had accorded him the honorific.

He looked at her. "You can ignore them for only so long, but sooner or later, they will pull the door open and get out." He looked at Bill. "I need a beer, babe. I need a lot of beers."

Without a word Bill went behind the bar, opened the refrigerator, and started lining them up.

"Okay if I borrow your pickup, Uncle?" Kate said to his back. "I won't be long."

He waved his hand without turning around.

Kate touched Jean's arm. At the door, Kate realized that Mutt wasn't with them and turned.

The 140-pound half wolf-half husky was standing on her hind legs, her forepaws on Moses's stool, her nose pressed against his cheek, a low sound that was neither whine nor growl rumbling up out of her breast. Across the bar, Bill watched both of them with a bleak expression.

"Mutt," Kate said.

Mutt waited a moment longer and then gave Moses a big, juicy lick up the side of his face, provoking a roar of profanity that was almost Bobby-worthy.

Satisfied with having made her presence felt, Mutt romped across the floor and shouldered her way out the door.

Kate's eyes met Bill's.

If she was not mistaken, the older woman's eyes were filled with tears.

The apartment over the Grant garage was a palace by comparison to the hovel Jean had been sharing in Adak. "The rent's paid up through the end of the month," Kate said. "So is the ATV."

Jean's tongue became unstuck long enough to say, "What about the landlady? Is she going to be okay with this?"

Kate thought about Tina Grant, the wealthiest woman in Newenham, the woman with the dead daughter, the dead husband, the daughter in the hospital, and the worthless son. "Long as you pay her in cash."

Jean was almost inarticulate with gratitude. "I don't know when I can pay you back."

"Don't worry about it," Kate said. "I'm going to be reimbursed for my expenses." She hoped. She stuffed her few belongings in her pack. "The ATV's parked under the stairs, the keys are on the hook here."

"Hey," Jean said.

Kate stopped on the stairs, hand on the doorknob.

"It was bad in Adak," Jean said. "Really bad."

"I had a feeling," Kate said.

"I owe you," Jean said.

"You owe yourself," Kate said.

Kate pulled up at the trooper post and Mutt, remembering good hunting from the last visit, vanished once more into the underbrush in pursuit of the not-so-elusive ptarmigan.

Inside, Campbell and Mason were interrogating Boyd. She dropped her pack in a corner and perched on the vacant desk.

Boyd, sweating profusely, was loud and repetitive in denying any knowledge of the contents of the totes. "They were sealed when they were loaded onto the aircraft in Anchorage," he said. "All Finn hired me to do was fly the plane from Anchorage to Adak, with a fuel stop in Newenham."

"Where did the load originate?" Mason asked.

"I don't know," Boyd said. "My job was to haul the freight from Anchorage to Adak. That's all."

"Were you going to be flying the bigger planes when Grant bought them?" Kate said. "And didn't you tell me yesterday that you were a partner in Eagle Air?"

Boyd wouldn't look at her, and didn't answer.

"What bigger planes?" Mason asked.

"The girl, Tasha Anayuk, out at Eagle Air, told me yesterday that Finn was buying some bigger planes. She didn't get more specific."

Everyone looked at Boyd. This time he gave Kate a look that should have turned her into a crispy critter on the spot and said, "I want a lawyer."

Kate laughed. "You need one." She looked at Mason. "Finn Grant has been shipping stolen American arms and selling them to buyers in Asia. He started out small, perfecting the route and proving he could deliver." She glanced at Boyd. "From what Boyd let drop, the pilots he hired were mostly ex-military, disillusioned with the missions in Afghanistan and Iraq. If they had any qualms, pretty sure they went away when he offered them an ownership stake in the company. I'm guessing there was a pretty nice profit-sharing plan."

"Bitch," Boyd said.

Kate beamed at him. "My middle name." She looked back at Mason. "He bought Chinook Air Force Base with an eye toward making large deliveries on big planes. The bigger the plane, the more cargo he could ship, and the more cargo, the higher the profit margin. It's simple economics. Also, and what I think would have been more important to him, the bigger the plane, the longer the range. It would also mean he could lift the arms from a base, say on the West Coast, Washington, Oregon maybe, direct to Newenham, thereby bypassing Anchorage altogether. Anchorage, as it does, playing host to way too many nosy federal agents, FBI, U.S. Customs, like that." She paused, and added, "If you aren't already, I'd be looking for a base of operations on the West Coast. Doesn't have to be fancy, just a big warehouse on a commercial airport with enough traffic for Eagle Air flights not to cause comment."

Mason meditated, hands clasped loosely in his lap. "We've always been worried about western Alaska." He raised his eyes and gave a faint smile. "It's just so damn big, and so wide open, and so close to Russia. It's the fucking Wild, Wild West," he said, unconsciously echoing Campbell's words spoken in another context a week before in the Park. "The Russians are broke, and the Russian Mafia pretty much owns the infrastructure. Since it doesn't look like they're ever going to give the Russian army a decent retirement plan, the Russian army officer corps has been providing for itself by selling everything from small arms to tanks on the black market ever since the Wall came down."

"Eventually, they're going to expand their horizons," Campbell said.

Mason nodded. "And one of those horizons would be right off their eastern coast. There's already an infrastructure of sorts. People in eastern Russia would starve without a black market. It's just a matter of Finn Grant and Eagle Air tapping into what's already there."

"And who says no to the Russian Mafia," Campbell said, "especially on their own ground. It would be, what, a thousand air miles from Adak to, what's the nearest Russian port?"

"Petropavlovsk," Kate and Mason said at the same time.

"A town of about two hundred thousand people," Mason said. "With a history of moving goods in and out unobtrusively. And most conveniently placed for Asian markets."

"How many miles from Eagle Air to Petropavlovsk?" Kate said.

"Fifteen hundred," Campbell said, looking up from his computer. He sat back with his hands linked behind his head, meditative eyes on Boyd's sweating countenance. "And on the U.S. side, no prying eyes at a remote FBO three hundred miles from the nearest population center big enough to support a regulatory and enforcement structure. All the runway you needed. Plenty of fuel storage. Accommodation for pilots and crews on layover."

"And, no offense," Mason said, "there's only, what, three hundred and fifty Alaska State Troopers?"

"Three hundred and eighty," Campbell said. "And at present only one in Newenham."

His and Kate's eyes met and held. "You might want to ask around," Kate said. "Maybe your getting no help on the job wasn't an accident."

He wanted to deny it. It was right there on his face for all to see. But he didn't.

"So, a wide-open frontier, a rudimentary law enforcement presence concentrated on local offenses, and a modern air base," Kate said, thinking out loud. "A smuggler's dream."

"None of this was cheap," Mason said.

"Yeah," Kate said, "I'd like to know where he got the money, too." Again, her gaze met Campbell's.

"I may have a line on that," Mason said unexpectedly. "I got a message from a friend yesterday. You know her," he said to Campbell.

"Let me guess," Campbell said, reaching for his phone. "Jo Dunaway?"

Ten minutes later, Jo Dunaway walked in the door. She stopped short at the sight of Mason. "James," she said.

"Hey, Jo," James Mason said, looking pleased, and not in a platonic way, either. "I, ah, got your message."

"Oh, hell no," Kate said.

"I have to say I wasn't expecting this quick a response," Dunaway said. "I thought you got transferred out of state."

"Ah, overseas, actually," Mason said, gray eyes warm behind his glasses. It looked to Kate's critical eye as if, absent present company and press of business, the special agent might be inclined to get a room.

Dunaway looked at Campbell, green eyes narrowed, blond corkscrews bristling with hostility. "What's going on, Liam?"

"Tell us about the embezzlement story you're following, Jo."

"Why should I?"

Campbell sighed. "Because it might be a lot more than just an embezzlement story." He glanced at Mason. "And if it is, you get it all." He raised an eyebrow.

Mason looked from Campbell to Dunaway, lingered for a long moment, and then gave Campbell the nod.

Dunaway thought about it long enough for the others to get restive, Kate thought not because she was thinking it over but because she was enjoying having a hold over three law enforcement professionals, and said, "Okay. You know I used to report on the criminal courts," she said.

"To my cost, yes," Campbell said.

Kate just looked at her.

"Yeah, yeah." Dunaway waved off both of them. "I'm doing more general reporting now, but I made a lot of contacts over the years and they keep in touch. A source, and that's as close as I'll come to naming them, a source at Chapados, Reid, Reid, McGillivray and Thrall told me they thought there were some shenanigans going on with Alexandra Hardin's trust fund."

Mason looked puzzled. "Who's Alexandra Hardin?"

"The heir to one of the biggest fortunes ever made during the Klondike Gold Rush," Kate said, "and doubled over the next three generations in natural resource exploitation and transportation. I think her dad was a lease-owner at both Swanson River and Prudhoe Bay." Along with Emil Bannister, Erland fucking Bannister's father.

"What's the estate worth?" Mason said.

"Half a billion dollars," Dunaway said.

"Jesus Christ," Mason said.

Campbell's jaw simply dropped.

"More than enough to finance the overthrow of half a dozen third-world nations," Kate said, who was made of sterner stuff. "Who or what is Chapados, Reid Squared and Whoever?"

"The law firm handling the Hardin estate. A very old firm, in Alaskan years, and very reputable."

"Alexandra not watching her own bank balance?" Mason said.

"I'm sure she would be," Dunaway said, "were it not for a little problem of early-onset Alzheimer's."

Everyone winced.

"As it happens, Chapados, Reid is also—" Dunaway paused for effect. "—the law firm for Dagfin Arneson 'Finn' Grant and Eagle Air Enterprises."

"Who's Grant's lawyer?" Campbell said.

"Hugh Reid," Kate and Dunaway said at the same time.

"Who is administering the Hardin estate?" Campbell said.

"Hugh Reid," Kate and Dunaway said again, and frowned at each other.

Kate thought back to the safari-clad suck-up she'd met at Eagle Air her first day on this job. "I met him," she said. "He doesn't seem like the type to orchestrate a massive embezzlement scheme and parlay it into an international arms-smuggling operation."

"He's a halfwit," Dunaway said. "He flunked the bar exam five times and the rumor is that he passed the sixth time only because his father, the first Reid in Chapados, Reid, Reid, McGillivray and Thrall, finagled it. The first Reid took our Reid into the firm because chances were he wasn't going to get a job anywhere else. My informant says he got the Hardin estate because it was supposed to be a no-brainer, just counting the money coming in and out, and making sure Alexandra Hardin was well cared for."

Mason's brow furrowed. "Where is Alexandra Hardin?"

"That," Dunaway said, with all the air of one who knew she was about to create a sensation, "is the half-a-billion-dollar question."

Kate didn't know Campbell very well, but she saw the slow burn. "Where is Hardin?" he said.

Dunaway looked like she was thinking about sulking, but the story was too good not to continue. "My source didn't have much except for a printout from the Hardin trust account showing transfers of figures in six and sometimes even seven zeros moving out of the account into a dozen different accounts scattered all over the planet. Each transfer was authorized by Alexandra Hardin. As it happens, Alexandra Hardin left the state of Alaska over two years ago, almost immediately after her father died. It took three months, a forensic accountant—and she wasn't cheap—and a lot of sweat equity before I could even locate the banks that held the transfer accounts. Usually by the time she got there, the funds had moved on. But I kept looking."

Kate couldn't resist. "Many Bothans died to bring us this information."

Campbell laughed. Mason looked like he wanted to but didn't dare. Dunaway ignored her. "One transaction was the same amount every month, and it went to the same account. In Bermuda."

She waited for someone to ask her. No one did. She huffed out an indignant sigh, and Kate saw Mason hide a smile. If the FBI agent actually had a thing going with the muckraker, Kate might have to take remedial action of some kind. Maybe get the special agent into the hands of a deprogrammer. That or pluck out her own eyes.

"It's a place called the Circle of Life," Dunaway said. "It's a long-term full-care facility for Alzheimer's and dementia patients."

"Is it the real deal?" Campbell said.

"So far as I can tell from here, yes," Dunaway said. "I talked to someone in the Bahamian government with oversight responsibility for social services and he says he'd put his grandmother in Circle of Life if he could afford it."

"Who signed her in?"

"Her nephew," Dunaway said, and smiled. "Hugh Reid. His father, the senior Reid in the firm's name, was Alexandra's mother's brother."

"They certainly kept it all in the family," Campbell said after a momentary silence.

"I talked to the admitting nurse," Dunaway said. "The nephew brought a friend along to help him with his aunt on the journey from Alaska. A big man with a buzz cut and a loud voice. They had to tell him to keep it down because he was disturbing the patients."

"Finn Grant," Campbell said.

Dunaway nodded, too caught up in the story now to resent interruption. "I didn't know it was him right away. After I found Alexandra, after I learned she was in no shape to sign checks, I started following the money again. The forensic accountant finally managed to trace one of the sums through half a dozen dummy corporate accounts and I think it was like a dozen banks and then—"

"Bothans, dying," Kate said.

Dunaway glared at her. "It was deposited in the Eagle Air corporate account in the Last Frontier Bank in Anchorage. Where Finn immediately started writing checks on it. Big ones, I think mostly for planes, and payroll."

"Pilots and mechanics," Campbell said.

"The guy I talked to in the Bahamas?" Dunaway said. "The one in social services? I got him to contact his opposite number in whoever oversights aviation in Bahamian airspace and I got the tail number off the jet they flew in on."

"Who was the owner?"

For the first time Dunaway looked a little disgruntled. "Haven't been able to trace that yet." She rattled off the number without referring to her notes. The first letter of its registration number was a *C*.

"Not American-owned, then," Mason said. He sighed. "We can probably help with that."

Campbell looked puzzled. Dunaway looked exasperated. "I don't even believe you're married to a pilot."

"All U.S. tail numbers begin with an *N*," Kate said to Campbell. She jerked her head. "Talk to you a minute?"

They went out on the porch. "Did you run down all those names on Grant's thumb drive?" He nodded. "Anything?"

Campbell shook his head. "They were all dead, in jail, or out of town in the twenty-four-hour period surrounding Grant's death, or they have strong alibis with credible witnesses. I tracked down Artie Diedrickson and Leon

Coopchiak. They put you in the Dumpster, by the way."

"Figured," Kate said.

He laughed, and shook his head. "They were looking for the thumb drive. Leon saw Finn with it once. And then Artie saw part of Leon's starring role over your shoulder at the library. And Artie and Leon winding up at Bill's at some point during every day is pretty much a given."

"Now I think about it, I think I sold them both a beer," Kate said.

"You could have suffocated and died in that freezer," he said.

"But I didn't," Kate said. "Fortunes of war."

Campbell shook his head again, maybe in disapproval, maybe in admiration, maybe both. "Finn was definitely blackmailing everyone on that list, and successfully, too. They all had plenty of motive, most of them had means, but none of them had opportunity."

"Then I'm done here," Kate said. "This—" A wave indicated the other side of the door. "—puts a whole different light on Finn Grant's death. When you hired me to investigate it, you had a guy dead in a plane wreck who had had a very public fight with your wife the day before. Now you've got a guy who made a career out of bullying and blackmailing everyone within a two-hundred-mile radius, who is also an international arms smuggler."

"You have certainly expanded the list of suspects, I'll grant you that," Campbell said.

"Which takes the heat off your wife," she said. "Which was why you wanted Grant's death investigated in the first place."

"I suppose so." Campbell considered. "There's still the matter of the wreck, and if it was an accident."

"If there is a way to prove a certain person loosened the nut on that oil screen," Kate said, "the FBI, god rot 'em, is a lot more likely to find it. It is possible, hell, even given his reputation as a pilot and a mechanic, it is far more likely that Finn did it to himself. Even the best pilot screws up now and then. Mostly it doesn't kill them. Sometimes, though..." Her voice trailed off, as she thought about that cold winter day. It would still have been dark at that hour of the morning, and freezing cold, but Grant would have had his Super Cub parked in Eagle Air's Newenham hangar, where there would be heat and light. Of course, that's why the lone toolbox was still there, so Grant would have tools at hand should repairs be necessary.

Convenient for a killer wanting to loosen the nut on an oil screen, too.

In her mind's eye she watched over Grant's shoulder as he preflighted his craft, checking the fuel, doing the walkaround to check the control surfaces, unbuttoning the cowl to check the oil and for leaks. He'd been flying all his adult life. It would have been second nature to him by then.

Kate remembered a chapter in a book on flying written by William Langewiesche, the son of the man who had written *Stick and Rudder* and a pilot in his own right. He'd said that one of the biggest mistakes an experienced pilot could make was getting too comfortable in the air. She thought that might hold true for a pilot who commuted to work in a Piper Super Cub he maintained himself.

"So," Liam Campbell said, "should I ask how much this is going to cost me?"

"You should not," Kate said, and smiled. "I just connected the dots for the FBI on an international arms-smuggling ring. I see a large check coming my way from the federal government. I'll just head on home and get right to working up my bill."

He laughed, and she admired the scenery when he did. The creases on either side of his laugh were so deep, they were almost dimples. He really was totally hot. Gabe McGuire, movie star–matinee idol–*People* magazine cover icon that he was, wasn't anywhere near as good-looking.

As if he had plucked the name out of her mind, he said, "You want me to whistle up Gabe for a ride home? Least I can do."

"No," Kate said. Perhaps she spoke with more force than absolutely necessary because his eyebrows went up. "You seem pretty sure he's in the clear. I'd be curious to know why. He is a partner in Eagle Air."

"Coerced," Campbell said. "Gabe talked to his attorney this morning, and they turned over the entire Outouchiwanet correspondence: emails, text messages, phone logs, offers, counteroffers, every substantiated word Gabe McGuire and Finn Grant exchanged on the subject of Outouchiwanet Mountain Lodge. It's pretty clear that Finn wasn't going to sell Gabe the lodge unless Gabe became a partner in Eagle Air, and unless Finn could use Gabe's name to publicize the business." He shoved his hands in his pockets and shook his head. "You couldn't call it blackmail, precisely, but it's making someone else do something they don't want to do to get what he wanted. And as we know now, Finn was very good at that."

"There are other lodges," Kate said. "McGuire could have walked away."

"He could have," Campbell said. "He didn't. It's also pretty clear from the evidence they turned over that Gabe is a minority shareholder who was many steps removed from operations. What's with you, anyway? You've really got the needle for poor old Gabe. You've already had one ride more than I have in that very nice private jet of his. You that sure you don't want another?" He seemed a little amused about something, but he didn't offer to share the joke.

"No thank you," Kate said, more politely this time but no less decidedly. "I'll grab the last commercial flight to Anchorage."

"Have you checked to see if you can get a seat?"

She eyed him suspiciously. "It sounds like you already know the answer to that."

"Mason already called," he said.

"Crap," she said. "And I gave my room away."

"Well, as it happens, Mason hired Wy to take him and his two prisoners to Anchorage this evening. Her Cessna's a six-seater. Room for all, and—" He nodded at Mutt. "—Mason gets help riding herd on Boyd and Shorty."

Kate smiled. "Got her number?"

31

JANUARY 22

Newenham

Jo Dunaway was still interrogating what Kate felt was a very patient Special Agent Mason. She was just relieved they weren't in a clinch when she and Campbell walked back in the door.

"I need to talk to you," she said to Campbell. "And you," she said to Kate, although getting the words out seemed to hurt her.

"Love to," Kate said with as much insincerity as she could infuse into her voice, "but I'm outta here."

An hour later Chouinard was preflighting the Cessna at the Newenham airport as her passengers arrived in two vehicles, one a rental driven by Dunaway, and Chouinard's pickup, which carried an extra passenger, a woman with long, dark, not very kempt hair sitting in the front seat of the darkened cab. Kate got only a glimpse of her. "My stepmother," Campbell said in passing, "Wy said she wanted to get out of the house." He escorted Boyd and Shorty into the middle row of the Cessna and strapped them into their seats. Mutt and Kate climbed into the back and Mason rode shotgun.

Campbell came to the door as Chouinard was closing it up.

He reached in to shake Kate's hand. "I appreciate the help." An eyebrow quirked. "If I deplore the methods."

Kate grinned at him. "Take a number."

He nodded and stepped back. He and his wife exchanged a kiss that Kate admired with a connoisseur's eye, made Shorty and Boyd despair of ever kissing a woman again, and Mason pretended not to see. "Fly safe, babe."

She smiled. "Always do."

Campbell closed the door and walked away. "Everybody buckled up?" Wy said. "Good. Got two extra headsets. Who wants them?"

Mason took one, Kate the other. Chouinard faced forward and the propeller cranked over and moved quickly into a steady, comforting roar, pulling the nose down. Across the runway Kate could see Finn Grant's old hangar, dark now. Gabe McGuire's Gulfstream was gone, too, probably tucked safely away in the hangar at Eagle Air. If not carrying McGuire to his next red carpet appearance. Wherever, Kate was deeply relieved to be on a heading in the opposite direction.

Just why she was so relieved was not something she cared to explore.

The Cessna gave a little jerk and began to roll forward.

It's the fucking Wild, Wild West.

Kate looked at the surrounding landscape of the Nushugak River delta, the wide mouth of glacial runoff spilling into Bristol Bay, the richest salmon fishery in the world. She thought of the harbor with the boats rafted together in twos and threes in their slips, of more boats shrink-wrapped in storage yards.

Chouinard's voice crackled over Kate's headphones, and the Cessna pulled out onto the end of the runway.

She remembered the photos she'd seen on the walls of Jeannie Penney's library, of the boats so thick on the water, you could have walked clear across Bristol Bay without getting your feet wet. The story Jeannie had told her of the three fishermen exchanging shots over fouling their nets in someone else's propeller.

The Cessna's engine accelerated, and the propeller spun into invisibility.

She thought of the near-shooting war between the local Native corporation, Alaskan environmentalists, fishermen, and everyone who just wanted a job over the proposed platinum mines in the Togiak Wildlife Refuge. She thought of the seventy-five-year-old homesteader headed for his cabin upriver with a load of groceries and supplies in his skiff, who had been enticed into pulling over to help what he thought was a boat in distress, only to discover it was two National Park rangers faking engine trouble so they could force inspections on a good Samaritan who was sap enough to pull over. Shots had been exchanged, big surprise, and the old man and one of the rangers were in the hospital in Anchorage, with a strong public sentiment in favor of, as the delicate phrase went, making the rangers' services available to the industry.

The Cessna began to roll, picking up speed.

Everything out here seemed to involve the business end of a rifle or a pistol or a shotgun. It wasn't like Park rats didn't shoot each other, but the Bay rats seemed to be that much quicker to reach for a .357 to punctuate an argument.

They rose smoothly into the air. The lights of Newenham fell away. The Cessna climbed quickly and easily to altitude through a clear, calm sky and rolled out on a heading for Merrill Field.

And now one of Southwest Alaska's leading citizens, posthumously perhaps but nevertheless, was found to have been gunrunning, using a vast, unpopulated wilderness and an endless and for the most part unpoliced border to ship stolen automatic weapons to the highest overseas bidder. Which were used at least occasionally, if Special Agent Mason was correct, to shoot and kill American soldiers.

The twilight threw the landscape crawling beneath them into shadow. Distance and inaccessibility were better cloaking devices than anything a Romulan could think up. Dozens of unmarked airstrips for transportation, hundreds of quick-running streams for power—she'd seen a group of hikers come into the Park with a backpack power plant weighing less than thirty pounds that could generate five hundred watts from any stream four feet deep. What couldn't you do with a reliable source of electricity? The tech was so there for self-contained, anonymous camps tucked away in remote corners of the state, conducting their business far from watching eyes. Where there was one Finn Grant, there had to be more, although she doubted there could ever be another so well financed.

You can imagine the effect on some poor grunt whose ride home gets taken out with a weapon manufactured two states over from where he was born.

At that moment she became aware that the Cessna's engine was running rough. She sat up straight.

There were black streaks coming up over the windshield.

Oil. The engine was leaking oil, and it was running rougher now, rough enough for Kate to see the cowl shaking, rough enough for her to feel the fuselage begin to vibrate beneath her feet. Chouinard's voice crackled over the headset. "Newenham tower, Cessna six-eight kilo, declaring an in-flight emergency, requesting immediate clearance for return and landing."

She sounded tense but not panicked. It seemed to Kate in the few seconds before Newenham tower responded that the engine started shaking even harder. They were already wing down in a hard right bank and in the distance Kate could see the lights of Newenham airport. Too far?

Mutt, who knew what a smooth-running airplane engine sounded like as well as any frequent flier, added her own into the mix with a big "*Woof!*" that in that small, enclosed space approximated the decibel level of a sonic boom. It sounded far too close to the unprotected ears of the two men sitting in front of her, and it was followed almost immediately by the distinct, acrid smell of fresh urine.

The engine ran rougher, the aircraft starting to shake like a maraca in a salsa band. For all her hours in the air, Kate had never been in anything even remotely approaching an accident, but what bothered her most was that there was absolutely nothing she could do. It was all up to the plane and the pilot now.

Correction. Shorty started yelling and lunging in his seat. Boyd started cursing. Kate grabbed them both by the hair and banged their heads together as hard as she could. It didn't have much effect, so she did it again. This time they shut up.

She used their hair to pull them apart so she could see out the windshield. The oil had streaked it so heavily by now that she didn't see how Chouinard was going to be able to see to land. The lights of the Newenham runway seemed much closer through the oily film, and she looked out her window to see the tops of the scrub spruce passing a foot beneath the right wheel. The rate of descent seemed to be a lot faster than usual and *bam!* they hit the runway on all three wheels hard enough that Kate thought the gear might come right up through the fuselage. It didn't, but she bit her tongue.

In the meantime Chouinard cut the throttle and the engine and the Cessna coasted down the runway until the friction of the tires on the pavement and the drag of air against the fuselage brought them to a halt.

Chouinard killed the engine, ripped the headset off, and turned to glare at the two men in the middle seats. "Did one of you sonsabitches actually just pee in my airplane?"

Neither of the prisoners said anything.

A sound from Mason sounded suspiciously like a groan. He was hunched over in the shotgun seat, holding his head. "Oh great, what, you hit your head? Did you hit any of the instruments?"

"No," Kate thought she heard him say, but he was still holding his head and his voice was muffled.

A pickup with its headlights on bright bore down on them at speed, followed by the screech of rubber on pavement, a door slamming open, and running footsteps. Campbell had the pilot's door open and Chouinard unbuckled and hauled out of her seat. In the next moment her face was mashed into his shoulder with his hand at the back of her head and his other arm cinched around her waist, her legs dangling in the air. "Jesus, babe, jesus jesus jesus," was all he seemed able to say, over and over again into her hair.

She was still trying to get her face out of his shoulder when Kate climbed out on the tarmac. She busied herself with getting Shorty and Boyd out of the aircraft. She left Mutt to guard them and went around to the other side to scoot Mason's seat back and help him out. His nose was bleeding and one eye was swelling but he still had all his teeth and he was mobile.

"I'm okay, babe," she heard Chouinard say. "I'm okay, we're all okay."

There was a shaky laugh. "I know. I know. Jesus, when I heard your call."

When Mason and Kate got around to the other side of the aircraft Chouinard was saying in a soft voice, "You were on the scanner?"

"I always am when you're in the air."

"I didn't know."

"Just because you're fearless in the air doesn't mean I am, as you well know." Campbell saw Kate and she could tell it took a physical effort for him to release his wife. "Kate. You okay?"

She managed a smile and hoped no one could see how badly her knees were trembling. "They say you aren't really an Alaskan until you've walked away from at least one airplane crash."

"We didn't crash," Chouinard said indignantly. She glared at Boyd and Shorty. "Although somebody did pee in my plane. Do you know how hard it is to get that smell out of the seat cover?"

"What happened?" Campbell said.

Chouinard's expression darkened. "Oil pressure started dropping, oil temp starting rising. Next thing I know, there's oil all over the windshield and the engine's running rough." By then other trucks were arriving, including Newenham's one crash truck, and there was more than enough light. Someone had a stepstool and Chouinard used it to unbutton the cowling and take a look at the engine. A moment later she stepped down, her expression angry and baffled. "The oil filter adapter separated. I know I checked that when I did the last change."

"I know you did, too," Kate said.

Everyone looked at her askance.

"He was murdered," Kate said.

"Who was murdered?" Campbell said.

"Finn Grant," Kate said.

Campbell looked from her to Chouinard, to the Cessna, and back to Kate.

"I know why he was murdered," she said. "And when you know why, you know who."

32

JANUARY 22

Newenham

"I'M SUCH A MORON," Kate said. "What's the first thing I learned on the job, what's Morgan's First Law? 'The nearest and the dearest got the motive with the mostest.'"

"Huh?" Campbell said.

They were speeding down the Icky Road, on their way back to Newenham, leaving behind an apoplectic Chouinard, an FBI agent with what was now a magnificent shiner, and two terrified suspects, one of whom needed a change of pants.

They hadn't left behind the stepmother, who was riding shotgun next to Campbell. Kate and Mutt were in the backseat, Kate with her nose pressed against the security screen. She noticed that the brunette's belly barely fit in the space between the dashboard, the passenger side door and the shotgun bolted next to the gear shift. "Wow," she said, "you're really pregnant."

"Tell me something I don't know," the other woman said, hanging grimly to the hand strap. "Could you take it a little easier on the gas, Liam?"

"You're the one who wanted to get out of the house, Stepmama," Campbell said.

"Stop calling me that!"

Campbell looked in the rearview. "Who's Morgan?"

"We're taught to always look at the spouse first," Kate said. "For good reason."

"Tina?" Oncoming headlights appeared and Campbell transferred his gaze back to the road. "Yeah, plenty of motive, but we agreed early on Tina's not a pilot or a mechanic. Plus she's got an ironclad alibi."

"No, she doesn't," Kate said.

"What do you mean?"

She still hadn't answered him when they pulled up a little down the street from Grant's house. The day Kate had moved into the apartment over the garage next door seemed like a year ago. The house next to it looked the same, harshly new, overweeningly ostentatious, and eerily empty in spite of all the lights on inside.

Kate headed for the front door. "We don't have a warrant," Campbell said behind her, sounding a little out of breath.

"If she doesn't want to let us in, she doesn't have to let us in," Kate said, and knocked on the door.

"At least you knocked," Campbell said. "More than I expected."

They heard footsteps on the other side of the door. It opened. "Hello, Jeannie," Kate said. Mutt shouldered between Kate and the door, forcing Jeannie back a step, and trotted inside. Kate promptly followed.

Behind her, Campbell made an effort not to roll his eyes. He doffed his cap and gave an indignant-looking Jeannie Penney an apologetic smile, but he stepped inside, too. Something told him that Kate Shugak was following a hot lead, and he wanted to be there when it paid off. He had become accustomed to closing cases in Newenham, and he didn't want to ruin his record.

"Where's Tina?" Kate said in the hallway.

"She's not really feeling up to visitors," Jeannie said, not quite glaring.

"Who is it, Mom?" The door to the TV room cracked, and Oren looked out. "Oh, Jeannie, hi. Didn't know you were here." He saw Kate, and Mutt, and Campbell. "Oh."

He shut the door.

"Neighborly," Campbell said.

"Or a guilty conscience," Kate said.

"No one was expecting visitors," Jeannie said, glowering.

Kate brushed by her like she wasn't there, walking down the hall to a door on the left. She opened it without knocking. "Hello, Tina."

Jeannie transferred her glare to the trooper. He refused to wilt beneath it, waiting until he heard Tina Grant's low-voiced greeting. It definitely wasn't a shrieked "Get out!" He followed Kate into the room.

Kate was looking at a gun rack hanging on a wall opposite the desk, behind which Tina was sitting. "Where is it?" she said.

"Where's what?" Tina said.

"The M4," Kate said. "I saw it here the other day."

Tina shrugged. "I don't know."

"I saw one just like it out at Eagle Air, too," Kate said.

If Tina had seemed bewildered, or looked to Jeannie or even Campbell for help, he would have stopped whatever was going on right now. But she didn't. She looked exhausted, washed out, leaden of thought and movement, as if she didn't have enough energy to get out of her own way. She looked like she had come to the ragged end of her endurance.

All that could have been explained away by her recent double loss and by her second daughter's assault, and Jeannie Penney's increasingly volcanic glare demanded a recognition of them. But his gut told him there was more. He waited on Kate Shugak to tell him what.

"I thought it was odd," Kate said. "One I could understand, but two brand-new M4s seemed excessive, even for a collector, which it is obvious your husband was."

"Yes," Tina said, her voice a monotone. "Yes, he collected rifles, shotguns, assault weapons."

"Tina," Jeannie said, "you don't have to—"

Kate crossed the room and leaned against a corner of the desk. When Tina raised her eyes to look at Kate, Campbell wasn't certain that blank gaze was really focussing on anything. Tina looked as if she ought to be feeling around for her cane.

"Your daughter was killed in Afghanistan," Kate said. "A sniper took out her helo with an RPG."

"Yes," Tina said, still in that dead-and-alive voice. "That's what they told me. Her commanding officer. What he wrote in the letter."

"Tina." Jeannie Penney marched around the desk and put her hands on her friend's shoulders. "You're tired. You should be in bed."

"But it wasn't an RPG, was it." Kate walked over to the filing cabinet and reached for a file folder that sat on top of it.

"Illegal search and seizure," Campbell almost said, but some quality of Tina's immobility, combined with her lack of protest, stopped him.

Kate opened the folder. There were two pieces of paper inside it. She held the first one up. "The condolence letter from her commanding officer." She put it back and held up the second one. "A letter to Tina from one of the soldiers Irene was supposed to fly out with that morning."

"Put that back," Jeannie said sharply.

It wasn't Jeannie's house, Campbell thought, it was Tina's, and she still had nothing to say. They were probably still constitutionally okay.

"They recovered the sniper's weapon. It was American made, a Colt M203, a variation of the M4 automatic rifle. He sounds pretty bitter about it. Can't say I blame him much. You don't travel halfway around the world and expect to get shot at with your own gun."

Campbell's eyes widened.

Kate nodded. "Remember what Mason said? That the Taliban were using American-made weapons to shoot Americans and leaving the weapons to be found as a means of disrupting morale?"

He nodded.

Kate looked back at Tina. "I guess the next question is, when did you find out your husband was smuggling them out of the country and selling them to arms dealers who were selling them in Afghanistan?"

Campbell drew in a sharp breath.

"And," Kate said, "that the very weapon that killed your daughter Irene might actually have been shipped there by her own father?"

Tina closed her eyes. Later, Campbell thought he would never forget that moment, that scene. Tina sitting behind the desk looking like the walking dead. Jeannie standing behind her chair, back to the window, hands on Tina's shoulders, looking like an avenging Valkyrie. Kate Shugak standing in the center of the room, the overhead light turning her short cap of thick hair an iridescent ebony, casting shadows beneath those high cheekbones, thinning the line of that wide mouth, a quality of expectance, almost even of invitation in her silence.

Next to her stood the enormous gray dog, equally unmoving, yellow eyes fixed on Tina Grant, appearing nothing less than an extension of her mistress' will.

Four strong, powerful women, suspended somewhere on the border between terra firma and hell. It was like something out of Euripides.

Campbell himself stood just inside the door, out of the light, filled with foreboding and a rising tide of dismay.

When Tina finally spoke, her voice was uninflected, disinterested, as if she were relating something that had happened to some other family in some other town. Campbell thought later that treating the story as one step removed might have been the only way Tina could face it.

"He had all that money," Tina Grant said. "He wouldn't tell me where he got it from, but of course I knew it had something to do with Hugh Reid. Hugh was always around, even before, but these last two years..." She looked around at the room. "This house. The air base. All those airplanes. I used to keep the books for Bristol Bay Air, but two years ago Finn shut me out." She opened her eyes and looked at the laptop in front of her. "He put passwords on all the accounts, and he told me he only wanted young, pretty women working at the FBO, something about eye candy for the pilots. After all the work I'd put in, I deserved to retire, he said. Take it easy, go to Hawaii or Arizona, someplace warm, we could afford it now." She drew in a long, careful breath, and Jeannie's hands tightened on her shoulders. "So for the past two years, I've been able to pick up only bits and pieces of information. Then one day..."

Jeannie started to say something and Kate gave her a fierce glance. The librarian's mouth shut again with an audible snap.

"I took the ATV out to Eagle Air. I made up some excuse, I just wanted to see how the remodel was coming, something like that. It didn't matter, Finn wasn't there. But one of the new cargo planes was. When the pilot went inside, I looked inside one of the totes and saw the guns."

Kate looked at Jeannie. None of this was coming as a surprise to her.

"I didn't know what to do," Tina said. "I didn't know where they came from. I didn't know where they were going. And then Irene..."

"She wasn't tracking really well after that," Jeannie said, her voice soft but her eyes still daring Kate to say one condemnatory word.

"They shipped her body back, and we buried her," Tina said. "And then the letter came. It was the first time anyone told me exactly how she had died. Her commanding officer just said she'd been killed by sniper fire."

She fell silent again. Kate Shugak didn't say a word, didn't stir a muscle, so far as Campbell could tell didn't so much as bat an eyelid. With infinite, inexhaustible patience, she waited, and sure enough, Tina Grant was compelled to fill the vacuum of silence the other woman created.

"She might have been killed by one of the weapons her own father smuggled to the insurgents. Do you see?" Tina appealed to Campbell. "Do you see?"

"Yes," Campbell said heavily. "I see."

"You were angry," Kate said in a neutral voice.

"Of course she was angry," Jeannie said hotly, "what mother—?"

"Shut. Up," Kate said.

Jeannie shut up.

Campbell wondered if he could get Kate to teach him that trick.

To Tina again, Kate said in that same neutral voice, "You

were angry. You were so angry that you decided Finn had to pay. You've been around airplanes all of your life. You knew just what to do to make it look like an accident. And you did it."

"She was staying with me," Jeannie said, spacing the words out deliberately. "She'd just found out and she came to my house to tell me the whole story and try to figure out what she should do next. About the guns," she said, emphasizing the last three words and looking fiercely at Campbell. "Like call you. She'd just gotten home when Tasha called to say that Finn was overdue. She had no opportunity to mess with his Super Cub."

Kate looked at Campbell. He wasn't buying it. Neither was she, but she couldn't find the pry bar that would break Tina Grant open, especially not with Jeannie Penney standing so literally and figuratively behind her.

The door opened. Everyone turned to look.

It was Oren.

It was also the M4, which in the way it focused everyone's attention seemed to walk in the door on its own.

He was carrying it loosely, carelessly, across his body. He wasn't really aiming it, but even Jeannie had seen enough television to recognize the curved clip of ammunition protruding from in front of the trigger guard.

Kate's mouth went dry.

"Of course she killed him," Oren said. "My loving mother. My loving father's loving wife. Not that he didn't deserve it. Bad man, my father. First-class, government-certified Grade A asshole, actually. But he knew how to make money, that's for sure."

"Oren," Campbell said in a voice that was just this side of soothing, "why don't you hand over the rifle." He put out his hand.

"Lots and lots of money," Oren said, stopping just out of reach and taking a long pull on the bottle of beer he held in his other hand. It was obvious that it was not his first of the evening. Kate could smell the alcohol oozing out of his pores from six feet away. "I drove Dad out to the hangar that morning. Taxi service. It was about all he trusted me to do. But what the hell." He gestured with the carbine. "It kept me in beer and basketball. One time he even got me courtside seats to a Laker game. Laker side, too, must have cost a fortune. Jack Nicholson was yelling so loud, he spit on me. I didn't wash for a week."

"Put that gun down, Oren," Jeannie said sharply.

"Shut the fuck up, bitch," Oren said. "And you, shut your fucking dog up, too."

Not that drunk, Kate thought, and took a firmer hold of Mutt's mane. Mutt had been growling since Oren walked in the door. Kate believed in Mutt, but she believed even more in the stopping power of the M4 Oren was holding so carelessly in his hands. "Stay, girl," she said. "Quiet, and just ... stay."

The slavering roar died to a rumble, but it didn't go away completely. To distract Oren's attention, Kate said, "Did you see your mother sabotage the Super Cub?"

Oren gazed at her blankly, the resemblance between himself and his mother never stronger. "No," he said. "Didn't have to. Had to be her. She hated him. I didn't like him much myself, but she's always hated him. She never would have married him if her parents hadn't made her." He burped, loud and long, and added as an afterthought, "She hated us, too."

Tina didn't say a word.

"All except Irene," Oren said. "The golden girl. Evelyn was always just going to keep her head down, and I was always going to be the family fuckup. But Irene, it was her self-appointed destiny to make Daddy and Mommy proud. Even if it killed her." A tear ran down his cheek. "And then it did."

Jeannie looked at Tina, who seemed incapable of speech. "Oren—"

"I said shut the fuck up!" He raised the gun in her direction and everyone cowered, Kate included. The safety had to be on that thing, to not punch holes in everyone and everything in that room at such rough and inexpert usage. Didn't it?

She sneaked a quick glance at Campbell. His face was set like stone. The sight did not reassure her.

Mutt continued to growl low and deep in her breast and strain against Kate's hand. "Stay," Kate said, hoping very much that Mutt wouldn't let Kate just pull all the hair out of the back of her neck and attack the crazy little bastard anyway.

She saw a shadow move in the hallway. She looked away immediately, but she thought it might have been Fred Grant.

And then, for a very brief moment, she wondered why she was so sure it was Fred Grant.

"It about killed her," Oren said. "Irene. When I told her where the money was coming from."

Those words did seem to reach Tina. Her brow puckered anyway.

"Jesus, Mom, didn't you ever wonder why she volunteered for a second tour? She wanted as far away from here, as far away from Dad, as far away from you—" He spat the word out. "—as she could get."

"That's not true," Jeannie said, her voice quiet now. "Tina, it's not true."

"Sure it is," Oren said. "That's the other thing I'm good for. Sh-sounding board for my sisters. Dad, too. They could tell me everything because they knew I wouldn't tell anybody." He laughed. "Who would listen?"

"I'll listen," Campbell said. "Hand over that weapon and I'll listen to anything you have to say, Oren."

"You know what she wants to do, don't you," Oren said. "She wants to give it aaaaaaall back. First she's going to catch them all, of course. She's just waiting for the last pilot to come through so she can get his name. But then she's going to give back all that lovely money Dad ripped off from some old rich broad who's too crazy to spend it herself."

He took another drink, or tried to. The bottle was empty, and he tossed it behind him. It shattered on impact and everyone jumped. "S'why Evelyn went out there the other night. I told her about that thumb drive of Dad's and she was determined to find it and get rid of it. She doesn't want to go back to being broke anymore'n I do."

"You understand," Oren said, peering at them earnestly, "the crazy broad doesn't need it. Dad and Hugh said she didn't even know she's got it. But good old Mom's gonna give it all back." There was a wealth of drunken contempt in the look he bent on his mother. "Dear old Mom's gonna put everything up for sale. The hangar. The planes. The base. She's gonna give back all the little businesses Dad ripped off from all those dumb bastards in town. One big Kmart Special." He looked at his hand and seemed puzzled that there was no bottle in it. "No matter that the rest of us will go hungry, dear old straight-arrow Mom has to make it all right."

Kate looked at Tina. "So that's why you wanted my rent up front in cash."

Oren burped again. "'Course it was. Mom wouldn't let Evelyn or me or Uncle Fred touch any of the money Dad had. She wouldn't, either. I will, though. I served enough time for it."

He saluted Tina with the M4 and Kate managed not to flinch. Another shadow moved in the hall. What the hell was

Fred Grant doing out there, waiting for Godot? Maybe the shadow had been only her imagination, or maybe he was as paralyzed by the big black cannon being waved around by the drunken little dweeb as the rest of them. She caught Oren's eye and said, "Big talk from a man who still lives with his mommy."

Oren looked ugly. When the barrel of the M4 began to swerve in Kate's direction Tina stood up and pushed away from the desk, crowding Jeannie into the left-hand corner of the office. In a purely instinctive move Kate felt herself crouching, preparing to launch herself into the opposite corner where the desk might afford her a little cover, too.

And then as she was moving she saw the shadow in the hallway coalesce to slip soundlessly inside the door of the office. There was no way Oren could have seen him or heard him, but a sound like furniture being shoved across the floor came from the hallway behind the shadow. Oren did hear that, they all did. He swung around, rifle at the ready, just before the shadow reached him. A second more and it wouldn't have mattered. A second more, and everyone would have lived.

Kate, frozen in midleap, felt time slow down again in the same horrible way it had only that morning in that bedroom in Adak, only this time it was as if everyone was moving through thick tar. Campbell was reaching for his sidearm in slow motion, Tina's arms were spreading in front of Jeannie, over her shoulder Jeannie's mouth was opening wide, Mutt's ears were taking forever to lay themselves flat against her head. In the hallway Fred Grant stepped forward into the light, face pallid, eyes staring. But then who was it who had come into the room?

Recoil from the first shot pushed the barrel up out of the inexperienced hands holding it. It kept climbing, high and right on full automatic, the first round impacting the shadow, the second the doorframe next to Fred Grant's head. Fred Grant flinched from the flying splinters, the film playing in Kate's head still running at half speed. She had all the time in the world to watch, her head following the trail the bullets left up the wall, across the ceiling, down the left-hand corner behind the desk.

The recoil that pushed up the barrel also pushed Oren's body around to his right. His balance was already unsteady from the alcohol, and the recoil made him lose it altogether, but not his grip on the trigger. He fell backwards, the bullets still spraying out of the rifle, breaking a recessed light above the bookshelf, shattering an ivory otter on a shelf below, breaking a shelf in half and sending a dozen books to the floor. One of the books caught a bullet and shredded into confetti, exploding into a cloud of white bits of paper. Tina was hit by one of the last fired, high up on her left side, going through her to shatter the window behind the desk.

The casings were spitting out to Oren's right rear and as he moved they arced in Kate and Mutt's direction. Mutt tried to dodge them by jumping in several different directions at once and instead got in their way, her startled "*Yip!*" cutting through even the deafening sounds of rifle fire when one hit her square in the nose.

Some malign chance of physics caused one of the casings to ricochet off the back of Kate's collar and fall down inside her shirt. It was hotter than hell and felt like it was raising blisters on the tender skin of her back, and time resumed its normal flow with a vengeance. She couldn't remember screaming, which Campbell later assured her she did, but she definitely remembered dancing around trying to pull the hem of her shirt from her jeans to let the casing fall out.

And then Campbell finally got himself airborne and hit

Oren Grant with all the force of his six-feet-two-inch, 180-pounds mass and both men flew horizontally across the floor and into the opposite bookshelves with a crash that knocked more shelves down, books cascading afterwards. A falling clock made from a slab of jade hit Oren in the head and he finally lost his grip on the trigger and the shooting mercifully stopped.

Later Campbell told Kate that it had taken only a few seconds to empty out the thirty-round clip of ammunition. It had felt like much, much longer. They also discovered that Oren hadn't stopped firing, he'd only emptied out the clip.

Campbell looked up from the floor and said something to Kate. "What?" she said. Her ears were ringing, and she couldn't hear her own voice, either. There was a faint drift of smoke, and the room smelled funny, almost sweet. She looked at Campbell and tried again. "What?"

She felt a cold nose press into her cheek and looked down at Mutt, staring up at her with anxious yellow eyes. A wet tongue followed the nose, and Kate realized she was still in a half crouch, ready to leap. The muscles in her thighs began to tremble. When she realized that, all her muscles began to tremble in unison.

Campbell finished cuffing Oren Grant. "Check on Tina," he said, and this time she heard him.

She stood up on shaky legs and went around the desk, hoping no one noticed that she was using it to hold herself up.

The two women had slid down the wall into the corner. Tina was cradled in Jeannie's arms, her back against Jeannie's breast. The bullet looked like it had shattered the entire left side of Tina's torso and Kate couldn't believe she was still breathing, raggedly, bubblingly, but breathing. There was nowhere she could see to apply pressure, there was just too much torn flesh, too much bone showing, too much blood.

Jeannie was covered in it, bits of it staining blond hair, matte skin. A piece of something indescribable was caught in her left eyelash. She looked up at Kate, her eyes pleading.

"Are you hurt?" Kate said.

Jeannie shook her head, dazed. "I … I don't think so. No. Tina shoved me out of the way, and then I guess she fell on me."

"Tina," Kate said.

The woman's eyes fluttered. Her skin was pasty white, her lips blue.

"Tina," Kate said, "did you kill your husband? Did you kill Finn?"

"I told you," Jeannie Penney said fiercely through her tears. "She was spending the night with me. She'd had a fight with Finn and she came over to my house. It wasn't the first time."

Kate looked at her and knew she would go to her grave swearing it was so.

Tina's eyes opened suddenly. She looked straight into Kate's, opened her mouth, and died.

Kate stood up, feeling suddenly and completely exhausted.

"Oh Jesus, Moses, Jesus," she heard Campbell say, his voice on the edge of agony.

She went around the desk to find Campbell holding the shadow in his arms, the shadow who was Moses Alakuyak, who had taken two shots, also on his left side, one lower and one higher than Tina's. His blood was splattered over the doorframe all the way out into the hall. It had saturated Liam Campbell from his hair to his boots.

Oren had pushed himself up on his left side, his hands restrained behind him. "The family fuckup fucks it up again. If Dad could only see me now."

Kate imagined the toe of her boot kicking in his front teeth and found her leg drawn back to do it before she managed to get herself under control. "Shut up," she said. "Just shut the fuck up."

She turned and saw Fred Grant standing in the doorway. "And where the hell were you?" she said. His eyes were wide and staring, speechless at the carnage in the office of his brother's house. He was evidently incapable of reply.

"I fucked up," Moses said. "Shit, Liam, I so totally fucked up. All those years practicing form and I couldn't take down a useless little shit like Oren Grant."

"I think Oren had help," Kate said, still looking at Fred Grant. In a sudden moment of clarity, she distinctly remembered the sound of furniture being moved across the hall floor just before Moses had slid into the room. Someone bumping into the corner table, perhaps, the one with Irene's picture on it. Just enough sound, just loud enough to alert Oren, the crazy guy with the weapon, before the old ninja came into the room like an avenging archangel. And was slain for it.

Fred Grant was still staring at the two men on the floor. He raised his eyes and saw Tina for the first time, and his face changed. "Tina! Oh my god, no, Tina, no no no!" He flung himself across the room, tumbling to his knees next to her body.

"Don't you dare touch her!" Jeannie shouted. "Don't you dare!"

"Bruce Lee wouldn't have had a chance against an M4 on full auto, Moses," Liam said. "You of all people should know that, you dumb bastard." He was trying to dial 911 on his cell with a shaking, bloodstained hand. Kate took it from him and made the call.

"Bill is going to be so pissed," Moses said. His right side looked worse than Tina's. Kate couldn't believe he was still breathing, either, let alone talking.

"No shit," Liam said, "and I don't have the guts to tell her you died, so you hang on, you cranky old bastard, do you hear me? You're tough, you can do it." The desperation was audible in his voice.

"Tell Wy I'm sorry," Moses said. "I never wanted her to have any part of the voices. Fucking genes."

"Don't worry about that now, Moses, just hang on."

Moses smiled, blood welling from his mouth to spill down his chin. "I'm outta here, boy. You treat her right."

"You know you can't trust me to do that without supervision," Campbell said. "You've got to stick around and make sure. Moses!"

Moses' eyes were closing. "At least the goddamn voices'll leave me alone now," he said, his voice slurring.

Kate squatted next to them. "The ambulance is on its way." It wouldn't be in time. She had seen that look before.

"Moses," Campbell said, pleading. "Come on, man."

The old man's eyes opened and looked straight at Kate. "You know he didn't do it, right?" he said, his voice strong and clear. "Jesus, you can't be that slow."

He looked at Campbell and said, "Your uniform's a mess. You're a sartorial disgrace to your service, son."

And then he died, too.

"Liam?"

Kate and Campbell both looked up at the sound of that shaken voice.

The pregnant stepmother had shoved past an immobile Fred Grant to stand in the doorway, staring at the office with a shocked face.

Her beige pants were soaked all the way down the insides of her legs.

33

JANUARY 23

Anchorage

IT TURNED OUT KATE would get another ride on Gabe McGuire's jet after all. This time all the seats were filled, with all the previous passengers except Jean and including new passengers Oren Grant and Fred Grant. Evelyn, still in the hospital, still not talking, and Jeannie Penney, along with Tasha Anayuk, were left behind, although Special Agent Mason made it clear that agents would be in Newenham to interview them all within twenty-four hours, and to please make themselves available for however long the FBI would need them.

The flight was less than an hour. Once McGuire came back to talk to Kate. He looked at her face and returned to the cockpit.

They were met at Million Air in Anchorage by an FBI van and driven to the FBI headquarters on Sixth Avenue, where they were conducted into separate interview rooms.

Kate dictated her statement in a level, expressionless voice and signed where they told her to. Gamble, the FBI agent she had had dealings with in the past and who seemed to have pissed off his superiors in D.C. badly enough to earn himself a lifetime posting to the Anchorage station, came into the room at one point. He looked at her and then looked away again, as if averting his eyes from something indecent. She didn't know what was the matter. She'd showered and changed her clothes before she'd got on the plane. The odor of placenta could have lingered on, she supposed, and looked down at her hands. She'd never really understood the phrase *baby catching* before. At least Katya had taken a decent amount of time in making her appearance. This kid had slid into the world like she was Tommy Moe coming off Chair 6 at Alyeska. For one terrified moment Kate had been afraid she was going to drop her.

Campbell's stepmother, whose name Kate never did learn, looked almost indecently relieved. Campbell himself had turned an interesting shade of green and had retreated into the hallway after he'd hoisted stepmama onto the couch in the television room.

Fifteen minutes afterwards Joe Gould, Newenham's lone EMT, showed up, too late for the deaths, too late for the birth. He pronounced Tina and Moses dead at the scene, which seemed a little redundant, and ventured a mild joke on Kate's skill at midwifery. Between the three of them he was lucky to get out of there alive.

And then Wyanet Chouinard showed up, white faced and red eyed, with Jo Dunaway in tow, and Bill Billington, who looked to have aged a hundred years in the space of a single phone call.

Mason wanted Dunaway to come with them. Dunaway flatly refused. Kate thought he should have insisted, but he didn't, and later she admitted to herself that he was right. Whatever knowledge Dunaway had, she would be more than happy to exchange for exclusive rights to what was going to be the biggest story of the year. But she would support her friend first, her friend who had just lost her grandfather in a gun battle. Much as she would have liked to, Kate couldn't fault her instincts.

And write the story she would. A month later, Kate and the rest of the state read the five-part feature in the *Anchorage News*. From almost the moment of the death of Alexandra Hardin's father, followed by her inheritance of his considerable estate, Hugh Reid and Finn Grant had been bilking it for funds, not only to build Eagle Air FBO and to buy new aircraft but pretty much anything else that took their fancy, including two recreational helicopters (until then Kate hadn't known there was such a thing), a fancy sailboat in San Diego, an apartment in New York City, and weekends in Vegas for them and their steadily increasing amounts of new best friends. Not to mention high-end escort services for Grant in particular, wherever he shopped for aircraft. The FBI staged raids of two airplane hangars, one in Anchorage and one in Portland, where had been found retail quantities of weapons from grenades to the ubiquitous M4 to rocket launchers, body armor, and missiles, surface-to-air and airborne.

Hugh Reid was in custody by then, of course. Reid said that Grant had hired Reid's firm to form a holding corporation, which firm's solid reputation had attracted other investors. As it always does in certain circles, Reid said, word got around. One of the men Grant had served with in the army had gone into the acquisition of arms from poorly guarded U.S. armories in a big way. He already had buyers, but he was always looking for a secure, efficient, and profitable means of distribution. When he sniffed out the existence of Grant's suddenly deep pockets, he approached Grant with a plan, contacts, and merchandise. Greed only begets more greed, and despite Reid's reservations—or so Reid said, and as Mason pointed out, he was the last man standing—Grant jumped on the opportunity for triple and quadruple profits.

Boyd cut a deal and had given up the warehouse in central

Washington State, conveniently located in a business park six blocks off a major highway and not a mile from a railroad line. The weapons had been stolen in small lots from a lot of different armories located in a dozen states, which, again according to Mason, had army security in a bit of a tizzy. Grant hadn't been thinking small, according to Boyd. The plan all along had been to use small arms to establish his ability to sell good product efficiently and discreetly, in small lots, defining and testing the safest route as they went. Later, they'd move on to bigger ordnance on bigger aircraft.

Kate had told him about Tasha and the Herc while she was giving her statement in Anchorage. "What was next," she said, "army tanks on C-5s?"

"He was a robber baron, essentially," Mason said, Kate thought not without a certain amount of misplaced admiration. "He would have fit right in with Carnegie or Rockefeller or Astor." He shrugged. "Many a respectable fortune was built on far less savory beginnings."

"You had an informant, didn't you," Kate said. At his look she said, "Oh, not someone you knew about, over there in the middle of the war. But someone was working this from this end, weren't they? Someone you found out about after we got here. I saw Gamble look in earlier. And they had flipped someone involved in Eagle Air in exchange for information."

Mason met her eyes. "How did you guess?"

"Jo Dunaway knew about the investigation into Alexandra Hardin's estate. First thing any good reporter does is check with primary sources, and the primary source for interstate fraud and racketeering is always going to be the FBI." She shrugged. "I know Gamble. He likes reading the news and knowing he's 'a source high up in the investigation who spoke on condition of anonymity.'" She paused. "Was the informant Fred Grant?"

Mason said nothing but his expression spoke volumes. Kate said, "He's got a thing for Tina, that's for sure. Or did have," she added bleakly. "Plus, I doubt he would have minded stepping into his brother's shoes as the owner and proprietor of Eagle Air. It's why Grant's operation was still going on when I showed up. Not because Tina wanted to get the names of all the pilots so she could turn them in to you, although I'd bet large that Fred told Gamble that. Did you give him immunity?"

His expression this time was even easier to read. She laughed without humor and shook her head. "Because I'm pretty sure he's the one who shot Evelyn at Eagle Air. Oren knew about Grant's thumb drive, the one with all the evidence of his blackmailing on it. According to Oren, Tina meant to give them all their businesses back. I think the loose-lipped little bastard told Evelyn about it, and I think she went looking for it. Could be she wanted to hide the evidence of her father's wrongdoing. Could be she was just as concerned over Tina's determination to strand the whole Grant family high and dry, financially." Her mouth twisted. "Although I'm pretty sure when you talk to her now, she's going to say she meant to turn all that information over to the proper authorities."

"If any of this is true, how did Fred find out what she was doing?"

"Try the usual suspect. Oren's the common denominator. And Fred probably wanted a bone to throw Gamble, something to throw the FBI off the scent of the arms-smuggling operation so he could bank a few more checks. Blackmail on the scale practiced by Finn Grant would have been a pretty good diversion."

"Well," Mason said, at something of a loss. "At least he didn't kill her."

She looked at him. "Or us."

"Us?" he said.

"He was there when we got back from Adak. You saw him. Chouinard's tie-downs are a minute's walk from Grant's old hangar. Which hangar is conveniently supplied with a full toolbox." At his incredulous expression she said with some exasperation, "Who else do you think sabotaged Chouinard's plane? The one carrying an FBI agent and two witnesses essential to the gunrunning case he was building?" *Not to mention me,* she thought, and what she found far less easy to forgive, *not to mention Mutt.*

"But—"

"In Adak, Shorty said something to Boyd about the boss. This was—" Was it only two days ago? "This was when I flew down with Boyd. Shorty seemed real concerned about the boss. Finn Grant died last month. What boss was he talking about?"

For the first time, she'd managed to shake Mason free of his habitual calm. "I—I don't—Hugh Reid?"

Her laugh was mirthless. "You haven't seen him yet, I take it. No one is ever going to be afraid of Hugh Reid, I promise you. But I can see someone being afraid of Fred Grant." And she was certain Fred Grant had made a noise in the hallway as Moses Alakuyak was coming into the room, in hopes that Oren the family fuckup would kill everyone standing and put Oren away, leaving only Evelyn in between him and control of Eagle Air. And he'd already shot her once.

She remembered his outburst when he had seen Tina's body. There had been real grief on his face.

So perhaps not everyone.

"Can you prove any of this?" he said.

"You probably could, if you tried," she said. "But you won't, because somebody here gave him immunity, so why bother." She tossed down the pen and got to her feet. "You people never get it right."

"You know, Kate," Mason said as he waited with her at the elevator, "Hollywood action movies notwithstanding, there isn't much anyone can do against an M4 with a full clip on full automatic, even if a moron's holding it."

"Maybe especially if a moron's holding it," she said.

34

JANUARY 25

The Park

SHE AND MUTT SPENT the night in Jack's condo, and took a cab to Merrill early the following morning. George took one look at her face and put her on shotgun, where she wouldn't frighten the other passengers.

The high that had been hanging over Bristol Bay for the last week seemed to have teleported itself to the Park. At any rate, the view was all the way to Canada before George began the descent into Niniltna. A river, yes, but not a delta, and the body of water it flowed into was only an edge of blue on the horizon. The Quilaks rose like a wall on the east, terrifying and comforting in their jagged proximity. The undulating landscape was lush with trees under a blanket of white. As George made his final, coming in over the river from the south, Kate saw a snowmobile head upriver, passing a four-wheeler headed down.

Jim was waiting for them at the airstrip. Mutt was first out the door of the Single Otter and crossed the space between in a single bound. When Kate, moving a little more slowly, brought up the rear, Mutt had both paws on Jim's shoulders and was savaging his face with a serious tongue bath. He was laughing and trying not very hard to fend her off.

He looked over Mutt's head and saw Kate. He grabbed the huge gray paws and said, "Okay, enough, glad to see you, too." He settled her down on the hard-packed snow. He seemed oddly relieved. "Hey."

"Hey," Kate said, and suddenly, inexplicably, began to weep.

She'd brought home a print-out of the front page of the morning newspaper with Dunaway's story in it.

FBI Busts Alaska-Based International Arms Smuggling Ring by Jo Dunaway
jdunaway@anchoragenews.com
Published: January 24, 10:34 P.M.
Last modified: January 25, 6:37 A.M.

Local attorney Hugh Reid was remanded into federal custody today pending charges of wire fraud, embezzlement, money laundering, theft of government property and illegal transportation and sales of arms in the ongoing federal and state investigation of Eagle Air, Inc. Reid is a partner in the law firm of Chapados, Reid, Reid, McGillivray and Thrall in Anchorage, which firm was also the administrator for the estate of the late John Neville "Wes" Hardin, Alaska businessman, entrepreneur and philanthropist. An unnamed source high in the FBI said agents are only beginning to unravel the story of a group of Alaska entrepreneurs who were apparently in the process of building one of the biggest illegal arms dealerships in history, based on theft of American arms from military armories across the United States, and transporting them to sell to terrorists overseas.

In related news, Anchorage District Attorney Brendan

McCord petitioned the court to appoint a guardian ad litem for Alexandra Hardin, the heiress whose estate it appears Reid bilked for upwards of $200 million over a period of two and a half years. Hardin is the daughter and last living relative of John Neville "Wes" Hardin, and currently resides in the Bahamas in a long-term care facility for Alzheimer's patients.

"Mason was right," Jim said. "Nothing you could have done."

"I know," Kate said. "I know he was right."

They were at the house. Kate and Jim were on the couch, Johnny on the floor with his head pillowed on Mutt's flank. She'd told them everything, the whole blackmailing, gunrunning, chest freezer- and Dumpster-diving, fish hold freight container, hitchhiking, flight-sabotaging, illegal arms–selling story.

Well. She'd made only passing reference to Gabe McGuire, and that only because she couldn't avoid it. He hadn't been mentioned publicly in connection to the case, at least not yet, but it was only a matter of time. Or Liam could mention him in passing when he was talking to Jim, and then Jim would want to know how she could possibly have left him out. So she said he was just like he looked in the movies. Hadn't talked to him much. Seemed like an okay guy.

"But you got to ride in his private jet?" Johnny said, stars in his eyes. "Twice?"

"Me and a bunch of other people," Kate said, conscious of Jim's eyes on her.

"Sweet," Johnny said.

She didn't mention that she'd let her inexplicable reaction to Gabe McGuire nearly push her out of Newenham too soon, before she'd finished the job.

"I'm just glad the little fuckup with the M4 missed you,"

Jim said, pulling her under his arm.

"That'd be me, too," she said, curling up next to him and putting her head on his chest. The reassuring beat of his heart thumped against her ear.

"That'd be me, three," Johnny said soberly. "Dumpsters and chest freezers are one thing."

"Don't forget the freight container, and the near miss with the Cessna," she said. She smiled at him. He didn't smile back, and in his youthful face she saw again the echo of his father's.

The faint echo of another man's. Or was it? Maybe she just wanted Gabe McGuire to look like Jack Morgan so as to make her attraction to him seem a rational reaction. She hoped he was back in L.A., or on his way there. She hoped the feds seized every single piece of property Finn Grant had ever owned or ever thought of owning or ever had owned, including Outouchiwanet Mountain Lodge, and sold it all off to pay Grant's back taxes. She hoped Gabe McGuire never had cause to cross north of the fifty-third latitude ever again.

There was the movie about the gold rush, but Nome was a long way from Niniltna. There was no reason their paths should ever cross again. She never wanted to see another one of his movies, if it came to that.

I think you're just as attracted to me as I am to you, and because you think of me as a face on a magazine cover, and in spite of that self-confidence you clank around in like a suit of armor, I think you don't know what to do about it.

It wasn't bad, as lines went. But it was only a line. Probably written by a screenwriter, delivered in a film of his she hadn't seen. She rubbed her face against Jim's chest, the pilling of his ancient sweatshirt rough against her cheek. This was real, this was here, this was now. A movie star was someone who couldn't pass a mirror without checking their hair.

Oblivious, Jim was still reading the newspaper, and craning her neck she saw that he had moved on to the obituary page.

> Grant, Clementina "Tina" Tannehill. Wife, mother, businesswoman.
>
> Donations in her memory may be made to a special account at the First Frontier Bank branch in Newenham, Alaska.
>
> For further information, contact her son, Oren Grant, also of Newenham, Alaska.

"A loving son," Jim said, tossing the newspaper on the floor.

"Yeah," Kate said. "One thing his father got right."

Mutt snoozed on her quilt. A log popped in the fireplace.

Jim took a deep breath and blew it out. He scooted his butt to the edge of the couch and got his feet beneath him, just in case a quick getaway was called for. "Remember the day you left, the little jet parked in front of George's hangar?"

"Uh, yeah," Kate said, a little bewildered at this seeming change of topic.

"It was Erland Bannister's jet, Kate," Jim said.

Kate stiffened.

"It might even have been the jet he was shopping for when he ran into McGuire shopping for his, who knows? Anyway, it was his jet, and he was on it."

"What," Kate said, spacing the words out, "was Erland Bannister doing in the Park?"

"You won't like it," he said.

Kate looked at him, eyes like flint.

"He's invested in the Suulutaq. I'd guess in a fairly substantial way, because he had Truax on board."

Kate didn't say anything. After exchanging a glance with Johnny, who had learned all this before Kate had and who had been and remained now extremely apprehensive as to her reaction. Jim said, "Just out of curiosity, I got hold of a copy of Global Harvest Resources' annual report. There's a list of non-majority shareholders in it. One of them is Arctic Investments."

Kate's face was wearing a strained expression.

"I checked with George," Jim said. "The jet's papers are in the name of the aforementioned Arctic Investments. They're a registered corporation in Alberta. And Erland Bannister is its majority shareholder, as well as its president and CEO."

"Arctic Investments?" Kate said in a queer voice. "Are you sure?"

"Pretty sure, yes," he said. "Or I should say, Kurt Pletnikof is. I, ah, availed myself of his services. Figured you wouldn't mind. Why?"

"Because," Kate said, feeling suddenly tired all over, "Arctic Investments is one of the partner companies in Eagle Air." She stopped.

"What?" he said.

"His tail number," she said. "Did it begin with a C?"

He frowned. "Yeah. It's registered in Canada. Kurt said it was probably a tax dodge."

She closed her eyes and shook her head.

"What?" he said again.

"I'll have to check with Mason," she said. "But remember the reporter I told you about? Jo Dunaway?"

"I remember," he said.

"She said Alexandra Hardin was brought to the Bahamas by two men, from their descriptions Grant and Reid."

Jim nodded. "And?"

"And she said they came in a private jet, piloted by Grant."

"Tail number start with a C?" At her nod, he swore.

"My sentiments exactly," she said. She raised her mug in a toast. "Here's to Erland Bannister, who has the best eye to the main chance of anyone I've ever met." She drank the rest of her cold cocoa and set the mug down on the floor with a savage thump. Mutt snorted and almost woke.

"I apologize in advance," Jim said.

"Honest to god," she said, spacing out the words, "I'm not sure how much more I can take."

"Axenia was on the jet with Erland."

She stared at him. "My cousin Axenia? Axenia Shugak? Mathisen?"

He nodded.

She let her head drop forward into her hands. Jim exchanged another look with Johnny. It was silent until Jim reached for a large manila envelope.

"Just one more thing about Bannister, Kate."

Her voice was muffled by her hands. "I don't want to know."

"This, you do." She raised her head and watched him open the envelope and extract an eight-by-ten photograph, black-and-white, although it had yellowed with age. It felt brittle to the touch. One of the corners had broken off.

It was a picture of a room in a house, a large sitting room. There were built-in bookshelves along the walls filled with a lot of leather-bound books with gilt lettering on the spines, the kinds of books that were only for show, never read. There was a lot of furniture that looked as if it was covered in some dark leather, and there were half a dozen tall, narrow display tables, beautifully crafted with scrolled legs and beveled glass, artfully placed in an implied path so as to entice a viewer to walk from one to the other.

At middle left there was an overturned wooden desk.

The desk had a body beneath it, a middle-aged man with a bit of a paunch, dressed in a suit and tie. It was a black-and-white photograph, but Kate was guessing that the stain on his clothing and on the carpet beneath him was blood. He didn't look like anyone she knew.

She looked up, a question in her eyes.

Jim nodded. "Emil Bannister." He handed her a second photograph. This one was a close-up of the desk, which was still overturned, although the body had been removed. "Look at the corner of the desk, here." He pointed.

Kate followed his finger. It was hard to see in black-and-white, but it seemed to her there was a spot of something on one corner. She looked back up at Jim.

He got up and got a magnifying glass from the kitchen. "You can see it better with this."

Through the glass the stain looked gummy. "You think it's blood," she said.

"I do," he said. "What's more, I think it's Emil's blood. Which means he hit his head on it after he either fell or was pushed, or possibly struck. I don't see any bruising on his face but these aren't the most detailed crime scene photographs I've ever seen in my professional life. Not surprising, since they're sixty-odd years old."

"Where'd you get them?"

"I got Brendan to sniff them out for me," he said. "Wasn't hard. Remember you told me that you told Victoria Muravieff she ought to look into her brother's parentage? Apparently she also looked into her grandfather's death."

"Why?" she said.

"If you'll recall," he said, "Erland's statement was that his father had interrupted a burglary."

"Yes," she said. "He said his father had caught the burglar in the act, that the burglar had attacked him."

"Not a burglar's style, first of all," Jim said. "Usually the smart ones aren't even armed. Erland's statement, taken at the scene—" He fished a single sheet of onionskin from the envelope. It was covered closely with print from a manual typewriter, faded almost into illegibility. "According to Erland's statement, "in the struggle one of the exhibit cases was broken and the desk got knocked over. Erland says he got to the room in time to see the desk fall on his father. He ran to his father and the burglar got away."

"Yes," Kate said. The burglar, as Jim well knew, had been Old Sam Dementieff, Kate's teacher, mentor, father figure, éminence grise, and lifelong friend before he had died the previous October. Old Sam had broken into Emil Bannister's house because Emil Bannister had possession of the Sainted Mary, the Russian Orthodox icon that had been stolen from Kate and Old Sam's tribe by Old Sam's father thirty years before the break-in and Emil's death. "Jim," she said, "are you saying—?"

"Look at that desk, Kate."

She looked at the desk, her heart beginning to thump in her ears. "It's big," she said.

"It's very big," Jim said, "and very heavy. If I had to guess, I'd say it weighed somewhere between a hundred and fifty and two hundred and fifty pounds. I submit that it is highly unlikely that a desk of that size and weight gets knocked over in a fight, especially when one of the fighters is doing his level best to shag it out the door."

He watched her face darken slowly, and waited, showing more calm than he felt.

"There is no way," Kate said, forming the words slowly

and distinctly, "that Old Sam deliberately turned that desk over on Emil Bannister. Knocked him down in the struggle, maybe. And maybe Emil did hit his head on his way down. But Old Sam did not turn that desk over on him."

"Agreed," Jim said, and handed her the first photo again.

She looked at the photo, scrutinizing it for details she might have missed. There was a sense of wrongness about it, and she said, puzzled, "This was a photograph taken by the Anchorage police, right?"

He turned the photograph over and pointed at the APD stamp and the date scrawled beneath it.

She turned it faceup again. "Why is his body still under the desk? Why didn't Erland try to…"

Her voice trailed away, and he watched her eyes widen and her face drain of color as she realized what she had just said.

Moses Alakuyak's voice echoed so loudly in her ears, it was as if the old man were standing next to her, shouting. Which he had done in Newenham, hadn't he, a time or two?

You know he didn't do it, right?

35

JANUARY 26

Niniltna

KATE WALKED INTO THE Niniltna Native Association a couple of days later. Phyllis Lestinkoff was pleased to admit her into the inner sanctum.

"Hey, Annie," Kate said.

Annie waited for the door to close behind Kate. "Was that you in Newenham?"

"How'd you guess?"

Annie raised an eyebrow. "Jim said you were on a job, and once I heard mayhem and murder, I knew it had to be you."

Unwilling, Kate felt a smile cross her face.

"Plus you didn't return any of my calls," Annie said. "So you must have been busy."

"I'm sorry," Kate said. "Did you need to talk to me about something?"

"Not today, but I'd like to know I could call you if I really needed to." Annie gave her a level look. "I wasn't the one who threw you off the deep end when you got landed with this job. Don't take it out on me."

Kate's jaw dropped. "I wasn't."

Was she?

She drew herself up. "By coincidence, that's sort of why I'm here today."

"Really?"

"You know that emeritus position you mentioned at the shareholders meeting?"

"Yes."

"Is that a paid position?"

ACKNOWLEDGMENTS

In no particular order, my thanks to:

Retired FBI Agent Bob Baker, who e-galloped to my rescue with some badly needed last-minute information on the M4 carbine.

FBI Agent Eric Gonzalez, for introducing me to Bob and for turning a gratifying shade of white when I ran the plot by him.

Larry DiFrancesco, pilot, who helped with photographs and details of Gabe McGuire's Gulfstream.

Cathy Rasmuson, for introducing me to Larry.

Jim Eshenower, A&P mechanic and pilot, who conspired with me to murder Finn Grant.

And pilots Wes Head and Stephanie Anderson, for introducing me to Jim.

Any errors that remain are mine.

THE PROLOGUE

TWO VILLAGES, WHERE TWO rivers meet.

A geologic age before, the runoff from Alakan Glacier high up in the Quilak Mountains chewed through a granite ridge to form a narrow canyon fifteen miles long.

A millennia before, a massive earthquake exacerbated a fault in the ridge. Half of it cracked and slid off to the southwest. It left behind a V-shaped wedge between the confluence of two watercourses, which would one day be named Gruening River on the south side and Cataract Creek on the north.

The tip of the V pointed due west. The surface of the wedge was flat and topped with a thick slice of verdant soil raised a hundred feet in the air by the earthquake. That earthquake had also fractured a way to the surface through the granite uplift for an underground spring. The spring's outflow trickled down the south face of the wedge, over time carving a channel for a little stream too steep to support a salmon run and too shallow to be good for anything but watering the blueberry bushes that grew thickly along its sides. In spring this slope was first to thaw, snow and ice giving way to a fairyland of wildflowers, the brash orange-and-yellow florets of western columbine, the shy blue of forget-me-nots, the noxious brown blooms of chocolate lilies, the elegant pink paintbrush, and the dignified purple monkshood.

By luck of the geologic draw the land across the river

remained largely undisturbed by the earthquake, a flat marsh covered in thick grass, cattails, and Alaska cotton. Over time glacial silt carried downriver filled in the marsh, and alder, diamond willow and cottonwood grew out to the water's edge. The force and flow of the combined currents of river and stream undercut the banks to provide habitat for river otters, mink, and marten, and carved tiny tributaries to be dammed by beavers and colonized by salmon.

Two hundred winters before, the Mack family walked up the frozen river. It was a wide river, not too deep, with a good gravel bottom. When it thawed that spring, even on a cloudy day an endless silver horde was visible through the peaty water, a solidly packed, seemingly inexhaustible mixture of king and red and silver salmon moving inexorably upstream. Tobold Mack, the little clan's patriarch, had led them south from the Interior, where a wasting disease had affected the moose population. A decade of famine had led to inter-tribal competition among the local Athabascans over the remaining food sources, and a disastrous decline in population of man and beast alike.

That summer Tobold looked long on where the white water rushed to join the brown, at the arrows in both left by the dorsal fins of the struggling salmon, the birch stumps left by the beaver and the willow stands gnawed down by the moose. He looked up at the mountains that cut into the eastern horizon, beautiful and terrible, and yet comforting all the same in their solid impenetrability. With mountains like those at his back, a man felt safe.

"We have walked far enough," he said.

They built a weir and a snug dugout on the south shore of the river. Drying racks were next, for fish in summer and moose meat in winter, and caribou when the Quilak herds came down to the river to calve in spring. Babies were born and lived, and elders survived long enough to contribute their accumulated wisdom to the tribe, and for everyone in between there was enough food easily available that there was time to sing and dance and play and laugh. Time not only to make a birchwood bowl for eating, but time to carve decorations around its edge. Time not only to make a parka from beaver skins warm enough to withstand the worst winter could throw at them, but time to embroider the parka with trade beads and dentalium shells.

This village they named Kushtaka.

Seventy winters before the present day, Walter Estes and Percy Christianson came up the river, trappers looking for beaver. They were new to the country but not to Alaska, being Aleuts displaced from the island of Anua by the war the Japanese had brought to the great land. Walter and Percy had fought together in the islands and knew firsthand how little there was to go back to. Now they looked for a new place to call home.

The Macks, like any Alaskans happy to see a new face in the long dark doldrums of winter, made them welcome. Estes was half-Italian and Christianson was half-Norwegian but they both comported themselves as men should, sharing the game and the fish they took in equal measure with their hosts. There was still more than enough for all, then.

Five years later, Walter and Percy moved across the river and built their homes on top of the big wedge of rock rising in the V between the creek and the river.

The Macks approved. Ownership of any part of river and creek and its adjacent lands was not a concept the people of Kushtaka understood. They hunted the moose that browsed through the willow and the caribou that calved on the riverbanks, they trapped the beaver and the river otter and the muskrat, they gathered the crowberries and the blueberries that grew on the south-facing slope of the wedge, and they cut the wood of the spruce and birch and alder for fuel. They took enough, never too much, because there was always next season, and they knew from hard experience handed down from Tobold Mack himself that there was always the chance that the next season could be a bad one, with the long cold returning, scarce game, and too many mouths to feed. In this vast land there was still plenty of room for all, and a good neighbor was always welcome in hard times.

Percy sent for his bride, Balasha, who was half-Russian, a plump, lively woman who settled down to smoke salmon, weave grass baskets in the fashion of the Aleuts, and pop out healthy children at the rate of one every two years. Walter married Nancy Mack, who joined him up on the wedge, in the log cabin he built for her.

They called their village Kuskulana. It was not as conveniently placed as Kushtaka, being a hard slog uphill from the salmon-rich waters of river and creek, and a longer, harder slog uphill when burdened with the hindquarter of a moose. But the spring that bubbled up provided much better drinking water than the Kushtaka wells, which were brown and brackish, and its sharp point hid a good-sized plateau that widened to the east, a good site for an airstrip. Walter, inspired by the sight of the fighters and bombers who had filled the air over the skies of the Aleutians during the war, was determined to learn to fly and promptly hacked an airstrip out of the alders, tied a red flannel shirt on a pole at one end for a windsock, and bought one of the first Piper Super Cubs.

Twenty winters on, President Eisenhower signed Alaska's statehood act, and among other things the federal government began to build post offices in the Bush. Air taxies all over Alaska got federal mail contracts. Kuskulana and Kushtaka both applied for the post office, which went to Kuskulana because they had the airstrip, and Walter's son Walter, Jr. got the mail contract.

And because the post office was in Kuskulana, a Christianson got the postmaster's job, a rare prize in Bush Alaska, full-time federal employment with a steady paycheck and benefits.

Twelve years after statehood, President Nixon signed the Alaska Native Claims Settlement Act, in which Alaskan tribes gave the federal government a right-of-way across aboriginal lands from Prudhoe Bay to Valdez for the TransAlaska Pipeline, built to bring North Slope oil to market. In exchange, the tribes received 44 million acres and almost a billion dollars.

Some Alaska Natives claimed that, with the formation of tribes into corporations, their homes, their ways of life, their very cultures would be forfeit, requiring them to become white in an already white world. But land and money, those two possessions by which white culture measured itself, were powerful inducements. As most tribes did after enduring three hundred years of forced secondary status, Kuskulana opted into the agreement.

Kushtaka was one of the handful of Alaskan villages that did not.

ANCSA money flowed into Kuskulana coffers and the village blossomed out with new houses and the villagers with new skiffs and drifters and four-wheelers and snowmachines.

Kushtaka rechinked the steadily increasing gaps between the logs on their fifty- and hundred-year old cabin walls, and made do with boats and snogos inherited from their fathers.

Kuskulana was given its pick of parcels of prime land in the area, and every Kuskulaner of any age from six months to sixty years became the proud owner of a five-acre lot, many of them on the Gruening River and several of which encroached on the land where Kushtaka's fish wheel had stood for generations. Roger Christianson, Sr. even tried to lay claim to the fish wheel site itself. Said claim was quickly quashed but the Kushtakans didn't forget. It didn't help matters when Kuskulana built their new boat landing almost directly across the river from the Kushtaka fish wheel. The wash from the Kuskulana skiffs muddied the water near the fish wheel, and frightened the salmon.

Dale and Mary Mack at Kushtaka opened a little store in their living room, stocking it with items they bought in bulk from Ahtna and Anchorage and selling them at a modest markup, dry and canned goods, cases of pop and potato chips, aspirin and Bandaids.

And then Roger Christianson and Silvio Aguilar opened a full-service store in its own building in Kuskulana, with everything the Macks' store carried plus fresh fruit and vegetables and even fresh milk.

The Macks' store was out of business in three months. Dale Mack and Roger Christianson bumped into each other at Costco in Ahtna and had words that were witnessed by people from both villages, words that lost nothing in the retelling and only hardened the attitudes of everyone who heard it second- and thirdhand. You couldn't trust a Kuskulaner not to steal your idea and cheat you out of your business, the Kushtakans said. Those Kushtakans, said the Kuskulaners, they hadn't really made it into this century yet, you know? Probably wouldn't ever, the rate they were going. They hadn't even managed to muster the wherewithal to pay for a power line across the river, and there wasn't a flush toilet in the entire village.

Whereas every new house in Kuskulana had hot and cold

running water.

Teenagers of both villages, quick to pick up the elder vibe, began a series of hormone-driven confrontations at various potlatches. Outnumbered five to one, the Kushtakers took home the majority of the bruises, but so long as the hostilities were confined to the occasional tribal celebration held far away from either village the adults were inclined to look the other way.

Two years ago, the world's second largest gold deposit was found sixty miles north-northeast of where the creek and the river met.

Before the first backhoe was airlifted into the Suulutaq mine, the population of Kuskulana climbed onto its many four-wheelers and beat down a serviceable trail between their village and the mine site. With ready access winter and summer, the trail made their people more attractive as employees to mine management. Given the working airstrip, Kuskulana became the designated alternative landing site in case Niniltna and Suulutaq were both socked in at the same time. Which made the Kuskulana strip eligible for federal funds for runway improvements, an electronic weather-reporting station and the construction of a hangar.

Kuskulana was, therefore, enthusiastically pro-mine, and their people came home to spend their paychecks.

Kushtaka, on the wrong side of the river, sent fewer workers to the mine. Those that went seldom returned, preferring to resettle in Kuskulana and Niniltna and Ahtna and even Anchorage, where there was cable and Costco, and Beyonce concerts only a 737 ride away. Kushtakans, fearing the drain on their population and resenting the ever-increasing wealth of their parvenu neighbors, came down hard against the mine, on the side of the fishermen and the environmentalists and the conservationists who were devoting their considerable resources to stop it.

That September Zeke Mack was out moose-hunting on the south side of the river. Inexplicably, he missed the bull with the four brow tines on both sides and instead put a hole through the trailing edge of the right wing of Joe Estes' 172. Joe having just taken off from the south end of the Kuskulana airstrip and at that time a hundred and fifty feet in the air.

Joe got back down in one piece, but it soon became known in both communities where the shot had come from, and there was some subsequent conversation about just how bad Zeke's eyesight was. A lot of laughter accompanied the conversation in Kushtaka. Laughter was conspicuous by its absence in Kuskulana, whose pilots started taking off to the north.

The following May, the state announced that they were closing the Kushtaka school because enrollment had fallen below ten students, and that Kushtaka students henceforth would attend the Kuskulana school. Truth to tell, Kushtaka had been fudging the numbers for years. Roger Christianson, Jr. in Kuskulana and Uncle Pat Mack in Kushtaka, on the whole sensible men, did think privately that perhaps some of the hostility between the two villages might abate once the kids started having to sit next to each other in class.

That, of course, was before someone tried to set the Kuskulana Public School on fire with a five-gallon can of gasoline and a blow torch.

And last September, Far North Communications built a cell tower in Kuskulana. They dedicated one of the antennas on the tower to Kushtaka.

Geography informs who we are.

Kuskulana, flush with ANCSA, state and federal dollars and land, a post office, an airstrip, a store, a school, a cell tower, on the same side of the river as a world-class industrial development and with a trail navigable by ATV and snowmachine between the two, flourished.

Kushtaka...did not.

ACT I

Tuesday, July 10th

Kushtaka

TYLER MACK WAS AN eighteen-year-old stick of post-adolescent dynamite just waiting for the right match. He was smart in all the wrong ways, using his intelligence chiefly to conspire with Boris Balluta, his best friend and coconspirator since childhood, on ways and means to avoid manual labor.

Of medium height, built mostly of muscle and bone, Tyler had thick dark hair that flopped into dark brown eyes that always seemed to be more focussed on his next deal than the person he was talking to. He was a shirttail relative of Auntie Edna in Niniltna, which made the entire Shugak clan part of his extended family in Byzantine ways known only to its elders. Auntie Edna considered him a member of her personal tribe and was quick to grab him up by the ear when word of his activities came her way. Tyler, as quick as he was lazy, took good care to keep his ears out of her reach.

But this morning he hadn't been quick enough, his Uncle Pat having dumped him out of bed at sunup, which in mid-July was 2 A.M., and booted him into his clothes and on his way upriver without so much as a mug of coffee to get his heart started.

It was a beautiful morning, clear and cool. Mist smoked up

from the surface of the water, broken temporarily by the bow of the skiff moving upriver, closing in again behind its stern. Night, in summer only a suggestion of twilight between midnight and 2 A.M., gave way to an intensifying rim of gold on that part of the horizon stretching from the northeast all the way around to the southwest. Uncle Pat's outboard was so finely tuned and so diligently maintained that its muted purr was barely audible above the rush of water beneath the skiff's hull. Eagles chittered from treetops. A moose cow and two leggy calves foraged for the tenderest shoots of willow on one bank. Around a bend a grizzly boar sleeping peacefully on a gravel bar woke with a snort and glared around nearsightedly. He rolled to all four paws and gave himself a good shake, his thick golden pelt moving almost independently of the rich layer of fat beneath, and lumbered into the water to bat out a morning snack of red salmon.

Tyler noticed none of this. He hated working the fish wheel almost as much as he hated getting up before the crack of noon. Working the fish wheel was way too wet and entailed way too much heavy lifting for a man clearly meant for a cushier life. Uncle Pat was well able to tend to the fish wheel himself, eleven hundred years old or not. Tyler had had plans for today, plans that involved Boris and a scheme that was going to make them both rich enough to escape the influence of old farts like Uncle Pat and Auntie Edna once and for all and set their feet on the path to riches and the high life. Park Strip condos in Anchorage, fitting themselves out in Armani at Nordstrom, parties at the Bush Company, weekends in Vegas. They'd be MVP Gold on Alaska Airlines before the year was out, and then everyone who'd ever showed Tyler Mack the back of their hand had better by god look out. Tyler was on his way to the big time, and no one and nothing was going to get in his way. He'd already proved that once, and he was ready to do it again, any place, any time.

He imagined Uncle Pat coming to him for a loan for a new kicker or a new shotgun, and smiled to himself. Of course he would give him the money. Of course he would. He only hoped the old man would stroke out trying to say thank you.

Two miles above Kushtaka village, the river had carved a wide loop in the face of the landscape. Cottonwood grew in clumps on the curve, thick trunks covered with coarse bark looming thirty feet over the alder and diamond willow jostling for place below. The soft wood of the cottonwood tree made it prone to snap off in high winds. Cottonwood scrags formed bridges for the alder and willow to lean on and trail leafy fingers in the water beneath. Together they cast welcome shadows over the gravel shallows for weary salmon returning home to spawn.

The Mack family had had a fish wheel just below that gravel bar since 1901, when a stampeder, one Joshua Malachi Smith, had struck out panning for gold and got lost on his way to Valdez for a boat home. Daniel Mack found him trying to catch salmon with his bare hands, and the Kushtakans took him in before he starved to death or died of exposure, whichever came first. In return, he taught them how to build a fish wheel, a series of buckets on a wheel caused by the current of the river to rotate on an axle. The buckets scooped up the fish on their way upriver and dumped them into a chute that led to a holding pen. When the salmon were running, the holding pen had to be emptied two and three times a day. During a good run, sometimes more.

The first fish wheel was made of woven willow, which did not stand up well to a current made swift and strong by runoff from a winter's worth of snow, and had to be rebuilt every spring. Today, the Mack fish wheel was made of stainless steel and mesh, held together with nuts and bolts. It was indestructible as well as portable, designed to be removed from the water at the end of each season and rebuilt at the edge of the river again every spring.

A fat red jumped on Tyler's left, falling back against the water with a rich, full smack! The sun peeped over the Quilaks just in time to turn the resulting flash of droplets into liquid diamonds, suspending them momentarily in midair before they fell back into the river, itself a moving, jeweled surface pregnant with mystery and treasure.

None of which did Tyler take any notice of, and this in a year in which king salmon were scarce and cloudy, rainy days plentiful.

What he did see as he nosed the skiff into the bank next to the fish wheel, was Jennifer Mack in a skiff on the other side of the river. The wrong side of the river, which is what you might expect from a girl, who had no business anywhere near a fish wheel anyway.

He opened his mouth to ask her what the hell she thought she was doing — maybe he could blackmail her into working the wheel today while he was at it — when he caught sight of a second figure, a man standing in the alders at the foot of the set of stairs leading down to the gravel bar that served as Kuskulana's landing. The man stepped forward to catch the bowline she threw and hitched it to a tree branch.

It was Ryan Christianson, and the outraged yell died in the back of Tyler's throat, unuttered.

Pat Mack's outboard was so quiet that neither of them heard or saw Tyler, or maybe they were just too concentrated on each other to be aware of anything else. They vanished into the undergrowth as if they'd never been there. He would have doubted his own eyes were it not for the skiff, the name, Jennifer M., painted plainly across the stern for all to see. Or rather, her father's skiff. Even without the name, Tyler would have recognized that elderly New England dory with the blue paint fading to white anywhere between here and Cordova.

He realized his own skiff was drifting out from shore and he gunned the outboard to nose it back in. The aluminum hull grated against the gravel and he hopped out and tugged it up out of the water close to the fish wheel, all the while his mind busy with speculation. What was his cousin, Jennifer, a Kushtaka Mack, doing meeting Ryan, a Kuskulana Christianson? And at this hour of the morning?

He pulled on rough rubber gloves that reached well past his elbows and hooked the suspenders of his hip waders over his shoulders. The water next to the fish wheel's bin was teeming with salmon and he didn't even sigh at the sight.

Give him credit, he tried to be fair. He tried to think of all the reasons why Jennifer would be meeting Ryan on the wrong side of the river this early in the morning, and in the end could only come up with the obvious. If there had been any doubt, it would have been wiped clean by the way Jen's hand went into Ryan's, sure, easy, familiar. She'd put the boat in at his feet and he'd been standing in exactly the right spot to catch her bow line, too. It wasn't the first time they'd met there.

Tyler's eyes narrowed. So, he knew something he hadn't before. What was in it for him?

He'd have to talk it over with Boris. Boris always had all the best ideas.

He waded into the water and plunged his hands into the holding pen, grabbing the salmon by the gills and tossing them with a practiced throw so they thumped hard into the plastic tote sitting amidships of his uncle's skiff. He was good at it, because he hated it so much he'd figured out the most economical way to get the job done as fast as possible. It was a good catch, maybe twenty-five reds weighing an average of eight pounds, and still pretty fat for having traveled all this way upstream.

He was so focussed on getting the salmon out of the pen and into the tote that he didn't even hear the boots crunching into the gravel behind him.

Pat Mack was, indeed, eleven hundred years old, but there was nothing wrong with his eyesight, and when that worthless grandnephew of his hadn't shown up by four o'clock that afternoon he went grumbling down to the beach and climbed into Tyler's tiny, trash-filled skiff, having sent Tyler upriver in Pat's own skiff because it was big enough to hold a fish tote. The kicker, new when Eisenhower was invading Normandy, took a dozen tries before it caught and with a sound like a chainsaw giving birth ripped a shrieking hole in the serenity of the afternoon. Tyler hadn't probably changed the oil since spring. Useless little fucker.

He pushed the kicker as hard as she'd go, which amounted to about half a knot per year. The sun had traveled to the other side of the sky and was making its usual empty threat to set by the time he got to the fish wheel. His mood, already bad, didn't improve when he saw that the fish wheel was jammed, the current battering it and rattling the above-water baskets in their brackets.

"Goddamn good-for-nothing little shit," he said, and beached the skiff.

His own skiff was there, drawn up on the gravel next to the fish wheel, and tied off to a scrub spruce growing out of the edge of the bank.

Tyler wasn't, which only fueled his ire.

The tote held at least a dozen fish, red salmon, almost a hundred pounds of fish. Pat's temper spiked when he saw that they were all dead and had been sitting in the sun without ice. He poked at them. All day, by the look of them. It'd been a warm one, and they were starting to smell.

"Tyler, you useless little fucker, you'll be lucky if you're able to walk ever again when I get done with you!"

His bellow echoed across the water and startled a flock of pintails into the air. There was a rustle in the bushes across the river and he snapped his head around, one hand reached for his rifle. This time of year there was enough fish for everyone, but bears were not reasonable creatures.

It wasn't a bear, it was a man, ducking back into the alders behind the Kuskulana landing on the other side of the river. Pat squinted. Some Kuskulaner, most likely a Christianson, since most Kuskulaners were Christiansons, with a few Halvorsens and last he heard still one lone Romanoff thrown in. Might have been Roger's son. They all looked alike to Pat anyway. Although he had heard tell of a couple of new families totally unrelated to the existing population moving in. Which wasn't surprising. Kuskulana had everything Kushtaka did not and a functional airport besides, so you could get the hell outa town when you had to.

He saw them at their landing on the other side or driving by in a skiff from time to time. Sometimes they waved. Sometimes he waved back. Sometimes he even said hi. The longtime rivalry and resentment between the two villages was a lot of damn foolishness anyway, although he'd never be able to convince his nephew, Dale, of that. Or any of the other Kushtaka men for that matter, young or old.

Sometimes Pat Mack thought of moving out of Kushtaka

himself, by god, to Niniltna, maybe, or Ahtna, or all the way Outside. The Macks had family, albeit distant, in rural Oregon. Probably didn't snow as much there, and if there were family feuds, well, he didn't have to opt into them. In the Park birth, community and history forced him down on the Kushtaka side of the fence whether he considered it the right side or not.

He stamped over to the fish wheel and looked into the holding pen. Still some fish in it, although not many. And where was that useless little fucker, Tyler? Nowhere to be found, as usual.

Muttering curses, Pat pulled on hip waders, sleeve protectors, and rubber gloves and waded in. The current wasn't as swift near the bank as it was center stream, but it had rained hard last week and the water was running high and dirty, so that he couldn't see beneath the surface. It was plenty fast enough to pull at his legs, which were not as young or as reliable beneath him as they used to be, and it was cold enough to instantly chill his flesh through multiple layers of protection. He took a minute to get and keep his balance, leaned against the current, and bent down to feel his way down the curved edge of the wheel.

Two of the baskets were submerged, one partially, the other entirely. The partially submerged basket was clear of debris, although an eight-pound red that would have looked a lot better in the tote swam out and away as he was feeling around. The second basket was wedged firm.

"What the hell?"

There was something long and rigid thrust through the basket and into the riverbed, a branch or something. Probably a limb broken off a scrag. Although it felt awful solid and inflexible. It sure was stuck, good and hard. The current must have brought it downriver at a fast enough lick that it had somehow jammed itself through the open mesh of the basket and become wedged into the river bottom, bringing the entire fish wheel to a halt.

He heard the sound of an outboard engine and looked up to see a Kuskulaner idling by in his skiff, watching him with a curious look on his face. He looked back down and wrapped his hands around the branch and tugged. It didn't move. He wasn't altogether sure he had enough upper body strength left to make it move but Pat Mack never lacked for stubborn. He set his jaw, squared his shoulders, dug his heels more surely into the gravel, and tugged harder.

It came free with a whoosh of water. He dropped it and staggered back up the beach, sitting down hard half in and half out of the water, looking at what was in his hand. "How the hell—"

The current pulled at the wheel. The freed basket scraped across the gravel, still not moving normally.

"Well, shit," Pat said, and pulled himself to his feet.

And then stood there, openmouthed, as the basket lifted free of the water to reveal the body of Tyler Mack crumbled inside it.

ABOUT KATE SHUGAK

KATE SHUGAK is a native Aleut working as a private investigator in Alaska. She's 5 foot 1 inch tall, carries a scar that runs from ear to ear across her throat and owns a half-wolf, half-husky dog named Mutt. Resourceful, strong-willed, defiant, Kate is tougher than your average heroine – and she needs to be to survive the worst the Alaskan wilds can throw at her.

To discover more – and some tempting special offers – why not visit our website? www.headofzeus.com

MEET THE AUTHOR

In 1991 Dana Stabenow, born in Alaska and raised on a 75-foot fishing trawler, was offered a three-book deal for the first of her Kate Shugak mysteries. In 1992, the first in the series, *A Cold Day for Murder*, received an Edgar Award from the Crime Writers of America.

You can contact Dana Stabenow via her website: www.stabenow.com

DANA STABENOW
A COLD DAY FOR MURDER

DANA STABENOW
A FATAL THAW

DANA STABENOW
DEAD IN THE WATER

DANA STABENOW
A COLD BLOODED BUSINESS

DANA STABENOW
PLAY WITH FIRE

DANA STABENOW
BLOOD WILL TELL

DANA STABENOW
BREAKUP

DANA STABENOW
KILLING GROUNDS

DANA STABENOW
HUNTER'S MOON

DANA STABENOW
MIDNIGHT COME AGAIN

DANA STABENOW
THE SINGING OF THE DEAD

DANA STABENOW
A FINE AND BITTER SNOW

DANA STABENOW
A GRAVE DENIED

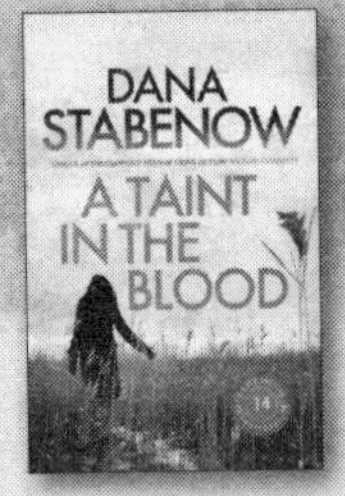
DANA STABENOW
A TAINT IN THE BLOOD

DANA STABENOW
A DEEPER SLEEP

DANA STABENOW
WHISPER TO THE BLOOD

DANA STABENOW
A NIGHT TOO DARK

DANA STABENOW
THOUGH NOT DEAD

DANA STABENOW
RESTLESS IN THE GRAVE

DANA STABENOW
BAD BLOOD